Look Before You Leap

Also by Virginia Heath

Look Before You Leap

A Novel

VIRGINIA HEATH

ST. MARTIN'S GRIFFIN
NEW YORK

First published in the United States by St. Martin's Griffin, an imprint of St. Martin's Publishing Group

LOOK BEFORE YOU LEAP. Copyright © 2025 by Susan Merritt. All rights reserved. Printed in the United States of America. For information, address St. Martin's Publishing Group, 120 Broadway, New York, NY 10271.

www.stmartins.com

Designed by Gabriel Guma

Library of Congress Cataloging-in-Publication Data

Names: Heath, Virginia, 1968– author.
Title: Look before you leap : a novel / Virginia Heath.
Description: First edition. | New York : St. Martin's Griffin, 2025.
Identifiers: LCCN 2025005766 | ISBN 9781250896094 (trade paperback) |
    ISBN 9781250896100 (ebook)
Subjects: LCGFT: Romance fiction. | Novels.
Classification: LCC PR6108.E1753 L66 2025 | DDC 823/.92—dc23/eng/20250210
LC record available at https://lccn.loc.gov/2025005766

Our books may be purchased in bulk for promotional, educational, or business use. Please contact your local bookseller or the Macmillan Corporate and Premium Sales Department at 1-800-221-7945, extension 5442, or by email at MacmillanSpecialMarkets@macmillan.com.

First Edition: 2025

10 9 8 7 6 5 4 3 2 1

For all the people like me—eternal optimists and dreamers who tend to jump in with both feet and rarely ever look before they leap. May you always seize the day with a smile, with boundless enthusiasm and with joy in your adventurous, hopeful hearts.

And most especially, this is for Lucy, Alison, and Liam— my fellow *carpe diem*–ers—who have encouraged me to leap time and time again during our raucous, authorly dinners at the pub and our gloriously questionable writing retreats by the sea. May you all never change, may your wine always be chilled, and may you all hit the bestseller lists!

Chapter
ONE

WHERE IT ALL BEGAN, SEVEN YEARS BEFORE . . .

ood gracious me! What on earth is all that muck on your shoes, Charlotte?"

Trust the eagle-eyed Miss P to appear in the hallway at the precise moment Lottie was trying to sneak back up the stairs.

"You really need to start looking where you are going, Charlotte, and how you go there." The owner of Miss Prentice's School for Young Ladies, Lottie's new home for the foreseeable future, peered at the mud-covered toes of Lottie's boots in resigned despair. "When you bound about everywhere at the speed you tend to, unpleasant things splatter." Then her nose wrinkled in exasperated disgust. "A proper young lady should always avoid mud at all costs, dear. It isn't seemly to be wearing it. It hints at a complete lack of *decorum*." The older woman huffed out a sigh, shaking her head before repeating, as she seemed to do hourly, with the resigned patience of an absolute saint, her mantra and the ethos.

"You are one of my protégées, Charlotte. Handpicked because *I know* that deep down you have so much potential to succeed." She glanced at the shoes again and shuddered. "Very deep down. But to unleash all that potential, to become the crème de la crème and a true protégée of this school, you have to start embracing and embodying all of the Four *D*'s." While Miss P launched into the already familiar lecture, Lottie bit the inside of her lip so that she would not give in to the overwhelming temptation to roll her eyes and tell her new mentor that she was probably wasting her time. There wasn't anything genteel or subdued to be found in Lottie's character and you could place all that she knew about behaving like a proper young lady on the head of a pin. And there would likely still be space left on it.

"The Four *D*'s are the pillars that define who we are, Charlotte. Duty. *Decorum*. Diligence." Miss Prentice counted each word on her upheld fingers. "And discretion at all times! At. All. Times!" The index finger wagged now. "It needs to become a habit, dear. It needs to be ingrained until it is second nature. That"—she wafted a regal hand to encompass the entire building—"is what makes *my* graduates so special. What ensures that they are the most-sought-after employees in any great house. There are run-of-the-mill governesses, or secretaries, or lady's companions, Charlotte, and there are *my* protégées." Miss P's chin lifted with pride, and rightly so. Being a protégée guaranteed one of her girls earned double the salary of all the run-of-the-mill governesses, secretaries, or lady's companions serving the ton.

That was the single biggest reason that Lottie was determined to make a success out of her stint here, despite all her many glaring character failings.

That and the inconceivable fact that Miss P had seen something in her to handpick her.

Her!

Lottie Travers!

Tomboy extraordinaire.

Nobody had been more shocked than she had been when the letter of invitation had arrived out of the blue at the family farm a month ago, and while her father and brothers had almost wet themselves laughing at the prospect of her training to become one of the crème de la crème, they had all been unanimous. It was an amazing opportunity too fortuitous to turn down. Especially when fortune and the Travers clan were virtual strangers and, through no fault of their own, money ran through their hands like sand through a sieve. This could, if she really, really, *really* tried to suppress practically everything that made her uniquely her, help her family financially.

"You have been given a great opportunity here . . ." Those wily schoolmistress's eyes dropped to Lottie's boots again. "Yet all that mud makes me wonder if you are paying any attention at all in your deportment lessons."

"I am paying attention and I will try harder in them, Miss P, I promise. It's just . . ." There was no point denying some of the unfortunate truth she was trying so hard to contain. "I grew up on a farm and therefore, I suppose, I don't really pay much attention to mud because it is everywhere."

Miss P sighed, her exasperation softening. "I know, dear, and I should make allowances, no matter how much potential I see in you. Let us blame my passionate reprimand on the morning grumps when I am most prone to lecture." She gently reached out to tuck one of Lottie's errant blond waves behind her ear. "You have years to become a true protégée and I am expecting too much for you to be proficient in the Four D's in just a week."

"I will try harder, Miss P, I promise." For both Miss P and for her five menfolk struggling to make ends meet back in Kent.

"I know you will, dearest."

Eager to escape now that the mood had changed and before Miss P questioned her further, Lottie offered a grateful smile before she turned. She went to dash up the stairs, then remembering that decorum seemed to be her biggest nemesis, stopped her feet from running to attempt a suitably decorous ascent instead. She managed all of three stairs before Miss P decided to ask the question she'd been dreading anyway.

"But where exactly have you been to get so muddy at"—she glanced at the grandfather clock, incredulous again—"six o'clock in the morning?"

"I couldn't sleep." With an awkward shrug, Lottie turned and then crossed her fingers behind her back to negate the necessary lie while she shuffled her filthy feet beneath the hem of her dress. Cursing herself for not having the wherewithal to clean them outside while simultaneously hoping that her kindly new mentor wouldn't notice that the boots, which were caked in mud, were also, in fact, not the dainty sort that any decorous young lady should be wearing here in Mayfair at all.

Instead, they were sturdy men's boots.

To be more precise, they were her youngest brother Dan's riding boots. Shamelessly pilfered from his wardrobe and stuffed in her trunk along with several pairs of breeches liberated from each of her other three brothers' closets on the morning she had departed the family farm. "I went to watch the sunrise in the garden." Another lie she made sure to cross her fingers to mitigate against. Because according to the gospel of her twin middle brothers Matthew and Luke, if you could get away with crossed fingers without someone demanding to see them, that went some way to canceling the lie out. A falsehood went from being a lie to being a fib, and fibs weren't quite as bad. "I am never good at sleeping in a strange bed."

Another lie, her third in quick succession and one that would have definitely had her called out at home. Both her father and her four brothers knew that she could sleep anywhere—even upright if necessary—never mind that her new bed here was an absolute delight. Plump feather pillows, an even plumper mattress, a thick and cozy eiderdown, and sheets so smooth and crisp she sighed with unadulterated pleasure every single time she slipped between them. Lottie would even go as far as to say that she had never slept so soundly in her life as she had in the six nights she had been here and, from someone who always slept like the dead, that was saying something. No doubt the rich and frothy bedtime cocoa that all the students were plied with also helped her swift drift into blissful dreamland too.

She had a decent bed at home, of course, and Papa worked his fingers to the bone to ensure that none of his five children had ever gone to bed cold or hungry. But the sheets in Aylesford were old and well-darned and nobody had ever taught Lottie how to make cocoa. If her mother had known, she had taken that secret to the grave with her, because there was no recipe for it in the stuffed notebook of collected wisdom dear Mama had written for her when her daughter had been barely ten and she had known the end was near. As that precious tome included a recipe for a salve to soothe a snakebite, when there weren't any snakes in Kent and probably weren't any in the entire British Isles either, her practical and thorough mother hadn't had the first clue about cocoa either. Which was a great shame because Lottie knew she would have loved it. So would her brothers. And Papa.

A wave of homesickness hit her hard.

Lord, how she missed her menfolk. The noise, the laughter. The incessant teasing. The freedom that came with living in an all-male household two miles outside of the village. Back home, alien concepts like decorum didn't exist to trip her up and remind her of how little knowledge she had about behaving like a lady. Which in turn made her suddenly mourn her mother all over again.

As that pain must have shown on her face, Miss P reached up for her hand and squeezed it tight. "It is perfectly normal to feel overwhelmed, dear, especially when all this is so new. But it *will* pass, I promise. And it's not as if you are never going to see home again, is it? You'll be back with your family for Whitsun and Christmas and Easter. A whole month in the summer with no pedantic old ladies nagging you about the need for avoiding mud."

"I know," said Lottie, feeling guilty at Miss P's sympathy when it wasn't in any way, shape, or form deserved this morning. "But there is something about the hour before dawn that reminds me of home. Maybe because it is the only time that London is truly quiet and I'm a country mouse at heart." One used to galloping across her father's fields at the precise moment the sun poked its head above the horizon.

Nothing woke you up better than the glorious exhilaration created by thundering hooves beneath you while the wind rushed over your face. It was even better if you could race someone beyond competitive, like Stephen, who considered himself the best horseman of the family, and then beat them. But alas, her eldest brother was a day's carriage ride away from Mayfair. A crying shame when he was a huge fan of a morning gallop too, and thought himself the best at it.

Which of course he wasn't now that his baby sister had trounced him on their last steeplechase—and she had been on the lesser horse.

"Well, there is no harm in watching the sunrise out in the fresh air here. So long as you stay within the sanctuary of our garden. If a worldly-wise woman like myself isn't safe on the streets of London in the dark from those who lurk in the shadows ready to take advantage, I dread to think what would happen to a naïve and unchaperoned country mouse of barely sixteen. How on earth would I ever face the families if something happened to one of my girls?" Miss P tensed as she contemplated that horror, making Lottie want to wince again.

Because she had, indeed, learned firsthand this very morning that there were lurkers in the dark shadows of Mayfair ready to take advantage. Half Moon Street might well be the home of the respectable, and the whole area might well be a well-to-do and leafy enclave during daylight hours, but she had certainly seen some evidence of the dissolute in her fast jaunt through the parks that abutted it this morning! Certainly enough to confirm that it wasn't the sort of place a genteel and delicate young lady should venture alone until the rest of the world woke up.

However, one of the advantages of growing up in a house full of brothers was that she was also as far from delicate as it was humanly possible to be. She had her father's height, so she towered over most women, and a lifetime of farmwork had made her muscles strong. With so many overbearing and quick-tempered siblings all vying to be top dog, she had also always known how to fight. She had a wicked right hook and a decent enough left one if Dan's now wonky nose was any gauge. Besides, from the moment womanhood had begun to blossom and the local boys had come sniffing around her, her overprotective brothers had taught her how to hone all those things to fight *really* dirty. That was why she knew every weak spot on the male body and how to turn a randy stud into a gelding quick sharp—and had done so on more than one occasion.

The miller's son, especially, back in Aylesford, had certainly been able to hit some very high notes in church for several weeks after he had attempted to take some liberties with her person at the last harvest festival, that was for sure! Or at least more liberties than she was comfortable granting. A stolen kiss or two was one thing, because a kiss was harmless in the grand scheme of things, but she had drawn the line at his hand up her skirts!

"Should I ask cook to save some breakfast for you so you can grab another hour of sleep?" Miss P's concern and generosity were doing nothing to ease Lottie's guilt. Guilt that she was lying. Guilt that she had snuck out. Guilt that she had broken several school rules in her quest for an hour of familiar freedom when she really appreciated being here. And yet more guilt at not being ladylike enough despite all her best intentions. "Two if you need it. I could inform your first teacher . . ."

Lottie shook her head. Talk about killing her with kindness! "No need. I am wide awake now." She smiled at her new mentor as she extracted her hand from Miss P's concerned grasp and backed up the stairs, the shame at her outright disobedience now somehow outweighing her need to be at one with the great outdoors again. Perhaps because that unbearable itch had been scratched? She certainly hoped so because this was too good an opportunity to ruin with her usual wild ways.

"But as I am up, I might as well make myself presentable and then go help Miss Denby set up the classroom for our deportment lesson—where I promise I will make a concerted effort to soak up every word and then act on all of them from this day forward." She resisted the urge to cross her fingers again and instead clasped both hands primly out in front, determined that she had told the truth rather than a lie because she really would try. Papa would tell her never to look a gift horse in the mouth, and she appreciated that becoming a governess one day would give her the life that he wished he could've given her. Fine clothes. Fine company. A decent salary and no more backbreaking work in the fields alongside her brothers. "I am determined to make everyone proud."

"That is very good to hear, Charlotte. Once you've learned to curb that unfortunate streak of wildness inside you, I have every faith that you will be a *protégée par excellence*."

Ready to get on with her own day, Miss Prentice spun on her heel and headed toward her office and Lottie sagged in relief as she plodded upward to her bedchamber.

That had been too close a call for comfort.

Now she knew that Miss P's day started at six o'clock, if she ever ventured out on another morning jaunt again—which of course she wouldn't—Lottie would be sure to be back by a quarter to, next time. She also needed to find a secure place to store her brother's boots where she could swap them out for more appropriate footwear before she came back in.

And in view of the fact that Mayfair before dawn was nowhere near as safe as Kent was and the ne'er-do-wells had seemed much worse, she should probably also consider taking some sort of weapon with her if there was a next time too. A stocking filled with a few marbles would be small enough to conceal about her person but still effective enough to deliver a decisive wallop if she needed to whack any lurking scoundrel—

"Where the hell have you been?" Her new friend and roommate, Portia, emerged from their bedchamber door and grabbed Lottie by the shoulders, simultaneously shaking them as she dragged her inside. Only once she had kicked the door closed did Portia hiss, "We've all been worried sick!" She jerked her pretty, dark head at Lottie's abandoned bed, the plump eiderdown now yanked back to reveal the pillows she had arranged to resemble a sleeping body beneath the covers. Behind that, the worried faces of her other two new friends and roommates, Georgie and Kitty, added several fresh layers to her already massive guilt. "We were on the cusp of raising the alarm and thought you'd run away back to your farm!"

"*We* thought she had run away," corrected Kitty with a pointed look at Portia. "*She* thought you'd snuck out to indulge in some clandestine petting with that stable lad we all collided with in the park yesterday because Portia always likes to think the worst."

"Who can blame me?" Portia shook Lottie's shoulders again. "You *were* flirting with him outrageously! For almost an hour too! And while I think that the rules that society expects we women to follow are archaic and that our reputations shouldn't be the be-all and end-all when character is more important—the rest of society is yet to wake up to that unfairness." Her friend's finger wagged just like Miss P's had. "You still have a reputation to protect if you want to become a protégée and I am sure I overheard you agree to meet that stable lad today when I had to practically drag you away from him! Is he who you were up to no good in the small hours with?"

Lottie considered trying to lie again until she realized it really wouldn't wash. She had hoped to sneak in and change before her three friends woke, but as they were all clearly wide awake now, that horse had bolted. Emotions were obviously also running high, so she was unlikely to get any privacy now to strip out of the muddy breeches concealed beneath her skirt, which would undoubtedly give the game away anyway. And she couldn't *not* change out of Dan's riding boots before she ventured downstairs again because they were another dead giveaway of what she had been up to. Any more than she could completely deny the accusations about the stable lad, when she had gone out of her way to flirt outrageously with him. Would have probably even kissed him if he'd asked, if it ensured that he lent her a horse. Would have probably kissed him even without the promise of a horse, truth be told, because he had been rather handsome despite his lack of cleverness and there really was no harm in kissing—so long as nobody else found out. "Yes—*but*—" Her three friends gasped in unison.

While Georgie's and Kitty's jaws dropped in shock, Portia's finger jabbed before Lottie could finish her sentence.

"I knew it!" Portia sank to Lottie's unoccupied mattress, squashing the pillow corpse as she put two and two together and made six hundred and fifty-six. "Oh, good heavens above. You actually *did* sneak out in the small hours for a clandestine meeting with a boy! What were you thinking?" Scandalized eyes locked with hers with touching, friendly anguish, reminding her so much of the supportive bond she had once shared with her mother. "Have you been . . . *ruined* now, Lottie?"

The other two gasped again at the ramifications of that possibility, and this time Lottie couldn't help but roll her eyes at their ridiculous overreaction.

"Of course I haven't been ruined! I am not an idiot, girls! I have no intentions of rolling around in the hay with Albert." At their further gasp at that unladylike retort, she realized that her new friends had lived much more sheltered lives than she had, confirming that Miss P's comment about Lottie's "wildness" did perhaps hold more merit here in polite society than she had originally feared. "Nor do I intend to." Which was also sort of the truth. Handsome Albert might get a stray kiss here and there in the future, especially if he kept lending her horses like he had today—if she was ever silly enough to do that again—but she did have some standards. That meant that Lottie was resolute that while a kiss was just a kiss, she would reserve any sort of hay rolling only for someone special. "I like Albert—but I don't *like* him in that way!" Only true love could convince her to lift her skirts and she knew herself well enough to know that a man needed to be more than just handsome to touch her heart. He had to be . . . *perfect.*

"Then why risk your reputation for him in the first place?" Kitty's question was a fair one. "Why flirt with him and then sneak out to meet him at a wholly inappropriate hour unchaperoned?"

"Because he has unfettered access to a stable full of horses and I've missed riding mine." A truth which, even to Lottie's own ears, sounded mercenary as she blurted it. "I flirted outrageously with him so that I could borrow one this morning. That is all." Another benefit of growing up in a house full of men was Lottie knew how their minds worked. A pretty face, some batting lashes, and the opportunity to feel attractive and impressive were all most men needed to be twisted around a woman's finger.

Was it wrong to use that weapon against one if he was daft enough to be so easily manipulated?

Probably. But . . .

"You've been out *riding*?" Portia said it with more incredulity than she had said "ruined."

"Yes." Lottie offered a weak smile, hoping they would understand that her motives weren't actually malicious—more medicinal. "I really needed the wind in my hair." So much she physically ached.

"I see," said Portia in a clipped tone that suggested she really didn't see at all. "You've made us *all* worried sick since dawn." She pointed at the exposed pillow corpse in disgust. "And you've lied to us all too."

"I have never lied to you and I resent the implication!" Although the guilt at the string of whoppers she had just told Miss P with crossed fingers called her a hypocrite. "All I am guilty of is sneaking out for an hour to ride around the park for the sake of my sanity, and that is hardly a crime."

"In a court of law, a lie by omission is still a lie, but that is by the by. I personally think that it is a crime that you willfully betrayed our trust in disappearing without any prior words of explanation, and you abused our friendship by preventing us from raising an alarm because we didn't want to get *you* into any trouble." Portia's eyes narrowed. "And you forced us to do all that because you *missed* riding your horse?"

"Well . . . when you put it like that, you make a short and harmless canter sound thoughtless." Which had always been Lottie's main problem, according to her papa. He always nagged her to think about the consequences of her actions before she acted, whereas she tended to dive in headfirst. Worrying, in her humble opinion, solved nothing. It just made you feel miserable and Lottie wasn't one for misery. "And selfish."

"That's because it *is* selfish!" Portia surged to her feet again, her outraged finger prodding afresh. "What were we supposed to say to Miss Prentice or one of the other teachers if they had wandered in here and asked where you were? Or do you deny that you expected your friends to lie to cover for you?"

"Well . . . I . . ." Suddenly, the seemingly necessary feel of thundering hooves beneath her while the wind whipped her hair didn't feel quite so necessary as keeping her three new friends her friends.

"Forget being ruined, you could have been kidnapped!" Always the most fanciful of the four of them, Kitty's eyes filled with tears that wounded far worse than all of Portia's incensed but correct accusations. "You could have been murdered, Lottie!"

"Which as you can all see, I plainly wasn't."

"More by luck than judgment." Georgie stood now too, folding her arms and sounding exactly like Miss Prentice in the full throes of one of her lectures on the Four D's. Cool, calm, but oh-so-cutting. "But we all make mistakes and the important thing is to learn from them. Promise us that this is a one-off, Lottie. That it was a hideous mistake that you bitterly regret and that you will never do anything this *reckless* or *thoughtless* or unbelievably *selfish* ever again." Worse, Georgie had Miss P's disappointed schoolmistress countenance down to a *T*. It was potent enough to make Lottie wither with shame beneath it.

"Because we are your best friends and we love you . . ." There was an invisible butter knife loaded with more guilt now hovering in the room that was being spread liberally and, arguably, not unjustly. ". . . and despite the unfair and untenable position you placed us all in this morning, which could very well have risked our own places in this school, the last thing we would ever wish to see is you squander this wonderful opportunity that you have been given to better yourself. Never mind what your lovely father would have had to say if you ended up getting yourself expelled simply because you couldn't control your childish urge to ride a horse."

As self-loathing settled like lead in Lottie's tummy, Georgie went for the jugular without once raising her voice. "To ensure that we all *stay* best friends, we are going to need that promise right this minute, Lottie, or you will leave us no choice but to confess all of our righteous concerns to Miss P about your future safety. For your own good. Isn't that right, girls?"

"Right!" Portia and Kitty said as one, mirroring Georgie's folded-arms stance but nowhere near mastering her reasonable tone. All three friends obviously so disappointed in her that she could hardly bear it.

"Then I promise," said Lottie, hoping it was the truth.

But just in case it wasn't, and her innate wildness got the better of her again sometime in the future like it always did, she made sure that her fingers were crossed behind her back while she made that solemn promise.

Just in case.

MISS PRENTICE'S SCHOOL FOR YOUNG LADIES, 21ST AUGUST, 1820 . . .

on't let Papa know that I told you—but things here are currently direr than . . .

Lottie allowed the letter to drop to her chest to stare at her bedchamber ceiling some more. Her youngest brother's words had haunted her for two entire days and nights and the worry for her menfolk was eating her from the inside.

If the circumstances were different, she would have hotfooted it home as soon as Dan's missive arrived. To roll up her sleeves and try to help in some way or simply to be there while they all put their heads together to find a solution. But her friend Georgie was getting married today and Lottie was the maid of honor, so she was stuck here in London. Unable to do anything practical and doomed to worry about her family in Kent until somebody came up with a viable way to make the best of this latest calamity to befall them. Ideally a miraculous cure that would turn back time and stop all the early summer rain that had pummeled the Garden of England for most of the summer. Because it had been that which had caused the majority of their barley crop to succumb to the dreaded mildew and die.

The Travers clan had always counted pennies. They were experts at making do and making the best of things without having to contend with the failure of one entire crop as well. Now the lack of money from the barley, on the back of the failure of half of last year's wheat crop, guaranteed the upcoming winter months were going to be tough. The thought of her beloved, if irritating, menfolk living hand to mouth, struggling to pay the rent while she lived in sublime comfort here in Mayfair thanks to the ceaseless largesse of Miss P, filled her with guilt. That they were always relieved to have spared her all the trials, tribulations, and hardships of a farming life these last seven years made her feel worse.

Ordinarily, and much to Papa's chagrin, Lottie would send three-quarters of her wages back home to them to help in some small way. Sometimes he told her off and pressed all the money back into her palm the next time she visited and other times he didn't because he had needed it. There was no doubt he desperately needed her wages now, but she had none to give him. Thanks to her own headstrong stupidity combined with the rebellious streak of wildness that refused to die within her, she was between jobs.

And, thanks to Dan's letter, Lottie was presently kicking herself twice as hard for being lured—once again—by the overwhelming pull of a good gallop across the park at dawn, which had enticed her into her former employer's stable. Especially when she had rather enjoyed her short stint as a governess at his Berkeley Square house, even if the master himself was a complete and utter arse. It might not be her fault that Lord Chadwell's odious son had tried to blackmail her onto her back before breakfast, but it was very definitely her fault that she had given the libertine the ammunition to blackmail her with in the first place.

If she had thought about the consequences of her actions and not put thinking about them off to tomorrow, she wouldn't have borrowed Lord Chadwell's stallion that fateful morning and she wouldn't have been caught red-handed by his frisky heir trying to return it. She wouldn't have had to kick that despicable scoundrel hard in the crotch to escape his unwelcome ardor. No matter how much she relished the memory of the randy twit rolling around on the floor of the stables in tears afterward as he had clutched his aching, but thankfully freshly flaccid, genitals, the image did nothing to alleviate her current guilt one jot. Because the son had then tattled to the father that she had been riding his horse without permission and Lord Chadwell had dismissed her on the spot for her insubordination.

All in all, it had not been her finest hour and now, thanks to her seemingly unconquerable recklessness, her family was paying for her stupidity while Miss P was charitably paying for her keep.

Again.

Because this was the second time in her career as a governess that Lottie had been dismissed for the want of a good gallop. Although in truth, thanks to her own lack of willpower and wildness, it could very well have been the hundredth. Even after seven years of trying, the need to ride like the wind at the slightest provocation had refused to subside.

Just when, exactly, was she ever going to learn her lesson? Or to put off thinking about tomorrow because she much preferred today?

Furious at herself, she reached for the old pocket watch she kept on the nightstand and almost sighed aloud when it told her that only ten interminable minutes had passed since she had last checked it. It was only a quarter to five and after her second sleepless, anxious night in a row since Dan's letter had arrived, she was wound as tight as a spring.

Worse, she couldn't offload all her worries on her three soundly sleeping friends like she normally would. Because this was Georgie's wedding day, for pity's sake, and Lottie would not spoil that happiness for anything!

Pretending to be deliriously happy had taken every ounce of her effort last night when they had all gathered here at the school for their final night as four single ladies. In honor of the occasion, Miss P had also put the four friends in their old dormitory, where they had reminisced and laughed until the small hours. All a little tipsy thanks to the two bottles of champagne that Portia had smuggled out of her employer's well-stocked wine cellar, which she had been adamant he wouldn't miss. It would have been a truly excellent night, too, if Lottie hadn't been so consumed with worry and guilt. She would probably confess all to Portia and Kitty once the bride left for her honeymoon, and then maybe that would make her feel better. But until then, she had no choice but to bottle it all up inside and paste on a smile.

Silently, she slipped out of her bed and padded to her own bedchamber to dress. She fully intended to don one of her day dresses before she watched the sunrise in the garden—but the moment she opened her wardrobe door, one of her riding boots fell out. Tempting her like the serpent had tempted Eve to do the unthinkable again.

Except . . .

Perhaps it wasn't quite so unthinkable today.

It wasn't as if she currently had a job to lose, and a good gallop through the park would undoubtedly help blow some of the cobwebs from her exhausted but overly busy mind. Perhaps it would also help her think of a solution to fill the empty Travers coffers because she had always done her best thinking at speed in the saddle . . .

No!

Not today, Satan!

She would push that alluring idea aside.

She had to.

<hr>

*T*here was plenty to loathe about London, but its large, leafy parks weren't one of them. Especially at this ungodly hour when Guy Harrowby had them all to himself.

With the early morning mist and the unspoiled chirping of the dawn chorus, it reminded him a little of his estate in Kent. Acres of empty green. No clogged roads. No crowds. And best of all, at the hours he chose to use this route, no bloody irritating people who might recognize him either. Which was probably why, whenever business forced him to come to this godforsaken place that he much preferred to avoid like the plague, he only ever ventured in and out of it via the parks where he rode at such a lick that he didn't have to meet anyone.

It was a constant mystery to him why the residents of overcrowded London never availed themselves of this splendid shortcut either. Because within three minutes of leaving his house on Grosvenor Square, he was in Hyde Park. Which conveniently led into Green Park, which in turn took him directly into St. James's Park, a mere hop, skip, and jump away from Westminster Bridge. Not twenty minutes after he crossed the river, and he would soon be on the Kent Road, headed home. Then the fetid capital, and most especially the cloying and supposedly polite society contained within it, would be an ugly blot on the horizon behind him. Out of sight and, most especially, out of mind.

Just the way he liked it.

London—and Mayfair specifically—always set his teeth on edge. This place made him feel small. No mean feat when he stood three inches above six feet and, according to his mother, blocked out all her light each time he dared to loiter in a doorway. Yet this city had the power to diminish him until his skeleton shrunk to a withered shell inside his skin.

Although why he allowed this place to do that to him still was a constant mystery, when he had long ago decided that London—and Mayfair specifically—was beneath him. It was filled with petty gossipmongers who had nothing better to do with their day than look down their noses at people in judgment. And warped judgment too, because a man was measured here by his title first and his fortune second and while Guy arguably had both—then and now—he likely still did not possess enough of either to impress them.

Nor did he want to.

No indeed! The days of him dancing to the beat of the snooty ton's drum were long gone.

Thank goodness!

He was no longer a member of any of the gentlemen's clubs, refused to attend balls, or soirees, or even the supposedly "intimate" dinners he still occasionally got invited to. And he wouldn't be caught dead here during the dreadful cattle market the self-proclaimed great and the good called "the season" for all the tea in China. He eschewed them all out of principle nowadays and he was a much happier fellow as a result.

Much happier.

In fact, his life had been positively charmed since he had had the good sense to liberate himself from all that nonsense, and he was beyond fulfilled as a result.

Content in his own skin.

In control of all aspects of his life.

Master of his own destiny.

Happier than he had ever been.

Which, if true, was doubtless why he was still skulking in and out of the city of his birth nine years after he had left it heartbroken and humiliated. And why he knew he wasn't really that happy at all. Wasn't, in fact, anywhere near close. Not even in Kent but especially not here. Because here was where all the memories were strongest and always held the power to make him feel ashamed, and he loathed that almost as much as he loathed this place.

This place that suffocated him.

This place that shrunk him.

This place that had weighed him, measured him, and found him sadly wanting.

Even now, all alone in this pretty park after a full year of avoiding this place, the weight of London this fine morning was almost too much to bear. Somehow worse than usual and sadly, he knew why.

It had been that stupid snigger.

The one Guy had heard after he had reluctantly tipped his hat to an old acquaintance and his new wife whom he had collided with yesterday as he had left the infuriating grain merchant's office. An intimate bubble of laughter which, arguably, had had nothing to do with him whatsoever. It could have simply been a shared joke between a husband and a wife about absolutely anything. The sorts of jokes he had used to swap with his own family once upon a time, back when he'd still possessed a sense of humor. But in his cynical mind nowadays, not ten yards clear of them, the joke had been about him. Or at least the old him. The gullible, naïve, fresh-faced, keen-to-impress, and much too impetuous him that had foolishly allowed himself to be a pawn in a chess game where he had romantically fancied himself the knight. The him that had made such a catastrophic error of judgment and had made himself both a laughingstock and an object of pity.

Nine years on and he still wasn't sure what was worse.

Unless it was his own flabbergasted fury at his staggering idiocy that infamous season, which still lingered to torment him. Whichever it was, it still held the power to make him need to flee from the god-awful place with his tail between his legs as fast as he could.

Suddenly keen to escape it even quicker, Guy nudged Zeus into a gallop, sucking in deep, calming breaths as his horse flew effortlessly across the dewy grass like the wind. So fast, the morning mist blurred the wall of trees rushing beside him into a watercolor smudge of green and brown.

Yet still that wasn't fast enough today, so he pushed Zeus harder. Gave the powerful horse permission to have his legs because he sensed they both needed to let off some steam. The sheer exhilaration making him throw back his head, close his eyes, and gulp in more air in the hope that it would cleanse all that pent-up shame which just one day in London had made new again.

Because he understood that he needed to forget it. That the only person he was hurting by holding on to all that festering self-contempt was himself. Knew he needed to leave his unfortunate but mortifying misstep in the past fully if he was ever going to find himself again and—

The second horse burst out of a gap in the trees scant feet before him, shocking him into an unmanly yelp. A similarly startled Zeus reared with such abrupt force that the next thing Guy knew, he was flying backward in the air.

Weightless.

Powerless.

Flailing.

Until the earth smacked into him with a thud, knocking every bit of air out of his lungs and causing a million stars to explode behind his eyes. The impact making his ears ring so loudly he could hear nothing else but their chime.

In an oddly silent haze, he saw the idiot who had unseated him struggle to remain in his saddle as he fought his own rearing horse into submission. A battle which only took moments before a fuzzy silhouette stared down at him. Mouthed something that the church bells ringing within his head totally drowned out, then stayed him with a raised palm when Guy tried and failed to sit thanks to the spinning ground he lay upon.

It was only when the other rider kicked his horse back into a gallop and left him there that Guy realized that Zeus had bolted too.

Marvelous.

There was fat chance of catching him now! Zeus was as temperamental and skittish as he was fast, and when spooked would likely run frantic rings around this park for the next hour before he calmed down. Which also meant that Guy no longer had a hope in hell of reaching the Kent Road in twenty minutes. Or of leaving London and its unpleasant memories behind in a cloud of dust before the residents of this cesspit awoke to start their day.

Thanks to the recklessness of that other rider, he was well and truly stuck here, in this dreadful place he despised, for goodness knew how long now. A prospect that made him feel sick.

The last time the blasted horse had done a runner, it had taken three hours to find the brute. But that had been at home, on his own quiet acres, not here in the capital. It was quiet now but in another hour or so, the streets surrounding this park would be busy and his nervous stallion wasn't used to that sort of city chaos at all. Worse, if Zeus decided to bolt out of the sanctuary of the park, then the consequences didn't bear thinking about.

Guy had to get up and search for him.

He groaned in frustration and pain as he gingerly reinflated his lungs. As the whirling stars behind his eyeballs began to subside, he tested his limbs. Rotated his ankles, flexed his knees. Stretched out his arms. Twisted his upper torso and neck. Nothing seemed to be broken beyond his pride, and as he had none left here anyway, he supposed that shouldn't really count—yet it did.

His poor arse, however, was a very different story. It had taken the full brunt of his fall and it throbbed as he pushed himself to sit on it. The morning dew seeping into his breeches did little to relieve the pain in his pelvis. The base of his spine screaming in protest at being made to move at any speed faster than a snail's.

It took a couple of minutes, but he managed to creak himself upright and began to massage his aching buttocks while he waited for the dizziness to subside, all the while scanning the park for any sign of Zeus. At full tilt, the brute could be halfway to Paddington already. Then what?

As hours and hours of futile searching loomed on the horizon, the other rider suddenly emerged from a clump of trees several yards away. By some miracle, trotting along beside him, bucking and fighting the taut reins all the way, was a less-than-impressed Zeus. Yet despite the horse's obvious temper tantrum, to add insult to injury, the other rider still managed to control him from atop their own saddle on a black stallion so huge it made Zeus look like a child's pony by comparison.

Guy limped to meet them, simultaneously relieved that his horse was unharmed and furious that he had been separated from him in the first place. But then pride always came before a fall, and once fallen, pride was the only thing you had left to cling to that might get you through it.

"Do you always ride so recklessly in a public place?" He reached for Zeus's reins and wound them tightly around his gloved fist in case the damned horse tried to bolt again, and glared up at the idiot. Squinting against the sunlight that pierced his retinas and rendered the dangerous fool faceless. "They make bridle paths for a reason! So that everyone knows where a bloody horse is going to be! You could have killed someone going at that ludicrous speed over ground you had no place riding on!"

He could see enough of the surprisingly lithe and slight rider's work-worn attire to know that this wasn't a gentleman—more a stable lad out exercising his master's best horse. "You could have killed me with your unbelievable carelessness, idiot!"

"You were hardly cantering sedately yourself, sir." The shock at hearing the curt but unmistakably female voice made Guy squint some more. "In fact, I would counter that you were galloping even faster than I was else you'd have been able to stop in time."

"But I was on the bridle path, madam!" Not that he could yet discern if this hellion was a madam or a miss. "And you weren't!"

"If you had been paying proper attention and had actually looked where you were going rather than staring straight up at the sky whilst galloping, you might have been able to control your horse before he threw you."

"But I wouldn't have been thrown if *you* had been on the bridle path like you were supposed to be!"

She brushed that outrage away with a regal flick of her wrist. "Arabians are notoriously difficult to handle and only a real idiot forgets that whilst on the back of one! Especially at the speed you were going."

"Are you trying to say that this is all my fault? When I was riding my horse precisely where I was supposed to and you were not." He flapped his hand toward the gap in the trees she had exploded through.

"Briefly, and for that I obviously apologize." Although she didn't look particularly sorry. Even shrouded in the rising sun's piercing silhouette, he could see her chin tilted defiantly, and she was very definitely regarding him down her nose with disdain.

"Your recklessness almost killed me! I could have broken my neck when you unseated me!"

Using just her trim thighs—thighs showcased outrageously in a tight buff pair of men's breeches and weathered riding boots—*she* maneuvered the fearsome and snorting black stallion out of the painful sunlight. Turned to face him and something odd happened to Guy's innards.

They instantly bunched up inside him and then seemed to sigh in unison as they immediately relaxed, as if they had been waiting his entire life for this moment. For this woman. Even the muscles in his jaw gave way and he felt it hang in bemused wonderment.

Bloody hell, but she was stunning!

Even with her golden curls tucked into a tatty brown cap and her rich, honey-colored brows furrowed as two striking big blue eyes glared at him in disgust, she fair took his breath away.

Not that he had much left to steal after his abrupt collision with the ground.

Which was probably why he felt so lightheaded again.

Why peculiar things were happening in his chest.

He was too world-weary and jaded to be irrevocably dazzled by a woman's beauty anymore and after his fall, it was hardly a surprise that his heart kept skipping a beat either. Thanks to her, he'd almost had a brush with death, so it wasn't any wonder he was suddenly more off-kilter than he had ever felt in his life.

"You were unseated because you lacked the skills necessary to stay in your saddle, sir. Because you bought yourself a horse that you haven't the first clue how to control. If anything was at risk of dying this morning, it was that poor animal. Spooked, and running wild like that he could have been severely injured on the back of your ineptness." She wagged her riding crop at him with such vigor it made him blink and take a step back. "If he had been, I can assure you that you'd have felt the sting of this!" The black stallion she sat astride—*astride* when all ladies rode sidesaddle—snorted his agreement and began to dance on the spot ominously as if he were about to lash out too. Then instantly calmed when she smoothed his neck. The taut, equine veins softening beneath her touch, almost as if she possessed magical horse-whispering powers.

It took Guy another moment of gaping at her elegant fingers stroking the now docile behemoth of a horse before he could haul his jaw back up. "I beg your pardon!"

Had she really just threatened to whip him? After insulting his prowess as a horseman and knocking him on his arse?

She waggled the whip at him some more. "An animal like that needs to be treated with care and respect, *sir.*" The respectful addition of "sir" couldn't have been more disrespectful if she'd tried. "Frankly, a grown man who can afford to purchase such a magnificent beast should also have the good sense to know how to handle one! Whoever sold you this horse should be shot because your lack of skill in the saddle just now was as shocking as your lack of concentration."

Guy wanted to argue. Almost did—but that blasted whip sliced the air again before he could find the right words to convey his outrage.

"For the sake of your poor horse, and any pedestrians unfortunate enough to collide with you while you attempt to ride him, I suggest you immediately invest in some proper lessons. If you are too proud or too stupid to do that"—her expression left him in no doubt she believed he was the latter—"I genuinely think you should consider buying yourself a slow nag to ride instead—as a feisty, energetic Arabian is obviously beyond your inferior capabilities. While you are about it, you might also learn some manners, you rude oaf!"

"I-I . . . um . . ." It was on the tip of his tongue to apologize despite his outrage because there was something about this veritable Valkyrie that brooked no argument. But the words wouldn't come and he instead gaped at her like a fish. Completely dumbfounded. Because he honestly could not remember the last time someone had spoken to him like that.

"I think the complicated sentence you are struggling to spit out, *sir*, is 'Thank you for rescuing my horse.'" That defiant chin tilted again, drawing his gaze to the swanlike curve of her neck. "I would say that it was my pleasure to fetch him for you—but it isn't, because I am not sure that I have done your horse any favors in returning him!"

With that terse admonishment issued, she turned her snorting stallion sideways with the merest nudge of a shapely, breeches-clad knee, and set off again at a gallop toward the Serpentine.

Slim shoulders lifted, graceful spine stiffened in righteous indignation, and without so much as a backward glance. Forcing him to watch her delicious peach of an arse bouncing in the saddle in perfect synchronicity with the giant horse beneath it while he wondered what the holy hell had just happened.

And why it felt quite so profound.

❦

*G*eorgie was a beautiful bride. Despite all Lottie's inner turmoil, made worse after her unfortunate near collision with that insufferably rude, ungrateful, incompetent, but ridiculously handsome horseman in the park this morning, the wedding had been lovely. Made all the lovelier by its unconventionality.

With no blood relations, the bride had been walked down the aisle by Miss P, which had felt fitting. It did not matter what you did, and Lottie could personally vouch for this, Miss Prentice always welcomed you back with open arms until you were in a position to leave again. Once a student of her school, you were also always part of the sisterhood it created. That was why Georgie's lack of blood relatives hadn't mattered today one jot. Her side of the aisle had been filled with a sea of smiling family made up of past alumni and present students. Even the first-years, who were all only sixteen, had been invited to the nuptials and the wedding breakfast along with the groom's young nieces and nephew, giving it all a wonderfully inclusive feel.

The addition of three boisterous children had certainly made the usual matrimonial formalities livelier, even if some of the guests had raised some disapproving eyebrows at so many breaks with tradition.

Now, bellies stuffed thanks to the excellent wedding feast, the amassed guests were milling about and sipping champagne in Miss P's drawing room, some spilling into the hallway while they all awaited the bride and groom to reappear ready to leave for their honeymoon.

Portia and Kitty were upstairs with Georgie, helping her change to leave and no doubt reliving the best bits of the day. Lottie hadn't gone with them. As delighted as she was for the new Captain and Mrs. Kincaid, seeing them disappear on their honeymoon in a shower of rice and rose petals suddenly couldn't come soon enough. Maintaining the cheerful façade was exhausting and Lottie couldn't wait to be able to strip off this constricting silk bridesmaid's gown, along with its even more constricting undergarments, and be all alone with her worries in her bedchamber.

Dan's letter had still played in her mind despite her best efforts to do her usual and postpone worrying about tomorrow until tomorrow. While it was true that worrying was usually a futile pursuit, this problem seemed insurmountable. Lottie hated feeling impotent, and despite her eventful morning gallop and no matter how hard she had racked her brains, she still hadn't come up with anything that would help her family through this latest crisis. In the absence of no better plan and no money to help her papa, she had decided to head home to grieve the demise of this year's barley crop in the bosom of her family. It was too late to leave for Kent tonight, but if she caught the early morning post with Portia, whose current employers were spending the summer with family in Gravesend, she'd be back in Aylesford before supper. Maybe then she'd be able to think of a solution.

"Do you see that lady over there?" Miss P's sudden whisper beside Lottie's left ear made her jump.

"Which lady?"

"The old lady sitting on the chair directly to the right of the fireplace."

There were several ladies who could fit that description but only one looked truly old. At least eighty by Lottie's best guess if the snow-white hair and saggy, papery jowls were any gauge. "The one with the ludicrous foot-high purple ostrich feather stuck in her hair and the expression of complete disapproval on her overpowdered face?" For this octogenarian appeared so displeased with everything and everyone around her she might as well be chewing on a wasp.

"Must you be so literal?"

"I am merely saying aloud what we both see." Lottie shrugged unrepentantly, watching the curmudgeonly old lady with interest now that she had been pointed out. Whoever that *grande dame* was, and there was no doubt from her expensive purple gown, superior demeanor, and commanding posture that she was a fearsome, blue-blooded woman who was not to be trifled with. She was also clearly one used to being deferred to because those matrons unlucky enough to be seated nearest to her all wore tight smiles and seemed too frightened to speak at all unless spoken to. As Lottie stared, one brave soul did and was rewarded with a glare from the old dragon that made the misguided speaker instantly wither on the vine.

As always, that pompous superiority rankled. Lottie might not be as opposed to rank and aristocratic status as Portia was, but she never had time for those who were so up themselves, they believed the world revolved around them.

Much like that incompetent but much too attractive idiot had this morning!

It took a special kind of inbred, aristocratic arrogance to blame her entirely for a careless mistake which both of them had had a hand in. He had been so obnoxious and insufferable a fellow despite her risking her neck to retrieve his bolted horse, she had thoroughly enjoyed knocking him down a peg or two as a reward. Had given him both barrels, in actual fact. Because having the excuse to righteously shout at someone rather than curse the ethereal and silent forces of fate had felt cathartic at a time when her emotions were all over the place.

It had also, in a strange sort of way, provided her with a welcome distraction from the other problem that refused to be ignored. She only had to picture that ridiculously chiseled jaw of his dropping in shock that someone so obviously far beneath him had the temerity to call him a rude oaf, and it made her smile. Because he *had* been a rude oaf. An unspeakably rude and ungrateful oaf, and she had probably done him a greater service in telling him than she had in returning his poor horse.

The arrogant fool did have excellent taste in horses though, despite his inability to control them; she had to give him that. That high-strung Arabian had been one of the finest and fastest specimens she had ever seen. It would make an exceptional racehorse or a racing stud. Not that she suspected his useless owner realized his animal's full potential. That jumped-up, pompous, and rude oaf had probably only bought that horse because the Arabian's whiskey-colored coat had perfectly matched his stunned, blinking eyes.

"That is Lady Almeria Winthrop." Miss P dragged Lottie's thoughts reluctantly back to the rude old lady they were discussing instead.

One of the first-year students who had been tasked with handing out glasses of sherry ventured too close to the battle-axe and was uncere-moniously shooed away with a snarl, prompting Lottie to once again say exactly what she saw. "Well, lady or not, she reminds me a bit of a grumpy terrier we used to have on the farm years ago, who hated everyone and everything. Although I cannot help but wonder what has got her dander up here? Doesn't she realize this is a wedding? A time for joyousness and celebration? She couldn't radiate more displeasure if she tried. Who wasted an invitation on the ungrateful witch?"

In line with the Four *D*'s, which she upheld with every fiber of her being, Miss P discreetly ignored all those literal observations, but Lottie could not help smiling at the fact she didn't disagree with any of them. "She is also the Dowager Viscountess of Frinton."

"So?" asked Lottie with another shrug. "Being a dowager viscount-ess doesn't excuse her atrocious behavior." Once again, an image of the outraged horseman from earlier skittered across her mind, making her wonder if he possessed a title too. It would explain a lot if he did.

Except he hadn't possessed the physique of a member of the aristoc-racy. Aristocratic males weren't usually so . . . imposing. They rarely pos-sessed such broad shoulders or so many obvious muscles. When you grew up in a house full of men, you knew the difference between real muscles and padding, and despite his thoroughly unpleasant manner, he had filled his coat very well.

"*So.*" Miss P nudged her, forcing Lottie's mind away from the rude oaf and back onto the rude battle-axe. "I have just discovered that Lady Frinton is in the market for a lady's companion, *so* I have told her I happen to have just the candidate ready to go already."

"Oh, you cannot be serious!" Making no attempt to hide her disbelief, Lottie sighed at her mentor. "You only have to look at her to see that she will eat poor Kitty alive." Like Lottie, her friend Kitty was again in between jobs and living temporarily back at the school on Miss P's charity.

Kitty had been dismissed from her latest position as a lady's companion for gross neglect of her duties—for the fifth time. Because for Kitty, daydreaming wasn't so much a pastime but a full-time occupation. At least Lottie could suppress the urge to ride an illicit horse for weeks on end before she succumbed to it, and even when she did, she never ever rode one during working hours. Kitty couldn't go more than a day without her mind flitting to the fanciful pastures of her imagination, usually during working hours.

"That sour-faced old matriarch will gobble up kind, gentle Kitty like a canapé." Lottie snapped her teeth shut to emphasize that point. "It will be like sending a lamb to the slaughter."

"Oh, I know that," said Miss Prentice, yanking Lottie by the elbow. "Kitty wouldn't last five minutes with a gorgon like Lady Frinton. That is why I am going to introduce *you* to her, dear."

Lottie planted her feet and scowled at that. "Have you lost your mind, Miss P? We both know that my character and temperament have always been better suited to running around after a nursery full of boisterous young children than it is to fetching the slippers for a crotchety old woman who believes the world revolves around her. I am a governess to my core and most definitely *not* a lady's companion in any way, shape, or form."

"Actually, dear, you *were* a governess and now, thanks to your own rash stupidity and continued lack of decorum, you are once again unemployed. Beggars cannot be choosers, Charlotte. Especially when there are rumors that Lord Chadwell has vowed never to employ one of my protégées again after he was forced to dismiss one who stole his horse."

"Stealing suggests I did not bring it back and I very much did."

"Whether you did or didn't steal the thing is moot when he claims that he paid through the nose for a supposedly superior governess, trained by me, who, rather than uphold the ethos of this school, instead continually neglected her duties while she indulged in mad gallops across Hyde Park."

"I most definitely did not neglect my duties. Not once in the six months I worked for him, so that is unfair too."

"I notice you do not deny the galloping, Charlotte." Miss P gave her one of her legendary exasperated looks. "And do not get me wrong, I think it is most ungallant of Lord Chadwell to besmirch your name or mine after what his disgusting son did, but Mayfair is a very small place and mud like that sticks! Enough that I am unlikely to find you another position as a governess here for some considerable time if the rumor spreads. Which it will! For exactly how many wild galloping governesses are there in this city who terrorize the parks on horseback?" She glared at Lottie until she bowed her head in shame. "Your improper galloping habit aside, at five feet and eleven inches, you hardly blend in, dear, do you? Not that you have really ever tried to."

As Miss P had her there, Lottie huffed out the last of her outrage with a hefty dollop of petulance. "It is hardly my fault that I am tall and I genuinely do *try* to curb my wild side."

The older woman smiled. "You are certainly *trying*, Charlotte Travers, and always have been, in your uniquely exasperating but lovable way. However . . ." And back came the schoolmistress with a vengeance. "You have created a problem for yourself and for me, and I am doing my best here to fix it. Lady Frinton needs a companion urgently for her upcoming trip to Scotland after her last one ran screaming for the hills. As she seems to chew through companions with worrying haste, this is unlikely to be a permanent position."

A statement that made no sense whatsoever in view of Lottie's current predicament and Miss P's claim that she was trying to fix things. "Exactly how employable do you think I will be after being dismissed twice in quick succession by two of Mayfair's supposed finest?"

A protest that was brushed aside with a flick of Miss P's fan and a wink.

"Certainly more employable than you will be if you are unmasked as the Infamous Galloping Governess! Thankfully, as Lady Frinton's horrendous reputation with the help is legendary, nobody decent would bat an eyelid to discover that she had dismissed you. To be frank, most would be impressed that you managed to stick with her longer than a week, so there is nothing to worry about on that score. It many ways, a stint in her employ would actually do you a favor as it shows you have gumption. But on the other score . . ." Miss P's lips pursed. "It is imperative that we have a few weeks' grace for those *swirling rumors* about the scandalous behavior of one of my protégées in Hyde Park to die down in order for you to become a halfway employable governess again. Something that will not happen"—Miss P slanted Lottie one of her I-know-everything-young-lady-so-do-not-bother-denying-it schoolmistress glares—"if Lord Chadwell's wild former governess persists in going for her ill-considered dawn gallops across Hyde Park."

"How did you—" There really was no point in attempting to question Miss P's raised palm further so she simply huffed again and braced herself for the rest of the lecture.

"I really did hope that when that idiot stable lad friend of yours got himself promoted to a groom he would cease lending you horses from his master's stable!" Because of course Miss P knew about Lottie's main supplier of borrowed horses just as she seemed to know about everything else. She was either omnipotent or she had a vast network of spies covering the whole of Mayfair. "But did you really have to court further scandal by galloping across Hyde Park *again* this morning when your dismissal is still so fresh? And in breeches too? Could you not have at least worn a skirt to cover them like you usually do?"

"I forgot." Lottie winced at that lie, considered crossing her fingers behind her back, and then gave up. She had known Miss Prentice for seven years so also knew that when the jig was up, it was up. "I didn't forget. Petticoats always get in the way and I'm sorry. I just . . . needed to go fast this morning."

"Why?" Instantly Miss Prentice was concerned. "Is something else wrong, dear?"

"Nothing is wrong . . ." Miss P stroked Lottie's arm and the dam holding up all her fraught emotions burst. "*Everything* is wrong. The barley crop has failed and thanks to my own rash stupidity and continued lack of decorum, I currently have no wages to send home to help my family through the crisis."

"Oh dear. Your poor papa." Miss P squeezed Lottie's arm in sympathy. "But his misfortune is all the more reason to meet Lady Frinton with all haste. I cannot deny that she is likely to be a horror to work for, but if she hires you, dearest, I hear the wages that she pays are excellent. That said, to set your expectations I must warn you that that is currently a very big *if* indeed with all the rumors about you flying about. Lady Frinton is very well informed of all the latest gossip and she is as notoriously picky as she is infamously difficult. But it has to be worth a try."

Thanks to the allure of excellent wages, Lottie let Miss P drag her across the room but didn't hold out much hope that she would impress the old dragon who was already eyeing her with distaste. Not when Miss P's suspicions were right and gossip about her was indeed swirling about the ton, and apparently at a rate of knots too. She'd been asked by three complete strangers here today if she knew which of Miss Prentice's protégées had been dismissed by Lord Chadwell. She had denied all knowledge of it, of course, but her mentor's point had been proved. Mayfair was a very small place that was fueled by gossip, and she was not only *the* guilty party, she stood out.

Her latest impropriety wasn't going to be a stain that was easily removed now that a version of events had leaked their way out of Chadwell House. If one of the scandal sheets printed it then it would go from idle gossip to the gospel truth in a heartbeat. If it did, it would be better all around if Lottie was miles away when it happened. Miss P did not deserve to suffer because Lottie had, once again, put off worrying about the consequences of her actions.

"Lady Frinton—allow me to introduce you to Miss Charlotte Travers."

Rather than say "How do you do?" like any normal person, Lady Frinton responded by lifting her quizzing glasses and giving Lottie a thorough, head-to-toe once-over. Only when that was done did she scowl. "Did you grow up in a greenhouse, gal?"

"No, my lady." She forced herself to smile past her immediately gritted teeth and tried not to take offense at the single most unimaginative insult that had plagued her since childhood. "A farm."

"Where I presume you slept on a bed of manure alongside the carrots." The magnified eyes perused her once again as if Lottie were some sort of exhibit in a museum of curiosities. "Because you are unfashionably tall for a female." Lottie decided there and then she disliked this woman. But as Miss P had stated, beggars could not be choosers and she seriously needed money.

"My father is tall, ma'am. So was my mother."

"Was?" The magnified eyes narrowed behind the lenses. "Did you kill her coming out?"

"No, ma'am." As this interview was already going badly, Lottie decided to answer that direct and tactless question with an equally direct answer in the hope it stopped this intensely personal line of questioning stone dead. "Consumption killed her when I was but ten."

"That is unfortunate for the both of you. A girl needs her mother at that age." For the briefest of moments, there seemed to be a flicker of humanity in the old dragon's eyes until they narrowed again. "My acquaintance Mrs. Wilson here"—Lady Frinton jerked her head toward a startled-looking woman who instantly tried to blend into the wallpaper— "lives on the corner of Brick Street and Piccadilly." A sentence that sent a shiver down Lottie's spine because the family her longtime accomplice at the stables worked for also lived on Brick Street. "Her bedchamber window overlooks the park and she is convinced that you must be the gal who was recently dismissed from the service of Lord Chadwell for horse theft because she swears blind that she has seen you take a horse out a time or two before."

"It is true that when at home, *in Kent,* I like to ride." Lottie did cross her fingers behind her back now. "But, alas, I have never had the pleasure of riding here in town."

"Then there must be another ridiculously tall, golden-haired woman who gallops about at dawn as if the hounds of hell are nipping at her heels." Lady Frinton pinned her with a glare that called Lottie a liar. "Do you have a twin, gal? Or would you like a second chance to set the record straight? As I'll warn you that I cannot abide liars."

As that damning question was the official death knell of this interview, along with any chance the rumors about her now not turning into an outright scandal for the school, there seemed little point in denying it. "I didn't steal it, more borrowed it so that both I and that neglected Thoroughbred could take some well-needed morning exercise." She turned immediately to Miss P. "I am sorry, Miss Prentice. I have brought shame on your school and thus, I shall immediately pack my bags and will never darken your door again."

As Miss P did a wonderful job of acting completely surprised and horrified by that confession, Lady Frinton scoffed. "So now you claim it was more an act of charity than a theft?"

Lottie shrugged, guilty color infusing her cheeks, which she desperately tried to ignore. "A horse like that was born to run and not languish in a stable."

That was met with stony silence that Lady Frinton stretched several seconds longer than was bearable. "I approve of that honest answer, Miss Travers." Something akin to mischief danced in those ancient eyes now. "Most especially because I have a soft spot for all things equine and I have always thought Chadwell is far too fat for a Thoroughbred."

A statement that was too insulting, too outrageous, and far too true forced Lottie to bite back some wholly inappropriate laughter. Laughter which soon died in her throat when the woman skewered her with a glower that was much too intuitive. "I do hope that you will indulge me with more honesty, Miss Travers, when I put it to you that I suspect there is more to the tale of your sudden dismissal than the *common* gossip suggests?" The emphasis on the word "common" made Lottie wonder if Miss P's network of spies had nothing on this old dragon's. "For I smell shenanigans, young lady, and my nose is never wrong."

She was sorely tempted to answer with the truth but Miss P's elbow in her ribs urged caution.

"Surely, borrowing a Thoroughbred without permission, no matter what the provocation, would be considered shenanigans enough for any employer to terminate employment?" Lottie made sure to stare the woman straight in the eye.

"Under usual circumstances, most would think so, Miss Travers. But I am not most people and the fact that it isn't so much Lord Chadwell as his son who currently wants your head on a spike is what makes this so unusual." The old woman's lips curled at the mention of Chadwell's odious heir. "Did that scoundrel take liberties?"

Despite the hard press of Miss P's elbow in her side, Lottie's gut told her to be honest. Even if it did mean that she had to kiss goodbye to a much-needed job and remove herself from this school for the foreseeable future. "He attempted to, Lady Frinton—but it did not end well for him."

Lady Frinton threw her head back and roared with laughter. Her cackles were so loud, they made the other fifty or so wedding guests stop what they were doing to stare. "I like that answer even more, Miss Travers!" Then she turned her attention to Miss Prentice. "She'll do. Have her packed and waiting outside my house in Grosvenor Square on Thursday. We leave for Scotland promptly at noon."

Chapter
FOUR

꧁ ꧂

*S*eeing as we are nearly three weeks out, how would you like to cele-brate your birthday, darling?"

Guy almost groaned aloud at his mother's seemingly casual and over-bright question because he knew what was coming next. She always saw his birthday as an excuse for festivities, whereas he hated them, for obvi-ous reasons. Aside from the hideous social interactions that were foisted on him by the woman seated opposite, birthdays for him only reignited bad memories he would prefer to forget. In fact, if he could magically erase the fourteenth of September from the calendar for the rest of his life, he would. Then they wouldn't have to have this yearly argument.

Instead of groaning aloud, however, he focused on cutting his ba-con. All hopes of a peaceful breakfast now as dead as a dodo while she dredged the fetid riverbed that he preferred not to disturb. "The same way I celebrated it last year. Quietly." An answer which he knew already would go down like a bag of gargled nails.

His mother's teacup clattered into its saucer. "Oh, for pity's sake, Guy! It is your thirtieth! A milestone! For once I want to celebrate it with a proper party and people! At our Mayfair house like we used to."

"Then you have my blessing to celebrate it that way."

"Really?" Hope lit her eyes.

"And I shall celebrate it my way. Here." The hope died and he was instantly guilty—just not guilty enough to acquiesce.

"Is it any wonder that I am ill!" And so the dredging started. "For heaven forbid my curmudgeonly only son ever do one thing his poor *widowed* mother asks of him?" For good measure, she also pushed her untouched plate away. "I hope that you are proud of yourself for ruining both my breakfast *and* my life."

"I decline a birthday party a day's ride away in that polluted cesspool I loathe and suddenly I have *ruined your life*?"

He put down his own knife and fork because his breakfast was ruined now too. Histrionics and guilt always played havoc with his system, as did any mention of London. Put them in the same sentence as his birthday and it was a surefire recipe for indigestion. "You know that late August is one of the busiest times for the estate. It is harvesting time, after all." He spread his hands in the placating manner which had always worked so well for his father with this woman, despite never working for him. "The wheat needs to be cut, those fields plowed and fertilized. The winter barley crop needs drilling. The lambs are weaning. The apples ripening. The hay needs to be cut, baled, and stored. The cows need to be brought in from the pasture."

"You employ countless talented people to do all of those things for you."

"But I still need to be here to oversee it all." Which wasn't strictly true because he did employ countless talented people, none of whom needed to be managed constantly. But he had to be strategic. "Why don't we have a nice birthday dinner here instead?" Seeing as he would have to throw her a bone to get her to back off, he offered her a concession. "Let's push the boat out and fill the dining room." Which would be tortuous. "Invite the Spencers and the Atkinsons." The only two tolerable families nearby. "And your friends the Mayburys—of course." Guy would honestly rather spear his forehead with a fork than endure an entire dinner with the fawning, overly familiar, and flirtatious Miss Abigail Maybury, who had long made no secret of the fact she fancied herself his wife. An unpalatable match his desperate-to-get-him-wed mother had begun, much to his complete horror, to encourage.

"You mean we should spend it with the same people we usually dine with when you deign to dine with anyone? How is that *pushing the boat out*?"

He feigned some enthusiasm, hoping that was contagious. "What better way to celebrate a birthday than with friends, Mama?" Another concession was clearly needed. "I'll even agree to all those silly parlor games you love." Lord, kill him now. "Charades and blindman's bluff."

"So you can abandon me to the Mayburys, Mrs. Spencer, and Mrs. Atkinson the second I put the blindfold on while you disappear off with their two husbands to talk about dreary things. Like the shocking price of flour and the latest newfangled farm equipment?" There was no point countering that he found neither of those topics as dreary as an infantile parlor game. "You could take a few days off for a *milestone* birthday, Guy. It wouldn't kill you."

It likely would if it involved London.

"I do not see this birthday as a milestone, Mama." Like a ship in a storm, it was clearly time to change course yet again even though he knew he was headed for the rocks. "A half century is a milestone. Seventy is very definitely a milestone. Any year after that is a blessed miracle to be rejoiced. But thirty is . . ." He searched for something profound which would minimize the achievement of managing to exist for a paltry three decades, and when nothing sprang to mind, changed tack once more. "Why is thirty suddenly more important to you than twenty-eight and twenty-nine were?" As soon as he said that he regretted it because it gave an opportunity that his clever mother could exploit.

Being his mother, she didn't disappoint.

"Because nine years ago, on his twenty-first birthday, my only son—*my only child*—solemnly promised me that I would have a house full of grandchildren by the time he turned thirty! That's why!" The first bucket of mud was dragged up from the fetid riverbed. "*You* made it a milestone when you made that solemn promise and then you reneged on it!" He had hardly reneged, he'd been unceremoniously dumped, but he bit his tongue rather than give her more ammunition. "So now the absolute least you can do to make up for my interminable, lonely, and *grandchild-less* existence is humor me with one measly birthday party in Mayfair—seeing as the last one of those was nine years ago too!"

An occasion so monumentally awful he needed no reminder of it.

Except now there was fat chance of that happening this morning. The dredging bucket appeared again, filled with a cringing memory of himself going down on one knee in their packed Mayfair ballroom. Proffering a ring whilst spouting such awful, flowery romantic guff he couldn't bear to think of the words let alone the huge crowd's delighted reaction to them. Then her expression. Triumphant and calculating and not at all what he had imagined after she had led him on during their whirlwind three-week courtship where he had been convinced it was love when it had actually been nothing of the sort.

"If you continue to allow one silly, youthful faux pas to hold you back, Guy, you will never find a wife!" Because of course she went there. Minimizing that life-changing blow to a mere faux pas. "You do know that lightning doesn't strike in the same place twice, don't you? Just because one woman behaved atrociously, doesn't mean that all women will!"

As the acid roiled in his gut, he was forced to remember the worst part of the humiliating debacle—the real object of her desire tapping him on the shoulder. After which, Guy had had no choice but to stand up and step aside because she'd fallen into the other fellow's arms. The silence in the ballroom as he had walked out had been deafening. The aftermath just as brutalizing.

All excruciating enough to make him so queasy he feared the little breakfast he had managed to consume was on the cusp of reappearance.

Obviously, his mother knew precisely what he was thinking about. She had been there, after all. As shocked and stunned as the rest of the ton at his sheer stupidity.

"If everyone else has forgotten your . . . blunder . . ." For heaven forbid she ever call the total obliteration of his heart, confidence, reputation, and pride the monumental disaster that it had been! ". . . it is beyond me why you haven't. It is long past time you opened your heart to love again as there are plenty more fish in the sea."

Except the sea was now poisoned and he had learned his lesson well that love was for fools.

It had certainly made a fool out of him. Such an outstanding one, he had even been featured in a satirical caricature in the *London Tribune*, complete with a jester's hat and bells on his boots as he had plighted his troth surrounded by a bejeweled crowd in hysterics.

"My private affairs are not up for discussion."

Before he could surge to his feet and storm out of the room like he always did when fish and sea and love appeared in the same sentence, his mother surged instead. "Then let us discuss mine!" She pointed a quaking finger at him. "Thanks to you, I haven't only missed out on the blessing of grandchildren to dote upon, I have also missed the joy of nine entire seasons as well! I am sick of wandering in the social wilderness because my only son cannot spare any time away from his stupid wheat, or barley or sheep or horses or whatever else he fills his entire year with to avoid having an actual life!"

"The social wilderness!" He would have laughed at that if the accusation hadn't been quite so preposterous.

Yes, he hadn't yet managed to furnish her with the next generation of Harrowbys as he had stupidly promised all those years ago as a fresh-faced viscount, but he had hardly held her back either. His mother wasn't so much a social pariah as she was a social whirlwind. Each time the post arrived, Guy had to wade through all her piles and piles of invitations to find his own correspondence. He was lucky if he received two letters a week. His mother received so many she kept the local post office in business!

"Which of the seasons did you miss, Mama?" He glanced around the dining room as if searching for one. "Because I cannot recall a single season in my entire living memory where you have remained here and not disappeared to Mayfair for months on end. Why, I barely saw you all last spring because you insisted on attending so many soirees in town!"

"There is a big difference between attending and *attending*, Guy. When, as the mother of an eligible viscount, I should have been attending *because* of you and not *in spite* of you! How are you ever going to beget any heirs if you refuse to meet any equally eligible young ladies?"

"I'll meet one in my own good time!" Guy wanted to hurl his eggs at the wall but had too much respect for all his hardworking servants to do that, so had to make do with slapping the table only hard enough that the crockery rattled. Not that his protest registered with his mother.

"This year's crop of debutantes is particularly good."

Debutantes!

Lord, give him strength!

As if he, a very jaded ancient with almost three decades of life and a satirical cartoon under his belt, had the patience to spend all eternity with a vapid and giggling girl of eighteen. He hadn't spoken to a single debutante since he'd been turned down flat by the last one and he was a very different man now from the idiotic, green milksop he had been then. Now he knew how the world worked, and more importantly, he had grown some common sense.

Anticipating he was about to take issue with the vast difference in his "milestone" age compared to this year's latest crop of calculating husband-hunters, his relentless mama pivoted before he could raise his own outraged finger and get the words out.

"If you'd prefer a more mature young lady, there are some promising candidates from the previous few seasons still single too. A couple of which I would have high hopes for if you ever agreed to meet them, as they are clearly sensible and discerning young women who are waiting for the right gentleman to come along." As she lowered herself back into her seat, she treated him to the yearning expression of a homeless puppy. "Young women you could meet if you'd allow me to throw a party for you in town . . ."

"Mother, I—"

She cut him off with a raised palm and alarmingly watery eyes.

"You might still be in your prime, Guy, but I am not getting any younger and now that my health is in rapid decline, I will not live forever."

"You suffer from heartburn, Mama, not heart failure."

"Well, it often feels like more. It's hard to tell when my poor heart is broken to begin with and hasn't mended since your father died." She idly rubbed her chest in the vicinity of that organ, her eyes suddenly far away. "I miss him so much."

Guy knew that to be a fact, so reached across the tablecloth for her hand. "We both do. He was taken too soon." And too fast. One minute he had been a hale and hearty force of nature, until the persistent, niggly cough he had had for the better part of six months had morphed into something much more serious. Then his seemingly infallible, larger-than-life papa had spent his last six weeks bedridden in frightening and rapid decline.

"He has left a big, gregarious hole in our lives, the wretch. I am still furious at him for leaving me like that when he had promised me faithfully that we would grow wizened together. Instead, he left me a widow at fifty." Close to tears, his mother grabbed her teacup again as an excuse to compose herself. For all her histrionics, she had never been one for weeping and wailing. One small mercy, he supposed, that stopped him from strangling her.

"In the decade since, I had hoped for the welcome distraction of grandchildren by now. But alas . . ." She rubbed her chest again, pulling a face. Her voice uncharacteristically small. "Such is life." She said that as if hers really was ebbing away. "There is still nothing whatsoever on the *barren* Harrowby horizon to look forward to that might keep me going." She stared off at an imaginary horizon with a wistful but worryingly resigned expression. Then she flapped that away. Stoically. Her forced chuckle hollower than he had ever heard it. "With so much disappointment in my life, is it any wonder I have *constant* acid?"

Constant? That couldn't be good! "I'll summon the physician again today and—"

"There is no point, darling." She flicked that offer away too, refusing to meet his eyes. "He is adamant there is nothing else to be done for my . . . condition. Beyond reducing my motherly anxieties over you, of course. He is convinced my malaise is aggravated by stress."

"I thought Dr. Arden said that it was your overindulgence of cheese that set it off?"

"That is what I *told* him to tell you, dear, because I didn't want you upset." The blame for all her suffering now firmly laid at his door, she sipped her tea while rubbing her chest once more for good measure, looking thoroughly pained and pale in the process. *Could one feign paleness?* "Despite your lack of concern for ruining my life, I have never wanted to ruin yours. You would understand the power of parental sacrifice if you had children of your own."

Guy was certain she was playing him like a fiddle, just as she had played him and his father all their lives with her meddling and manipulations, but the alarming ring of truth to that comment still plagued him exactly as he suspected it was supposed to.

She *had* protected him from his father's dire prognosis until it could not be hidden. Which obviously made him wonder if the heartburn the physician was currently treating her for was in fact something else. Something more sinister that she was keeping from him.

But on the other hand—she had always been as sharp as a tack. So she must have noticed the way his concerned eyes had followed her fingers to her chest where they still rubbed and, to get her way, he would not put it past her to milk his concern for all it was worth. She might draw the line at weeping and wailing but she was a better actress than most of the lauded thespians who trod the boards on Drury Lane.

But she was unusually pale . . .

As if she read his mind, she martyred some more. "Before I leave this mortal coil, I want to honor the promise I made to your father on *his* deathbed . . . that I would do everything in my power to see you happy." A statement guaranteed to exacerbate all his new worries and smother him in guilt. "Which I have failed to do thus far."

"Mama, I can assure you that I am quite—" And now he was talking to her palm.

"What? Bored? Restless? Unfulfilled? Miserable? Lonely?" Accusations a little too close to the bone for comfort. "It isn't healthy to cut yourself off from people in the way that you do, my darling. Your withdrawal from the world has become out of hand and you are a shadow of your former self. You used to be such fun. As gregarious as your dear father but all work and no play has made Guy a very dull boy indeed."

"I do have an estate to run. A hundred and forty-four employees and tenants who depend on me. Papa raised me to take those responsibilities as seriously and as diligently as he always did—and I do. He taught me my strict work ethic. I learned it at his knee, and I promised him faithfully on *his* deathbed that he was leaving it all in safe hands." If she was going to use his paternal guilt so shamelessly against him, then what was sauce for the gander was sauce for the goose. "Or would you have me dishonor *his* legacy—his life's work—by putting myself first instead?"

Her eyes narrowed and for a moment, he took that as a sign that he had won. Edward Harrowby had been the epitome of excellence as a land-owner and master. Not even his mother, who could argue pink was blue in perpetuity, could get out of that one.

"How dare you use your father's legacy as an excuse to live like a social pariah!" Her cup clattered to her saucer for a second time. "Yes, he worked his fingers to the bone—but he also lived his life to the fullest! He never did anything by half measures, irrespective of whether that was get-ting the harvest in or being the life and soul of the party. These walls used to ring with the sound of gaiety and laughter—even when he was ill—the guest bedchambers upstairs were rarely empty and our London parties were legendary. The Harrowby Ball was *the* invitation of the season. *Every-one* came to it. The preparations for that ball, I might add, he insisted on being involved in because he adored hosting it so. He had such fun coming up with the themes. Choosing the music. The most difficult dances. The bizarre food. Causing havoc with the seating plans just to enjoy watching old foes attempt to make polite conversation or, even better, give each other the cut direct."

A smile pulled at the corners of Guy's mouth at those memories. "Papa did have a warped sense of humor." And the loudest, most in-appropriate laugh. Especially when he played a practical joke on Guy's mother—which was often. Almost as often as Guy had played them on her. Back when he had been gregarious and fun. And a blitheringly stupid romantic idiot.

Reading his mind again, his mama sighed. "When was the last time you did anything daft just for the sheer joy of it, darling?"

"Er . . ." Guy racked his brains and came up empty. "I do plenty of things that I enjoy. I ride. I read. I . . ." Good grief—was he really that boring? "I love to learn and I continually expand my mind. I exercise. I relish good food and occasional good company and—"

"Listen to yourself! You sound like a man in his dotage, making do with his pipe and slippers, and not one in his prime living his life to the fullest like your father used to. There is no excitement in your life, Guy. No *joie de vivre*. No passion. No silliness. Not a single sparkle resides in your eyes anymore when they used to dance like his did. Every day is the same. Your routines have become so entrenched, your life so isolated and safe and predictable, I wonder how you can stand it."

Pride made him rail against that despite knowing she had called his situation correctly. "I'll have you know that I indulged in a reckless and mad gallop through Hyde Park only yesterday, just for the sheer fun of it." Sort of. And had almost got himself killed in the process. "It was most exhilarating." If being thoroughly shown up and then dressed down by a harpy in breeches could be considered exhilarating.

It had been . . . extraordinary, however. Enough that he wasn't fully over it yet.

Or her.

There had been so many sparks in that hellion's exceptionally fine but condescending cornflower eyes that she had positively crackled. So bursting with *joie de vivre* and passion, she could barely contain it all as she had galloped off. Good grief, but he envied her that!

"When was the last time that you laughed? Danced? Took a risk? Grabbed the bull by the horns and *indulged* your wild side."

"I don't have a wild side."

"You used to."

As Guy really didn't want to think about the gullible, reckless fool he had been back in the day, he rolled his eyes as if he were the disapproving parent instead. "Thankfully, like the pimples I also used to suffer from, I quickly grew out of it."

"By withdrawing into yourself and pushing people away."

"I do not push—"

"You have become the archetypal lion with a thorn in its paw. Unsociable and withdrawn. Intractable and ill-tempered. And when you use that volatile temper of yours, you lash out and alienate people. You are *so* unforgiving." More home truths that were difficult to swallow.

He preferred to think of himself as no-nonsense but some of his behavior in Hyde Park yesterday still bothered him. That Valkyrie might not have been using the bridle path as she was supposed to, but they had both been galloping recklessly. Yet he'd immediately lashed out because he had been embarrassed. He'd fallen on his arse right in front of her and the humiliation of that indignity alone had caused him to lose all sense of perspective and reason.

He could and should have handled the whole affair differently. Been more gracious. Nobody had died and she had brought his blasted horse back, after all. Knowing what an unpredictable handful Zeus was, at the very least he should have thanked her for risking her neck to go fetch him despite the fact that the hellion had almost broken his by knocking him off his horse. But he hadn't thanked her, he'd bellowed in her face, and that shamed him when his father had raised him to be a gentleman. Which was probably why he couldn't stop thinking about her . . .

"All I am asking for is the chance to throw my beloved son one little party." His mother rubbed her chest again as if she were indeed in pain. Certainly pained enough that the actual state of her health needed some thorough investigating. "For a milestone birthday, is that really too much to ask?"

Was she really ill or manipulating him?

He suspected the latter, because experience had taught him that that was what most women did. His mother had always been adept at twisting both him and his dearly departed father around her little finger when she wanted something, but he could not bear the thought of the former being true either.

Guy knew the voice screaming at him in his head was right, but the guilt from her sudden paleness had him tied in knots. "You know I loathe London."

"Then forget I even mentioned London, darling! Let's agree on a compromise and hold the party here instead."

"Well . . . I . . ." Why the blazes had he stupidly made this all about London? "There is the harvest—"

"Don't I deserve a little happiness? I so love planning a party. It would remind me of all the joy I had planning parties with your father. You won't have to lift a finger. I'll do everything and will make sure that nothing interferes with all the important work you have to do here, I promise." She looked so happy and hopeful it was killing him. "Please say yes as this is such short notice I will need to get the invitations out immediately or they won't arrive in time for people to come!"

It really was short notice, so hopefully that would prevent his mother's plans from getting out of hand. Everyone who was anyone was rusticating in their own country estates before the next season started again with a vengeance. As those estates were dotted across the entire British Isles, it was unlikely that many would be prepared to travel all the way to Kent just for one evening. Surely that would work in his favor? "I suppose if the guest list was small, a tiny party here wouldn't—" He didn't even get to finish that sentence because his mother leapt from her seat, clapping her hands, and dashed around the table to hug him and smother him in sloppy kisses.

"Thank you, Guy! *Thank you!* You have no idea how much this means to me!" She squeezed his cheeks together like she used to do when he was a boy, instantly as hale and hearty again as she had seemed yesterday. "A party here will be more than perfect!"

"A *small* party, Mother." Experience told him that he had to set the strictest boundaries despite the scant three weeks' notice. She had the reputation for moving mountains when she set her mind to something, and he was already regretting this. "Nothing elaborate and for no more than say . . ." *Oh good grief, what had he done!* This was a mistake. A huge mistake. Perhaps his biggest in nine bloody years! "Twenty guests maximum."

That earned him *the look*. The one that she had used when she thought he was talking gibberish. "Twenty is a dinner, darling. A party *starts* at forty."

"How about we split the difference then, and agree on thirty? One guest for each of my years on this earth." But his dear mama was now a woman on a mission and he was already talking to her back while she practically sprinted from the room. Leaving Guy all alone with his growing indigestion, a large dollop of remorse, and an escalating feeling of dread.

What the hell had he done?

Chapter
FIVE

꧁꧂

With Scotland and the requirements of being a traveling companion entirely unknown entities, Lottie had given up trying to pack light for the trip. On Kitty's advice, she had prepared for every conceivable eventuality. Her friend had warned her that the hardest part of being a lady's companion were the whims of the particular lady concerned. Apart from being a prizewinning battle-axe, the only thing that she knew about her new employer was that the old lady spoke her mind and seemed to like honesty. But as the hackney pulled up outside Lady Frinton's vast double-fronted town house and she spied the small but regal purple, black, and gold carriage waiting outside it, she regretted bringing such a large trunk. With that strapped to the back, there would be precious little space left for any of Lady Frinton's belongings.

She briefly considered getting the hackney to turn around so that she could repack in something a third of the size, but the old dragon had specified noon sharp and it was already a quarter to. The last thing she wanted to do was anything that displeased the famously fickle old witch today. Even if that meant putting on every essential garment in her trunk and leaving all the rest of her belongings on this pavement.

Her enormous trunk was in the process of being unloaded when a very harried and hook-nosed fellow clad in black appeared at the front door. "Miss Travers?"

"Yes." She pulled herself to her full height, trying her best to look professional and unintimidated by the glimpse of opulent grandeur of the cavernous hallway behind him. After two years of working as a governess in Mayfair, she was accustomed to the wealth of some of its inhabitants, but Lady Frinton was clearly in a different league if the sheer size of her house was any gauge. Only the wealthiest crème de la crème could afford Grosvenor Square in the first place and this residence positively dwarfed all its neighbors. Lady Frinton must be as rich as Croesus! "And you are . . . ?"

"The long-suffering Longbottom. I have the great misfortune of being her ladyship's butler. A post that I have miraculously held for close to two decades now, although why I stay is beyond me as it is hell on earth here—but nevertheless—welcome to Frinton House." A sentence that made her like the man instantly.

Longbottom looked her up and down, the ghost of a smile playing at the corners of his mouth as his eyes settled on her face. "Her ladyship tells me you have spirit, which reassures me greatly as you will need it in spades to survive her. Employment here is not to be recommended for the fainthearted." An addition that made her like him more. "If you are of a delicate disposition, easily offended, or under the foolhardy misapprehension that this isn't going to be the worst job that you have ever had, then this is your last chance to run." When she didn't, he grinned and Lottie felt as though she had passed a test. "On your own head be it then, Miss Travers, and don't ever say that I didn't warn you. Lady Frinton is impatiently awaiting you in the drawing room." Unexpectedly, he gestured for her to enter via the grand front door and not around the side at the servants' entrance.

The hallway was every bit as intimidating as the glimpse of it had suggested. The floor was highly polished white marble. Two sweeping stone staircases flanked it on either side, their banisters covered in gilt, and twisted upward through four floors toward a ceiling decorated with painted cherubs floating in naked splendor amongst the fluffy white clouds of a bright blue sky. A whimsical scene completely at odds with the two terrifying suits of Japanese armor standing guard on either side of an uncomfortable-looking, narrow sofa upholstered in purple velvet. Both wielding raised, unsheathed, and razor-sharp samurai swords as if ready to slice any unwelcome intruder who dared sit on it to shreds.

"Her ladyship bought them to discourage uninvited callers," said Longbottom as he caught her looking. "And by and large they work."

"Good heavens," said Lottie as, frankly, she had no other words.

"Good heavens indeed." The butler hurried her past them at speed. "Although I'm not convinced it is the warriors' swords that scare them all away as much as the sharp tongue of their owner."

"I only met her briefly, so I really cannot comment beyond saying that I noticed she was rather forthright."

"A very diplomatic way of saying rude, Miss Travers." The butler chuckled as he continued to race her down the hallway and then stopped outside an imposing pair of double doors with a wince. "I'll give you fair warning that her ladyship is not in a good mood today, so gird your loins and try not to take it personally. But as she hasn't been in anything but a foul mood for the last fifteen years, you should probably get used to girding them."

"I heard that!" Lady Frinton's voice came from beyond the doors and Longbottom grinned briefly again before he flung them open and, rather tellingly, made no attempt to apologize to his mistress, who sat glaring at him from a wingback by the fireplace. Bedecked from head to toe in the same purple as her compact little carriage and hallway sofas.

"Miss Travers, my lady."

Lottie immediately dipped into a respectful curtsy that would have made Miss P proud.

"You're late, Travers!"

A quick glance at the clock on the mantel confirmed that she wasn't. "You said noon, my lady, and I did not want to inconvenience you by arriving too early."

"Well, it has inconvenienced me," said Lady Frinton, pushing herself to her feet with the aid of a gold-tipped walking cane. "Because I decided this morning that I wanted to leave earlier and your tardiness has thwarted that." She hobbled toward Lottie with a face like thunder. "But better late than never I suppose."

As it seemed expected, Lottie followed Lady Frinton back down the hallway, resisting the urge to make polite small talk. By the time they got to the threatening samurai, the foyer was now a hive of activity. Almost as if Longbottom knew that the lady of the house had only been waiting for her new companion's arrival before she could take leave of it. There was a swarm of footmen, surely more than any residence could possibly ever need, all carrying something outside. She counted at least five trunks coming down the stairs, all twice the size of Lottie's, along with enough hatboxes to open a milliner's shop. So much luggage, in fact, that it would need a separate carriage of its own to take it all to Scotland.

"The post has just arrived." Longbottom held out a silver salver laden with a tied stack of letters the size of a brick. "Would my lady like to read them before or after her holiday in the Highlands?"

"Give them to Travers to bring with us." Lady Frinton jerked a gloved thumb back at Lottie as she hobbled through the door. "She can read them all aloud and answer them in the carriage."

Lottie hadn't thought to pack either paper or pens and that must have shown on her face because Longbottom came to her rescue with a roll of his eyes. "I'll fetch her ladyship's traveling lap desk too then, seeing as we've already got everything else bar the kitchen sink." As he said that, two footmen came down the stairs carrying a rolled feather mattress that was trussed like a ham and so heavy that they were both out of breath, while another juggled a tower of pillows.

What sort of person traveled with their own bed on a holiday to the Highlands?

"Stop gawking, girl, and come help me!"

"Yes, my lady." Lottie hurried outside, convinced that she had seen everything, then her jaw practically fell to the floor. Because now, three more and significantly larger carriages were all lined up behind the smaller one at the front. All in various stages of loading and all sporting what she assumed was the Frinton family crest on their smart purple, black, and gold livery. It was ostentation in the extreme and quite preposterous. Unless they were traveling with another ten people. Which obviously they had to be to warrant four whole carriages. She swept a hand to encompass them all. "Who else is traveling with us today, my lady?"

Lady Frinton frowned. "What a silly question! I certainly wouldn't need the services of a paid companion if I was bringing more interesting company along, now, would I? And I can hardly expect my staff to travel by cart when the Scottish weather is famously unpredictable."

"I suppose not." As her new employer was waiting with her hand outstretched, Lottie took it and helped her into the carriage. Despite Lady Frinton's constant rudeness, she could not help finding her amusing. There was something quite refreshing about her disregard for all the expected social niceties and her determination to live her life exactly how she pleased.

No sooner was the dragon seated than she was breathing fire. "Do stop dallying, Travers. I want to get going!"

Reasoning that she could hardly read out and respond to her demanding new employer's correspondence from up on the perch beside the driver, she climbed in behind her and sat opposite.

Instantly, the older woman took issue.

"No! That will not do at all. Your legs are far too long and are crowding mine. You'll have to sit beside me!"

"Very well, my lady." She did that just in time for Longbottom to return, laden with things.

He placed a footstool made out of more purple velvet and trimmed with gold beneath Lady Frinton's feet. A thick but soft blanket was handed to Lottie to drape over the old woman's legs while he placed a wicker basket on the seat opposite. Then he directed a footman to place a rather dainty but obviously expensive lap desk next to the basket, and with a final flourish, he produced the thick stack of letters and a solid silver letter opener, which he entrusted to her.

"I shall be in the next coach with the maids in case you need me. Our first planned stop is at an inn near Potters Bar. I shall see you there, Miss

Travers, unless her ladyship's plans suddenly change . . . or you throw yourself from this conveyance beforehand." As his mistress shot him daggers, he winked at Lottie. "Good luck."

The door closed, the carriage lurched forward, and the silence stretched as they turned out of Grosvenor Square. Silence that, as uncomfortable as it was, was certainly not Lottie's place to break.

Beside her, glaring straight ahead with a pinched expression, Lady Frinton huffed out a sigh. "Seeing as you are so obviously judging me, Travers, for your information, I loathe traveling with anyone who is not in my employ. It requires too much compromise, and I am too set in my ways. I also suffer from a bad back and need my own mattress else I'll be as stiff as a board for the duration of this trip."

"I wasn't judging you, my lady."

"Of course you were!" The old battle-axe nudged her with a bony elbow. "And frankly, so you should. I would be very disappointed to discover, after your promising initial show of spirit, that I'd employed a spineless chit with no discernible thoughts or opinions of her own. That said, it goes without saying that I expect you to keep your opinions about me to yourself. I pay you first and foremost to cater to my every whim, and I shall expect you to do that with a forced smile and a polite nod no matter how tempted you might be to wring my neck. It is your most important task."

"That indeed goes without saying, my lady." Perhaps there was something warped about Lottie's character, but she was already enjoying Lady Frinton immensely. She had assumed the life of a companion would be dull and boring, but it now seemed that there would never be a dull moment with this sour old dear. Ancient she might be, but this dowager was sharper than those samurai swords she had installed in her hallway and unlike anybody Lottie had ever met.

Still staring straight ahead, Lady Frinton adjusted her blanket. "Your opinions and insight about others, however, are always welcome and the pithier the better." There was that glint of mischief in those wily old eyes again, which she failed to fully disguise as she skewered Lottie with her glare. "I like my gossip, young lady, so know that snuffling it out is your second most important task. People expect me to be the first in the know and I expect you to subtly dig for every scrap of scandal and hearsay you can find to make sure that I am."

She looked Lottie up and down again and shook her head with disgust. "Ideally, I would prefer that you be one of those bland and insipid-looking gals who blend into the wallpaper as those usually make better spies. But as you are far too tall and far too pretty to do that, we shall have to use those attributes to *my* advantage. How are your flirting skills?"

An outrageously improper question when the dragon clearly expected her to use them disingenuously to "snuffle" gossip. Yet, having used them shamelessly for years to "borrow" horses from the finest stables in Mayfair, as well as flirting for the sheer fun of it whenever her head got turned, Lottie didn't have a problem with it. Flirting was a delightful and harmless way to pass the time. Especially if the fellow she was flirting with was handsome or charming and knew how to kiss. "If I say so myself, my lady, they are exemplary. I flirt almost as well as I ride."

The old lady's lips twitched. "I am glad to hear it." Then she gestured to the letters on Lottie's lap. "Now read me my correspondence—but only the interesting letters. You can deal with the dull stuff in your room alone once I retire for the night."

"How do I know which is dull and which is interesting?"

"By opening them, of course!" Then with another bristle she added, "Do try to use some common sense, Travers! You'll only annoy me otherwise."

Lottie smothered a giggle and set to work on the letters, but it soon became apparent that despite delegating the task, Lady Frinton wanted to be the one to decide which were deemed interesting or not. Beyond the obvious bills, which she was adamant she didn't care about, there was certainly no rhyme or reason to which she wanted Lottie to read aloud and which she did not. They were barely down Piccadilly when she realized that the simplest way to find out was to read the signature at the bottom of the missive, and that in itself was fascinating because the old dragon did not hold back her opinions on the sender.

She straightaway refused five invitations from various society matrons because they "had fluff for brains." Lady Arbroath bored her, as did Lord Renshaw, and Lady Peterson was apparently "still in purgatory" for some slight which was not elaborated on beyond that "it would do her the power of good to be ignored until the very last minute to teach her a lesson." And Lord Dorchester, whoever he was, was, according to Lady Frinton, "a pompous, self-righteous, and boring arse not worthy of my time." That missive had been snatched from Lottie's hand, screwed into a ball, and unceremoniously tossed out of the carriage window. Ten letters in and she hadn't needed to answer a single one, so the dainty lap desk remained unopened.

"This one is signed only Constance," said Lottie, frowning at the scant and cryptic contents of the eleventh. "But appears to have been sent express."

"What does it say?" Lady Frinton was suddenly all ears.

"My dearest Almeria . . . You were right! The threat of a party in London was all that it needed!"

"Good heavens above!" The dowager clutched her pearls as if she were shocked to her core. "What's the date?"

Lottie squinted at the note again. "It doesn't say."

"Not the date of the letter, idiot! The date today."

"It's the twenty-fourth of August."

The window was yanked down and Lady Frinton practically screamed out of it. "Turn the carriage around!"

No doubt terrified of the repercussions if he disobeyed, the coachman turned on a sixpence, sending Lottie careening into the old lady hard. But rather than tear her off a strip for crushing her, Lady Frinton threw her white head back and cackled.

"Have you ever been to Kent, Travers?"

Chapter
SIX

⟨◈⟩

*G*uy had been in the midst of a late-afternoon meeting with his estate manager on his top field when he'd seen Aunt Almeria's cortege trundle up the lane below.

It went without saying that he had groaned aloud at the intrusion. Not because he hadn't expected her to attend his enforced birthday party— his aunt always turned up like a bad penny for his birthday. More that she was a full fortnight earlier than usual and had, typically, packed most of her worldly goods for the occasion.

His mother's much older and crotchety half sister did not understand the concept of traveling light. Nor did she understand the concept of boundaries, overstaying her welcome, or the need for personal space. All three of those things were guaranteed to be encroached upon during her visit and sure to result in a jaw ache from the gritted teeth that had started when he'd spied that first gaudy purple-and-gold carriage.

All her servants and blasted baggage never failed to upset the harmonious equilibrium of his life here, somehow turning the peaceful order of his sanctuary into her space. Probably because she didn't so much visit as lay siege. And his mother knew that! Often complained about it herself! Yet the traitor had clearly invited his aunt behind his back to help her plan the awful party that he had been blackmailed into.

It was bad enough that his mother was making his life a misery with all her excited plans for the small soiree—but now he also had Aunt Almeria to contend with. Two overbearing and infuriating women whose only purpose in life seemed to be nagging him narrow about his many failings when one was quite exasperating enough.

There would be no surprises as to the main three topics of conversation for both tonight's painful dinner and the immediate excruciating future either. The pair of them would feed off each other as they gnawed on him like carrion birds on a roadside carcass.

Topic number one would be his distinct lack of a wife.

Number two would be his distinct lack of offspring because of his lack of a wife.

And number three, his absolute favorite, would be his continued and, to their minds, wholly unreasonable stubbornness to allow them to parade him around society like a prize bull up for auction so that they could find him a blasted wife! The subtext in that one was always as galling as it was as plain as the nose on his face—that he couldn't be trusted to find one himself because he had already proved himself to be more than incompetent on that score.

In petty protest of the additional fortnight of misery he was now guaranteed, he had delayed his homecoming this evening to ensure that dinner would *have* to be late. His mother was a stickler for dinner at eight sharp. His aunt wasn't so much a stickler as a fanatic about that dinnertime, hence it was now almost half past the hour. Childish his lateness may be, but it only seemed fair that if they were determined to grossly inconvenience him until he turned bloody thirty, that he should be able to inconvenience them in return.

He might even rebel some more and refuse to change for dinner as well because that would really get them both foaming at the mouth. Such disregard for the proper formalities would be a cardinal sin as far as his aunt was concerned, as she always dressed for dinner. Even when she'd had pneumonia last winter and had had to eat her meals in bed, she had still insisted on putting on a gown.

Well, he was his own man, despite the looming blasted birthday party he had been bullied into, and a little rebellion would prove to his meddling womenfolk that he wasn't going to brook any nonsense from either of them! Not only was he not going to apologize for his tardiness, Guy was going to sit at *his* table late, eating *his* food in *his* work clothes and *his* decidedly muddy boots after a long day in *his* fields, and the pair of them would just have to get on with it. It wasn't as if he had known to expect his aunt for dinner tonight. Like everything else about his milestone birthday celebrations, his mother had kept him in the dark about Almeria's much too early but contrived arrival, so what else should they both expect?

Trumpets? Rose petals?

No, indeed. They could take him as they found him or not at all!

He dismounted and handed Zeus to a waiting groom, then stalked across the yard and into the back of the house. He forced himself to smile and greet his poor cook, who already looked to be at her wits' end. Then he briefly considered the ultimate rebellion of sneaking up the servants' stairs and not turning up to dinner at all but knew that wouldn't wash if he collided with any of the enemy on the way. His own staff might well be loyal to him, but Aunt Almeria's entourage were paid handsomely to spy. Besides, he couldn't keep the pair of them in check on all things pertaining to the bloody birthday party if he wasn't there. The tighter he held the reins, the more chance he had of controlling the carriage.

Guy stalked onward, steeling himself for the ordeal to come. He intended to march into his own dining room as if he commanded it but paused midstep when he heard a raised voice inside.

"Somebody needs to tell your cook that tomatoes have no place in a soup, Constance!" Because of course Aunt Almeria had found fault with something already. "The start of a meal should be bland and inoffensive."

"If only the same could be said about you, aunt." Pleased with the irony of that statement, Guy shoved through the double doors determined to make a decisive, I-am-the-master-of-this-house entrance. Which backfired spectacularly when he immediately smacked into a person right in front of him.

A person carrying warm tomato soup that he was instantly doused in. "What the . . . !"

His arms instinctively windmilling to flail the warm liquid away even though the damage had been done, he staggered back several steps, then blinked down at the carnage. He was pretty much orange from chin to groin. His favorite buff riding breeches completely ruined unless the laundress could work a miracle of biblical proportions on the stain.

"Oh my goodness! I am *so* sorry!" Something about the voice sounded familiar and his head snapped up. Despite the shocked hands covering her face, his gaze locked with a pair of striking eyes the exact same unusual shade of cornflower blue as those belonging to the wasp-tongued, breeches-wearing, bridle-path-averse termagant who had almost killed him in Hyde Park.

"That right there is another reason why tomatoes have no place in a soup." Aunt Almeria cackled with delight as she pointed at the state of him. "Tomato stains are forever."

"Please forgive me, I . . ." The fine feline eyes belonging to the cause of those indelible stains instantly narrowed as recognition dawned for her too. "*Oh.*"

"*Oh* indeed, madam." He still wasn't over their previous altercation and had thought of this harridan frequently as a result in the days since. It wasn't every day that he was given a thorough dressing-down by a harpy wielding a horsewhip, and that stain on his pride was still fresh too. Especially as he had thought of at least a thousand pithy retorts to all her accusations in the days since that might have made him feel a bit less mortified about the incident if he'd had the wherewithal to say them rather than gape mutely. But to find her suddenly in his dining room made him embarrassed and outraged all over again. Especially as she had made a fool of him for the second time. "One of these days you might actually look where you are going, madam, and—"

"Oh, for goodness' sake, Guy!" His clucking mother bustled over, wielding a napkin that she thwacked him with before using it to smear the soup further around his face in an attempt to clean it. "Don't you dare be your usual beastly self to this poor young lady when this unfortunate accident wouldn't have happened in the first place if you hadn't just charged into dinner like a bull at a gate. What on earth were you thinking to fling both doors open with such brute force? You are supposed to be a gentleman, Guy, not a Viking marauder!" She gave up on cleaning the soup coating him as the lost cause that it was to fawn over the menace who had flung it. "Pay him no mind, Miss Travers. My son's bark is worse than his bite."

"This"—the harpy gestured at him with a disgusted flick of her finger—"is *your* son?" The cornflower eyes fluttered rapidly before she twisted to gape at his aunt instead. "*He* is your nephew? *Him?*" The word was laced with sheer horror.

"Sadly, yes," said Aunt Almeria, enjoying the sight of him soaked in soup too much to disguise it. "Travers—meet Lord Guy Harrowby, the thirteenth Viscount Wennington. Guy, I know it goes against the grain, but please try to be nice to my latest companion. We have only been together a day but I have high hopes that this one shows promise."

Promise in causing accidents with her reckless clumsiness, perhaps!

"My lord." Miss Travers's gaze once again locked with his as the vixen instantly dipped into a curtsy. The involuntary tic in her cheek and defiant stare telling him in no uncertain terms that she only offered him the expected deference begrudgingly. "My sincere apologies for . . ." The wrist flicked again. This time at the gloopy river of tepid tomato soup now dribbling down his thighs. ". . . the spillage." Just the spillage, he noted. Not for unseating him from his horse after willfully ignoring the rules of the road or calling him a rude oaf or besmirching his riding abilities or threatening to horsewhip him in Hyde Park. Or for looking at him right now as if he were something unpleasant stuck to the sole of her shoe. Then to add insult to injury, she smiled, though it did not touch her eyes any because those pretty blue irises had hardened to ice crystals. "It is a pleasure to finally meet you, my lord. Your aunt told me a great deal about you on our journey here."

It was clear she hadn't found anything at all impressive in what his aunt had told her. Which all rather suggested Aunt Almeria might have been too honest about him and that troubled him too. Although why he should care if Miss Travers considered him any more of a big joke than any other random stranger was a mystery—but he did and that rankled. As did her arrogance in pretending that they hadn't met because she clearly expected him to keep the skirmish she had mostly caused in Hyde Park to himself.

The insolent minx.

He should put her in her place right this minute by calling her out on it. Make her into the joke instead. That might teach her a lesson or two. She certainly deserved it.

Except she was employed by his aunt and the truth might lose her the job. An awful job she must really need to have accepted it in the first place.

Drat her.

But in the grand scheme of things, having to suffer his aunt Almeria was probably comeuppance enough. Frankly, if the Valkyrie lasted a week with his unreasonable relative, it would be a bloody miracle. And in regurgitating the story of how they had collided, he'd likely end up humiliating himself more as his aunt and his mother were bound to find his misfortune in Hyde Park funny. Just as they both currently found the incident with the soup funny. His mother was turning pink with her efforts not to howl with laughter.

"The pleasure is all mine, Miss Travers." He too could smile and not mean it, and he actually did take some pleasure in watching her fine eyes widen as his narrowed. "But please excuse me. Now that I have had my soup, I had best go and change for dinner."

Chapter
SEVEN

֍

*L*ottie gave up trying to go back to sleep, kicked her eiderdown to the bottom of her bed, and stared at the dawn shadows on the unfamiliar ceiling.

She'd had a restless night because there was no doubt that she was now in a precarious position. Viscount Wennington hated her. He had made no secret of that for the rest of the dinner after she had ruined his clothes with all that tomato soup.

Last night he might have kept their first unpleasant encounter to himself, but he wasn't over it. She had felt that in every brooding stare he'd sent her way. Each one making her skin prickle in the most disconcerting manner until she could barely stand it.

She supposed that would teach her to react without thinking. In sticking up for his poor horse, she had insulted him—she might have even threatened him, she had been so angry—and now she was an unwelcome guest in his house. Whether he had deserved the telling off she had given him or not—and he very much had—it was inevitable that if she put another foot wrong, he might very well send her packing. Then what? No wages to send to her struggling family, that was what. Family who were, ironically, fewer than ten miles from here.

She hadn't believed her luck when Lady Frinton's visit to Scotland had instead turned into a high-speed jaunt to her part of Kent. At the time, it had felt serendipitous that she would have both the opportunity to provide her family some funds and to be able to deliver them in person. Now, all that joy had turned into trepidation and suddenly she was walking on eggshells.

Lord Wennington had made her so uncomfortable with his nearly constant glaring that she had hardly said a word over dinner last night. Of course, as a companion, she was only supposed to speak when spoken to, so she hoped nobody had noticed.

She wasn't sure what it was about him, but she had never been so aware of a man in her life. He was big and surly and as much as she wanted to avoid his stormy, dark eyes, they seemed to draw hers like a magnet. Which was as mortifying as it was annoying. As was his overt and brooding attractiveness. He was a rude, arrogant, and all-around horrid man, and yet all the more compelling for it. The more she tried not to notice his strong jaw or broad shoulders or his impatient, blunt, tapping fingers, the more the wild and wayward part of her wanted to. Which was ridiculous when there was absolutely nothing about him to like otherwise.

Especially when it had been clear that the viscount had been in a foul mood last night and that he only sat at the table out of sufferance. He made no attempt to make any polite conversation, only answered questions specifically directed at him, and his responses were brief. Clipped. However, although she suspected that her presence was responsible for a great deal of that, she had also sensed another undertone for his curt manner.

The presence of his aunt seemed to irritate him almost as much as Lottie's did. Similarly, his upcoming birthday party caused him a great deal of consternation and any attempts by his mother to draw him into her plans for the event were met with exceedingly short shrift.

It was plain he didn't want one, thought the whole thing a complete waste of his precious time, and only became animated when he stated that he had no intentions of feigning any enthusiasm for it while it happened either. He also kept reiterating that there were only to be thirty guests as he mentioned that specific number at least four times before he made his abrupt excuse to leave the table the second the desserts were done. They hadn't seen hide nor hair of him afterward—but he had given Lottie one last glare before he stalked out.

One that told her in no uncertain terms that he wasn't the sort to forgive and forget and that he wasn't anywhere near done with her yet.

She presumed that meant that at some point today words would be had where he asserted his dominance, so she was already smarting at the unpalatable prospect of having to bite her tongue while he said them. Here, she had to remember her place, and until she and Lady Frinton left Kent, it would probably be a good idea to apologize profusely, then keep her head down. Try her hardest to suppress her wild streak and blend into the woodwork. But Miss P was right about one thing. Blending in had never been her forte and she didn't trust herself not to bite back if that arrogant wretch provoked her enough.

In which case, her only real hope was Lady Frinton, who despite being rather despotic and hard to please, wasn't the sort to get rid of a member of *her* staff because they had displeased someone else. People deferred to Lady Frinton; she was far too contrary to defer back. Lady Frinton had also found the incident with the soup hilarious and hadn't made any attempt to chastise her for it. Lady Frinton also knew that she had a penchant for borrowing horses so the fact that she had once again been riding in Hyde Park wouldn't come as much of a surprise. Therefore, Lottie sincerely hoped that if she dismissed her, it would be because of something Lottie had done or not done to displease her. And her alone. Therefore, rather than be intimidated by her employer's vexatious nephew, she should instead focus on working tirelessly to become the best lady's companion that the pernickety old dragon had ever had. The sort who anticipated all her employer's needs and was completely indispensable. No matter what tattletales her disapproving nephew might tell.

A quest she would start right this second if it wasn't six o'clock in the morning. She didn't know much about her new mistress's needs and peculiarities yet, today was only her second day after all, but Longbottom had warned her that the old dear did not rise before eleven. She liked a good ten hours' sleep and did not leave her bed without a soft-boiled egg, a slice of hot buttered toast, and at least two cups of tea inside her. Tea that Lottie would deliver personally this morning to Lady Frinton's exacting expectations. Just like the perfect lady's companion should.

In the meantime, she might as well use the empty hours productively. If she was going to become indispensable, she needed to know the lay of the land. This giant house was a baffling maze and she might as well learn where everything was, and who to procure things from.

Rather than trouble a maid, she washed in cold water and dressed in her plainest gown and even pinned her hair in a no-nonsense-I-am-part-of-the-wallpaper bun. Exactly like the hair of a dutiful companion should look.

Unsurprisingly, downstairs was already a hive of activity as the servants prepared for their masters to wake. As a companion, and therefore basically a servant herself, she was acknowledged with just a polite good morning as a footman hurried past going about his business.

"Have you seen Longbottom?" Lady Frinton's butler was the key to her becoming indispensable, seeing as he was apparently indispensable enough himself to have been dragged here too. He knew everything about the old bat and seemed the sort who might share his knowledge, given the right incentive. And what better incentive than teaming up and sharing the heavy load of Lady Frinton? A problem shared was a problem halved after all.

"I think he went to the henhouse, miss." Because of course he had! After fifteen years of service, Longbottom would know that only the right sort of soft-boiled egg would appease their fussy mistress, so it stood to reason that he would go and choose it himself. He probably also stood over the pot staring at his pocket watch while it boiled too!

Lottie asked directions and headed out the back door. The beauty of the morning slapped her in the face as she stepped outside, warming her heart. Oh, how she had missed these misty Kent mornings! The sun peeking over the gently rolling hills in the distance and bathing the wheat fields in front of them in diffused light, reminding her so much of her own home it brought a lump to her throat. Even the perfume from the roses blooming in abundance over the wall of the servants' yard smelled the same as those which twisted around her father's porch.

Except the Travers family farm wasn't anywhere near as grand as her current surroundings. Wennington Hall appeared larger from the back than it had from the front. She had been impressed by the classical symmetry of the whitewashed Palladian-style mansion as the carriage had pulled up to it early yesterday evening. Yet she could see now that what had seemed to be a large, rectangular house was in fact a flattened horseshoe because two big wings jutted out like twin arms hugging the grounds. It had to have at least twenty bedrooms and by the perfect, unbroken vista ahead, it came along with hundreds upon hundreds of acres.

Oh, how the other half lived!

She followed the gravel path to the left as she had been instructed, and would have also followed it past the stables had the stables not been enormous. By the clean look of the pristine brickwork, they were also very new. Beside them was an expansive exercise field surrounded by a sturdy wooden fence where a burly groom worked with an adolescent horse attached to a very long rope.

Lottie hadn't realized that she had veered from the path until she came up against the fence, she was so transfixed. By the powerful but lithe build of the animal literally chomping at the bit, it could only be another Arabian. Except by the way this one fought the line, he was clearly an unbroken one.

"How old is he?"

"Two and a half," said the handsome groom, happy to chat. "And a proper handful."

"Arabians can be. Especially in the wrong hands." Except one look at this modern stable complex and she already knew that she might have misjudged the vexing viscount's knowledge of horses. "Bred here?"

"Aye, miss." The groom let out the rope, giving the frustrated horse the opportunity to let off some steam. Instinctively it began to gallop around the exercise field in a circle. "Was it you I saw arrive yesterday with the dowager?"

"Yes. I'm her latest companion."

He offered her a pitying look. "Then I tip my hat to you." He did so with a cheeky wink. "For you're a braver soul than I am."

"I don't frighten easily." Her gaze followed the horse. "What's his name?"

"Hercules." The groom gestured to a pasture beyond, where another, much fairer-coated Arabian grazed amongst a scattering of different breeds, including a giant Shire horse and a tiny Shetland pony. "That's his mother over there—but Juno is as gentle as the breeze and he's inherited none of her calm temperament. He's every inch the son of the tempestuous Zeus, so being a handful is in his blood."

"Which is Zeus?" She squinted at all the horses in the distance, and none looked as majestic as this fine specimen or his beautiful mother.

"Out with the master. He's the only one with patience enough to ride him."

As the concept of patience jarred with the ill-tempered man she had met twice and didn't like, she frowned. "I don't suppose Zeus is the exact color of whiskey but with a jet-black mane and tail?" That horse had been so jumpy and combative he would try the patience of a saint.

"Aye, miss. That's him. Snorts and bucks like it's going out of fashion. This one's the same." Right on cue, Hercules took issue with the line and tried to twist out of his bridle. "Resents the rope and it still takes three of us to put him in a harness after five months of trying. We daren't strap a saddle on him as he'd likely break your neck soon as look at you. But he's a work in progress, as they say. We'll either break him eventually or he'll break us. At this point it could go either way."

"Maybe he's still a bit too young to train. Arabians have a great deal of energy and are often stubborn."

"That they are—even after they've been broken. The master has to saddle Zeus himself as that demon will only allow a chosen few to touch him. I've had bruises aplenty that prove that I am not one of them." The groom chuckled without any malice toward the animal. "More's the pity as I'd love to take him out and put him through his paces. But maybe Hercules will let me one day."

He slackened the line as he approached the horse and released it, then quickly opened the gate by swinging his whole body out with it. Hercules needed no encouragement to fly out of the confines of the exercise yard and gallop into the other field straight to his mother. Within moments, he went from an uncooperative devil to an angel as they watched the transformation in companionable silence. His chestnut tail swished as he munched on the grass beside the mare.

"He's always a different beast out there." The groom secured the gate. "Makes me wonder if he's just one of God's creatures who is meant to be wild."

Much like Lottie was.

She always tried her best to conform to the rules but something inherent and unstoppable within her made her break some. Being here in Kent, for example, amongst all the horses and lush, open fields made the urge to jump on the back of one of these horses and gallop so strong it made her heart race. *But not today, Satan!* While she worked for Lady Frinton, she was determined to be all restraint and decorum.

Restraint didn't mean that she had to be disinterested though. If she couldn't ride a horse, surely it couldn't hurt to just talk about them. "Was Zeus as boisterous and uncooperative at that age?"

He shrugged. "Who knows? The master brought Zeus home fully grown one day four years back. Went to Maidstone to buy a new plow and came back with a face like thunder, a black eye, and an angry Arabian instead. The hows and whys of the transaction remain shrouded in mystery and we all know better than to inquire. Ask anything that his lordship considers an invasion of his privacy and you'll likely get your head bitten off."

Much to her chagrin, Lottie found that story intriguing. But it did make her feel slightly better about the master of the house to know that it wasn't just her he was bad-tempered with. "And Juno?"

"Bought for a king's ransom a few months later—especially for Zeus—because none of the other horses dare go near him and, frankly, I don't blame them. But there's no accounting for taste in matters of the heart, is there? All that matters is that she seems to like him and him her." The groom sent a smile Lottie's way, his gaze now one of masculine appreciation. "I'm Bill, by the way. It is lovely to meet you."

"Lottie," she said smiling back with the merest hint of flirtation. Not really because she was drawn to the groom in *that* way, but because she always made a habit of keeping grooms on her side. Just in case she felt the overwhelming urge to . . .

No!

She was *not* going to ride any of Viscount Wennington's excellent stable. Especially not when he had it in for her.

"How come a pretty lass like yourself knows so much about horses?"

"I grew up with them. On a farm not ten miles from here."

"That explains why I immediately took a fancy to you." Bill folded his big arms, no doubt to impress her with the size of his muscles. "You're a Kent girl and Kent grows the best ones."

It was on the tip of her tongue to flatter his ego by telling him that Kent grew the best men too, but she bit it back and forced her eyelashes not to bat, because harmless flirting had always come as second nature to her, particularly where horses were concerned. However, as she was a changed woman, she smiled politely and ignored his blatant smoldering like a prim and proper lady's companion should. "I don't suppose you could point me in the direction of the henhouse please, Bill? Only I have to find the perfect egg for Lady Frinton or society might crumble." Not flirting didn't mean that she shouldn't be friendly.

Bill leaned one muscular elbow on the gate this time, leaning closer to her as he did so. "Can't I tempt you with a tour of the stables first? Knowing Lady Frinton, she won't be up for hours and I'm sure Juno would love to meet you."

*T*t was her laughter that Guy heard first. Earthy and unabashed, just like the woman herself. How he knew it was Miss Travers he could not say beyond an odd lurch in his gut as he wandered into the tack room to get what he needed to brush Zeus down. He rubbed a porthole in the dusty window and there she was. As bold as brass in his pasture, looking all effervescent and pretty while being adored by tiny Hamish, his usually grumpy old Shetland pony who never gave him the blasted time of day.

Because that was just bloody typical!

Why he'd been compelled to rescue the ungrateful equine curmudgeon from that traveling menagerie where he'd lived in a cage was one of life's great mysteries. Because after liberating him from incarceration at some not insubstantial cost, Hamish had hated him for it ever since. Now, to add insult to injury, the ingrate had taken a shine to that clumsy shrew! And she wasn't even feeding the traitor any carrots so the adoration was given for free. Totally gratis when he had to earn every scrap of notice from the most pointless horse he had ever owned.

It was enough to boil his piss.

And on the subject of adoration . . .

Guy's gut lurched again when Bill, his head groom, suddenly invaded the scene and said something apparently so hilarious that Miss Travers threw back her pretty golden head and roared. The smug smile on Bill's face and the way his ludicrously beefy shoulders rose with pride made clear that he had taken a shine to the woman too. The besotted fool reached for her hand to help her up, held it for far longer than was necessary, and she beamed at him in return. Offering Bill a smile so breathtaking, Guy found himself holding his.

With gritted teeth.

What the blazes was that all about when she boiled his piss too?

Furious at himself, he gave Zeus a vigorous brush down, then made sure to check out of the tack room window that the minx was gone before he ventured out. He was in no mood to face her just yet after she had decorated him in soup, and he still hadn't decided what he wanted to say to her.

Something definitely needed to be said about their collision in Hyde Park.

Something that set the record straight, righted the one wrong he wasn't proud of, cleared the charged air, and reinstated some of his battered pride. She'd made a fool of him twice now and that left him so off-kilter he honestly could not escape fast enough last night. Afterward, the image of her disdainful cornflower eyes was seared onto his mind. Tormenting him. Even while he'd slept.

Bloody woman!

He was leading Zeus out to join the rest of the herd when she and Bill appeared at the entrance of the stable. They both stopped dead, horrified to see him, which in itself spoke volumes. She offered him a wary curtsy as Bill doffed his cap.

"Good morning, my lord."

He acknowledged that with a nod. "Miss Travers." Then, because she made him inexplicably tongue-tied, decided to carry on doing what he had been doing and lead Zeus out.

"I'm just giving Lottie a quick tour of the stables." Bill smiled as Guy passed them, secure in the knowledge that he wasn't the sort of employer to get annoyed that he wasn't doing his duty every minute of every day, yet was blissfully unaware that the fact he was allowed to call the minx Lottie annoyed him anyway. Because of course the stable's most enthusiastic stud hadn't wasted any time charming the vixen so that they could drop the formalities.

Lottie.

He rolled the name around in his head as he crossed the yard and decided it suited her far better than Charlotte. Charlotte was such a conventionally proper name. Charlottes did not wear breeches and ride astride. They did needlepoint and played the piano, and she didn't strike him as the type for those calm pursuits. In fact, he'd lay good money that she'd never picked up a piece of embroidery in her life, and the piano . . . Well, that might provide him with an opportunity to get a bit of his own back. He might innocently request she play them all something tonight after dinner and then he could enjoy how badly she did it. Dent her abundant pride some to even the score. Not that he was one to enjoy another's discomfort normally—but he'd make an exception in her case.

Maybe.

And most likely maybe not.

Sabotage wasn't gentlemanly.

Annoyed at her, himself, and blasted Bill, he released Zeus into the pasture and, with a huff, closed the gate.

"I should have been on the bridle path." Her voice so close to his shoulder made Guy jump. As he spun around, her expression was contrite, long, delicate fingers clasped before her like a naughty child before her governess. "I also should have apologized for spooking your fine horse that morning when I galloped right in front of him. I was in a bad mood . . . distracted . . . and never slowed to look properly, so what happened was entirely my fault."

Of all the things he'd expected this whirlwind of a woman to say, an unsolicited apology out of the blue wasn't one of them. Unfortunately for her, he was too jaded to believe it was genuine. Not when she had been openly disdainful last night and was employed by his ornery aunt. "I see."

She stared at him for several seconds before she smiled. "This awkward silence is the part where you are supposed to apologize for not thanking me when I retrieved Zeus for you."

She really was a brazen one, even though he conceded she did make a valid point. "Thank you for retrieving Zeus for me." Why the blazes was his heart racing? Why did his skin not seem to fit his bones properly? What was it about this woman that unnerved him so?

"And . . . ," she said, turning her hand like a wheel, smiling. "I am sorry for being a rude oaf, Miss Travers, but you caught me in a foul mood too." Her cornflower eyes twinkled with amusement as she dared him to elaborate while providing him with an excuse for his ungentlemanly behavior. "Or is that too hard to say, when here I am, standing humbly before you, admitting all blame and desperately trying to meet you halfway?"

Currently, with his innards bunched and his stomach doing somersaults, everything was too hard to say, but thanks to his stubborn pride alone he managed to find his voice. Except what came out of his mouth wasn't at all what he wanted to say nor at all what he should have. "If you are worried that I will insist that my aunt dismiss you because of your recklessness, then don't. She'll probably do that soon enough without my help anyway."

Her smile melted and he instantly missed it.

Apologize, idiot! Take it back. Don't be a lion with a thorn in its paw.

But no words came out of his paralyzed mouth.

"Very true, my lord." Then she curtsied. Properly this time, with all the expected deference and respectfully dipped eyes that his stupid title supposedly warranted, and he hated it. Hated that he had crushed her olive branch with curt words and pessimism. "Thank you for listening."

And then she was gone.

Chapter
EIGHT

❧❧❧

*I*nsufferable man!"

Lottie stormed back toward the house, her quest to find Long-bottom to pick his brains forgotten.

What sort of person turned down an apology flat and then took plea-sure in insulting a person on the back of it? The sort who was so pompous and arrogant that he thought he was incapable of being in the wrong, that's who! Lord Wennington was worse than the rude oaf she had first pegged him for. He was a thoroughly nasty piece of work!

She took the back door into the house, then took the servants' stairs two at a time, so angry she needed to expel some of it before she was fit company to commence her duties calmly. Half an hour screaming bloody murder into her pillow while pacing her room might do the trick. Barefoot because she'd been placed in a small bedchamber next to Lady Frinton's palatial suite and didn't dare wake the old dragon up. Not when she had been explicit in her dislike of mornings in general and most especially any that started before nine. Thankfully, as it wasn't yet eight, Lottie had a decent while to rant with impunity.

But as she approached her bedchamber, a harried maid scurried out of Lady Frinton's room carrying a tea tray. Unwelcome evidence that the battle-axe was up and Lottie had already failed to attend to her mistress as a good companion should.

Swallowing all her anger left her feeling bloated and tense, but duty called. She pasted on a smile, lightly rapped at the door and, without thinking, sailed inside.

Lady Frinton squealed and clutched her bedcovers to her chest while her much younger sister, Lady Wennington, threw her body over a pile of papers on the mattress.

"Oh, I am so sorry!" Clearly she had interrupted something as now both women wore twin expressions of guilt as they blinked back at her.

"Come in, gal, and shut the bloody door!" Her employer's gaze went from shocked to narrowed in an instant, whereas Lady Wennington remained half prostrate on the eiderdown. "And for pity's sake, sit up, Constance! Travers is paid good money to keep her mouth shut and just might come in useful." As her sister rose and readjusted her clothing, Lady Frinton gestured for Lottie to drag over a chair. "What we are about to tell you is tantamount to a state secret, do you understand?"

"Of course, my lady." Now that all the apparently secret papers were exposed, Lottie could see that they were invitations. Some were written but most were blank. "My lips are sealed."

"Good! Because my bloody nephew has eyes like a hawk, his servants are too loyal, and if he gets wind of what we're up to, our best chance of getting the slippery blighter wed before he's too old to father any children will be gone."

"I see." Although she didn't. "In what way can I be useful?"

Lady Frinton's eyes flicked to her sister for permission to elaborate and the other woman nodded. "After years and years of refusing to attend any social occasions in town, my nephew has finally reluctantly agreed to a birthday party here. A *small* birthday party."

"I know that," said Lottie, wondering where this was going.

"He must remain in the belief that all we are planning is an intimate evening soiree involving just a few families on the day of his birth." She handed Lottie what appeared to be a short guest list.

As there were more invitations scattered across the bed than were needed for the few on the list, it did not take a genius to work out that these ladies had other plans. "I take it that is not the case?"

"Of course not!" Lady Wennington's voice was hushed but passionate. "How on earth is he supposed to meet and fall head over heels with the right lady in a few measly hours?"

Lady Frinton patted her slightly overwrought sister's hand in sympathy. "He can't, Constance, and enough is enough. All his shilly-shallying has to end. If he refuses to investigate all the eligible choices on offer in London, then we have a moral duty to bring London here." An outrageous comment that calmed the other woman down somewhat. "You have done all you can—but when it comes to women, Guy is useless."

Lottie wanted to add that he was obnoxious too but bit her tongue.

"That is why we are throwing him a surprise house party, Travers. A proper one. That will last a whole week."

"Which he will absolutely hate," added Lady Wennington, nervously fiddling with the pearls encircling her throat. "But what else can I do, Miss Travers, when he has become intractable on the subject of love and I am desperate to see him happy?"

They were matchmaking! Lottie knew enough about the curmudgeonly viscount already to know that he wouldn't just hate a house party. He would loathe it with every miserable fiber of his being, the rude and insufferable wretch. Which conversely cheered her right up.

"I would not normally go behind Guy's back like this, but desperate times call for desperate measures." Lady Wennington was knotting a handkerchief this time. "Especially when my son will be thirty on the fourteenth of September. *Thirty*." The way she said his age made him sound decrepit, which the irritant wasn't. As much as it pained Lottie to think it, for all his many faults, he was a prime physical specimen. And a viscount to boot. In London, and irrespective of his foul character, he would have to beat the debutantes off with a stick. Here . . . well, the prospect of him being hounded by a herd of hungry husband-hunters while unable to escape was just too funny.

Except, he had such a vile personality, she pitied the fool who caught him. You would have to be a very stupid or a very desperate woman indeed to willingly shackle yourself to that!

"I can assure you that I have tried absolutely everything to get him to find his soulmate, but he refuses to cooperate. If I try to steer him left, I can guarantee he will go right just to spite me. He's forced me into this."

"You are doing the right thing, Constance, so stop second-guessing yourself." Lady Frinton patted her sister's hand. "Sometimes, we mothers have to give our offspring a little nudge in the right direction but in stubborn Guy's case, that means pushing him off the cliff! We need to put temptation directly in his path and let nature take its course."

"My father had to do that with a reluctant bull once," said Lottie without thinking. "We had to surround him with cows in season before he worked up the enthusiasm to cover one of them—but once he started there was no stopping him. Ended up being the most randy bull we ever had."

One look at Lady Wennington's stunned face told Lottie that she had completely misjudged her audience and she winced. Lady Frinton, on the other hand, roared with laughter. "Indeed! One has to lead a horse to water to make him drink and we are going to supply him with an ocean."

"Exactly how much of London are you inviting?"

"As many as we can get, Travers." Lady Frinton rubbed her hands together with glee. "I have made a list of every good family with an unmarried daughter who could potentially be here by the eighth—which gives us just fourteen days to pull it all off." Then she deflated. "But that lofty ambition is not without its challenges at such short notice. We'll need to get all the invitations posted today to stand a chance of having a halfway decent turnout."

"That shouldn't be a problem here in Kent where the postal service to London is excellent." Lottie's letters always arrived in her family's hands within two days and their replies came back to Mayfair just as swiftly.

"Ah . . . yes." Lady Frinton turned to her sister. "Travers is a native of this county."

"Are you really?" Lady Wennington tried to show some interest even though her mind was on the party. "That's nice."

"Sadly, sending out so many clandestine invitations without Guy noticing is only half the battle." Lady Frinton threw up her palms. "While we can easily explain away taking a carriage into Maidstone this afternoon on the pretense of shopping, it will not be easy to hide the veritable mountain of replies from him. He'll smell a rat if Constance gets too many letters as he's capped her guest list at thirty and expects them all to be local."

"The servants are ridiculously loyal to Guy so one of them is bound to tattle." His mother tossed her handkerchief on the bed as if surrendering. "And before you suggest that we ask the postmaster in the village to hold them for us, Miss Travers, he's as loyal as the servants are and will not engage in any deception if he thinks Guy will be upset by it. Never mind that it's impossible to make proper plans unless we know precisely who is coming, as that would only result in chaos. Bedchambers will need to be covertly prepared for the most important guests lest we grossly insult them, inns will need to be reserved for everyone else in good time if we get more than I can house here, and then there is all the food to consider. A great deal of that will need to be ordered in—but not from anyone close who is liable to let the cat out of the bag. So you see, we've rather been scuppered by the first hurdle as everyone hereabouts adores my son."

Lottie struggled to believe that but did not question it because mothers were supposed to love their children unconditionally. Clearly Lady Wennington wore blinkers when it came to her objectional offspring. But that wasn't her problem, and this situation had provided her with the perfect opportunity to be indispensable.

"If you state plainly on the invitations that this is a *surprise* house party, you can instruct everyone to direct their replies elsewhere. My father's farm is less than ten miles away and no trouble at all for me to get to and fetch them for us. Especially as I am unlikely to be missed by his lordship." Avoiding him *while* being able to visit her family was a double bonus.

"Your father would do that?" Lady Wennington reached for her hand. "It seems like a dreadful imposition."

"Of course he would—but if you wish for me to ask his permission first, I could do that this afternoon and post the invitations en route. Aylesford is just outside of Maidstone and that is too busy a town for him to know every merchant."

"Oh, that would be splendid, Miss Travers. Thank you."

"Didn't I tell you that this one showed promise, Constance?" Lady Frinton settled back against her pillows and gestured for her teacup that was well within arm's reach on her nightstand. When Lottie dutifully passed it to her, she didn't get a thank-you. "If Travers is the intermediary on the guest front, Longbottom can return to London and take care of all the food that needs ordering and *my* maids can take care of the covert making up of the guest bedchambers nearer the time. Between us all we'll get it all done and Guy will be none the wiser. In the meantime, Constance, he must think that it is business as usual so you must do a very public job of organizing a small evening soiree on the day of his actual birthday while lamenting its mediocrity alongside his reluctance to allow you to do the deed properly."

"I can absolutely do that!" For the first time since Lottie had entered the bedchamber, Lady Wennington grinned. "He loathes me nagging him about finding a wife so much, he will purposefully make himself scarce if I am relentless." Then she giggled, mischief dancing in her eyes. "This is going to be such fun, isn't it?"

Lottie nodded, already enjoying herself immensely at the vexing viscount's expense.

Lady Frinton, on the other hand, scowled at them both over the rim of her teacup. "Well? What in God's name are the pair of you waiting for? Divine intervention? Pick up some pens this minute and start writing while I reel off the names of every eligible and gloriously single young lady of the ton."

———❦———

It was late afternoon when the Frinton carriage made its way up the lane to the farm. She could see her menfolk dotted around the fields, all watching the grand conveyance with interest because nothing like it ever visited, but it was her youngest brother, Dan, who saw her first and ran toward her, beaming.

"Well, look at you, Beanstalk!" He eyed the carriage first, taking in the unusual purple paint and gold crest. "All fancy." He hauled her into a hug and, in case the coachman heard, whispered, "I take it this smart gig belongs to the fire-breathing old dragon you've just started working for?"

"Lady Frinton is more hot air than fire—but yes, this is hers."

Knowing her only too well, he held her out at arm's length with a scowl. "Did she lend it to you or did you pilfer it?"

"Pilfered, and I kidnapped her coachman." She pushed him away, laughing. "Of course she lent it to me. I am here at her behest actually so this visit is all aboveboard, thank you very much."

"What could a *viscountess* want with the likes of us?"

Over her brother's shoulder, from all directions, she could see the rest of the family running toward her and knew the window of opportunity to talk to Dan alone was rapidly closing. "I'll tell you all that in a minute. First, tell me how dire things are here?" He was only a year older than her and had always been the brother least likely to be overprotective.

His expression shuttered. "I overreacted in my last letter, Beanstalk. We'll get by."

As she had since childhood, she quickly grabbed the hand he had hidden behind his back before he could stop her. Guilt instantly suffused his face when she stared down at his crossed fingers. "I thought as much. Spill everything before Papa gets down here or I'll break your nose again, liar."

"He's planning on selling half the dairy herd to tide us over the winter."

"But the milk makes money! Especially in the longer term." A fact her father knew better than anyone so things must be worse than she thought if he had to sacrifice that future income to pay for the months in between. "Surely that's a last resort?"

Dan shook his head. "The blight in the barley was bad, Beanstalk. Twice as bad as it was in the wheat two years ago, so we've lost that field for at least another year to give it a chance to recover. Not that we've got any seed or the money yet to purchase any to plant the damn thing. But the loss of this year's crop and now the next is going to hurt. We've been over all the figures and options over and over again and unless a miracle occurs fast, the cows have to go to cover the shortfall."

"Don't let him do it yet as a miracle might happen." What sort of miracle when farmers all over the country were going bankrupt in these unbelievably challenging times, she did not know, but she was an eternal optimist. Or perhaps a complete fool for believing something positive would come up when nothing had in years. Farming had always been hard, but it was getting harder and harder. Labor costs were sky high, thanks to the better wages in the newly industrialized towns, and the merchants banded together to extort lower and lower prices, which smallholders like her papa had to accept or risk their crops rotting away while they argued with them. Then there was the competition from foreign grain. All factors that worked together like a vise to squeeze farmers. And that was before a devastating disease like persistent blight killed every seed you tried to grow and poisoned your fields in the process.

But she would not focus on that as it was too depressing, so Lottie rummaged in her reticule and pressed some money into his hands. "Put this in Papa's money jar after I leave and deny all knowledge of it. Miss P insisted that Lady Frinton pay me a week in advance, seeing as she goes through staff like most people do bread. There will be more of this in a few days. I know it's not much but it's something."

"I can't deny that this will come in handy." Dan quickly pocketed the money as they both knew that her proud and protective father, who was mere yards away now, would rather starve than take it from her. "Don't let him know that I told you. He knows nothing about the letter I sent."

"I'll pretend to stumble upon the truth in my own inimitable way, just like I always do." She didn't need to paste on a smile for her father who, being a sentimental man, already had tears in his eyes.

"The prodigal daughter returns!" Arms outstretched, her papa ran the last few feet to get to her and wrap her in a tight embrace. "Why didn't you tell me that you were coming home so I could roll out the welcome mat and hire some trumpeters?"

Behind him came Stephen, her eldest brother. "A fanfare? For this long streak of nothing? A whistle will do and that would be pushing it." But despite his droll welcome, her feet lifted off the floor as he spun her around. "Nobody missed you, baby sister."

Then the twins, Matthew and Luke, bounded over and took impatient turns to smother her in love before Matty stole her bonnet and Luke ruffled her hair so hard it resembled a bird's nest by the time he had finished.

"Seeing as we've all been working hard and Lottie has been twiddling her thumbs while swanning around in that fancy carriage, who votes that she makes the tea?" Dan's arm was raised before he finished his question and every other hand shot up, so he frog-marched her toward the house.

Everything within was as it always was. Unchanged since her mother's day, save a little more clutter, and blissfully homey. A stew bubbled on the range, courtesy no doubt of Mrs. Parkin, who still came in every morning to take care of the housework while Lottie's menfolk worked in the fields. Thanks to Dan's letter, she knew that their part-time housekeeper was one of only a handful of essential employees that had been kept on now that the farm had to tighten its belt. Which in turn meant that her brothers and her father had been forced to take on more, and that bothered her. Especially as her father wasn't getting any younger and had always worked himself too hard.

The fresh burdens since the barley had failed showed on his face. His eyes bore more shadows and his shoulders were more slumped. As if he carried the whole weight of the world on them. It was clear he wasn't sleeping well. Stephen, too, looked more troubled than usual despite the steady stream of bantering insults he sent her way as the kettle boiled.

Yet irrespective of all her justified concerns about the state of their health and the depressing Travers finances, it was good to be back in the bosom of her family again. She hadn't seen any of them since her last visit home in June. Two months of distance was hard when they were all as close as they were.

"I can't say I ever pictured you as a lady's companion, Lottie." Her papa always blew on his tea before he took his first sip, no matter what temperature. "What happened with Lord Chadwell? I thought you liked being the governess to his children?"

Dan slanted her a conspiratorial glance that told her he had kept his word and hadn't told the rest of them the truth about her dismissal.

"Lady Frinton pays better," he said, compounding the lie.

"That's right." She tried to sip her tea as nonchalantly as she could while tucking her hand beneath her skirt so that she could cross her fingers. A ridiculous thing for a grown woman to still do but, like her brother earlier, it wasn't so much a habit but a compulsion she could not break. All the Travers siblings had done it since time immemorial and not doing it was unthinkable. Although what they thought would happen if they lied without crossed fingers was anyone's guess, especially when a lie was a lie. Yet somehow the crossed fingers lessened the crime and made them all feel better about it. "I am getting almost twice as much working for her as I did with Chadwell so if you—"

"Do not even think it." Her father's mouth flattened as he held up a warning hand. "That money is yours to save for when you are married and that is that. I do not need your misplaced charity. We're doing grand, aren't we, boys?" Four heads wearing varying expressions of convincingness nodded in unison.

"Governesses and lady's companions don't marry, Papa."

For a start, in the usual course of their duties, they never met anyone to marry. They lived a life of dutiful servitude, unnoticed and unimpressive, and had to make do with living a more than comfortable life instead. With most of the luxuries afforded to a young lady from the gentry but without all the status or the freedoms of one. Miss P had taught them to accept that as it truly was a privilege when so many would kill for such security in these difficult times. Yes, her friend Georgie had broken that mold in marrying her captain—but she was a rare exception to that rule. The only one out of the countless protégées of Miss Prentice to wed.

"Nonsense," he said, waving that away like he always did. "A pretty and clever girl like you will soon get snapped up, mark my words. A fellow would have to be mad not to want to marry my daughter." Because he knew Lottie would argue some more, he did what he also always did and changed the subject. "If you're not tearing your hair out trying to wrangle other peoples' children, what sort of things does this Lady Frinton have you do with your days?"

"That's not an easy question to answer as I've only worked for her for two days. But so far, there hasn't been a dull moment—which surprises me as I thought it would be a much duller job than that of governess. I was supposed to be halfway to Scotland by now, except that didn't happen after Lady Frinton read a letter from her sister. Before I knew it, we'd turned around and at lightning speed we headed here to Kent. Her sister lives just outside of Maidstone, less than an hour away. Hence I could come here to visit. Although it helped that I have been sent here on a covert mission."

"Covert?" Her father chuckled as he loaded his pipe with tobacco, the familiar scent filling her nostrils with a thousand memories of days gone by. "That sounds exciting."

"It is rather." Plotting shenanigans behind the objectionable Lord Wennington's back had given her a definite spring in her step. "We're planning a surprise birthday party for Lady Wennington's son."

"Wennington?" Her papa lit the barrel and sucked on the stalk to encourage his pipe to light. "Why do I know that name?"

"He's the one who organized that farmers' collective near Rochester last year." That came from Stephen. "The one who went head-to-head with the powerful London merchants, refused to back down when they turned the screws, and threatened to burn it all if they didn't pay a fair price for the crops. He planned to reimburse all the local farmers himself, so they all made a stand. He represented fifty farmers, if I recall it correctly, and only half of them were his tenants. It was all over the local papers."

"Oh, yes." Her papa sucked on his pipe contentedly. "He won too, didn't he? Called their bluff and stuck to his guns. He's a good man, that one. Sticks up for what's right and puts his money where his mouth is. I wish our local lord of the manor was as decent."

Decent! That couldn't possibly be *her* Lord Wennington. This paragon of the community they were raving about had to be a cousin of some sort. Or more likely Stephen had mixed him up with someone else. Her eldest brother had never been good with names. "Well, anyway—Lady Wennington needs a safe place to get her guests to send their replies so as not to tip her son off to the surprise. I suggested here! Would that be agreeable to you?"

"Agreeable?" Her father sat forward and grinned. "For a principled man like him, it would be an honor."

Chapter
NINE

꿏

The last thing Guy wanted to do was sit down to dinner with his aunt's companion again. He almost sent his trumped-up excuses and skipped it but his conscience wouldn't let him. He owed Miss Travers an apology after his uncalled-for rudeness this morning and had spent all day regretting it.

Except when he arrived for dinner, the menace wasn't there and his mother was holding the soup course expressly for him, so the little speech he'd worked out had to wait. He wanted to ask where she was but didn't want to give his relatives any inkling that he cared, and after he'd witnessed her flirting with Bill, he did care. Heaven only knew why. Most likely because Bill had the reputation of being both a lady's man and a bit of a heartbreaker hereabouts.

As much as he respected Bill as a man, as a gentleman it was incumbent on him to make sure that Miss Travers was forearmed before she allowed herself to be seduced by the handsome bugger. If she fancied Bill and knew the score, then fine, he would leave them to it. His head groom and his aunt's companion were both adults and they could continue their flirtation with his blessing so long as their liaison didn't interfere with the smooth running of this house.

Or so he kept telling himself despite the bad taste the thought of any such liaison left in his mouth.

"Why are you late?" asked his aunt before he could even take his seat.

He suppressed the urge to roll his eyes and instead snapped open his napkin with more vigor than was necessary. "I've been working." He gestured toward the window. "I don't know if you've noticed, but I have a large estate to run and we are a wasp's breath from harvest time."

"All he ever does is work." Because of course his mother had to have a dig.

Now that he was also a wasp's breath from turning thirty, anything he did that wasn't making her a grandchild was a cause of consternation. Not that he wouldn't mind indulging in the sport of baby making, because frankly it had been too long since he had rolled around on a willing woman's mattress, but he wasn't keen on making the actual babies if it involved one of those bloody childish young debutantes back in Mayfair that she seemed overly keen he shackle himself to. If he ever did find someone to shackle himself to, it would have to be a woman he could both live with and had things in common with. He didn't care how much it bothered his mother or how much she lamented his bachelorhood, he was not prepared to settle for one whose only discernible attributes boiled down to a pretty face who wanted to accomplish nothing beyond hooking herself a title. He had made the mistake of being blinded by the shallow exterior of one of the fairer sex over the more important interior once before and that had ended in disaster.

Which was precisely why he knew that Bill was welcome to the trying Miss Travers. She was too pretty by half. Certainly pretty enough to turn a naïve man's head and then turn him into a laughingstock once she had. She'd already made a fool of him. Twice. Thrice if he counted the irrational way he had reacted to her apology this morning.

"Do you know, Almeria, he has even pleaded work as the excuse why I cannot throw him a big birthday party in town this year. What a spoilsport he is."

"If you are going to nag, Mother, I shall rescind my agreement to the small party here as well."

"I wonder where the devil Travers has got to?" Ignoring their bickering, his aunt glanced at the clock on the mantel and frowned. "She left hours ago, and it will be dark soon."

Which typically raised Guy's brows. "Where did she go?" When the sun went down here it was as black as pitch, and he did not like the prospect of a woman out alone in it. There weren't usually any incidents with footpads in this quiet enclave in Kent but it wasn't unheard of either.

"I sent her into Maidstone on some errands after luncheon and thought she'd be back by now."

He felt his eyebrows disappear beneath his hairline at that. "Surely not on foot?"

"I am not a blasted idiot, nephew! Nor that unreasonable an employer that I would make her walk all that way there and back until her feet bled. Maidstone is a good ten miles away, so obviously I sent her in my carriage." Which went some way to calming his racing heart. Aunt Almeria's coachman was built like a prize fighter and probably drove with a pistol handy.

His pulse was on the way back to normal, and the soup course half finished, when Miss Travers appeared. All it took was one look at her and it quickened again thanks to the becoming flush in her alabaster cheeks, the tousled curls which had escaped their pins, and the rapid rise and fall of her delectable, compact bosom in the constraints of her tight, fitted bodice.

"You look like you've been dragged through a hedge backward, gal!" Unlike Guy, clearly Aunt Almeria was completely immune to the beguiling effects of a disheveled Miss Travers. "Why are you so late? Not only have I been greatly inconvenienced by your absence but you've made my poor nephew worry."

The minx shot him the perplexed look of utter disbelief before she treated his aunt to the same sort of disdainful expression that she always gave him. "I was running all the errands you sent me on and, unsurprisingly"— she was speaking slowly as if laboring a point, her cornflower eyes slightly narrowed—"all that to-ing and fro-ing took a while."

Before he could stop himself, Guy was defending the minx. "If you were inconvenienced by Miss Travers's absence, why didn't you send one of my servants or one of the battalion of your own that you brought with you to run your errands instead?"

"Because I do not wish for any of them to know my private business and because I entrusted Travers with it." Admonishment issued, his aunt leaned over to her companion, who was in the midst of taking her seat beside her. "Was *everything* completed satisfactorily?"

"Of course, my lady. Just as I said it would be."

"That still doesn't explain why you were so late back when you left at two." Aunt Almeria pushed her soup away. "I sincerely hope that the next time I send you on *an errand,* you'll be home in time to help me get ready for dinner. Especially when you were granted full use of my carriage."

In impressive, clipped tones, Miss Travers gave her surprisingly short shrift. "Your carriage can only go as fast as the roads it has to travel upon. Roads which were congested thanks to it being market day in Maidstone. Had your carriage been able to travel cross-country like a lone horse would, I'd have had *the errands* done significantly sooner and been back here to attend to you hours ago."

"She makes a valid point," said his mother. "We have more fields in this part of the county than we do roads and they are always a nightmare on market days."

"Days?" For reasons best known to herself, that seemed to perturb Aunt Almeria. "How many days is the market in Maidstone?"

"That depends on the market, sister. The fruit and vegetable sellers ply their trade every Monday, Wednesday, and Saturday because it is the county capital and everyone goes there. On alternate Fridays there is livestock—though I am not sure if that means that it will fall on this coming Friday or the next."

"How inconvenient is that?" His aunt seemed disproportionately incensed by that until she had some sort of an epiphany and pointed a bony finger at him. "You must lend Travers a horse, Guy. That is the only way around it."

"Er . . ." He wasn't sure what he felt about that. Especially as Miss Travers's much too pretty eyes instantly lit at the prospect.

"Of course he will." His mother squeezed his arm in a mock affectionate don't-you-dare-say-no kind of way. "Guy has more horses than he knows what to do with so it will be no trouble to allocate her one for the duration of her stay. Assuming you know how to ride, Miss Travers."

"By all accounts, she rides like one of the Four Horsemen of the Apocalypse. Isn't that right, Travers?" His aunt cackled with glee at that while her companion winced, sheepish. No doubt remembering how they had collided in Hyde Park. "So whatever you do, don't give her a sedate old pony as it will not be able to cope with her."

"Then it's settled," answered his mother. "She can use Juno, can't she, Guy?"

"Well . . ." If the thought of the whirlwind wandering alone on the quiet Kentish lanes gave him the jitters, the prospect of her cutting across them at speed on an Arabian gave him palpitations. "Juno is—"

"*Can't she,* Guy?" His mother's fingers dug into his forearm like talons, making it impossible for him to yank it away without an unseemly tussle.

"Surely you trust Longbottom to run your errands instead, aunt?" His question made the sparkle in Miss Travers's fine eyes dim and her plump lips flatten with disdain but she said nothing. She didn't really need to when her renewed dislike of him shimmered off her in waves. "It isn't safe for a young lady to travel all those miles alone."

"For pity's sake, Guy." Mama's claws retracted so that she could fold her arms and glare at him. "Why must you always be so difficult? All we are asking for is the lend of a horse—not your firstborn son. Although at the rate you're going, pigs will fly before you get around to providing me with one of those!"

"What does this"—he jabbed both pointed palms left—"have to do with that?" He jabbed them right. "Why does every single conversation with you currently get twisted to suit your agenda?"

Arms still folded, his mother stuck her nose in the air. "Because you would try the patience of a saint, Guy, that's why. I am honestly at the end of my tether with you. Your dear father would be turning in his grave to see the horrid man you have become!"

His jaw hung slack because honestly, it beggared belief how quickly this conversation had spiraled into him being the villain of the piece when he had had nothing to do with Aunt Almeria's blasted errands in the first place. "I am apparently the only person here who cares for Miss Travers's safety and that makes me horrid? If she were your daughter, would you allow her to ride unchaperoned to Maidstone, Mama?"

Aunt Almeria sighed. "I understand his reticence, Constance, even if it is overly cautious. Entrusting a complete stranger with a precious mount, irrespective of its breed, is not something a diligent stable owner like Guy should take lightly. His concern for my companion's safety is also noble." For a moment, he actually thought his aunt was about to see sense and take his side—until she ruined it. "Why don't we give Guy a demonstration of Travers's superior abilities as a horsewoman right this minute, and then that will put his mind at rest."

---

*B*acked into a corner and sick and tired of his mother's lack of grand-children being used as a stick to beat him with, Guy had done the sensible thing over the main course and partially relented before he beat a hasty retreat out of the dining room. He agreed the harpy could borrow a horse on two conditions. The first was that she could have a gentle mare and not a fast Arabian. The second was that wherever she went on it, she had to be back by six at the latest for the sake of her own security. It wasn't an ideal compromise but at least he didn't have to worry about her breaking her irritating neck on Juno, and he went to bed satisfied at his small victory.

This morning, now that he was watching Bill flirt shamelessly with the minx as she was introduced to the mare, he had some serious misgivings. For a start, he should have stipulated that she could only borrow the horse when she had errands to run for her mistress that could not be done by anyone else. He hadn't thought that far ahead in his hurry to escape all his mother's nagging histrionics last night, so he hadn't expected Miss Travers to take advantage of his offer first thing this morning when she had no errands to run whatsoever. Simply to ride. Just for the fun of it but cunningly dressed up as getting to know Blodwyn, the sturdy Welsh cob he had assigned to her.

What Blodwyn lacked in speed she made up for in intelligence and a sure foot. In other words, she was the sort of horse that his aunt's reckless companion was the least likely to get herself killed riding. Although now that Guy watched Bill insist on helping her onto the pony and enjoying the sight of her swinging one long leg over Blodwyn's thick body far more than was polite through the tack room window, he realized that he should have also insisted upon a fourth stipulation. A sidesaddle. Because nobody could ride like one of the Four Horsemen of the Apocalypse perched on one of those complicated and unbalanced contraptions.

Now that he knew the menace was going out astride, he wondered if it might be prudent not to visit his orchards at the farthest end of his estate and to follow her instead. For no other reason than to put his mind at rest that she wasn't in any danger.

Before he talked himself out of it, he quickly saddled Zeus and led him out of the stable just as Miss Travers trotted out of the yard. Besotted Bill was too engrossed in ogling her bouncing derriere to notice him at first and when he did, Guy gave him a stern look. "Why did you let Miss Travers use a man's saddle?"

"It seemed rude not to after she'd selected it herself and hauled it to Blodwyn's stall before I got there." The charmer grinned and wiggled his brows. "Those long legs of hers seemed to have no trouble sitting on it, so I reckon she's done it before." Then Bill winked and all of a sudden, they weren't just talking about saddles anymore. "She's a feisty one, that one, and a mighty fine filly to boot. Wouldn't mind going for a ride with her myself."

The flash of jealousy at the innuendo caught Guy off guard. "Do your courting on your own time and not mine. Be in no doubt, my aunt's companion is off-limits if you've set your wandering eyes on courting her!"

"Is she, now?" Rather than reel at Guy's cutting tone or jump to it because he had uncharacteristically pulled rank, the scoundrel flashed him a knowing smile instead. *"Interesting."*

"What is that supposed to mean?"

"Only that I've known you close to three decades and not once in all that time have you ever had a problem with where my wandering eyes have wandered, that's all."

"My point is merely that my aunt is very fond of her, though goodness knows why."

"Point taken." Bill chuckled as he turned to go about his business, then took his time leaving to gaze across the field at Miss Travers, who had now kicked Blodwyn into a canter. "And goodness knows why indeed. For what hot-blooded male wouldn't be interested in that fine filly?"

The wretch was still chuckling as he disappeared inside.

That outrageous misapprehension alone convinced Guy not to follow her. The last thing he needed was having anyone thinking his noble concern for the Valkyrie's safety—and by default poor Blodwyn's—meant more than it did. Especially as his only interest lay in getting the pair of them back in one piece.

He certainly wasn't interested in the termagant in *that* way.

He wasn't an idiot after all.

Or stark-staring mad.

He pitied the fool who took on that handful.

Reassured that Bill had the entirely wrong end of the stick, Guy turned Zeus toward the orchards. Trotted that way until the stables were well out of sight, then found himself veering after her regardless.

Chapter
TEN

⟨₯⟩

"Would you look at all this, Blodwyn." Who knew that once they crested the small hill, Lottie and her stout pony would be confronted by a shimmering expanse of water on the other side of it?

It wasn't so much a small lake as a big pond, but it was no less pretty for the distinction, and the wild fowl floating atop it seemed to like it, whichever it was. It was so shallow she could see all the stones carpeting the bottom. Thick bulrush and tall water reeds framed one side. Their blooming heads fluffy with cottony seeds now that it was near the end of their season. The opposite bank was all tall grass and late-summer wildflowers that split to frame either side of a well-trodden path. An inviting path to who knew where, that followed the edge of the pond until it disappeared beneath a vast weeping willow. Its long branches brushing the water and providing a haven for the two young geese playing a splashing game amongst them.

"If I'd have known about this, I'd have brought some bread." Blodwyn's ears twitched in agreement. "Would you like a drink, girl?" The ears twitched again. So Lottie guided her down until they were just feet from where the shallows kissed the shore before she slipped off the horse's back.

Blodwyn took no encouragement to wade into the clear water up to her knees, her thick tail swishing with joy as she sniffed the fragrant summer air around her.

Lottie removed her bonnet and the jacket of her riding habit and went to sit on the bank to watch her, then decided Blodwyn had it right. Why sit when you could wade? So she toed off her riding boots, bent to strip off her stockings and then, because the wretched thing would be more trouble wet than it was dry, she shimmied out of the heavy and voluminous skirt of her riding habit and rolled up her breeches as far as they would go.

Despite the early morning summer sun, the water was bracing. Cold enough to cause a thousand goose bumps to erupt all over her skin but not cold enough to dissuade Lottie from wading into it until it covered her knees too. There was something wonderfully liberating about being in the water—especially when she had the beautiful landscape stretching around her. Lady Frinton had been specific that the next clandestine planning meeting for the vexing viscount's surprise party was to take place in her bedchamber at ten sharp, so she had at least two hours to herself to soak all of nature's wonderment up.

Heaven!

Oh, how she had missed Kent! Almost as much as she had missed her family. Suffering Lord Wennington's occasional presence was a small price to pay for the luxury of both.

A dragonfly buzzed past her nose and then dipped to hover over the water as it whizzed toward the willow, drawing her eyes to the two splashing goslings again. Now that her ears were attuned to the sounds of the pond, one was squawking as it rapidly flapped its wings. The other was pecking at something under the waterline just beneath it.

Lottie smiled at the playing geese until something about it seemed off. For all the movement, the squawking bird wasn't moving an inch. Almost as if it was trapped on something.

"Are you stuck, little fellow?" She waded closer to check and could see that it was more distressed than playing. His friend appeared to be trying to free him.

It was probably a line left by a careless fisherman and if it was wound around the poor thing's feet, he was going to do himself a mischief if he kept yanking on it so violently. "I'm coming—try to keep calm." A ridiculous thing to say to a goose. As if it spoke English! But she hoped the reassuring sound of her voice would help it realize that she was a friend and not a foe.

The depth of the pond remained unchanged as she waded farther, thank goodness, but the gravel beneath her bare feet was sharp. "I'm almost there, little—"

"Stop!" She instantly halted at the loud and panicked bellow from behind, and spun around in time to see Lord Wennington galloping toward her at full pelt. "The bottom of the pond isn't—"

The end of that sentence disappeared as the shingle ledge beneath her feet slipped away with the speed of an avalanche and, because she was already unbalanced thanks to his unnecessary hollering, she yelped as she fell backward into the water. It all happened so fast and so unexpectedly, Lottie managed to swallow half the pond in the process.

She came up coughing and spluttering, unexpectedly having to tread water because this part was so deep.

"Try not to panic!" shouted Lord Wennington, who was obviously panicking as he threw himself off Zeus to run along the path. "I'm coming!"

She still hadn't caught her breath when his intent to save her became apparent, tried to wave her hands to stay him, but all to no avail. Fully clothed and while still in motion, he did an ungainly dive off the bank and, with a huge splash, joined her in the water.

He popped up gasping, no doubt in shock from the cold, and rather gallantly began to swim toward her. "Try not to panic," he repeated again, quite unnecessarily when she had stopped choking and was bobbing quite happily now that initial shock of her dunking was over. "It is impossible to float if you panic."

"Good advice." She wanted to laugh but held it in to mime a few calming breaths for his benefit, seeing as, for once, he meant well. But then she couldn't resist stretching out on her back and kicking her legs as the giggles escaped. "And good heavens above, it works!"

He stopped paddling and scowled. "You can swim."

"Like a fish," she sung, twisting to her front so that she could swim lazy circles around him as he treaded water.

"I thought you were drowning!" He seemed more annoyed than relieved that she wasn't.

"I did try to tell you, but you were flying through the air before I could get any into my lungs. But thank you for trying to rescue me anyway. It is much appreciated."

He huffed and swam the few yards to the shallow shingle ledge, then began to wade to the shore. "What sort of an idiot goes for a swim when the sun has barely risen and the water is freezing?" He tossed that insult masquerading as a question over his shoulder.

"The sort of idiot who is on a rescue mission of her own, that's who." With a huff of her own, she continued swimming toward the trapped gosling. "One of your birds has caught himself on some line."

"Oh."

"Oh, indeed." Under her breath she added, *"You rude oaf."* Then twisted her neck to check he hadn't heard. Which of course he hadn't because he was already halfway up the bank, muttering to himself. No doubt something unpleasant about her.

She was less than three feet away from the gosling when she heard the angry "Bloody hell!" and twisted in time to see him wrestle his trapped arm out of his coat before he slapped the sodden garment on the grass. By the looks of things, he was also about to strip out of his waistcoat, and while her wayward eyes were sorely tempted to stay right where she was to watch that, she had a bird to save.

"Keep calm, little fellow." She reluctantly turned and reached out a hand, only to have the gosling's frightened friend peck at it. She brushed it away, trying to wedge her body between the trapped goose and its protector, ignoring the pecks at her shoulder from one to grab the other who was indeed now so terrified, she feared for his foot.

As soon as she lifted its quivering body out of the water, the problem became apparent. It wasn't a fisherman's line but what appeared to be a strip of net that the gosling was caught in, and in the struggle, it had knotted itself around the leg.

One hand cradling the bird close to her chest while it fought her, she tried to untangle it, but her cold fingers achieved little. She was concentrating so hard that the first she knew of Lord Wennington swimming back up behind her was when he spoke.

"I'll need to cut it off." And lo and behold, he had a penknife with him, which he unfolded beside her. Their limbs brushed as they both treaded water, which was almost as disconcerting as him being back in the water with her. So close she could see the copper flecks in his whiskey-colored irises and the dark stubble on his chin. "Hold him still."

With no better plan, she did exactly that, keeping the gosling's wings from flapping while Lord Wennington held the trapped foot and carefully set about cutting each thread so as not to hurt it.

"Blasted poachers." His eyes flicked to hers briefly. "Like to help themselves to my carp but can't ever be bothered to clean up after themselves." She got the impression he was more annoyed at the litter they left behind than the theft of his fish. Then, in a more surprising turn of events, he paused the cutting to stroke the head of the young goose, those usually hard eyes uncharacteristically tender. "I won't hurt you, little one, I promise." Miraculously, that seemed to do the trick as the bird stopped struggling, allowing him to slice through a few more threads while he continued to soothe it. "Not long now. You'll soon be back with your mother." His eyes lifted to hers again, warily this time. "And on the subject of his mother . . ."

Lottie pulled a face, all too aware of how territorial and aggressive certain geese could be. "I've not seen her."

"Then keep your eyes peeled. After my dip in this ice bath I'd rather not be pecked to death today."

As if that warning summoned her, a very large, very angry goose immediately swooped down from the sky, plopped on the water inches away, and began to hiss. Her powerful wings arching, ready to attack.

"Marvelous." Bizarrely, Lord Wennington was surprisingly matter-of-fact about being pecked to death now that it was a very real possibility. Instead, he swiftly maneuvered his body so that his back was to the gosling's mother, his newly stiffened posture the only clue he was braced. "Just when you think your morning can't get any worse . . ." He winced as the adult goose went for him but still kept his focus on freeing her offspring. Although Lottie really didn't want to have to give him any credit for anything, his selfless dedication to the cause was rather impressive. "Hold him still, Miss Travers, for the love of God!"

"Easier said than done." Especially with the adult goose landing a few blows on her.

Several fraught moments later and the last of the net fell away from the gosling's foot and with considerable relief, she let it go. It hurried to its mother's side while both she and the vexing viscount waved their arms about to send the mother packing. To begin with, the goose refused to back down, but when her baby was well clear she swam away, her head turned backward as she did, so that she could hiss some more.

"Well—that was fun." Lord Wennington slicked back his dark hair. "I take it that a mermaid like yourself doesn't need my help to get back to the shore?" It was a rhetorical question because he had already set off, forcing her to follow behind.

She considered speeding up and racing him as she would have done with any one of her four brothers but quickly dismissed the idea. He might well have just saved a goose but the curmudgeon lived with a permanent storm cloud over his handsome head and no joy in his soul. He would find racing a pointless activity. He also likely wouldn't take kindly to her beating him. But she could be magnanimous if it was required, and diving in to save her and then being gentle with a goose did make him more agreeable.

When he hauled himself up to stand, however, as his wet linen shirt stuck to him like a translucent second skin, she could not help noticing that parts of him were more than agreeable. He had a magnificent pair of shoulders and a nice, tight bottom. As he waded toward the bank, he shook his head like a shaggy dog, raising his arms to squeeze the last of the water out of his hair, and Lottie's breath caught at the solid shape of his biceps as they bunched and flexed. Then he turned to check on her progress and she almost gulped in half the pond again. All because he'd lifted the hem of his shirt to wring the water out of it and she was confronted by the sheer, solid perfection of his naked abdomen.

His taut skin too golden to have not seen the sun, which suggested he wasn't averse to stripping his shirt off outside. An image she really didn't need but that now gave her vivid imagination scandalous ideas. All involving bunching muscles and nudity. While her mind conjured all manner of improper scenarios, her eyes shamelessly following the dark dusting of hair that arrowed down his flat belly and disappeared beneath the waistband of his breeches. Like a signpost promising more.

Conscious that she was now staring at his crotch, she wrenched her eyes upward, only to see through the wet linen of his shirt how that intriguing arrow of dark hair fanned to cover an equally impressive chest that caused highly improper things to happen in the region of her own crotch.

Good heavens above!

What he lacked in likability he more than made up for in raw and blatant masculinity. A soggy and half-dressed Lord Wennington was, not to put too fine a point on it, absolutely . . . sublime.

Thankfully, he read her dithering as difficulty getting out of the water rather than difficulty breathing because of all the shameless ogling she was doing at his fine physique. He rolled his eyes, letting her know with an accompanying huff that in no uncertain terms, he thought her the most dreadful inconvenience before he waded back a few yards. He held out his hand to yank her out of the pond and, to her complete disgust, she was more than a little off-kilter as she took it. Then, to her further astonishment, went from off-kilter to all aquiver in an erratic heartbeat when his sun-kissed wet skin touched hers.

Lottie knew what desire was because she had felt it a time or two—but was stunned to be feeling it for him.

Him! The most obnoxious and disagreeable man on the planet!

Her stupefaction must have showed because he frowned at her as he helped her onto the bank, immediately ripping his hand away the moment her feet left the water to fetch his sodden clothes. His ferocious scowl telling her that he wasn't happy with her at all.

"I have urgent business to attend to." He slapped his wet coat over Zeus's saddle. His mesmerizing muscles bunched again, still doing all manner of inappropriate, tingly things to certain parts of her body that annoyed her as he bent again to retrieve his boots and empty them of water. "Another set of perfectly good clothing ruined thanks to you!" Yet rather than glare at her in blame as she expected, he kept his face averted as he wrestled them on.

"I did not ask you to dive in, Lord Wennington. You did that of your own volition."

His only response was a grunt as he heaved himself onto the Arabian's back.

"I trust you can find your own way back, Miss Travers?" He glanced her way briefly, all furrowed brows and outraged prickliness, then quickly looked away when she nodded. "Splendid."

Then he was gone.

Galloping off with not so much as a polite nod, let alone a "good day." Leaving her oddly . . . flustered. Perhaps more flustered than she had ever been by a man because she felt . . . ripe. A state which, frankly, horrified her, but was hardly a surprise after his fine body in that translucent shirt had thoroughly seduced her.

Absently, she placed her flattened palm over the layer of damp linen covering her racing heart and had the most awful epiphany. Because if the bracing pond water had rendered his shirt so transparent that it left nothing to the imagination, then it had probably made her blouse transparent too.

One glance downward confirmed her worst fears, because her sopping-wet garment left nothing to the imagination either. Especially as she had, as usual, come out riding without the constraints of stays to cover her modesty. In fact, judging by the very visible and jutting pink peaks of her chilled and shriveled nipples, she might as well be topless!

And that really was mortifying.

For how on earth was she supposed to look that objectionable man in his irritating copper-flecked eyes ever again when he must have seen what her horrid brothers always mockingly called her bee stings?

In all their flat-as-a-pancake glory!

ELEVEN

᥎᥎᥎

*I*t is, as always, a pleasure doing business with you, my lord."

Guy stifled a yawn as he shook hands with the merchant, relieved that he had held his own with the vultures so far despite three days of practically no sleep. "I am glad that we could have this discussion privately. It has made things much simpler." After his disastrous meeting in London last week with Mr. Granger, the biggest, greediest, and most unreasonable grain merchant of all, picking off his rivals one by one seemed to be a good idea. The other merchants were inclined to be more reasonable as individual businessmen rather than as a gluttonous collective.

To avoid the unpleasant standoff he'd had with them last year, he wanted to ensure that all the local farmers he represented had a decent price for their wheat without him having to hold them to ransom again.

Something that was proving significantly easier without including that crook Granger in the discussions. Guy had one meeting to go and hoped that his going behind the most powerful grain merchant in London's back to cut him out of the deal wouldn't backfire on him. None of the Kent merchants liked Granger despite their collective tendency to bow down to the man, so he hoped this last one wouldn't need too much persuading to do some respectable business without him. Or tip Granger off about what Guy was up to. If they could all squeeze Granger out of this county, it would be better for everyone—merchants and farmers alike.

The bad news was that even while negotiating the livelihoods of all the local farmers who were depending on him to represent them at these critical discussions, his insomnia-addled mind had repeatedly wandered to *her* during the meetings. The blasted woman who was responsible for the insomnia despite all his best efforts to exorcise the vixen and her obscenely perfect breasts from his thoughts. Once she popped into his mind, he could barely concentrate on anything else and such an unwelcome distraction could not have come at a worse possible time.

Right now, he needed to focus on his work and not on the strange allure of her!

He had managed to avoid Miss Travers like the plague for four whole days already. The inconvenient changes he'd had to make to his usual morning routine were a small price to pay for his sanity, so he had happily hauled his carcass out of bed an hour earlier to avoid that early bird at all costs. According to Bill, who still smirked every time the menace featured in one of their conversations, *"Lottie"* arrived at the stables every day at eight sharp, so he made sure to have left there long before. Returning only after dinner was well and truly done so that he could sneak upstairs to bed. Again, eating his meals cold and on the hoof was a small price to pay to not have to see the menace.

For how exactly did one face the most infuriating woman in the world while he burned hotter than the sun with unwanted lust for her? So hot he feared he would spontaneously combust if he actually had to see her and her beguiling body ever again at close quarters.

The image of her emerging from the water, her shapely long legs bare to mid-thigh and her lush breasts as good as bare seemed to be permanently seared onto his mind. His thoughts kept drifting to that memory every waking hour and his dreams—which were excruciating in their vividness—were unmitigated torture. Because in those, dream-state Guy didn't have to just drool over those pert, pointed breasts and their saucy, dark pink raspberry nipples in his mind. He could suck them whole into his mouth and whirl his tongue around those tempting points while those long legs of hers wrapped themselves around him tightly, anchoring him in place while he buried himself inside her to the hilt.

And on the subject of unmitigated torture . . .

He subtly readjusted his breeches before he strode into Maidstone's market square, furious at her that he'd also had to walk around with an uncomfortable flagstaff instead of a cock since that fateful morning by the pond. Once his greedy eyes realized the water had rendered her blouse see-through, his frisky appendage had instantly stood to attention and had flatly refused to die down since. It was perpetually half-cocked. No matter how many times he'd had to take care of it. If the local vicar was right and the sin of masturbation robbed you of your sight, then Guy expected to be struck blind at any moment. He hadn't touched himself with such frenzied frequency since puberty!

Bloody woman!

Why the blazes was he so obsessed by her?

Common sense told him that lusting after a beautiful woman was a totally natural thing for a man to do when he had practically seen her naked and liked what he saw. Except there seemed to be more to it and none of it that he understood. She had a strange hold—

"Get out of the way, idiot!" The angry coachman shook him out of his reverie and with seconds to spare, Guy stumbled backward before the noon post ran him over. "Look where you're going!"

"My apologies—" Bloody hell, but that woman was going to be the literal death of him if he wasn't careful. Proof, if proof were needed that she needed to be both out of sight and out of mind or he was done for.

But as the carriage rattled past, he saw what he thought was her on the other side of the market square chatting to a stallholder.

Was his addled mind conjuring the menace now?

She had her back to him and a bonnet covered her hair completely, but there was something about the confident set of the distant woman's shoulders, the animated tilt of her head, and her unusual height that suspiciously suggested that she could only be his Valkyrie.

As the woman moved sideways to visit another stall, so did Guy, using the sea of people and market traders to hide behind in case she turned and saw him. Frankly, the last person he wanted to collide with was Miss Travers, yet the magnetic pull of her was too strong to ignore and as much as his head screamed at him to escape to the inn at all costs, his feet edged ever nearer anyway.

She wandered into a bakery, so he rapidly skirted the edge of the square to get a closer look, hoping against hope that it wasn't his aunt's companion so he could go about his business. He was loitering in a nearby doorway when she emerged carrying a big box of cakes, his back pressed into the shadows and the brim of his hat tilted downward lest she recognize him. Feeling utterly pathetic, his addled mind was already thinking of excuses to approach her. For the excuse to have a brief interaction with her. For the right words to make her smile at him in the same way she smiled at his flirtatious head groom.

What the blazes was that all about?

Suddenly her head whipped his way and she beamed.

As his breath caught and his stupid heart leapt, a fellow dashed past him. Tall and handsome and beaming too. Guy's foolish heart ached when Miss Travers threw herself at the golden Adonis, wrapping one of her arms around him as he spun her around while the other still held the string of the bakery box. Then the man—who Guy now hated with a vengeance— kissed her forehead as he lowered her to the ground. In return, she looked at the scoundrel with love radiating out of her pretty blue eyes.

Although barely ten feet away now, Guy couldn't hear a word of their much too overfamiliar conversation, but he tasted bile in his throat as she looped her arm possessively through the other man's. Then they sauntered off. Grinning at one another like a pair of besotted lovebirds as they shared a joke. One that he was paranoid enough not to wonder if it was about him.

Guy had no clue why he cared that Miss Travers clearly had a sweetheart—but he did. In truth, that new knowledge infuriated him more than the constant erection the minx had given him. He also should have left the pair of them to it and headed to his next meeting.

But he didn't.

Instead, he followed them at a safe distance, for no other reason than he had to. His jealousy was as irrational as it was misplaced but it was real and it was worrying. Especially when he had never been the sort to suffer from it.

Miss Travers and her beau turned out of the square and headed to the small patch of common land where several horses had been left to graze. Blodwyn, the mare he had reluctantly lent her, was there, and they both made a fuss of her. The Valkyrie produced an apple and her Adonis fed it to her horse, while Guy loitered behind a stall still in the market square, watching the pair of them as if his life depended on it.

After a good few minutes, her man friend grabbed her about the waist in the most overfamiliar way to lift Miss Travers onto her mount. Instead of horsewhipping the brute as she should have for taking such a liberty, she laughed. As if she didn't mind Mr. Handsome manhandling her in the slightest.

Within moments, they were both on horseback, grinning at one another as they trotted down the lane side by side. Out of busy Maidstone toward the secluded countryside beyond. Off to eat cake in private together. Unchaperoned. Where he was in no doubt that more than some forehead kissing and some overfamiliar waist grabbing would take place.

A prospect that nearly made Guy's head explode.

With an irrational red mist clouding his eyes and his judgment, he ran back to the stable at the inn where he had left Zeus, kicked him into a gallop as soon as they left the market square, and retraced their route.

Except by the time he reached the crossroads half a mile outside of Maidstone, there was no sign of either of them anywhere on the horizon. He was also half an hour late for his meeting with the last merchant he needed to get on his side. Leaving the man waiting was likely not the best way to forge a new alliance.

---

*T*o what do we owe this great and rare honor?" His mother blinked in shock when he walked through the door four hours later. "You do realize that it is still daytime? Aren't there fields or farmers or French beans in urgent need of your constant attention today?"

Guy was in no mood for her sarcasm after his fruitless wild-goose chase hunting down Miss Travers, but smiled regardless. "Is it suddenly a crime to take tea with my two favorite ladies in the world after work has forced me to neglect them for days?"

While his mother's eyes widened with disbelief, Aunt Almeria's narrowed. "He's either taken a knock to the head, Constance, or he's up to something as I've never known my nephew to willingly take tea with us in the middle of the day before. Not when there is always something more pressing that he could be doing as an excuse to avoid the rest of the human race."

The wily old witch had called it right because he was up to something. He was on a mission to find out more about the infuriating Miss Travers, who was still missing in action, but it would be a cold day in hell before he admitted it. Instead, he took a seat, shrugging. "I will admit that I do have a hundred and one more important things to do, but the guilt which my dear mama ladles on with the world's largest spoon has got the better of me this afternoon." In anticipation, he produced the latest note she had left on his nightstand and tossed it on the tea table between them so that her outrageous, angry words at his continued absence could be read by all. Except this time, it was his mother's eyes that narrowed while his aunt's widened as she picked up the damning missive, followed by the ever-present quizzing glasses that dangled from an amethyst-encrusted chain to match her customary vivid purple frock.

If you refuse to be sociable for me, the VERY LEAST you could do is spare the odd hour to socialize with my poor, aged sister. Or do you not care that Almeria is so decrepit she could die at any moment!

After several silent seconds had ticked by, during which his dear mama shot him daggers, his aunt lowered her quizzing glasses and nodded, unoffended. "She's right, of course. At my age, who knows how many afternoon teas I have left? So shame on you, Guy, for being such an absent host when

I dragged these ancient bones all the way from Mayfair to Kent specifically to spend some time with my favorite nephew before Heaven takes me."

"And I thought you came here because you are in cahoots with my mother to foist a birthday party on me that I do not want." He accepted the proffered tea from the meddling woman who had birthed him and toasted Almeria with the cup. "And we both know that when your time comes, aunt, it will be the devil who takes you."

She cackled at that. "Only if he is brave enough. He and the good lord might decide that I am too much trouble for either of them to bother with and leave me here for all eternity instead."

"Perish the thought." He sipped his tea and tried to look nonchalant despite dying to know when the Valkyrie was due to return so he could ask her . . . he didn't know what yet, but felt that some words needed to be had. But with his unwelcome lust and even more unwelcome jealousy, he was struggling to think of the right ones. Bloody woman had him tied up in knots and that really bothered him because he had thought that that reckless, passionate, and romantic side of him that burned for a woman was long dead. Smothered by betrayal, cynicism, and humiliation. Yet here he was, hoping against hope that Miss Travers wasn't as head over heels in love with her Adonis as she had looked and had a perfectly reasonable excuse to be galloping off into the sunset alone with a gallingly handsome man. "What have you ladies been doing with yourselves in my absence?"

"The usual," said his mother. "Catching up. Gossiping. Lamenting about you and your distinct lack of a wife. Or love in your miserable, closeted life. Have I mentioned that I want the old Guy back? The cheeky and incorrigible one who used to laugh."

In truth, he missed the old Guy too, but didn't know quite how to be him any longer. That Guy had been sucked inside the armored shell he had retreated behind and got lost. Which was a shame because Miss Travers probably would have liked the old Guy. "Surely not that tired old subject again, Mama?"

"It is you who has become tiresome." His mother pouted. "Tiresomely serious and tiresomely dull. Old before your years."

"Responsibilities do that, Mother." As did having your heart bludgeoned to a pulp in front of the world. "We don't all have the luxury of whiling away our afternoons drinking tea and gossiping. Some of us have to work."

As his mother let out a groan of disgust, Aunt Almeria chirped up. "I don't miss the old Guy. That reprobate used to put honey in my slippers."

"And spiders in my sewing box." His mother shuddered. "It took his father an hour to round up all those horrid creepy-crawlies. They had quite taken over the drawing room by the time he heard my screams." She pouted some more. "You deserved to be sent to bed with no supper that night!"

Except he hadn't gone to bed with no supper. Because his father found his only son's prank so hilarious he had snuck Guy in a veritable feast when he had come to "tell him off" after all the spiders had been evicted. Papa had ruffled his hair and then given him five shillings for giving him his best laugh in ages. Which had been Guy's motive for the crime all along because he had loved making that man laugh. A memory that simultaneously made Guy want to chuckle while making him miss his father all the more.

"No wonder there is no sign of Miss Travers this afternoon. You have bored her senseless with your constant litany of all the many ways I have disappointed you." Despite how unsettled all the talk of the old Guy made him, he was rather proud of the subtle way he had turned the topic to her. "Did she plead a sudden headache in order to escape?"

"Travers is running errands."

"Again? This late in the day?" Guy made sure to take a long, perturbed glance at the mantel clock. "It will be dark soon." Give or take a few more hours, but still. He dreaded to think what mischief she and her fancy man could get up to in four unchaperoned hours. "Are any shops still open at five o'clock?" He didn't want to outright tell tales on the minx, more sow some seeds of suspicion in his aunt's mind that might make her more diligent about the hours her companion spent away from her side. "Aren't you worried about her?"

"Not in the slightest." His aunt brushed his concerns aside. "I am more worried about you." She wafted a wizened hand at his face. "You look tired, Guy. Bordering on the haggard."

"That's because of all that *important work* he does while I'm gossiping over tea." Always ready with a stick to beat him with, his mother used the pretense of lamenting about him to her sister as a way to nag him by proxy.

"A crime tantamount to treason in this house, apparently," he said to no one in particular because neither cared what he had to say on the subject. "For heaven forbid a landowner tend his land when he could be drinking tea."

"Dresses like a common laborer some days too," continued his mother while his aunt shook her head in sympathy, "then thoughtlessly traipses mud all over the house once he's done simply to torture me."

"By traipses, she means I leave my boots at the back door and take the servants' stairs directly to my bath."

"That is unforgivable." Aunt Almeria patted his mother's hand. "What a thoughtless, tiresome son he is."

"I honestly do not know where I went wrong with him." His mother topped off his aunt's cup.

"You tried your hardest with him, Constance, so do not castigate yourself. You brought him up to be a gentleman but if he chooses to roll around in the mud instead of taking his rightful place in society as a gentleman, what can you do?"

"I am still here, you know." Guy waved in case he had suddenly turned invisible. "Can anyone hear me?"

"I can." Miss Travers sailed through the door looking all windswept and bright eyed. No doubt from all the exercise she had had all afternoon. She offered him a smile which, much to his chagrin and against his better judgment, warmed him from the inside out. "For what it's worth, I think its admirable that you work in your fields. My father always says that if you don't have a feel for the soil then you will not have any clue what to best put in it."

"What the devil kept you, gal?" Finally his aunt seemed concerned at her absence. Until she ruined it. "Guy has been worried sick about you! Haven't you, Guy?"

A statement that made it sound as if he cared about the vixen, which he was quick to correct. "I really haven't been."

"He was about to send out a search party."

"I really wasn't. I merely inquired as to where you were." Which also sounded like he cared. "Seeing as you left Maidstone hours ago." As soon as he blurted that he regretted it. "Assuming that was you that I happened to notice leaving the bakery in the market square earlier."

"You saw me at the bakery?" Her eyes darted to Lady Frinton. Guiltily, if her ferocious blush was any gauge.

"I did. You were carrying a big box of cakes."

"Ah, thank goodness!" That came from his aunt. "You managed to get my éclairs. Well done for tracking some down, Travers, for éclairs are a rare thing this far out of London."

"They are indeed, my lady. But I managed to finally find them in Maidstone." Miss Travers's smile was overbright as she nodded. Insincere. Trying to convince them all that butter wouldn't melt in her mouth. "That is why I took so long."

A likely story that did not explain why she had arrived back tousled and empty-handed. "Éclairs, you say. The perfect accompaniment to an afternoon tea. I could murder an éclair right now." Guy patted his stomach for effect, wondering how the lying menace was going to explain the fact that she and her paramour had devoured them—either before or after they had devoured each other on his trusting aunt's shilling. "Go fetch them, as I am starving."

Her awkward reaction did not disappoint. "I . . . well . . ."

"Go fetch your own éclairs from Maidstone if you want one." Quick as a flash, his aunt came to the temptress's defense. "Those are mine."

"All of them? Surely not. The box she had was huge and you eat like a bird."

Aunt Almeria bristled as if he'd insulted her. "Only in polite company, nephew, as is proper. Alone, I eat like a horse." She then turned to Miss Travers. "Did you get the rest of the items from my list?"

"More than expected." She beamed with staggering pride considering she had shirked her duties so brazenly. "Brazen" being the operative word when one considered how indiscreet and improper she had been, going off unchaperoned with that man. "I put everything in your room, Lady Frinton. Along with the éclairs."

Aunt Almeria chuckled and rubbed her hands.

"What else was on the list?" Because acquiring "more than expected" suggested Miss Travers wasn't quite done with making a meal out of running his aunt's errands and was doubtless contemplating a second trip to see her Adonis. "I'll send out one of my servants first thing to get them all for you, aunt. Save Miss Travers the trouble of *wasting* a whole afternoon in Maidstone again when I am sure that you need her."

"Personal things," answered his aunt for her when all Miss Travers could do was blink in response, and when he dared to query that with an arched brow, she clarified with a jabbing finger. "Personal *women's* things that are none of your damned business." A response that Aunt Almeria knew he wasn't brave enough to challenge any further. "Now if you've finished with your inquisition about where I choose to spend *my* money, Guy, I'm off to my room for a lie-down before dinner."

As she stood, his mother did the same. "I think I'll go for a lie-down too." This coming from a woman who not only never took afternoon naps but who had also nagged him narrow to be sociable. "I am sure that you could do with a rest too, Miss Travers, after your tiring journey to Maidstone."

"Oh, I'll bet she's tired," said Guy, pinning the minx with his glare. "You must be exhausted after all that *exercise*."

Both ladies had reached the door before a rather shifty-looking and still blinking Miss Travers went to follow, and she would have if he hadn't caught her arm. "Are you going to tell my aunt that you spent half of this afternoon galivanting with a gentleman unchaperoned, or am I?"

Her damning blush this time was crimson but the tilt of her chin was as defiant as ever. "I wouldn't dream of spoiling your fun, my lord." Disdain radiated from her lovely cornflower eyes. "I hope the telling gives you great joy." She tugged her arm away and dipped into an insolent curtsy. "For goodness knows I've never met a man in more dire need of some."

She sailed out of the room with her nose in the air, leaving him dumbstruck. He had never felt so insulted, petulant, and so thoroughly put in his place all at the same time.

TWELVE

❧

I've told you, Travers. Pay it no mind. If he comes to me telling tales, he'll get short shrift."

Despite it being the middle of the day, Lottie was in her mistress's bedchamber again while the two sisters added names to the seating plan they were creating for the first formal dinner of Lord Wennington's secret birthday house party on the night of what they now all referred to as *the Surprise*.

"She's right, dear," said Lady Wennington as she deliberated between two of the nine squares of paper that represented the eligible young ladies who had so far confirmed their attendance. "It is none of his business."

"But I was so rude to him yesterday." So rude she had definitely overstepped the mark—again—but the man never failed to get her dander up. Each time she attempted to be pleasant to him, he seemed to lose his temper with her more, and that brought out the worst in her. "When I suppose, technically, he only had Lady Frinton's best interests at heart." Begrudgingly, she thought it admirable that he didn't want his dragon of an aunt taken advantage of. There was some innate nobility in the curmudgeon despite his objectional character. The sort of man who looked out for old ladies and saved trapped goslings couldn't be all bad, even if he thought badly of her.

"What did you say, dear, that wasn't the truth?" His mother placed one of the paper squares on the seating plan two chairs away from her son. "Guy has, by increment, become a grumpy, impossible-to-please curmudgeon in the last few years. I genuinely despair of him sometimes as he never used to be like that. Once upon a time he was more like his gregarious father, with a ready laugh and an optimistic attitude, but he has changed. And not for the better."

"We blame *her*." Lady Frinton pulled a face and both sisters shuddered, then promptly returned to their study of the seating plan as if that was explanation enough.

"*Her?*"

"The woman we dare not mention in his presence." Lady Wennington dropped her voice to a whisper in case her son was listening at the door. "Conniving Florinda the Duplicitous Duchess. She led him on a merry dance to snare her duke, broke his heart, and he's never been the same since."

"She stole all the joy from his soul," added Lady Frinton, unaware that she had echoed something of Lottie's tart response to him last night. "And seems to have put him off women for life. Hence, we have to reignite his interest in them." She watched her sister place a square of paper directly opposite Lord Wennington on the plan and instantly took issue with it. "Who the blazes is Abigail Maybury? She wasn't on my list."

"She's a neighbor, so was on mine." Lady Wennington seemed pleased with her placement. "I sent the Mayburys their invitation before you arrived."

"I take it that as you've given the chit the best seat, sister, she is a preferred contender as your future daughter-in-law?"

"Good heavens, no!" Lady Wennington shuddered again. "She is the most irritating girl I have ever met. Doesn't laugh so much as bray like a donkey and does so to excess and at the slightest provocation. She will not do at all. Guy cannot stand her."

"Then why, Constance, have you given her that seat?"

Lady Wennington's eyes danced. "Because she is utterly shameless in her pursuit of him. Does nothing but fawn and flutter her eyelids and, given the chance, hangs on him like a limpet. Obviously, I've given her every chance to do so as an incentive to force Guy into finding his own bride just to spite me—all to no avail. However, I have high hopes that by putting her front and center at his celebration, not only will she make all the other ladies appear more attractive to him, she will also give them all the impetus they need to thrust themselves at him shamelessly too. The more temptation we put in his way, the more likely he is to be tempted."

"Well, in that case . . ." Lady Frinton placed another square on the other side of him. "We should also torture him with Lady Lynette Connaughlty."

"Will she tempt him?"

"She'll certainly tempt him to find swift solace with someone else." Lady Frinton cackled. "A more arrogant, pompous, and emotionally oblivious a chit as you'll ever meet. Fancies herself up there with the Queen of England and could talk the iron legs off a donkey. Mostly about herself." The old lady rolled her eyes. "Ad nauseam."

"Oh yes! She sounds perfect." Lady Wennington chuckled with glee. "Then if we sprinkle some halfway decent young ladies close by, he'll be automatically drawn to them because they cannot possibly be as bad!"

"Indeed, sister. The more strategically we appear to match him with the wrong woman, the more chances he has of finding the right one just to spite us."

Both sisters sniggered at that logic but Lottie couldn't join in. Not now that she knew Lord Wennington's heart had been broken and that he was noble deep down. It didn't sit right. Neither, suddenly, did this ruse that she was involved in. On the one hand, was it fair to meddle in the romantic affairs of a man who had been burned by love when he clearly wasn't ready? But on the other, maybe these meddling sisters knew best. All these machinations were designed with his future happiness in mind and they wouldn't be doing this at all unless they cared about him. Surely? Sometimes a person needed a push.

And sometimes, they didn't.

What was the right thing to do?

Which ultimately was the crux of the matter because what precisely could Lottie do? She saw both sides and had the added complication of being Lady Frinton's employee. One that had to do as she was told because her family was in dire need of her wages.

Maybe not pondering it was the answer and it would sort itself out? And maybe she should concentrate on being a proper lady's companion seeing as fate had thrown her this timely bone? It wasn't as if she held any sway on the outcome anyway.

"If I am not needed, my lady, I might take another trip home to see if there is any more post waiting." A solution that removed her from the problem today, at least, and one that would certainly take her mind off of it.

Lady Frinton did not even look up as she waved her off. "Good idea, Travers."

Lottie hurried out in case the old lady changed her mind and quickly dressed in her habit. She was on the way to the stables to fetch Blodwyn when she heard the commotion coming from the exercise field, turned, and saw two young grooms wrestling with Hercules.

Like Bill, who was running toward them from the direction opposite, she did not know which of the three to worry about the most.

"Let him go, idiots!" Bill got to the gate before her. "One kick from him could break your legs!"

They both did as instructed and backed away, leaving the horse still attached to the line, bucking to dislodge the flapping saddle they had tried to put on him.

"What the bleedin' hell did the pair of you think you were doing?" The head groom let rip as soon as he had dragged the second lad to safety over the fence. "I told you to exercise him, not try to ride him!"

"He seemed calm," said the boy, his face blanched and his voice shaking. "Never gave us a moment's trouble when we put the reins on him and was doing so well—"

"Fools! He ain't ready and even if he was, that wasn't your decision to make!" Quite rightly, Bill looked ready to pummel the pair of them for their stupidity. "Whose idea was it to leave the training lead on? You never attempt to saddle an unbroken horse with thirty feet of rope still attached!"

"We thought the long line might make it easier if he kicked." The youngest stared at his feet.

"Now I've got to try and take the blasted thing off him before he gets tangled in it and hurts himself!" Bill went for the gate to do just that, took one look at the frenzied movements of the spooked horse, and stayed put because Hercules was twisting as he bucked now, trying to bite the saddle off.

"You can't leave him! He's still attached to the line!" Lottie tried to shove Bill into the arena but he wouldn't budge.

He shook his head. "That horse needs to calm down a bit first. He's a danger to us all in that state."

"He's more a danger to himself! Hercules could break his legs if that line tangles around them!" And then the poor thing would have to be shot. "You have to help him, Bill!"

The groom folded his beefy arms and shook his head again. "When he's calmed down."

Which could very well be too late.

"Oh, for goodness' sake!" Before anyone could stop her, Lottie clambered over the fence and went to help the animal herself.

"Easy, Hercules." If she could catch part of the line, she could move as much of it as she could out of the young Arabian's way. "Easy."

"Lottie! Get the hell out of there! That's an order!"

She ignored Bill's holler to edge nearer. "Good boy . . . *good boy.*" She kept her movements slow and her tone soothing but made sure the horse could see her. He was panicked enough and didn't need any more unwelcome surprises. "Let me help you."

She was less than a foot away when Lord Wennington ran toward the gate, and in case his approach upset Hercules more, stayed him with a raised palm before he did something stupid like to try to rescue her again. In the same soft, musical tone, she sang, "I've almost got him."

To his credit, Lord Wennington stopped dead, although his arrival distracted the horse long enough for her to reach for the line. No sooner had her fingers caught it, and Hercules was off again. This time dancing in erratic circles which forced her to let go while he ran rings around her.

From the gate, which he looked ready to launch himself over, Lord Wennington copied her tone. "Miss Travers—I am begging you—leave him be. Trust me, I have known this animal since birth and he will not let you help him until he is calm."

"He's too much like Zeus," added Bill, and that gave her an idea.

"But he can be gentle like his mother too, I've seen it. Fetch her."

"You heard her! Fetch Juno!" To her surprise, it was Lord Wennington who was agreeing with her. "Fast!"

Lottie heard the thud of boots running across the cobbled stable yard but didn't dare take her eyes off Hercules until she heard his mother's hooves clopping back. Someone opened the gate, and in she came.

Miraculously, her presence was all it took for Hercules to slow. He trotted toward her, clearly still unsettled but not in the temper that he had been. Lottie bent for the line again, but rather than put any tension through it this time, fed it through her fingers as she walked toward him.

She was three feet away when he snorted and thrashed his head, ready to fight again, but his mother nudged him with her head. Almost as if she were reprimanding her offspring, and he stopped. Then he allowed Lottie to grab the bit and, a half minute later, let her stroke his neck so that Lord Wennington and Bill could also approach.

Between them, the men released him from the offending saddle so that Lottie, aided in no small part by Juno, could walk Hercules toward the gate to the pasture. A gate that was swung open by the viscount just as Lottie released the horse from his bridle.

Together, the two Arabians trotted into the field and the gate closed.

Lottie leaned on it, her gaze fixed on the horses as she sensed Lord Wennington rest beside her. "Shall we get your blistering lecture over with now, my lord, or would you prefer to tear me off a strip later?"

He huffed. "No lecture—merely a thank-you."

"A thank-you?" She turned to find him watching the horses too. "Are you sure? This is me, after all, and I do exasperate you."

"That you do." The corners of his mouth lifted as he continued to stare at mother and son. "But you saved the day, so it would be remiss of me not to give credit where credit is due. Bringing Juno into the fray was a stroke of genius."

"Gracious." She really hadn't expected that. "Did you just give me a compliment? Will wonders never cease?"

He laughed at her sarcasm. Not a full-bellied chuckle, more a gentle expulsion of air. "Try not to ruin this unexpected and unique moment we are sharing, Miss Travers."

She could not resist teasing him a little bit to see how he would react. "But I am all astonishment, my Lord Wennington. To get *praise*. From *you*. Good gracious. Who knew you had that in you?" She clutched at her chest as if overcome. "My *flabber* is well and truly *gasted*. In fact, it is so gasted I am almost speechless."

He rewarded her with a proper laugh this time and, to her actual astonishment, it suited him. It did lovely things to his eyes; enough that she found herself staring into them as she smiled back. Until his faltered and those mesmerizing dark irises broke contact to dip downward. "Then allow me to take advantage of that rare occurrence by adding an apology to go with that compliment."

"For what?" She was intrigued as to which one of his many rude misdemeanors he felt bad about. Especially after yesterday, when he had made it plain he thought she was cheating his aunt by wasting time fraternizing when she was supposed to be working.

"Where to start?" Was it her imagination, or did he look sheepish? "I owe you an apology for not looking where I was going in Hyde Park. For not thanking you for retrieving Zeus that same day and barking at you instead. For the unforgivable way I refused to accept your later apology when half the blame for what happened in Hyde Park rests squarely on my shoulders." His eyes lifted as he winced. "For my curtness over the incident with the soup and the debacle in the pond. For not apologizing sooner." His smile this time was awkward. And oh-so-disarming. "Basically, for being an insufferably rude oaf every single time we have collided."

"Gracious." Lottie was so staggered by his admission she had no other words.

"For what it's worth, I've wanted to apologize from the outset but . . ."

"But I would try the patience of a saint?"

"I have no doubt that you would, however . . ." He shrugged and stared at the horses. "It is a pathetic excuse, but I am never at my best when I feel foolish and, when I do, sometimes . . . most times actually . . . I react badly." He inhaled deeply, squared his impressive shoulders, and forced himself to face her. "I've repeatedly reacted very badly around you and for that I am truly sorry."

It was rather big of him to take ownership of his behavior without blaming her for it. His was also one of the prettiest and most sincere atonements she had ever heard. "Your apology is accepted, my lord." An answer that pleased him enough to earn her another smile.

"Thank you, Miss Travers. That is very decent of you."

She could not resist teasing him a little bit more. "Does this armistice mean that we need to make an effort to be civil to each other going forward?" She pulled a face as if she could think of nothing worse and he responded in kind with a grave nod.

"Sadly, yes. I believe it does. Within reason, of course, as I sincerely doubt you can curb your annoying forthrightness all of the time." There was a twinkle in his dark eyes now, and that suited him more than the smile.

"Any more than you could constantly avoid suppressing your inner curmudgeon. Or your outer curmudgeon for that matter too. But I shall grit my teeth and try to forgive you for it."

He did a poor job of disguising how much her cheek amused him. "Indeed. We must be realistic in our expectations. The best we can hope for, until I celebrate the day that you and my incorrigible aunt leave me in blessed peace, is feigned toleration and not a miracle."

"You can be as pessimistic as you want, Lord Wennington, as that is your dreary, doom-and-gloom, no-joy-in-your-soul prerogative. However— and I appreciate that this trait in me will only annoy you further—I am an eternal optimist to my core and I am confident in a miracle. So confident, in fact, that I will wager that you will not celebrate the day that I leave." Before she thought better of it, her errant index finger prodded him in the center of his chest. It was every bit as solid as she'd imagined it. "You will dread it instead. Because I am a veritable ray of sunshine and I am *determined* to make you—my perennially depressing storm-cloud nemesis—*like* me."

He folded his arms and regarded her with fake pity. "My poor, misguided Miss Travers. While I admire your ambition, you have more chance of touching the moon than you do my joyless soul." Then as if thoroughly fed up with her presence, he stalked off, tossing a mischievous insult over his shoulder as he went. "Enjoy the rest of your afternoon, *Miss Guided*. Mine is certainly all the brighter—simply because you won't feature in it."

Chapter
THIRTEEN

※◈◈※

A grinning Bill deposited a second saddle next to Guy's in the middle of the training yard. "Others around here might think it's *telling* that you're suddenly taking Lottie's advice, but I don't."

"Of course you don't." Guy tossed the heavy bundle of bridles and reins next to the saddles while biting his tongue. He had decided that trying to argue against his head groom's constant teasing was counterproductive days ago, because denial had only made things worse. As a day of stony silence hadn't improved things either, he now planned to blandly agree with everything the riling wretch said and spoil Bill's fun.

Except Bill was nothing if not tenacious and had redoubled his efforts.

As Guy stalked back to the stables to fetch the last of the equipment, his dog-with-a-bone groom skipped like a crab beside him so he could better watch his reactions. "I told them all that any interest you have in her is mutually and exclusively equine at its heart and not an expression of *your* heart in any way, as the gossips around this estate are suggesting."

"Thank you, Bill." Guy marched into the tack room and tried not to scream as his tormentor followed.

"I also told them that there is a big difference in being friendly with a woman and wooing her. Just because you smile more when she happens by doesn't mean you fancy her."

Guy agreed to that lie with a disinterested nod as he grabbed a few apples and shoved them in a saddlebag that he looped over his shoulder. Furious at himself for the bad case of unwelcome lust that he was inflicted with that was so strong, it was hardly a surprise Bill had noticed.

"And to all those who accuse you of hanging on her every word, I tell them that I think it's lovely that you hold her in such high esteem. Professionally, that is. For Lottie knows her horses. Nobody could deny that."

Guy nodded his agreement again rather than mutter all the obscenities lined up in his throat while he rolled his eyes in frustration. Frustrated at the lust. Frustrated at the minx who had caused it and frustrated—most of all—by the fact that Bill got to call her Lottie while he hadn't yet been invited to. "Miss Travers does have a unique way with them." And with people. Everybody liked her. Including him.

Not that he would ever admit that aloud.

"Horses aside." His head groom was closer than his shadow now that they were indoors and Guy had nowhere to escape, hovering like a bird of prey waiting for some chink in the armor that would allow him to swoop in for the kill. "I'm glad the pair of you seem to be getting on so well. Aside from the mismatch in your temperaments . . ." How had she described that? *The ray of sunshine and the storm cloud.* Guy couldn't deny her summation was likely as apt as it was galling. "You and Lottie have a great deal in common."

Bill loved to list things on his fingers, so he had shoved them in Guy's face. "You love horses, she loves horses. You're both happiest when in the great outdoors. Obviously, we know the fact that she is also a vivacious and beautiful woman to boot is by the by and that you are immune to her physical charms, so pay all those gossips no mind. It would take a special sort of woman to tempt you back into the courting arena and she isn't it. She's too pretty. Too clever. Too funny. Too"—Bill rolled his hand as if pondering the conundrum—"vivacious for a staid fellow like you. I know that it is coincidence and coincidence alone that you've collided here every day this week at the exact same times as she sets off for her morning ride . . ."

Because of course his wily head groom had clocked that small shift in Guy's routine after he'd gone out of his way to avoid her beforehand.

Why wasn't he avoiding the menace now? More importantly, why was he doing the exact opposite and doing his utmost to collide with her? It made no sense when she was everything in a woman he feared. Pretty, funny, clever, and vivacious were all adjectives that could be used to describe Florinda and she had used those attributes ruthlessly to make a fool out of him. But a niggling voice in his head kept reassuring him that his mother was probably right and lightning never struck in the same way twice and this was different.

She was different.

And he was likely an idiot for thinking it.

". . . I know that you've had genuine business here at the stable and it's not her that draws you like a moth to a flame. The gossips are simply imagining things because we've suddenly got a pretty and feisty young woman here and you're a single fellow who happens to enjoy her company occasionally. There's no harm in that and people shouldn't try to speculate as to your intentions. Let one of them dare say to me that when you think nobody is watching, you gaze at her like the first sunrise after a long, cold winter, and I'll give them slanderous scandalmongers both barrels."

"I cannot tell you what a comfort it is that you've got my back, Bill." He had to choke out that insincerity because they both knew the wretch had painted a target on it and wanted to be the first one of those scandalmongers to fire the bull's-eye.

Guy grabbed a pair of horse blankets and strode out again, determined to take control of the conversation before he gave in to the urge to strangle the observant bastard. Except the second he stepped back into the stable yard he almost walked smack-bang into Miss Travers.

Just like the ray of sunshine she had claimed to be, she beamed and the world was a better place. "Good morning."

"Good morning." He tried not to sound as stiff and awkward as he felt with Bill watching while the lust caused an unwelcome twitch in his breeches.

"It's always a good morning when it starts with you in it." Bill, of course, didn't feel the slightest bit awkward and flirted with her as usual.

No doubt to rile Guy some more. "And might I add that while you are always a sight for sore eyes, you are looking particularly lovely this morning, Lottie?"

"You might." Miss Travers gave the rascal a flirty smile back, clearly pleased at the compliment enough to do a little twirl while she patted one of her loose blond curls.

"What's different?" The groom swept the length of her with an appreciative gaze. "A new dress? A new bonnet perhaps?"

"Just eight solid hours of glorious, uninterrupted beauty sleep."

"That's what his lordship needs—but alas, sleep eluded him last night." How Bill knew that was a mystery. "Apparently, you lit a flame within him last night at dinner," he added, grinning like an idiot, "and it's been burning ever since."

"I did?" Miss Travers's bemused gaze darted from Bill's back to Guy's as guilty heat rose beneath his collar. There was no way his groom could truly know how the vixen had haunted his dreams. A snippet of the most vivid instantly sprang to mind to aggravate the twitch in his breeches further. It involved long legs, bare skin, thrusting, raspberry-tipped breasts, and Miss Travers's lithe, tight body pulsing around his as she rode him with the same reckless abandon as she had that stallion in Hyde Park. "How?"

In case Bill could actually read his filthy mind, Guy tossed the blankets at him, hitting the devil's grinning face before he steered her away. "I couldn't stop thinking about what you said about Hercules, and how both of his parents influence his behavior but how his mother, especially, always manages to calm him down. That got me thinking—"

"He's lain awake all night because of you," said an unrepentant Bill from right behind. "Tossing and turning. Just look at the shadows under his eyes."

"I actually slept like the dead too . . ." Guy was going to torture bloody Bill before he wrung his neck! With a red-hot poker as he pulled each of his fingernails out with pliers! "But as the sun came up it suddenly occurred to me that perhaps we are trying to train Hercules all wrong

and that maybe we could literally *rope* in his parents to help break him."
Nerves had him chuckling lamely at his pathetic pun as he tried to be less
of the storm cloud, and when Miss Travers paused by one of the stalls to
idly pet a horse, he shot Bill warning daggers. The sort that he hoped said
he would dismiss the devil on the spot if he continued. "I thought I'd try
to train Hercules alongside his parents as an experiment."

She pondered that for a second, then nodded. "It's definitely worth a
try. Hercules is a lot like his father in his character, but Juno has as much
of a calming effect on Zeus as she does on their son."

"The right woman can tame even the most savage beast—and they
enjoy being tamed," said Bill, staring straight at him with suggestively
wiggling brows. Before Miss Travers noticed, Guy sandwiched himself
between her and his head groom as they filtered out of the stable door,
then made sure to slam it shut on the nuisance.

"I was thinking that to begin with, to ease Hercules's fear of the saddle, it might be a good idea to take him out without one—alongside Juno
and Zeus—so that he can see for himself that being ridden isn't such a
bad thing. He'll watch them both be saddled, then watch us mount them
and—"

"Us?" She stopped dead as Bill reappeared. "As in you and *me*? *You*
are going to entrust *me* with riding one of your prized Arabians?" Guy had
never witnessed a smile quite like the one that bloomed on her face and
had certainly never experienced the ripple of delight which shot through
him as a result.

"Well . . . I . . . um . . . had planned to do it with Bill this first time."
The dazzling smile dimmed, and he couldn't stand it. Not when he held
the power to bring it back. "But as he's a good-for-nothing shirker, there is
plenty he could be doing instead that's been left undone, so if you do not
mind accompanying me in his stead . . ."

"Mind?" The dazzling smile returned and she was suddenly a fizzing
ball of excitement. She clutched at his sleeve, her lovely eyes shimmering.
"I would *love* nothing more than to finally ride an Arabian!"

"And I am sure his lordship would love nothing more than an invigorating morning ride with you, Lottie." Bill was so delighted by all the fresh ammunition that had just been gifted him, it was a wonder he didn't dance a jig on the spot. They both knew Guy was going to pay for his rash, spur-of-the-moment invitation later. "I'll go fetch the horses."

"No need." Miss Travers bent over for a handful of bridles and dashed toward the pasture, laughing. "The quicker those Arabians are saddled, the less time their overprotective owner has to change his mind about letting me ride one!"

They watched her skip off—or rather Guy watched her skip off and Bill watched him watching with another smug grin. "I should probably leave the pair of you to your own devices then." Bill tugged his forelock with a wink then walked away, chuckling.

Fewer than ten minutes later, after agreeing on a flat, mile-long loop for this first experiment, they were leaving the paddock. Her on Juno, him on Zeus, and Hercules sandwiched between. Typically, the only horse behaving in this new situation was the one Miss Travers sat on.

"Hercules has never ventured this far from the pasture before." As the house disappeared but the horses' behavior did not improve, Guy felt compelled to defend both of his erratic animals. "And Zeus is . . . Zeus. Crochety and impatient and set in his ways."

"Much like his master, then." She chuckled at her own joke, never missing an opportunity to tease him. "Although to give you some credit, Bill did tell me that he was fully grown when you acquired him and much worse until you trained some of the temper out of him."

"He was an absolute nightmare, that is true. Unpredictable, uncontrollable, and dangerous. Nowadays he's just temperamental, which frankly, is a miracle."

"I suppose I shall have to say well done, although, as I am sure you can imagine, giving you a compliment galls."

"I felt much the same way when I was forced to compliment you the other day, so I feel your pain." Was it wrong that he enjoyed sparring with her? Or that already he was uncharacteristically comfortable around her? Or that she made him want to smile?

Inch by inch, Guy could sense his guard coming down and he wasn't sure how to feel about that. Yet he couldn't muster the enthusiasm to shore those defenses back up again this morning. She'd be gone in a week, so it wasn't as if this unlikely friendship that had kindled between them could develop into more, and he certainly wasn't stupid enough to act on his attraction. Knowing Aunt Almeria, Miss Travers wouldn't last in her employ anyway, and she'd have a new companion in time for her next visit to Kent, so what was the harm? Irrespective of Bill's close-to-the-bone teasing, there really wasn't one, so why was he overthinking things?

"Had Zeus been mistreated?" Her intuitiveness impressed him.

"He was previously owned by an idiot who tried to race him but used the whip too freely rather than learn how to control a horse respectfully."

She slanted him a knowing glance, as if she saw straight into his soul. "Is that why you bought him? And Hamish for that matter too. Then you purchased Juno for a king's ransom so that Zeus would have a friend because all the other horses hated him and you couldn't stand that."

"I bought Juno as I have lofty ideas to breed champion horses." An ambition he had never admitted aloud up to now. Yet, somehow, he knew she would understand it and not think him silly for doing it.

"To race or to sell?"

"Both, I suppose. Except my first attempt"—he gestured to the jittery Hercules—"isn't the sort of horse I could do either with."

"Hercules is just young and headstrong. With the right training, I think he has the potential to win the Derby. Just look at him." He knew she would understand because she knew horses. "Look at his bone structure and muscle tone. He has an impressive gait too, and his father's lengthy stride. I'll wager he will fly like the wind on a straight track and love it if he's taught properly." Her focus shifted from the horse back to him. "I can see you as a breeder and it makes sense to spend good money on good horses." Then she shot Guy a mischievous glance that went straight to his groin. "But that doesn't explain why you purchased the arthritic, limping, ancient cart horse that Bill calls Old Nag six months ago for no other apparent purpose than to allow him to spend his twilight years munching on grass?" She grinned before he could answer. "For all your bluster and the perennial angry storm cloud lingering over your head"—she gestured to it as if she could see it—"you are a softhearted rescuer, aren't you?"

He wasn't prepared to admit to that aloud, so he sidestepped. "I simply like horses, Miss Travers. Dogs and donkeys too. Sheep, cows, pigs. Cats at a push."

"So basically any creature, so long as they have four legs."

He shook his head, enjoying her company. "I'm not a fan of vermin and they have four legs, but I don't dislike birds and they only have two."

"Must you always be so contrary?"

"I fear I must when your accusation holds no substance. I could list several two-legged creatures that I like. Humans, however . . ." He shrugged with a half smile and let the rest of the sentence hang. "And certain humans, like yourself, for example, have such little to recommend in them and are so tedious to be around that I find them impossible to like."

"Nobody could find me tedious, my lord. We both know that I am a veritable delight and my sunshine is a balm to the soul." Zeus thrashed some more and she used that as an excuse to insult Guy again. "You would much rather have me ride you than your unpleasant owner, wouldn't you, Zeus?" And of course the blasted traitor calmed straightaway at her soothing tone while Guy's fevered imagination pictured being ridden by her once more. "We both know that you would be an absolute sweetheart for me."

"It took four months of constant work to convince Zeus to allow me to sit on him. Even now, several years on, he's still a handful and as you saw that fateful morning in Hyde Park, it doesn't take much to elicit a tantrum." He was certainly making Guy work this morning and, right on cue, decided to whinny his disapproval at this unfamiliar situation and thrash his head. "In short, he's not an easy horse to control."

She waited until he had settled the beast before she responded. "I notice you still don't carry a whip though."

"I value my neck too much to risk one. Or even have one within Zeus's sight. Bill walked past him once with one idly dangling by his side and got kicked clean across the paddock for his troubles. Couldn't sit down without a cushion for a week afterward." A memory that, after the ribbing the reprobate had given him this morning, made Guy chuckle.

"Poor Bill." But she found the story funny and he realized, with a start, that he enjoyed making her laugh. Had made it a bit of a quest, in fact. Much like he used to do with his father. "Has he worked for you long?"

Was that a conversational question or one that hinted she had interest in Bill, the man? She had certainly been a bit flirty with him this morning. Enough to make Guy pathetically envious of the easy rapport the pair shared. And the flirting, when she had never so much as fluttered her lashes at him. "His father worked for my father, so I suppose we as good as grew up together."

"Hence all the teasing and door slamming." Because of course she had noticed Guy fling the stable door back into his smirking groom's face.

"*Hence* I am stuck with him because I liked his father and suffer from a misplaced sense of obligation."

"Really?" She didn't believe him. "I suspect that you are not a man who cares overmuch for airs and graces and therefore, you not only respect and like him, you consider him a friend."

"I most certainly do not." Guy wasn't sure how he felt about her ability to read him like a book. "Whilst I am very definitely *not* a man for airs and graces, that scoundrel is not my friend. At best, I feel I must tolerate him. At least until his father dies, of course. Then it will be goodbye, Bill." As she seemed determined to use this ride to chisel past his protective exterior to the too-softhearted core within, Guy changed the subject again. "Speaking of tolerating, how are you getting on with my awful aunt?"

That made her grin. "Perhaps I am peculiar, but I genuinely *do* like her. She pretends to be awful, and probably is to those not made of sterner stuff, but she has such spirit and is unapologetically herself all of the time."

"Much like you, Miss Travers." He had never met a woman as unapologetically herself as this Valkyrie. She wasn't just a dazzling ray of sunshine and a fizzing ball of energy. She was a breath of fresh air too.

Her eyes locked with his again. "Much like you, more like, as her bark is worse than her bite."

If she thought she was turning the topic back to him again, she had another think coming. "Has she finally run out of errands to send you on?"

"Don't be silly." Miss Travers leaned sideways to give the fractious Hercules's ears a stroke and he calmed instantly. "She has a perpetual list of requests. Some of them necessary, the other half nebulous, and at least a quarter, wholly unreasonable—but I like the challenge. She likes to test me, and because I am ridiculously competitive by nature, I love to exceed her expectations."

"Aunt Almeria has always been a hard taskmaster. Only she would send you miles and miles to Maidstone just for éclairs."

She winced. "About that afternoon—"

He held up his palm, annoyed that he had inadvertently injected some awkwardness into their pleasant exchange. "There is nothing to explain. It was none of my business and I should have added that to my apology the other day. Who you choose to . . . um . . ." *Why the blazes had he brought bloody Maidstone up? Latent jealousy? Futile hope? Pointless when his relationship with Miss Travers was blessedly transient.* ". . . spend time with has nothing to do with me."

"The man you saw me with—Dan—"

"Oh, Mr. Handsome is called Dan, is he?" The curt note of sarcasm in his tone was unconscious, so he tempered it with a chuckle in case she thought he was jealous of her Adonis. Which, much to his chagrin, he was. Enough that the invisible storm cloud over his head rumbled with thunder. "You must know him very well to be on first-name terms."

"Daniel is my brother." She was too focused on steering Juno around a molehill to notice his visible relief at that. "One of them, anyway.

Because the universe clearly wanted to punish me, so it gave me four of them. All older and all beyond irritating. Dan is the youngest and the closest to me in age. Only one year separates us, so, yes—I do know him very well. Sadly."

"Ah." Guy tried to mask how overjoyed he was at that welcome revelation. "Then we must add me making improper assumptions to the list of things I've not reacted well to. My apologies again for jumping to conclusions."

By the emphatic shake of her head, Miss Travers made it plain she wasn't going to accept it. "I should have explained when you queried it and told you that your aunt knew I was going to briefly visit my family that afternoon. They are dealing with"—her eyes clouded briefly before she forced those clouds away—"some difficult things at the moment and so I bought them the cakes you saw me with to cheer them up." Her gaze flicked to his, contrite. "They live just a few miles from Maidstone. In Aylesford, actually. But rather than correct your misapprehension, I was curt and rude to you, and I shouldn't have been."

"Yes, you jolly well should have." If she could be humble in her honesty, so could he. "I was typically rude and ungentlemanly, had unfairly besmirched your character, and had as good as accused you of impropriety. Therefore, I thoroughly deserved to be put in my place."

"That is very decent of you—even if impropriety is my middle name." She sent him a grateful smile that quickly morphed into one of mischief. "Please desist being decent or I might have to like you, Lord Wennington, and that wouldn't do at all."

She liked him? How . . . marvelous. "Am I allowed to ask what sort of difficult things your family is dealing with at the moment, or is that another impertinent invasion of your privacy?"

"They are farmers and, as I am sure you know, farming isn't always easy."

"Is that the mind-your-own-business answer, Miss Travers?"

"It was actually the I-won't-bore-you-with-the-details answer, Lord Wennington. Unless you have a burning desire to hear a tale of woe about persistent blight, that is."

"Blight can be a blighter." Before she did, he rolled his own eyes at that pathetic pun. "How persistent is it?"

"It first reared its ugly head three years ago and ruined a third of the wheat crop. My father left the infected field fallow for twelve months, hoping that would sort it, but it didn't. This year, it decimated the entire barley crop." As if he wouldn't understand how devastating that was, she sighed. "We don't have infinite land or infinite resources, so the loss of both the crop and that field for the foreseeable future is a blow."

"I am sorry." And he was. Farming was hard and those with small-holdings suffered the most. "Is there anything I can do to help?"

"*No!* No, of course not but thank you for offering." He hadn't meant to embarrass her but could tell he had. "We can manage."

As it wasn't his place to press the issue, Guy racked his brains for something else to talk about in the five minutes they had left before their loop was completed. But it was Miss Travers who filled the void.

"By 'we,' I actually mean my menfolk because my father is too stubborn and overprotective to include me in his plans. If Dan hadn't written, then I wouldn't even know that they were struggling and I wouldn't be able to give them my wages to help." An admission that touched him and bothered him in equal measure. "Not that my father yet knows that Dan took my money, of course, as he'd have returned it with a lecture. He would rather starve than bother me with our family's collective woes. Never mind that I want to help—and can. Honestly! Why are men so . . . idiotic?"

"We prefer the term 'proud' when we are being insufferable."

"Even though pride always comes before a fall? It is exasperating to have to go to all the lengths we women must go to in order to circumvent that collective obstinacy and get them to see reason." For the first time since he had known her, her confident, bold, effervescent ray-of-sunshine façade slipped and he witnessed how burdened she was beneath it. "And it is so frustrating to be left out of things simply because my family thinks that they know best. Because surely there is something that they haven't thought of that could prevent my pigheaded father from having to sell half our dairy herd to the butcher? That is just robbing Peter to pay Paul when their milk is worth more in the long run than the beef."

Guy couldn't argue with any of her logic because she wasn't wrong. But commiserating wouldn't help. "There are many new ideas for all manner of pests detailed in the farming journals. Does he subscribe to those? What else has he tried beyond leaving the infected field fallow?"

She shrugged, exasperated, as the paddock came back into view. "All I know comes from the snippets Dan deigns to share with me and even he tends toward overprotectiveness too if the mood strikes him."

"But if I could find a newfangled treatment that they haven't tried in one of my journals, Dan would be able to convince your father to give it a go?"

"I suppose so. Dan is a man, after all, and so are you. In this world of men, that seems to be the single qualification a person needs to be taken seriously." She huffed out her irritation to offer him a wry smile. "Good heavens above, now I sound like Portia."

"Who is Portia?"

"A friend. One so outspoken she makes me look like a shrinking violet."

Guy pulled a face of disbelief and she giggled. "A fair point. I am more a gaudy sunflower than a shrinking violet." Then a very different expression softened her features. "But despite your rudeness in pointing that out, thank you for allowing me to vent and for trying to help when none of this is your problem. The Travers clan are no strangers to adversity, and we always manage to overcome them. I apologize if my outburst just spoiled what has been, up to now, a very lovely ride."

"I meant what I said. I will try to find something." In this precise moment, he was prepared to slay dragons for her, so hunting through over a hundred journals was the least he could do. "It really is no trouble. In fact, it gives me an excuse to escape that tedious hour after dinner while my mother castigates me for ruining her life because I have curtailed all her hideous plans for my birthday."

Her golden brows kissed as she frowned. "A birthday celebration planned with love isn't hideous, my lord."

It was on the tip of his tongue to ask her to call him Guy. "I'd honestly rather stick pins in my eyes than suffer through the small gathering I *have* condoned, let alone the sort my mother would have thrown given half the chance."

"Suffer?" She brushed that away. "It will be fun. You'll see."

"It might be fun for someone like you who is comfortable in your skin around others, but I loathe being the center of attention." Why had he admitted to that last part? Now he sounded pitiful. Socially inept and out of his depth in front of a woman who was neither but who he was still, pathetically, keen to impress. The only way out was to make a joke out of it. "A dull, serious, and curmudgeonly storm cloud like me would much rather read about blight. And who knows, I might find something useful."

Her smile was unconvincing. "I cannot deny that a miracle, sometime around now, would be welcome."

"Wouldn't it?" But as he gazed at her, he was starting to wonder if one had already happened. Because there was an odd stirring in his wary, shriveled heart, and much to his surprise, it didn't completely terrify him.

Chapter
FOURTEEN

❦

𝔗t was after seven by the time Lottie returned from Gravesend where she had rendezvoused with Longbottom to appraise him of the final preparations. Almost eight before Lady Frinton and her sister finished quizzing her about whether or not he had managed to procure everything needed for *the Surprise*. They wanted to know every minute detail, so it took forever before she could dash away to change for dinner. Their inquisition left her with no time to do more than throw on a frock and splash some water on her face and because she was running so late, she tried her best not to revisit the guilt at her part in this which had plagued her for days. She might well now consider Lord Wennington a friend but she had to be realistic. He was a viscount. A member of the blue-blooded aristocracy. In the normal scheme of things, a viscount and a lady's companion weren't usually friends and just because he was finally being civil did not mean that he thought her one. She was employed by Lady Frinton and would leave with her next week regardless, she could not jeopardize that, so it really wasn't her place to tip him off about tomorrow—no matter how much she wanted to.

So she would jolly well put off thinking about it until then!

Ignoring her still nagging conscience, Lottie took a cursory glance in the mirror. After a day on horseback, her hair was an unsalvageable disaster. With no time left to start it again from scratch, Lottie shoved a handful of pins into the bird's nest on her head. Who was she trying to look nice for anyway? Two older ladies and a handsome viscount too far above her station to take any notice.

More was the pity.

The clock in the hallway began chiming eight as she ran down the stairs and hurried toward the open dining room. She was almost there when a grinning Lord Wennington appeared out of the music room door and beckoned her over with a finger to his lips. He grabbed her hand and tugged her inside, gently kicking the door closed behind them.

"Peas," he said.

Or at least she thought that was what he said because he was still holding her hand and that was all it took to make her pulse have a conniption. It had quickened so much she couldn't think straight. "I'm sorry?"

"Peas . . . or beans." He shrugged, still smiling, the soft light from the only lamp in the dim room making the copper in his irises heat, much like her flesh was heating beneath the loose grip of his fingers.

"Er . . ." Gracious! She was so off-kilter from the effects of his touch that she had missed the most important part of that odd question—if it even was a question? That had never happened before. Not even a thoroughly good kiss had ever had the power to scramble her wits like the feel of just her hand in his. "As in which do I prefer?"

His deep chuckle sent a shiver through her. Like a trickle of warm honey over flesh already sensitized because he still had her hand. "My apologies, in my excitement and because I've been preoccupied with it for the last two hours, I assumed you would know immediately what I was talking about. Peas or beans. Whichever grows better in your father's soil. That is the apparent solution to his blight problem."

He paused and glanced down, bemused, to where their hands joined as if he had only just realized that they were, before he slowly severed the contact. "Er . . ." His brows furrowed for a moment before he took a couple of steps back, and her body instantly mourned the closeness. "They apparently work better than leaving an infected field fallow and the crop earns you more money in the long run as well."

He rocked on his heels and folded his arms, looking every inch as awkward as she felt, making her wonder if he had experienced the same peculiar reaction to the unexpected contact too. "The journal I just read actually recommends two years of legumes to begin with for really persistent blight." Arms still folded, he flicked his fingers in the rough direction of his study. "It also recommends adding a legume of some sort into the regular crop rotation even if you haven't got blight as it does wonders for the soil. Legumes are a wonder crop apparently."

Lottie couldn't resist punching the air. "All hail the legume!" As she had hoped, that broke the odd tension in the room and made him laugh. "And all hail the man that can string so many sentences with the word 'legume' in it together so seamlessly. Especially when I was ignorant of the existence of the word 'legume' not five minutes ago."

"Well, they do say that you learn something new every day, Miss Travers."

"They do." She was certainly learning, and fast, that an animated, smiling Lord Wennington was a dangerous thing indeed. Especially when he was standing so close and smelled absolutely divine. Clean and fresh like spring rain but with a hint of spice too. Earthy. Masculine. Extremely attractive. Of their own accord, Lottie's feet took a step closer to better inhale it and she almost sighed aloud when she did because it was also headier than a glass of champagne on an empty stomach.

Was that all him?

Or him mixed with cologne?

Did he always wear cologne?

Surely she would have remembered a scent this potent and seductive if she had encountered it before?

She found her gaze dropping from his eyes to his lips as her errant mind wondered if he tasted as good as he smelled, then blinked when she saw them moving. ". . . with you later."

"I'm sorry?" She had no clue what he was suggesting he do with her later, but frankly, she was now up for anything.

He stared at her bemusedly now. "Have you even listened to a word I've said?"

"I'm . . . a bit distracted." Which was absolutely the truth but it probably wasn't wise to let him see that she was thoroughly distracted by him. "I've been running countless errands for your aunt all afternoon and only recently got back, so my head is still spinning from it all. Kindly repeat what you just said—I got the bit about using legumes in the crop rotation."

He sighed without any malice. "Then you've got the gist. All I added was that I'll give the journal to you later so that you can pass it on to your brother."

"Ah, yes. Thank you. I look forward to reading it myself after dinner. On the subject of dinner . . ." She gestured to the shadowed clock on the mantel. "We are late." Because frankly, if she spent another minute alone with him in this intimate, darkened room, she wasn't sure she'd survive it with any dignity left intact. "And you know how your mother and her sister feel about tardiness to the table."

Lottie spun around to exit, unaware that the dangling hem of her hastily donned petticoat was trapped beneath her shoe. She lurched backward as it twisted taut, tried to steady herself, and failed miserably. Her flailing hands grabbed nothing but air.

With a lunge, he caught her before she met the floor, and somehow that was so much worse than her cranium hitting the carpet. Her semi-reclined position left her not only overwhelmed by his presence but engulfed in it. Her arms clinging to his shoulders, his arms wrapped tight around her ribs, her breasts squashed intimately against him. Faces inches apart. Wide eyes locked. Her positively drowning in his heavenly scent while all manner of improper sensations ricocheted around her body.

Lottie swallowed and so did he, his Adam's apple bobbing. Something strange was happening to all the air in the room because it felt suddenly heavier and seemed to crackle around them. With anticipation and . . . excitement. The thrum of his heartbeat against hers, mirroring and matching. Almost as loud. Almost as erratic. The copper in his eyes like fire, molten against his suddenly much darker irises.

Had desire darkened them?

Had it darkened hers too? She had no clue, but it pooled in the most scandalous recesses of her increasingly wanton body regardless.

Were they having a reckless and magical moment?

She sincerely hoped so because she was ripe for it. So ready to be kissed breathless by this vexing conundrum of a man that her nipples puckered against his chest in shameless invitation and she wasn't the least bit inclined to stop them.

His gaze raked her face until it settled on her mouth. He edged lower until his warm breath whispered over her cheeks while she willed him to close that last inch of distance.

She had the urge to lick her tingling lips. To caress his face and run her fingers through his hair. To arch up and close the gap herself. To be brazen and instigate the kiss she was now convinced they both desperately craved—but didn't. In case she was reading all his signals wrong in her intoxicated, discombobulated, and ridiculously aroused state.

Finally, the tip of his nose grazed hers, but as her eyelids fluttered closed, in the space of a single heartbeat the moment was gone and he was dragging her upright. As soon as she was horizontal, he briskly stepped away.

"Crisis averted," he said, looking every which way but at her. "I thought I was going to drop you."

"Yes . . ." Her voice was breathy. "Thank you for catching me . . . and clinging on." And because the crackling air bursting with promise had now been replaced with an oppressive cloud of awkwardness, Lottie stumbled toward the door, doing her best to fill the mortifying void with the most cringeworthy vomit of words possible. "I do hope your cook will be serving us legumes for dinner. After all that talk about them, I could murder some peas."

Chapter
FIFTEEN

❧

$\mathcal{T}$he Traverses' farmhouse was larger than Guy expected. It was no smallholder's tied cottage. It was a gentleman's house. However, from the few missing roof tiles, lack of any servants rushing out to greet him, and the overgrown roses cascading over the porch, it was clear the family money that had once purchased this house and land was long gone. That observation didn't mean that the place had gone to rack and ruin from mismanagement either, as it was well-kept and homey, the yard neat and tidy. A nearby barn looked to be almost new, and he was surrounded by well-tended fields. This was the home of an obviously hard-working agricultural family and he admired that.

Although he had no idea why he was here. Not really. His only excuse was tenuous at best, but after an almost-kiss, some very real warring doubts, and yet another sleepless night craving her, he'd had to come. Had to see where the vixen came from.

"Can I help you, sir?" The man emerged from the barn, wiping his hands on a rag as he smiled. He was a big bear of a fellow of around his mother's age. Late fifties, perhaps early sixties, but as fit as a butcher's dog. Tall and broad with the sun-burnished skin of one who spent most of his time in the fields, a thick mop of graying sandy hair, and what could only be his daughter's bright blue eyes.

"Mr. Travers?"

"I am indeed. And who might you be?"

"Guy Harrowby, sir." Not wishing to intimidate while he looked down on her father from Zeus, which for all manner of worrying reasons was not the first impression he wanted to give this man, he dismounted and held out his hand. "Or Wennington. I answer to either."

Rather than incline his head as many did when they learned of his title, Mr. Travers's smile only widened in recognition as his enormous work-roughened palm gripped Guy's. "It's nice to finally put a face to the name. It's also an honor to finally meet the man who took on all those bloody grain merchants last year and won. Good work! Made it so much easier for many of the farmers of Kent to get a fair price for their crops." He pumped Guy's hand enthusiastically. "We all owe you a debt of gratitude. I should also offer you my condolences as I'm told that you currently have the unfortunate pleasure of my daughter as a houseguest."

"I do indeed."

"Please tell me that you're not here because Lottie's driven you mad with her willfulness and you're hopeful that I can use my fatherly influence to make her less so. Because trust me, I've tried for three and twenty years so far and nothing's worked." He chuckled with obvious affection. "I know I should've beaten her as a child, because lord only knows she gave me plenty of reason to—and still does—but I was brought up never to strike a woman and now the whole world is paying for my saintly restraint."

Mr. Travers feigned exasperation, but his eyes danced with amusement. This was a man who clearly loved his only daughter to distraction and enjoyed the way she was. It also proved where she got her sense of humor from. "What's the firebrand done this time?"

"Nothing." Apart from mining under Guy's skin and most of his defenses and leaving him so conflicted inside that he didn't know which way was up. "At least nothing recent." He grinned and Mr. Travers chuckled back. "Although she *is* the reason I am here."

"I see." Mr. Travers looked him up and down, his ready smile flattening, suddenly every inch the protective father who knew that his daughter was a prize and who wasn't going to allow her to settle for a man who didn't deserve her. "Do I need to sit you on a low chair in my study, loom over you in a menacing fashion, and quiz you about your intentions?"

Maybe.

And maybe not.

Guy still hadn't made up his mind about that. He had been engaged in a full-scale war between what his sensible, battle-scarred head and his clearly still reckless but equally battle-scarred heart wanted. He'd veered both ways since he had almost kissed her last night. Part of him—the part that terrified him the most—was furious that he hadn't just said to hell with it all and tasted her mouth.

Because they had both wanted him to.

Of that he was sure.

Guy might not be the expert womanizer that Bill was, but he had been with enough women to know when one was willing! Miss Travers had enjoyed being in his arms. He knew that because she practically melted against his body the second he'd caught her, just as his body had instinctively fused against hers—as if it was meant to be there. Then, rather than scramble out of his arms and acting all missish about their compromising clinch, she'd looped hers around his neck while she had waited for him to make the next move. Lips parted. Breath expectant. Her lush body languid and compliant, inviting him to continue without any hint of disapproval at their intimate position. She had even stared at his mouth while she waited. All clear signposts that she wasn't averse to being kissed.

He certainly couldn't ever remember wanting a woman more—and that was what troubled him the most. Nobody had ever heated his blood like she did. Not even Florinda, who had gone out of her way to heat it in all manner of highly improper ways. That conniving woman's overt seductions hadn't seduced him half as much as the desire in Miss Travers's lovely eyes.

But as the comparison with Florinda popped into his mind a split second before he gave in to the urge to kiss Miss Travers, it panicked him enough not to. The last time he had jumped headfirst into the murky waters of love—again after a ridiculously short acquaintance thanks to far too much temptation—he'd been made a fool of. Only a complete idiot would rush into it again with a woman he barely knew, simply because he wanted her in every way possible. Which he supposed was part of the reason he was here. He needed to know precisely who Miss Travers was before he gave too much of his wary heart away again. Hoping against hope that lightning wouldn't, couldn't possibly strike so destructively twice. Especially as Miss Travers—Lottie—wasn't anything like the conniving and social-climbing woman whom he had made the fatal mistake of proposing to.

"There is no need for you to loom today, sir. I come here as a fellow farmer and not a prospective suitor."

Yet, said the impetuous and increasingly loud voice in his head. But he might be. He could admit that to himself. Feeling his way slowly—with sensible caution—despite the overwhelming longing he was suffering from that urged him to rush in and make his aunt's latest but unconventional companion his. A turn up for the books likely so scandalous that it would make it into the dreaded gossip columns because viscounts didn't tend to court lady's companions. At least not as a general rule. But as he had eschewed all the stupid rules of the ton when he had exiled himself from them, if she was the elusive one that his lonely heart had been looking for, he wouldn't give two figs what those jumped-up, judgmental, preening fools thought.

"Just as well as I'm not in the mood for looming today." Mr. Travers's shoulders relaxed as he sighed in relief. "You do not strike me as mad and you'd have to be to want to shackle yourself to my Beanstalk. I love my daughter more than life itself, but she's a handful."

The mention of a handful reminded Guy of how perfectly she had fit in his arms last night and how desperately he had wanted to fill his hands with every soft, womanly part of her. Thighs, bottom. Those saucy, pointed, raspberry-tipped breasts that begged to be teased and licked and . . .

Good grief! What the bloody hell was the matter with him? The menace hadn't just seduced him, she'd thoroughly bewitched him because nothing would shift her from his mind. He certainly shouldn't be fantasizing about all the things he wanted to do to the woman in front of her father!

"Your . . . um . . . daughter mentioned that you have persistent blight and I happened across an article in one of my farming journals the other day that I thought you might find of interest."

Glad of an excuse to escape Mr. Travers's gaze, Guy retrieved the journal from his saddlebag, where he had put it after she had failed to turn up for her usual dawn ride. After she'd avoided him all through dinner and afterward last night.

His fault. He had embarrassed them both last night by withdrawing from the kiss and he figured he owed her some sort of explanation for his behavior. He hadn't fathomed the exact words he needed to say yet but recognized that she deserved to know that his failure to kiss her wasn't because he didn't want her.

In fact, nothing could be further from the truth.

There was something about Miss Travers that called to his soul, as well as his body, in a way that had never happened before. Something that transcended all his lust. It was hard to categorize what it was he felt for her, especially as every sensible part of him warned him to run away and to deny what was happening. All he knew was that there, alongside his intense physical attraction to her, was a unique connection between them, as if they were kindred spirits in some way. Someone he could be himself with. Someone he was tempted to entrust his heart to.

He just needed to prove that.

Perhaps the only way to do that was to court her?

A sudden epiphany which absolutely terrified him.

With a tense swallow, he passed the journal to Mr. Travers. "I marked the page and will leave you to read it at your leisure, but the gist is that farmers who plant infected fields with peas for a season find they recover better than those who leave the field fallow." Was he really already contemplating forever? "Your daughter said you'd already left it fallow last year to no avail." Lottie was definitely the forever sort. The sort a man could build a life with. A future with. A family with. *Stop running before you can walk, man! Look before you leap!*

"Aye, we did. Blasted blight." Guy forced himself to focus on her father and not the churning ball of fear spinning out of control in his gut. "Left it to rest for fourteen months this second time and the damned disease only grew stronger in the ground." Mr. Travers flipped to the article, clearly interested in a potential solution. "I've never grown peas, have you?"

"I was going to, a few years back," answered Guy truthfully, "but never got around to it." Because peas needed staking. Protecting from birds. Handpicking. Peas were a handful, just like this man's effervescent and bewitching daughter. A commitment he hadn't quite been ready for.

Mr. Travers pulled a face, almost as if he could read Guy's thoughts "I've heard that peas are a lot of work for a short season. But I'm not afraid of hard work and neither are my boys, so if they get rid of the blasted blight . . ." His eyes scanned the charts, taking in the figures and the yields with what seemed to be a promisingly open mind. "Then maybe it's worth the faff to fix things. The things that take the most effort are always the most rewarding in the end."

Like a proper all-cards-on-the-table courtship with his aunt's latest companion.

He was going to have to have a very frank discussion with her, wasn't he? The baring-the-soul sort. The I-think-you-and-I-might-have-something sort.

Guy was queasy just thinking about it.

"Lord knows nothing else has worked on my bloody blight so far and I'm worried it might spread to the rest of my land." Mr. Travers's frustrations dragged Guy out of his panicked reverie and back to their conversation.

Thank goodness, because his epiphany was giving him severe palpitations. As was his next step. Going home and asking this man's daughter, a woman he had known for only eighteen days and been cordial with for just a week, if she was up for being wooed.

He sucked in a calming breath that did little to make him calm. Because a week was fast by anyone's standards to fall a little bit in love. Perhaps even more than a little bit. "If you turn to the next page, sir, there is another chart that suggests that blight-free fields that are regularly rotated with peas also yield more grain. They also sell well to all the fancy tables in the capital, and for an excellent price too while they are in season. I hear they even stock the things at Fortnum and Mason."

"The king's own grocer? Really?" Mr. Travers liked the sound of that, which pleased Guy as he already liked Mr. Travers and wanted him to like him back. "I bet the seed is expensive though." He said that with the determined nonchalance of someone who probably couldn't afford to invest in any after the blow the blight had dealt him this year. He closed the journal, which confirmed it, and pasted on a brave smile so reminiscent of his daughter's last night after Guy had rebuffed her, it plucked at his heartstrings. "I shall give this a proper read later and give it some serious thought. Thank you for taking the trouble to personally deliver this to me, my lord. It was good of you to do so."

"It was no trouble at all, Mr. Travers. I had business in Maidstone today anyway, so was passing." If "passing" was the correct term for going four miles out of his way. "Besides, we farmers should always stick together. Especially with something that affects us all." Like a golden-haired firebrand that they both adored. Albeit in decidedly different ways.

"Is everything all right, Pa?" Two men approached. One Guy instantly recognized as the Adonis he had seen her with that day at the market. Daniel, she'd said his name was. Dan? The other was a few years older but no less handsome than his younger brother. Both were tall. Both had the same dark blond hair as their sister. Both were displaying similar wary expressions.

"Of course it is!" Mr. Travers beckoned them over. "This is Lord Wennington, the nephew of the lady our Lottie is working for. He's come with some ideas for our blight."

"Today? Today of all days?" Dan's eyes widened until his brother gave him a firm nudge as he strode forward, hand extended.

"Pleased to meet you, my lord. I'm Stephen. Lottie's eldest brother."

Like his father, there was a protective edge to that statement. "My sister has told us all about you."

"Then I dread to think what she has said." If they were a close family, they might even know everything, and he wasn't sure how he felt about that. *Yet.* Any more than he was sure how he felt about her *yet* either.

Could I really already be in love with the minx? This fast? This thoroughly?

The very idea made his head spin and his heart . . .

His poor, bludgeoned, guarded heart . . . was singing.

God help him!

"She said nothing too bad," said Daniel, stepping forward to shake his hand too. "I'm Dan and I beg of you not to judge all of the Travers clan by my troublesome sister's horrendous example. I'm sorry she covered you in soup, got you attacked by a goose, and threatened to horsewhip you." Clearly she *had* told them everything.

"She threatened what?" At his father's outrage, Dan winced at Guy. "I forgot that Lottie swore me to secrecy about that part; don't tell her I did or she'll likely horsewhip me too."

"If my daughter threatened to horsewhip you, my lord, then—"

"It's Guy, Mr. Travers." If he was going to be courting his daughter, and wanted this man's approval to do it, then "my lord" didn't feel right. "I've always been more a farmer than a viscount and while she did once threaten me with her whip, I can assure you that I deserved it. I was most ungentlemanly to her that day and—"

"Then maybe you did deserve it." Suddenly, Stephen's face was like thunder as he obviously didn't know the whole story and had assumed "ungentlemanly" was a politer way of saying he'd taken a liberty. Which he hadn't—but he wanted to.

Really wanted to.

"We collided while riding in Hyde Park one morning." He supposed honesty was the best policy with her menfolk from the outset. "We were both going too fast, both weren't looking where we were going, and when we almost ran into each other, our stallions got spooked. Zeus here . . ."

He shook the reins in his fist. "Threw me off, then bolted. She gave chase and managed to catch him, which was no mean feat, I can tell you, with this unpredictable brute. She brought him back and instead of saying thank you, I told her off for reckless riding. Things deteriorated from there. It wasn't my finest hour."

"Nor hers, by the sounds of it. She's always been hotheaded and always rides like the devil is on her tail." Her oldest brother's wry smile told Guy that he was now suitably appeased. However, the story hadn't done the same for the father, who glared at Dan.

"What was she doing on a blasted stallion? She's been borrowing horses without permission again, hasn't she?" When Dan winced again, the older man shook his head. "Is that why she's now a lady's companion and not a governess? She got herself dismissed again, didn't she?" He pointed an accusing finger at his youngest son. "And she told you not to tell me! Because you two have always been as thick as thieves." Mr. Travers was so agitated he was turning purple. "Why does that girl never think of the consequences of her actions? She'll be getting a piece of my mind when I see her."

"There's a bit more to it this time, Pa," said Dan with a pointed look at first his father and then his brother, who had obviously also been kept in the dark. "So what happened wasn't entirely Lottie's fault."

"Still—"

Before Mr. Travers continued to rant, his eldest son intervened with a warning glance at his father that stated that this wasn't the time or the place. "Your horse is an Arabian, isn't it?"

"He is."

He stepped forward to stroke Zeus's neck. "I'll bet Lottie loves him. She's always had a soft spot for Arabians. We used to have a neighbor who bred them." He gestured north with his head. "She was there all the time as a girl, constantly dropping by his stables just to spend time with them." Guy smiled because he could imagine her doing just that. "She was there so often he ended up putting her to work just to get her out from under his grooms' feet."

"Took advantage of her passion for his mounts, more like, and never paid her a penny for all the hours of work she did for him, the skinflint." Now Mr. Travers was aggrieved about something done to his daughter rather than what she had done. "Let her brush them down, feed them, and even asked her to muck out their stalls but never let her ride one of them. What sort of person does that? When he would have known it would have meant the world to my little girl."

"That was his problem." Stephen rolled his eyes. "He knew she was a better rider than anyone in the county and he wanted to believe he was so he didn't want to be shown up." He turned to Guy with a wry smile. "But don't you dare tell her I said that as it'll go to her big head and I'll only deny it."

"She knows she rides better than anyone already, idiot." Dan laughed at his brother. "I've lost count of how many times she's beaten you at a steeplechase. That's why none of us bet on your races anymore. It's pointless. We all know Lottie will win. Even if she was on the back of a cumbersome cart horse with a limp, she'd get the best out of the animal and find a way to finish first. Our sister has always had a unique bond with horses, almost as if she can speak horse. For goodness only knows they respond to her in ways they don't with anyone else."

"She'd make a better horse trainer than she makes a well-behaved governess, that is for certain." Mr. Travers huffed, still not over his initial annoyance. "Please tell me she has your permission to be riding Blodwyn?"

"She does." Although now that he knew her better, Guy had to admit that Blodwyn wasn't really the horse for her when Juno had suited her more. He would tell her that when he got home too. Offering up Juno would guarantee him one of her most dazzling smiles and might go some way toward convincing her to give him a go.

"Then what bad thing has she done to bring you here?" It was Stephen who asked it, but Dan leaned in to nod as if he too expected the worst.

"A good thing!" Their father waved the journal. "A potential solution to our blight problem. Peas, of all things. Who knew?" Mr. Travers explained what the article said, likely only out of politeness now that he realized the cost was prohibitive, and Guy embellished it for all he was worth.

"Anyway, I thought it might be worth a try." Now that they had thoroughly exhausted the topic of legumes, and the sun was inching ever closer to the horizon, Guy shrugged and decided that he had likely outstayed his welcome. He really wanted to help further, and at least buy them the seed that they would doubtless struggle to afford or loan them the money plus some extra to tide them over, but knew these men wouldn't allow it. Guy empathized. It took one to know one, and nobody knew how important, yet fragile, a man's pride was better than he did. "If you do and it works, let me know. It was nice to meet you all."

They said their goodbyes and walked him to the lane. He was about to mount Zeus when he had an idea. "You know . . . I've a feeling I have a couple of sacks of old seed peas in a barn somewhere." A lie. "So old, I wouldn't be surprised if they don't grow, but a few might germinate and so you're welcome to them if you want to conduct an experiment. They're doing nothing in my barn apart from slowly rotting, so someone might as well make use of them."

The two sons instantly looked to their father, their interest clearly piqued, but the older man shook his head and squared his shoulders. "I won't take them for free but I'll pay you a fair price for them."

"I think a fair price for old seed that might not grow is nothing, Mr. Travers." A response that made the patriarch of the family set his stubborn jaw. So Guy scratched his as if weighing up his options. "But if it does, seeing as it's technically *my* seed, although arguably all your land, your labor, and you'd have to find the market to sell it, I'd be happy to take . . . five percent of your profits once you have it as compensation." He deliberately went in low because he had a feeling Mr. Travers would insist on increasing the percentage to save face.

He didn't disappoint.

"Ten percent. I won't take it off your hands for less."

"Ten it is, then." Guy stuck out his hand and they shook on the deal.

"I'll get one of my lads to deliver it." Just as soon as he bought it. "Have a good evening, gentlemen."

"We won't be having as good an evening as you." Dan's comment earned him another dig in the ribs from his older brother and he winced again. "Assuming you are doing something good, that is. But whatever you are doing . . . um . . . I hope it goes well for you."

"So do I." Especially as what he was doing involved plighting his tentative troth to Dan's baby sister. "And I hope I see you all soon." Where, no doubt, if tonight went really well, they'd all want to loom over him and quiz him on his intentions.

Chapter
SIXTEEN

⁀ঌৣৣৡ⁀

*N*ot long now, Lady Harper, I promise. Please return to your room until you are summoned. We don't want to spoil Lord Wennington's surprise now, do we? I am sure your daughter's perfect coiffure will last until then." Lottie ushered the fretting mother up the stairs with a tight smile before she glanced at the hallway clock again.

It was already twenty minutes to eight and Lord Wennington should have been home an hour ago. Why wasn't he?

"Any sign?" Lady Wennington stopped pacing as soon as Lottie entered the dining room.

"Not yet, my lady, and your guests are getting restless. Trying to keep them all hidden is becoming a bit like herding cats in fog. No sooner do I send one back to their room, another appears on the landing."

With impeccable timing, Longbottom, who was trying his best to keep the surprise intact from the back of the house, slammed into the dining room too. His expression every bit as frazzled as Lottie felt.

"Your difficult French chef is adamant that his culinary masterpiece cannot be held until half past eight, Lady Frinton, and will be serving the first course at a quarter past as originally planned whether there are guests to eat it or not." From her butler's clipped tone, it was clear that words had been said. "He told me to tell you that he would rather quit than compromise the delicate quality of his *soufflés au quatre fromages*, which are already in the oven."

"Oh, poo!" Lady Frinton blew a raspberry. "Unyielding, my backside! François has threatened to quit at least a thousand times this last year alone. Go back and tell him to jolly well take the things out of the oven or I'll head to the kitchen myself to give him what for."

"I wish you would, my lady, as I'm this close to . . ." Longbottom made a brief fist before he clicked his heels together and bowed. "Very good, my lady." He shot Lottie a glare as he spun on his heel. One that very much suggested that even he had reached the end of his tether this evening.

"Where the devil is my son!" Lady Wennington was peeking out of the curtains now for any signs of life outside. "He knows dinner is always at eight sharp. Always!"

"He might have a good excuse. Or be injured in some way—" Lottie's concerned reasoning was cut off by a raised palm.

"He had better be close to death, the ingrate, because if he isn't, he soon will be!" As his irate mother began to pace again, another mother poked her head around the dining room door.

"Any news on when we all need to come down?"

"Not yet, Mrs. Maybury." Lottie smiled through intensely gritted teeth. "I told you that I would personally come and fetch you when the time has come." It took all her strength not to add the word "twice." "Hurry back to your room now, if you please." As soon as the woman left, she turned to Lady Frinton. "If we leave them up there much longer, not only will your surprise be ruined, there will be mutiny."

"Agreed. What's our contingency plan?"

At first Lottie assumed that Lady Wennington had that answer, but when both ladies stared at her, she realized they didn't. "We don't have a contingency plan, do we?"

"We don't," said Lady Frinton, bristling, "but I had hoped you would have had the foresight to prepare one, Travers, as that is what I am paying you for. I don't have a dog to bark myself, gal."

Dumbfounded, Lottie gaped, then huffed. It was pointless arguing over it as someone had to do something to salvage the situation and it clearly wasn't going to be these two. They had made camp here in the dining room over an hour ago and had done nothing but issue unhelpful instructions ever since. "Lady Wennington, would it be possible to begin to amass the guests in here without bringing them down the main staircase where your son might see them?"

She nodded. "There is, but it is a convoluted route down the servants' stairs and through the kitchen." She pointed to the discreet door in the paneling. "That will bring them out here."

"Longbottom will know the route." Lady Frinton said that with all the assurance of one who thought her butler knew everything. "Get it done and we'll play the rest by ear once Guy deigns to grace us with his presence."

Muttering under her breath, Lottie went to the kitchen to fetch Longbottom and found him in the midst of a whispered shouting match with the temperamental François.

"Do you 'ave any idea what happens to whipped *œufs* if they are interrupted during cooking, Monsieur Longbottom? *Pfffft!* They sink! Then it is *au revoir soufflé!*"

"Then serve the guests soup instead!" Longbottom was snarling now. "Soup is what every other cook makes as a first course!"

A comment that made the chef twitch uncontrollably. "François Cadieux would never serve something so predictable and *insipide* as soup at a banquet!" He shook his semi-clenched hand in the butler's face. "Besides, I 'ave not prepared any!"

"I have." That came from Lady Wennington's poor cook who was clearly at the end of her tether too. "Not enough but if I stretch it with some stock and cream, it will taste good enough. I'll put it on to heat."

"*Non!* Good enough is *never* good enough!"

"Sorry to interrupt—" Before François's head exploded, Lottie grabbed Longbottom. "But we now have another job."

"Please say that it's running screaming for the hills, Lottie, because if it isn't, I might just run screaming for them anyway."

"I wish it was, but sadly we need to go urgently herd some cats."

She explained her plan en route. They both agreed that retrieving the guests room by room would be too slow but trying to maneuver them all at once was madness. Especially as there seemed to be some competition between the fifteen unmarried young ladies who had been invited to tempt the birthday boy down the aisle and she did not trust them not to try and sabotage one another in some way. There could be no accidentally-on-purpose torn frocks or dawdling with him due home at any moment. Therefore, they had decided on three families at a time, which meant that they had to successfully orchestrate five clandestine trips through the bowels of the house to get everyone unseen to the dining room. "If I keep a lookout downstairs in the hallway for his lordship, I can distract him while you get everyone off the landing. Do not move anyone until I give you the signal." For ease, they had kept the signals simple. Lottie's hands would be clasped behind her back if the master of the house was in sight, and in front of her if the coast was clear.

For the next fifteen minutes, as she ignored the crushing guilt that came from her clandestine part of this and her increasing dread at his reaction, Lottie alternated between loitering at the bottom of the stairs for Longbottom and pacing before the front door, waiting for Lord Wennington's return. All the while praying that he wouldn't return on her watch because she still had no earthly idea how to react around him after she had done everything in her power to convince him to kiss her last night and he hadn't.

With hindsight, she was also mortified at her outrageous come-hither behavior to convince him to. He'd looked thoroughly horrified by it all as he'd extricated himself and couldn't bring himself to meet her gaze after. She had never seen a man spear his carrots with such determined focus as Lord Wennington had during dinner. But his brows had been exceedingly furrowed and his jaw exceptionally tight. She could only imagine what he had been thinking, and it obviously wasn't good. She wasn't the least bit surprised that an eligible viscount hadn't been inclined to kiss a companion of any caliber, let alone one with bee stings for breasts who did not possess a single modicum of decorum at all. Especially one as noble as Lord Wennington. That humiliation made her toes curl inside her evening slippers.

"Pssst . . ." Longbottom's hushed call from above startled her. "I'm about to take the last lot, Lottie."

"Excellent. Fetch me when it's done." She kept one eye on the front door as the last gaggle of overexcited young ladies and their parents scurried across the landing, wondering, not for the first time today, what Lady Frinton and his mother had been thinking when they had chosen these particular young ladies for him in the first place.

Lottie might not be Lord Wennington's cup of tea or in his league, but she knew him well enough to know that none of those giggling, fawning ninnies were either. They were all very pretty, one or two were stunning, but they didn't seem to have much else going for them. Most were as *insipide* as the soup François refused to serve and seemed to only care about pointless nonsense like gowns or dancing slippers or the perfect state of their *coiffures*. Whereas he was a man of complex layers. One who loved the great outdoors and horses and agriculture. He was all about the country and those silly girls only seemed to care about London and the countless balls they apparently spent their entire existence attending there. In short, not right for him at all, in her humble opinion.

But what did she know? Maybe eligible viscounts were predisposed to prefer aristocratic nincompoops over farmers' daughters. Maybe, amongst all his complex layers, Lord Wennington had the overwhelming urge to maintain the blue in his bloodline?

She jumped out of her skin for a second time as the front door opened and there he was. He strode in, distracted, then stopped dead when he saw her. By the way his face instantly blanched of all color, he was clearly still appalled by last night. "Miss Travers . . . I . . . um . . . I . . ."

Her toes curled some more at that horrified greeting. "Good evening, my lord." She bobbed one of her usual lackluster curtsies. There was nothing for it but to brazen it out, be her usual self, and pretend nothing had happened. "You have arrived just in the nick of time to change quickly before dinner." She pointed at the clock, which now read just two minutes to eight. "Very quickly unless you want to suffer the wrath of both your mother and Lady Frinton." She had to keep him away from the dining room at all costs, so used a sweep of her arms to shepherd him toward the stairs.

He edged toward her like a man who did not want to be within ten miles of her. "Um . . . before I change, can we . . . er . . . talk about what happened last night?"

"Last night?" A hot blush crept up her neck as she willed the ground to open and swallow her whole. "I cannot think of anything that happened last night that would require a conversation, my lord. Has something happened?" She was clutching at straws now, even though her face was already burning crimson.

His dark brows furrowed, doubtless until he realized what a gift she was trying to hand him on a plate. "Miss Travers, I . . ." Now he looked to be in actual pain, which was exactly how she was feeling as she contemplated throwing herself out of a window and running, screaming in mortification, toward those hills. And would have, too, if there had been a window handy. "I . . . um . . ."

"Please, my lord!" She was mortified enough that she might even run out the front door and not stop until she hit the White Cliffs of Dover. "It really doesn't matter."

"It matters to me." He grabbed her elbow and spirited her away from the staircase to the secluded alcove beneath it.

He sucked in an audible breath and stared at her. "The thing is, Miss Travers . . . *Lottie* . . ." He raked a hand through his hair. "The thing is . . ." He scrunched his eyes closed and she seriously thought about bolting. As if he sensed that, his hand slipped down to her hand and gripped it tight as he stared deep into her eyes with the maniacal look of a man who was dreading saying what he wanted to say almost as much as she dreaded hearing it.

"I must go . . . Lady Frinton needs me." She tried to tug her hand away and he held on tight. "My lord, I . . ."

"Guy . . . it's Guy, and I . . ." His eyes locked with hers and she wasn't sure which of them looked more uncomfortable. "I . . . um . . . er . . . oh, to hell with it!" Before she knew what was happening, he dipped his head and pressed his mouth to hers.

His lips were gentle at first, but as she sighed against them, he snaked an arm around her waist and hauled her closer, and she clean forgot all else.

Lottie had been kissed many times before, but never like this. This kiss was something special. Intense and complex like the man bestowing it and almost impossible to decipher all in one go. Desire meshed with tenderness. Haste mixed with restraint. Longing laced with wonder. Reverence. Impatience. Triumph and surrender. Almost as if he had been holding everything back for as long as he could but the dam had broken.

Her own flimsy dam had disintegrated the second their mouths met, so she welcomed everything, looping one arm around his neck while her other hand gripped his lapel. In case he did not get the message from that, she kissed him back with equal fervor until she was drunk on him.

She even moaned her appreciation when his hands went on a mission to explore her body. Parting her lips so that they could deepen the kiss as his palms wandered possessively up her back and then all the way down again. He tugged her hips flush to his as his tongue tasted hers. Letting her feel his desire hard against her pelvis before he filled his palms with her bottom and groaned his approval. "All I've done is think of doing this to you since yesterday." Heady words that were music to her ears and sheer torture for her body. "I should have done this then, Lottie. I wanted to."

It was on the tip of her tongue to return the sentiment, but his mouth was on hers again and she didn't want that to stop. So instead, she arched against him and buried her fingers in his hair, anchoring his lips in place as she thoroughly kissed him back.

"Lottie, we're—" They jumped apart at Longbottom's voice and he blinked at them in shock. It was obvious he had seen everything. "My apologies, my lord."

"Is that finally my son?" Lady Wennington suddenly rushed into the hallway, and like a stampede behind her, so too came all the impatient guests. The young ladies pushing each other out of the way in their eagerness to make that all-important first impression.

He looked to Lottie. Either stunned from the intensity of their kiss or stunned by the crowd coming toward them. "What's happening?" He sounded panicked. Looked panicked.

"What's happening?" Unaware of the intense, passionate moment that had just been interrupted, his mother enveloped him in a hug. "Why it's the party I've been planning for you for your birthday of course, darling! Surprise!"

Lottie got pushed by the wayside as the guests swarmed him and he was dragged into the drawing room. He glanced back, only briefly, the panic in his expression replaced by one of pleading. As if he was expecting her to somehow save him. Which of course she couldn't, not now, despite being desperate to. Someone closed the door, trapping him inside, and the bile rose in her mouth.

Alone in the hallway, she stumbled to the staircase and groped for a step to sit on. Her head spinning, both from the residual power of their kiss and from the overwhelming realization that what was happening in that room was all wrong and she had helped fling him to the wolves. There was a cacophony of noise from behind the door and she just knew he would hate that. Hate the intrusion into his privacy and being blindsided by so many strangers.

She had no clue how long she sat there wondering how to rescue him. She was so lost in conflicting thoughts it could have been one minute and it could have been a hundred. But the muffled voices suddenly increased momentarily in volume, so her head whipped to the door and there he was. As white as a sheet and so furious she could feel the intensity of his anger coming off him in waves.

Anger that seemed wholly focused on her.

"Guy, I—"

"How *could* you!" He spat the words, his stormy, dark eyes a world of pain. "How could you do that to me?"

She jumped to her feet and rushed to him, arms outstretched because she needed to comfort him. "I didn't have a choice. I—"

He swerved away from her a touch before he swiveled to face her, arms raised in frustration before slamming both fists to his sides. "You have a bloody tongue in your head! One you use often enough, madam, and for lesser crimes than this!"

"I wanted to tell you." She reached out to touch him and he stared at her hand as if it were a cobra before he pivoted to stalk up the stairs, forcing her to follow. "Please, Guy . . . Hear me out. I wanted to tell you but—" He stopped dead as she caught his arm and she almost slammed into him as he twisted.

"But you didn't, did you?" For a moment, he allowed all his vulnerabilities to show in his expression, until he yanked his sleeve from her grip. "When you knew I would loathe that . . ." He grimaced as he flapped his hand toward the noisy houseguests. "With every fiber of my being. I let you in and this—" He couldn't even finish that sentence, his emotions were so raw.

"I wanted to tell you but . . . you have to understand . . . it wasn't my place to. Your mother wanted to surprise you and I had no choice—"

"Don't you dare try to excuse this!" He wagged an accusatory finger at her. "Do not dare attempt to deny your part in this when you were one of the perpetrators of this vile . . . cruel . . . humiliating . . . *Urgggh!*" On that guttural grunt, he was off again. "You are a liar, *Miss Travers*." Somehow the pointed use of her surname again cut more deeply than him calling her a liar. "According to my mother and my aunt, you weren't just complicit— you were the linchpin. They apparently couldn't have pulled any of this off without you." His tone was laced with bitterness now. Betrayal.

Hurt.

That shamed her the most.

"That's not entirely—"

He spun around again and regarded her with complete disgust. "Then you deny sending out all the invitations, do you? Riding practically every single day to Maidstone to collect the replies? Of hiding every single one of those awful people down there in bedrooms in *my* house?" He shook his head and backed up the stairs. "And I thought you were . . ." He growled and his features hardened. "Just get out of my sight, Miss Travers. For I cannot bear to look at you."

"But—"

"And stay out of it until you leave, or I'll have you removed from my house."

Chapter
SEVENTEEN

॰ঌৣৣঌৣৣঌ

*T*he door to the dimly lit tack room swung open to reveal his aunt sporting an expression so sour it would curdle milk. "So this is where you are hiding?" Aunt Almeria leaned against the frame rather than her walking cane and skewered him with her glare. "Now that the mystery has been solved, the only question that needs answering is whether you are hiding out here like a pathetic coward or sulking in here like a petulant child?"

The jury was out on that one, as Guy wasn't sure himself quite why he was still sequestered here at ten o'clock at night, but he maintained an air of unruffled aloofness regardless. Instead of replying, he focused on the ledger he hadn't managed to focus on in the two hours since he had been pretending to focus on it, jotting a random number in one of the columns to make it look as if he had been. "As you can plainly see, I am working." He said that without lifting his head. "I had to relocate to a temporary study after the world and his wife laid siege to my house and rendered it impossible to concentrate." Which was sort of the truth and the excuse he had made to his poor footman, who had been sent to surreptitiously retrieve everything that he'd left on his desk there while everyone else was having dinner. In truth, he couldn't imagine the forty-odd people currently encamped in the house were quiet, but he hadn't ventured back there to check since he had stormed out of it at the crack of dawn this morning.

God, how he hated birthdays!

This one would certainly go down in history as one of the worst. What the blazes had his mother been thinking to invite fifteen blasted debutantes and their matchmaking mamas for a week? Did she seriously think he would just roll over and pick one? That he was either that shallow or that desperate in his dotage that just any woman would do? When most of those twittering, fawning, fluff-for-brains, spoiled daughters of the ton weren't his sort of woman at all! What precisely would he spend eternity talking about with a woman who only knew about ballrooms and Mayfair? The two biggest things he detested!

And as for the sort who was his type . . . he couldn't bear to think about Lottie's betrayal without wanting to punch the wall. Or wanting to flagellate himself with brambles for how close he had come to throwing all caution to the wind and leaping into the murky waters of romance with both feet again with a virtual stranger. So much for once bitten and twice shy! Or of lightning not striking in the same place twice. Thanks to Lottie, he had endured the second most awful public humiliation of his life! Clearly hadn't learned his lesson well enough the last time he'd donned the rose-tinted spectacles of besottedness and been made a fool of!

Last night, like the absolute blithering rose-tinted, spectacle-wearing idiot he obviously still was, he had foolishly thought he had known enough about her to take the plunge. Then she'd gone and stabbed him in the back. *Et tu, bloody Brutus!*

Thank goodness their kiss had been interrupted before he'd lost his head completely and bared his heart to the duplicitous witch. He owed Longbottom a debt of gratitude for saving him from that catastrophic mistake in the nick of time.

Except he didn't feel particularly grateful yet. Instead, after an entire day of licking his wounds, he felt stupid and foolish. Disappointed and hurt.

So, so, so very hurt that it made his poor, bludgeoned heart ache. "I presume you tracked me down at this late hour because you have something pressing to say, aunt, so kindly get it over with because I am busy." Busy feeling betrayed.

"Your mother went to bed in tears tonight after the unfair and disrespectful tongue-lashing you gave her."

"If you are referring to the private conversation I had with my mother when she ambushed me on my way out this morning, then it was hardly unfair." Although it had been more a tongue-lashing than a conversation. She'd complained that he'd bolted from his surprise dinner and then disappeared before the dessert without so much as a thank-you-all-for-coming-but-I-am-tired, and he had replied—shouted actually—something along the lines of "you're blasted lucky I even turned up for the meal and you can shove your stupid parlor games where the sun doesn't shine."

"I reluctantly agreed to a birthday dinner party on the day of my birthday, set strict parameters for the occasion, and she ignored every single one of them to put on a surprise she knew I would hate. Therefore, if anyone has disrespected anyone, then she is the guilty party."

His aunt's only reaction to that unpalatable truth was to roll her eyes. "She's also been close to tears all day trying to explain away your absence, despite the brave face she has put on for your guests, so I hope you are proud of yourself."

"They are not my guests." While he was filled with guilt at the news that his mother, who rarely cried, had done so because of him, he had to defend himself on that score too. He wasn't going to be painted the villain of this piece when he was the victim! "I did not invite one single person currently ensconced in my house to be there!" Each time he thought of all those people, he felt queasy. "They are her guests—and yours—and whatever plans she has made behind my back with them are her problem and not mine. As you can plainly see . . ." Guy swept an expansive arm to encompass his stack of ledgers, papers, and his moonlit estate outside. "I have a million more important responsibilities to attend to."

"Boo-hoo, poor you." His aunt clomped closer. "I suppose, in your tiny, closed-off mind, that justifies your failure to return to those guests last night? Legitimizes the temper tantrum you subjected your poor mother to when she had the audacity to tell you off for leaving a dinner that she, and a great many other people, worked hard to lay on for you? Excuses you from failing to attend every meal or activity today? Of failing to pop your ungrateful head into the room, even, for two minutes to say hello to all the people who traveled all the way here to see you? When the very least you could do is offer your profound apology for your unforgivable absence."

"To apologize, I would have to feel some regret at missing them."

"Do you take delight in insulting so many good people, Guy? Does it make you feel better about yourself?"

"'Delight' is too strong a word for the indifference I feel toward them, aunt."

"Indifference? To good people who have come here with no other motive than to help you to celebrate your birthday? Shame on you!"

Good people, his arse! "Are you claiming they have no other motive?" Guy's stunned laugh was bitter. "Do you and my mother honestly think that I was born yesterday? Or did you not consider me canny enough to notice that every family invited conveniently also has a single daughter of marriageable age to parade under my nose?"

That was just one of the things about Lottie's involvement in this awful situation that bothered him. Hurt him more than the surprise had. She had known it was a cattle market and that he was the prize bull up for sale and she still hadn't told him. Even when they had buried the hatchet and settled their differences and grown closer. Close enough that he had considered her a friend. Close enough that he had been compelled to kiss her last night and had come within a gnat's cock of asking to be allowed to court her!

If she had any reciprocal romantic feelings for him, it made no sense that she would be party to that. Nor would she send him into the lion's den without warning him. Ergo, he could only conclude that her loyalties lay elsewhere, his feelings weren't returned, and that he had wasted them on the wrong woman yet again.

"This whole mockery of a surprise house party is merely my dear mama's latest unsubtle attempt to get me to make her some grandchildren." Which, ironically, he would have been right up for last night with Lottie. But that was yesterday, when he'd not been thinking straight. Today, he didn't even want to look at her, let alone touch her.

A shocking lie which he hoped if he repeated often enough to himself, he might eventually believe!

"My dear mama has put me out to stud in a field full of mares and she doesn't care which one I mount so long as I mount one of them." Whichever way he looked at it that was insulting. And humiliating.

So, *so* very humiliating.

Aunt Almeria turned her nose up as if horrified. "Don't be vulgar, Guy!"

"Whyever not, when it is vulgar?" He had feelings, after all. And foolishly futile hopes and dreams about the sort of wife he wanted to spend eternity with. However, in one fell swoop, his mother had reduced him to the appendage between his legs and not the man who actually owned it! "Is it any wonder I want no part of it?"

Aunt Almeria pulled up a stool, and as soon as she perched upon it, sniffed the air with distaste. "It stinks in here! It's a wonder you can breathe, let alone work, with this acrid stench in your nostrils. It's making me gag." For effect, she did. "The smell is suffocating."

"I'm quite used to the aroma of a stable." He certainly preferred it over the bitter stench of betrayal. Thanks to all his stuttering and stammering before the kiss, Lottie also knew that she tied him in knots and he hated that he had given her that power over him. Feeling so emotionally exposed made him feel physically sick.

"Horses, I can stand." Aunt Almeria coughed some more, directly over his ledger too, forcing him to sit back rather than be sprayed. Forcing him to pay attention as she jabbed an incensed finger inches from his face. "The fetid aroma of burning martyr, I cannot. Now get your moping carcass out of that chair and go be the host your mother's efforts deserve."

"Do you need an ear trumpet, aunt? As you clearly didn't hear anything I just said about wanting no part of the charade being played in supposed honor of my birthday. I especially do not want the part of the leading man!"

"Leading man!" She slapped her hand on the table before she wagged her finger again. "Oh, for pity's sake! This is not about you, idiot! It has never been about you! You have some arrogance to even think that it is!"

Perhaps she was going senile rather than selectively deaf. Or had partaken of a glass too many of sherry after dinner. "Er . . . correct me if I am wrong, aunt, but isn't that mockery of a sham my surprise milestone birthday party? Or am I not the one turning thirty?" He glanced around the tack room and then under the table as if looking for the real birthday boy. "Don't tell me that my manipulative mother has another son that she wants wed but has kept that a secret from me for three decades? If she has, I certainly hope that my secret brother is feeling frisky enough to service all those braying fillies she procured for him. And in between breeding, he can jolly well pay for the unwanted debacle as well, as I dread to think how much it is going to cost to feed forty unwelcome mouths at least three meals a day for a week. He's welcome to the lot of them!"

"That's just as well as martyrdom, vulgarity, *and* sarcasm are the most unattractive characteristics in a potential mate." His aunt shot him a withering glance. "If you are going to be selfish and view things on the most superficial level possible, nephew, then yes, this event has been thrown in your honor. However, while I share my dear sister's frustrations that you have failed to do your duty, it is her that currently concerns me the most. I am extremely worried about her."

"If she's convinced you that she is ill, she really isn't." He threw his head heavenward and prayed for strength. "She's definitely got heartburn and not heart failure. I checked with her physician. He's prescribed her peppermint tea and licorice root and she'll take neither to ease it and still eats cheese!"

It was his aunt's turn to stare at the sky as she shook her head. "What day is it today, Guy?"

"Saturday. Which means I still have too many interminable days left of my mother's hideous surprise to endure and trust me, I am counting down both the hours and the minutes."

Now she was staring at him like he was daft. "The date, Guy?"

"The ninth."

"And tomorrow is?"

Was she really giving him a counting lesson! "The tenth—because any fool knows that ten always follows nine."

"Indeed it is. It is the tenth of September, 1820, to be exact."

"And that is pertinent to this discussion because . . . ?"

"Give it a moment to marinate, dear, and I am sure it will come to you."

Guy waited several and when nothing came to mind, was on the cusp of responding with a surly shrug when it slammed into him like a wall. "It is the anniversary of Papa's death."

"The *tenth* anniversary to be precise."

"I'd completely forgotten." And now he felt terrible. "To be honest, I've always tried to put it out of my mind." As it was one of the main reasons why he hated his birthday. He'd spent his entire twentieth birthday writing his beloved papa's eulogy.

"As you should, dear boy, because life goes on and your father would have wanted you to commemorate his life and not his demise. But your mother has been a widow for a decade and that's the real milestone here. She adored your father from the first moment she set eyes on him and when he died, a part of her did too. She's always tried to busy herself at this time of year, but it has hit her harder this time than usual. In fact, it's all she's talked to me about for months now and it is not like her to dwell on her grief."

"She's been dwelling?" His mother hadn't mentioned anything to him. Aside from that comment the other day about being furious that his father had reneged on his promise to grow old with her.

"Constantly. 'Ten years, Almeria, a lifetime, yet I still miss him so much.'" His aunt sighed, the worry in her eyes reminding him that her heart wasn't quite made of the granite she wanted everyone to think it was. "I knew she needed more of a distraction this year than ever before. I even planned a whole trip to take her mind off things and invited her to travel to Scotland with me. But she would have none of it because of you. She wanted to do something big to celebrate your milestone to take her mind off hers. That is why I did everything I could to help her arrange this *mockery of a sham,* as you have so ungratefully labeled it."

"Oh . . ." Guy wasn't sure what he felt about that. It was a lot to take in. His mother had always been such an exuberant force of nature it genuinely hadn't occurred to him to consider she was still in the depths of grief after a decade. "She should have told me."

"Of course she shouldn't! She's your mother and she doesn't want to be a burden to you. Especially at this time of year when you are always at your curmudgeonly best." His aunt rose to her feet so that she could glare at him like a naughty child. "However, now that you've gone and upset her even more, I suppose needs must. So if you could heave yourself out of your traditional, annual, solo, self-indulgent celebration of *oh, woe is me,* I would appreciate some tolerance on your part to make the next few days more bearable for her. Even if you just drag your scintillating sourpuss to dinner every evening and sit there in disapproving silence it would mean the world to her." She turned up her nose. "For reasons best known to your mother, she adores you as much as she adored your father, although why she does when you are such an ingrate is beyond me!"

That final barb issued, Aunt Almeria sailed out, leaving Guy to absorb the full extent of her bombshell.

He dropped his head into his hands in frustration, secure in the knowledge that if he had known how she was feeling, he would have come up with a far better way of distracting them both from September. Even if that had meant abandoning this estate at harvest time to trek to Scotland with her and his overbearing bloody aunt. Who also could have told him all this sooner! What was it with women that they did one thing when they meant another? They were all as unfathomable as they were bloody exasperating!

And he was an arse.

~✍~

*L*ottie almost fell off her chair when Lord Wennington strode into the breakfast room. He wasn't dressed for riding either, which was most unlike him in the mornings. Instead, he was wearing a smart forest-green coat that did wonders for both his shoulders and his coloring, a tan waistcoat, and buff breeches that hugged his powerful rider's thighs in a way that made her mouth water. He'd even tied a cravat when he was usually one for a simple country knot.

"Good morning, everyone." He bent to kiss his equally stunned mother's cheek. "And my apologies for neglecting you all yesterday but urgent estate business came up that I could not get out of. I hope you can all forgive me." But while he was smiling at no one in particular, his eyes scanned every pair seated around the table but hers.

"Of course we forgive you, my lord." Lady Lynette Connaughlty, the most dislikable of the invited debutantes present, simpered as Guy took his seat at the head of the table. Lottie had taken an instant dislike to her the moment she had shown her to her assigned bedchamber and Lady Lynette had pointed out all of the things she would change in the charming room as soon as she became the viscountess. The arrogance of the chit was astounding. " As I told everyone here repeatedly yesterday, you must be a very busy man."

And good gracious, did Lady Lynette love to pontificate! No sooner had she put her foot in the door than she behaved as if she owned the place while expecting everyone else to defer to her as if she were already the viscountess. If anyone dared continue their conversation while she interrupted, Lady Lynette would shush them with a frown. "An estate as large as yours takes a lot of running. Especially at this time of year when the carrots need harvesting. I spotted your workers plowing up those straightaway on our tour of the grounds yesterday. Those and the turnips." As Guy blinked at her, clearly unsure quite how to respond to that, Lady Lynette batted her lashes at him across the table. "Well done, you, for both carrots and turnips are such difficult crops to grow." That, in a nutshell, was why Lady Lynette was so dislikable.

Not only was she a dreadful know-it-all—which would have been quite bad enough in itself—she actually knew nothing at all. Carrots and turnips were harvested in July and not September, and any fool could see that his workers had been harvesting the wheat. With scythes and not plows. If any farmer was ever foolish enough to harvest his carrots with a plow, he'd have a crop of mush! And there was nothing difficult about growing them, beyond the backbreaking tasks of planting the seedlings and pulling them up by hand. But the self-appointed diamond of the last three seasons did love the sound of her own voice and was apparently an expert on everything.

"Thank you," he eventually stuttered when he realized that Lady Lynette was actually ignorant and not being ironic. "I . . . um . . . hope you enjoyed your tour."

"Oh, it was quite splendid! As usual." In case the awful Lady Lynette had scored some points over her, Miss Abigail Maybury, the Kent neighbor who was seated beside him and was possibly the most shameless young lady present, touched his arm with bold overfamiliarity. Exactly as his mother had hoped she would. "But then I have always loved your beautiful grounds, my lord." If her rival had simpered, Miss Maybury positively oozed take-me-I-am-yours eagerness. "It has been too long since we last took a turn about them. I would be happy to withdraw from the bowls tournament this afternoon if you fancied some proper exercise later."

"I would too." Lady Lynette batted her lashes some more.

"As would I," said two of the other young ladies in unison, as clearly none of them had any pride when it came to snaring themselves a viscount.

As much as that brazen behavior appalled her, Lottie was sorely tempted to toss her hat into the ring too. Not because she particularly craved exercise or because she wanted to attempt to compete with these awful women—although unsurprisingly after their spectacular kiss, she did—but because she was desperate for a chance to apologize to him again. She had hurt him and that had torn her to shreds, so at the very least, if he couldn't forgive her, she wanted him to understand that she hadn't had a choice.

As if he knew she was pondering how best to approach him, his stormy gaze briefly settled on Lottie's, then hardened before it snapped away.

"If the four of you are in such dire need of vigorous exercise, I suggest you all take some together this afternoon." That came from Lady Frinton, whose expression let the young ladies concerned know that she thought them all pathetic. "My nephew has already missed out on too much of his own birthday celebrations and cannot be spared to accompany you. Besides . . ." The old lady shot him a pointed look over her teacup. "He has promised to be my bowls partner, isn't that right, Guy?"

As Lady Wennington's head swiveled his way, incredulous, he looked from the debutantes to his aunt and back again, like a man who couldn't decide which activity he found the least horrifying. "Er . . . yes. I did, aunt." Then when Lady Frinton continued to glare at him, added, "Unless my mother wants me to be her partner, of course, as she should get first dibs."

"Really?" He might as well have just offered her the moon, Lady Wennington was so overjoyed. "You would partner with me?"

He nodded with all the enthusiasm of a man headed to the gallows.

"Then that's settled." Lady Frinton's smug smile suggested that the old dragon was up to something, although Lottie did not know what. "In this afternoon's league, mother and son will form one team. Travers and I the second." The slight tic in Guy's jaw was his only outward acknowledgment that he wasn't happy about Lottie playing. Or even being here when she was supposed to be keeping out of his sight. "But which two teams are brave enough to take us on in a best of three?"

Lady Lynette shot out of her seat like an eager firework. "Well, obviously my dear mama and I will make up the third. We are both excellent bowls players. Some might say the best in Mayfair." Because of course they were—especially if the arrogant Lady Lynette said so. "It's all in the wrists." She leaned over to waft one of hers in front of his face. Either to show him how superior her wrists were to all the other wrists present, or to attempt to entice him with her perfume.

Another young lady was on the cusp of volunteering, too, when Miss Maybury pipped her to the post, and who likely would have whacked all her potential rivals with a post too if she'd had one handy. "Count us Mayburys in. We need a second team from the Kent contingent, don't we?" She placed a possessive hand over Guy's sleeve again. "While I am sure Mayfair produces some excellent players, I suspect those from Kent have the edge. What say you, my lord?"

"Er . . ." Guy looked ready to bolt and likely would have if his breakfast hadn't arrived and given him the excuse to free his arm from her grip. "I suppose so."

"Will you be accompanying us to Rochester Castle this morning, my lord, or do you have better things to do?" The youngest but richest deb of the bunch, Miss Beatrice Yates, managed to ask her question with enough casual disinterest, as she toyed with her eggs, to sound as though she wasn't the least bit bothered about snaring herself a viscount.

It would have been impressive if she hadn't been the daughter of one of England's most successful canal builders. An ambitious man who had dragged himself up from nothing but his bootstraps. One who now only needed to inject some blue blood into his family to render his new money more palatable to the old-monied aristocratic ranks he aspired to complete acceptance in.

"He will," said Lady Frinton with a glower at her nephew. "Won't you, Guy?"

"Yes," he replied with an overbright smile and abject fear in eyes that were locked suspiciously on his wily old aunt's. "I am looking forward to it."

———◆———

*F*or reasons best known to herself, Lady Frinton personally organized all the assorted and amassed carriages headed to Rochester. It made no difference who owned the conveyance; if it had been commandeered for the trip, then she decided who sat in it. Obviously, her well-sprung, purple coach went first and had the most space in it as the only people allowed to sit inside were her, her sister, and her nephew. That also meant that all the other stuffed coaches had to sit impatiently on the drive while she allocated the seating from the front to the back.

If the old battle-axe had a plan, it only made sense to Lady Frinton and she didn't share it. That was why Lottie and the long-suffering Longbottom were made to direct all the accompanying parents to the last six carriages and all the debutantes were squeezed into the rest. There seemed to be some sort of ranking to those debutantes too, with the most annoying or most eligible all shoved in together in the second carriage, no doubt for Lady Frinton's own sport, and the most amiable or those who faded into the background grouped accordingly behind.

"Is that everyone?" A stupid question when the carriages were all now full and the driveway deserted.

"Yes, my lady. Apart from you, of course."

"And you." Her employer jabbed her with a finger. "We need to squeeze you in somewhere, Travers." Lady Frinton stared at her own conveyance as if considering putting Lottie in there. A prospect that horrified her because Guy had made it quite plain he wanted nothing whatsoever to do with her. Just as thirty minutes of taut silence and betrayed, accusatory looks loomed before her, the battle-axe shook her head. "Your legs are almost as long as my nephew's so you absolutely cannot ride with us. Being cramped flares my arthritis."

Lottie's inward sigh of relief was short lived, however, as she was presented with a fate worse than death.

"You can sit with that dreadful Connaughlty chit and her equally awful flirty nemesis Miss Maybury in the second carriage."

"But there are already five young ladies in that carriage, my lady, and I am not convinced I should even go." It was a long shot, but by Jove, she was going to do her best to wriggle out of this hell if she could. "You hardly need a companion today when you have your family and friends around you and I am not sure that it is appropriate that I—a servant— should attend his lordship's birthday festivities. Like Longbottom . . ." She grabbed the butler's sleeve like a drowning man would a piece of floating driftwood. "I am only here to serve you, after all, and I have plenty of chores I can be getting on with while you are gone."

"Plenty of chores," agreed Longbottom in solidarity.

Lady Frinton stared at them as if they'd gone mad. "When I hired you, Travers, I bestowed upon you just two solemn duties. The first was catering to my every whim and the second was snuffling out gossip. How, pray tell, do you propose to fulfill the latter, gal, if you are not immersed in the vipers' pit? That carriage"—she jerked a thumb back at the one where Lady Lynette's smug face was smiling at the window seat she had procured in the most unladylike fashion—"and with those appalling girls, is where all today's best gossip will be snaffled. Therefore, I am tasking you with the unenviable job of being their shadow for the duration of the trip instead."

As Lottie would rather swim in stagnant swamp water than spend hours in the company of those dreadful debutantes, she allowed her face to show that. "But my lady . . ." Honestly, she would beg on bended knee if necessary. "I am not *one of them* and my presence will not be welcomed. I also sincerely doubt any of them would dare let anything slip in front of a servant who they would see as a spy, so—" Lady Frinton held up a palm in front of her face.

"Most of them do not possess a modicum of subtlety and they are all bursting at the seams with one-upmanship, so I suspect you will find that they will be staggeringly loose-lipped. Especially if you behave as a good servant is supposed to and mutely blend into the wallpaper."

"I stand at five feet and eleven inches, so blending in is—"

"Oh, do stop whining, Travers, and accept your fate with some stoically servile dignity, there's a good gal. You are being paid to do my bidding, after all, and handsomely too, so accept that you are my well-compensated eyes and my ears and eavesdrop with impunity. I shall certainly be all ears when you report all their shenanigans and nonsense back to me later." The old lady cackled with delight. "Because mark my words, there will be shenanigans and nonsense aplenty now that Guy has deigned to join us. Those stupid fools will likely stop at nothing today to impress him while sabotaging their competition, and that means we are all in for some fine entertainment!" She cackled some more, then skewered Lottie with her glare. "Now get in the coach, gal, and stop trying my limited patience!"

"Ours is not to reason why, ours is but to do . . . ," whispered Longbottom as soon as Lady Frinton was out of earshot. They watched as her nephew solicitously alighted the carriage to help his aged relative into it. His big body obviously tensed as he braced himself for the ordeal to come and his gaze resolutely averted so that he could not possibly glance toward Lottie even though he must have known she was there. "Although I don't envy you your traveling companions today." They shifted their focus toward the second carriage in time to watch the shameless Miss Maybury—who had also wrestled herself into the window seat opposite her know-it-all rival—squint into a tiny mirror as she rearranged the tight curls artfully poking out of her ludicrously large but fashionable bonnet. "I fear there will be shenanigans aplenty and most of them either impertinent or improper. I pity you, of course, but I pity his lordship more."

So did she. He might have just given her the cut direct, but she understood why. "Poor Guy."

She hadn't realized that she had said that aloud until Longbottom grinned. "Oh! *Guy*, is it now? Are you two courting now as well as kissing?"

"Don't be ridiculous!" Her cheeks felt so hot, you could probably fry an egg on one of them and a slice of bacon on the other. Because Long-bottom wasn't daft and had plainly seen how passionate that kiss had been. "You witnessed an odd moment, that is all. One that will not be repeated." More was the pity.

"Of course it won't." He chuckled as he winked. "It is patently obvious that there is nothing going on between the pair of you." Before she could stutter any sort of denial, he yanked open the carriage door. "If you would kindly shuffle up, ladies, you need to make room for one more."

"*She* cannot come in here!" That came from the pompous Lady Lynette, who was displaying every bit of her Mayfair superiority as she sniffed down her nose at Lottie. "There is barely any space left as it is without one more. Especially one more of *her* stature." As that could mean she was either too lowly or too tall, Lottie decided to take offense at both statements but bit her lip rather than show it. Instead, she politely waited for Longbottom to deliver the bad news.

"As this is where his lordship's beloved aunt has expressly stipulated Miss Travers sits, I suggest you take that up with her. However, if you would like more space, my lady, there is plenty in some of the other carriages." He wafted a hand behind. "It would be no trouble at all to help you move."

From her sour expression, Lady Lynette did not like that answer, but she backed down. "As Lady Frinton expressly stipulated that I should also be here in this second carriage, it would be ungracious to go against her wishes." She shuffled a reluctant two inches closer to her precious window seat. "You can try and squeeze in here."

With gritted teeth, Lottie bobbed her thanks and did her best to wedge her lengthy frame into the smallest gap possible. Knees and elbows clenched in as far as she could clench them, she clasped her hands in her lap and stared at them. Doing her very best to merge into the upholstery as the carriage lurched forward. Feeling—in her sensible gray traveling dress amongst this crowded box full of the finest, most fashionable, boldly colored expensive silks available—very much like a common pigeon in an aviary of exotic birds.

Despite taking up more than her fair share of the limited space, Lady Lynette wiggled her bony elbows to eke herself out a little more the moment they started moving. "I sincerely hope Rochester Castle is worth all this discomfort. If it is naught but a ruin, I shall be most aggrieved at the inconvenience."

"Oh, it is a ruin," said Miss Maybury, "but a pretty one." Then with a superior expression, she couldn't resist staking her prior claim some more. "Being a local, I have visited here frequently with the Wenningtons. Our two families have always enjoyed a *special* friendship."

"As do we." Not to be outdone, Lady Lynette was keen to embellish her acquaintance to their hosts too. "Mama and I have often taken tea with Lady Wennington in her Mayfair house. And the occasional dinner, of course, during the season. Have you ever attended a season, Miss Maybury?" They all knew she hadn't. Miss Maybury's father was a country squire and not aristocratic enough for the ton.

"The odd ball, here and there." Miss Maybury flicked that blatant falsehood away with a superior chuckle. "But I confess high society holds little appeal. Like his lordship, I detest all the ludicrous pomposity of the ton. I much prefer life here in Kent than all the competitive and shallow silliness of London."

"Is that because you do not feel able to compete in London?" Miss Yates had now decided to enter what Lottie's brothers would call the pissing contest. Lottie might be more than a little envious of the heiress's beauty and status here today, but she could not help but admire her forthrightness. Miss Yates had clearly judged both the awful Miss Maybury and Lady Lynette and found them both wanting.

"Compete with what?" Even Miss Maybury's fake laughter made her sound like a donkey. "All the ladies there falling over themselves to secure a husband with a title? Much like yourself, Miss Yates. Why on earth would I do that when I have an eligible and titled gentleman right here on my doorstep already?"

"It is too bad that he shows you no particular favor though," said Lady Lynette, reaching opposite to squeeze Miss Maybury's hand in mock sympathy. "Know that I take no pleasure in saying that I witnessed he has displayed no particular partiality toward you so far. In fact—and please do not think me cruel in mentioning this, Miss Maybury—I thought he looked more disinterested than thrilled at your overt attempts to flirt with him this morning."

As catty barbs went, that one was so sharp and so sudden, everyone in the carriage except the maligned Miss Maybury and her tormentor took in a sharp intake of breath.

But rather than take offense or appear wounded by the uncalled-for comment, Miss Maybury laughed—brayed—instead. "That is because Guy"—she covered her mouth with her gloved fingers as if his Christian name had accidentally slipped out—"I mean, *his lordship* and I have known each other for a decade and are such good friends we usually do not bother with the formalities. In *private,* at least." She managed to say that with a knowing smile, as if they didn't bother with more formalities in private than merely using each other's names. "There is so much local speculation about the pair of us hereabouts, it is embarrassing. Although hardly a surprise since we have always been instinctively drawn to one another. Some have even said the frisson between us is palpable, hence we are feigning disinterest so as not to fuel the rampant gossip further."

Lady Lynette scoffed. "I witnessed no hint of any frisson this morning."

"Guy is a private man who keeps that side of himself to himself. He would never dream of *public* flirting." Miss Maybury smiled her secret smile again. "Which is precisely why I tease him with it at every available opportunity. Let it all build up within . . ." She now looked so smug, Lottie almost rolled her eyes. Miss Yates, to her credit, did roll hers. "Then wait for his feelings to erupt the next time we are alone." Miss Maybury stroked her empty ring finger. "I hate to be the bearer of bad tidings, ladies, but I suspect a proposal is imminent."

"If you are such a certainty as his future viscountess, why has his mother invited all of us here?" Miss Yates was nobody's fool and said exactly what Lottie wanted to. "If she was satisfied that you and he were a match made in heaven, she wouldn't have thrust fourteen other eligible ladies at him to take his pick from, would she?'"

That cold dose of reality thankfully shut Miss Maybury's flapping jaws like an insulted vise. But as one mouth closes, so another always opens.

"I take issue at the idea of a man picking me when, in my case, the shoe is very definitely on the other foot." Lady Lynette sat higher on the carriage bench as if she was about to chair a meeting. "I have several excellent beaus currently courting me in London. Most have titles and *all* have fortunes, and at least two of them would make me a very suitable husband should I deign to accept them. However, it is always prudent to weigh up all the options before one makes such an important decision. That is why I accepted Lady Wennington's invitation. If I feel that the viscount passes muster, I will give his suit due consideration."

His suit! The arrogance of the woman was staggering when Lady Lynette was the one throwing herself at him.

"As will I—if I can be the one of the fifteen of us to convince the viscount to turn his head my way," said Miss Yates with refreshing honesty. "So I suppose all that is left to say on the matter is may the best woman win."

"Oh, I will win." Miss Maybury's secret smile was back with a vengeance. "By hook or by crook, he will be mine."

ante was wrong.

There weren't nine circles of hell, there were sixteen of them. All bar one were part of the harem Guy's mother had curated to tempt him, and all bar one were currently vying for his attention in some way but not tempting him at all. The one—the only one he reluctantly still wanted—was currently uncharacteristically quiet and subdued while he tried his best to ignore her. An impossible quest he was failing miserably.

"This has always been my favorite view of the castle and the cathedral." Miss Maybury had attached herself to his arm a quarter of an hour ago, as they had toured the cathedral's crypt, and refused to relinquish it. No matter how hard he tried to prize it out of her viselike grip. Short of wrestling the woman to the ground, he was stuck with her until he could shove her back into the carriage. A moment that, frankly, could not come soon enough.

"The cathedral actually predates the castle. I believe there was one on this site as far back as the seventh century, which rather boggles the mind." Miss Maybury had also appointed herself the tour guide for this interminable trip and was leading the rest of the pack around while she tossed random bits of history to them as if she owned the castle too.

She was certainly behaving as if she owned him and he didn't like that at all. But listening to her witter on was marginally preferable to listening to Lady Lynette's self-obsessed droning. He had never met a person so in love with themself. Lady Lynette was the walking embodiment of Narcissus and likely still lacked half of that fool's charm.

Guy glanced longingly at the line of carriages waiting for them on the lane below and the promise of a couple hours' peace once they returned before the horror of the lawn bowls tournament began at four. He sincerely hoped that ordeal would not drag like this morning had. That had, so far, been the longest morning of his life! But at least his mother was enjoying herself. Each time she sent a grateful smile his way, he felt wretched for the eight years of birthday distractions he had denied her. Today was about being a good son. And so were the next five days—if he survived them. Then it would all be over.

And Lottie would leave with his aunt.

His gaze wandered to her again and that only compounded his misery.

She had tried twice to apologize to him since her betrayal and both times he had given her short shrift. This morning, and to his shame, he had even told her where she could stick her apology and reiterated that if she did not desist in bothering him, then he would send her packing.

He wasn't proud of himself in any way, shape, or form, but there was an ache in his heart and she had put it there, so he was trying to justify his ungentlemanly behavior as self-preservation.

He knew, in the grand scheme of things, that keeping him in the dark about this awful birthday party wasn't the crime of the century. But he had dropped his guard around her, allowed her to see some of the real him, and she had let him down. It was a trust issue and, for him, that was everything. How could he possibly risk all of himself to a woman who had proved herself so untrustworthy?

"Seeing as we have a few hours spare this afternoon, I intend to spend them in your rose garden." Miss Maybury's annoying voice dragged him out of his reverie, just in time to see they had been left behind by the rest of the group who were several yards away. "Just me and a book in the pergola."

The fingers gripping his elbow suddenly caressed his bicep. "It is a very dull book, so I would welcome a distraction from it."

How the hell was he supposed to politely respond to that hideous invitation?

"Er . . . then perhaps you should take a different book with you. There are plenty in my library for you to choose from." Guy tried to maneuver them forward but she refused to budge.

"Perhaps I don't want to read." Miss Maybury snuggled closer, pressing her left breast into his arm and dropping her voice to a seductive whisper. "Perhaps I want to—"

"Sorry to interrupt." Lottie appeared out of nowhere. "But Lady Frinton has a question about the castle that I could not answer and so I need to borrow Miss Maybury for a moment to pick her brain. Seeing as she is the expert."

"Of course." It took all Guy's willpower not to punch the air with delight. Before Miss Maybury refused, he extricated his arm and then fought the overwhelming urge to sprint away as fast as he could. "I shall go help organize the carriages."

Free at last, he marched toward them in the hope that it would chivvy everyone. All the while keeping one eye on his rescuer as she quizzed the shameless Miss Maybury extensively, wondering if she had rescued him on purpose.

Then wondering how he felt about it if she had.

Surely rescuing him was a good sign?

Lottie was either keen to make amends or had been jealous, or both. He could not deny that the prospect she had stepped in because of proprietorial jealousy buoyed his ego immensely. Not that Lottie had anything to feel jealous about with Miss Maybury. The absolute last woman he would want to clandestinely meet in his mother's secluded rose garden was her.

"I'm bored to the back teeth of Rochester and want my luncheon." His aunt Almeria was the first to the conveyances. "Be a good boy and go chivvy the rabble, would you? I am sick to the back teeth of them too."

"As am I." After an entire morning of reluctant socializing and dodging the most outrageous of the young ladies his mother had invited to tempt him to make babies with, some respite on the ride home was more than welcome. "I have suffered quite enough this morning."

"Oh, Lord Wennington! *Yoo-hoo!*" He stiffened at the screeched tones of the awful Lady Lynette, who was keen to stake her claim again loudly from two hundred yards away. "Could you settle an argument between me and my mama?"

"Clearly I haven't suffered enough." He shot his cackling aunt some daggers before he pasted the polite semblance of a smile on his face. "I will be happy to, Lady Lynette—over luncheon." Which he fully intended avoiding. "But I must obviously supervise the carriages first. I wouldn't want anyone left behind."

Except, of course, Lady Lynette.

And Miss Maybury.

And both of their equally annoying, cloying mothers and maybe six or seven of the most desperate debutantes could be forgotten too. Then, perhaps, the rest of Guy's day might be bearable.

Or better still, he could send them all back and leave himself behind. If he accidentally on purpose forfeited his ride home and walked at a snail's pace, he might even miss the lawn bowls. An idea that was very tempting.

Very tempting indeed.

"Are you having a nice time, darling?" His mother's hopeful question filled him with guilt and so he plumped for a diplomatic answer.

"This trip hasn't been as bad as I thought it would be." It had been worse. So much worse. "Have *you* had a nice time?" Because that was the most important thing.

"I have had the best time!" She kissed his forehead as he helped her into her seat. "So much fun and so much diverting company, today has been simply splendid, hasn't it? And the rest of the week will be even better, I promise." Guy felt a part of his soul wither and die at that but he smiled regardless before he excused himself.

He had hoped that getting everyone back into the carriages would be a simple affair. But that was because he had stupidly assumed that everyone would return in the same carriage as they had arrived in, like sensible people. After the awful Lady Lynette's equally awful mother muscled herself into the second carriage with her daughter, and then several of the most desperate debutantes refused to listen to reason and fought tooth and nail to join them, it became apparent that things had turned into a free-for-all.

It also became an excuse for many of those young ladies to need his personal assistance to climb into a carriage rather than accept it from the footmen paid to do it. Which meant he had to endure taking the hands of several in quick succession, then pretending not to notice how deeply the owners of them tried to stare into his eyes while their lashes batted. After the tenth such encounter, his fake smile had turned into a grimace and his patience was worn so thin, he was in real danger of howling at the sky.

Miss Maybury, of course, had witnessed the Great Carriage Kerfuffle from afar and so had hung back with Lottie to ensure that she was the last lady he would have to assist. Guy knew already she intended to milk that moment for all it was worth. However, as much as he wasn't looking forward to another cringing moment with his least favorite houseguest, Lottie was still with her. Would it be wrong to flirt a bit with Miss Maybury to see if he could make the Valkyrie a bit more jealous? He would feel a great deal better about things if he had the tiniest shred of proof to cling to that his feelings for her were requited. Proof that there might still be hope for them.

Because he was clearly still an idiot. And a blasted masochist to boot.

Guy racked his brains for something flirtatious to say, but quickly abandoned the idea. Just one look at the zeal in the limpet's eyes as she undulated toward him and he realized that flirting with Miss Maybury was a very bad idea indeed. She really needed no further encouragement to throw herself at him. Especially when her invitation to meet him in the rose garden had terrified him quite enough! And then there was Lottie, who he had childishly ignored all morning. What the hell was he supposed to say to her?

Bloody hell, but this was awkward! "I am afraid all the front coaches are already filled, ladies." The only sensible course of action now was to get both women into the carriages and beat a hasty retreat. He spoke to his brazen neighbor and tried to avoid all eye contact with the Valkyrie. "But there are two seats left in the back one." He gestured to it. "If you will just follow me."

Miss Maybury did not budge. "But Lady Frinton was most insistent about me traveling in the second, so somebody in there will have to move." She clearly took her relocation as a threat to her place as a contender for his wife, which was ludicrous when he wouldn't marry her if she was the last woman on the earth. "Let me see who has stolen my place and I shall personally evict them." She probably would have too if the second carriage hadn't chosen that exact moment to set off, closely followed by the third and fourth.

Miss Maybury blinked at them in outrage and likely would have chased after them if the fifth and sixth hadn't also begun to move. The departure of those revealed his aunt, who had decided to leave the comfort of the first, still stationary, carriage to take charge once again. "What on earth is taking you so long?" She threw up her palms as if he was to blame for this protracted debacle. "It shouldn't take twenty minutes to load up a few carriages!" It shouldn't, but it had, and that was more her fault than his. She'd invited this infuriating bunch of women in the first place. Something he would have stated in his defense if his unreasonable aunt hadn't turned her frown toward Miss Maybury and Lottie. "Hurry up and get in, gals, or you'll both be walking back!"

That threat finally encouraged Miss Maybury to move, although she made no secret of the fact that she wasn't happy as she claimed his arm again while he maneuvered her briskly to it. Especially when she saw that the final carriage contained only parents and none of her rivals. However, she stifled her irritation to make a meal out of being helped into the carriage, showing an unnecessary expanse of silk-stockinged leg before she turned and offered him her best come-hither smolder. "Don't forget to smell the roses later, my lord." Her gloved thumb caressed his palm for good measure.

"It'll be too dark to see the roses if we don't get a move on." That timely snide comment came from Lottie, who wedged herself between them, forcing Miss Maybury to relinquish Guy's fingers from her grip. Without thinking, he took her ungloved hand to help her up instead and instantly regretted it. Because Lottie somehow made all his nerve endings dance in a way no woman's touch ever had before and he wasn't anywhere near ready to accept that inconvenient truth either.

Unsettled, he instinctively yanked his tingling hand away with such force that she almost stumbled. Then, while he wondered how or if he should apologize, she shot him an exasperated look. Ashamed of his overreaction and out of ingrained politeness, he proffered his hand again but she glared at it like a snake. "I think I can manage a few steps by myself, *my lord*, so please do not put yourself out on my part." She stomped up them and was three-quarters in when his aunt shouted.

"Travers! For goodness' sakes, gal, can't you see that I need you?"

Guy heard her huff before she turned and stomped back down the steps with her pretty nose in the air. "I'm coming, my lady." By the way she averted her face as she marched past him, it did not take a genius to work out that she wasn't impressed with his behavior.

That made two of them. But then again, he wasn't impressed with hers of late either. Saving him, perhaps twice, from Miss Maybury's clutches did not make up for the fact that she had done her utmost to throw him to the wolves in the first place.

Furious at himself, Guy stalked back to his carriage to wait for his aunt to stop dithering, but as he turned around, ready to tap his foot with impatience, there she was.

And next to her was a very peeved Lottie.

"I've set the final carriage going," said Aunt Almeria unnecessarily as it trundled past. Which meant that Lottie was traveling with them. Thirty minutes of unwelcome and likely torturous enforced proximity loomed, which he really wasn't in any way prepared for.

His aunt leaned heavily on him as he helped her up, but instead of taking the forward-facing seat next to his mother as she usually did, she sat opposite. "The pair of you take up far too much space and Constance and I need to stretch out. Travers can deal with your ridiculously long legs, and you can suffer hers."

Unbidden, his mind pictured her bare legs at the pond. An image that had haunted his dreams and all his carnal fantasies ever since. Those ridiculously long and shapely legs clad in tight breeches rolled to mid-thigh. Paired with that soaking-wet linen blouse that had clung to her pert breasts like a second skin and left nothing to his imagination. He felt the beginnings of yet another Lottie-induced erection stir in his own breeches and seriously considered walking all the way home.

He attempted to assist Lottie and she ignored his hand and his gaze for the second time in as many minutes, preferring to haul herself up instead. She then stared any which way but at him as he climbed up behind her and did his best to arrange his own legs into the miniscule amount of space left without touching hers. The only way to do that was to spread his to either side of her tightly gripped knees as he lowered himself down. He pulled the door shut, rapped on the roof, and wished he was dead as soon as the carriage pulled away.

Because the scant inches of space that they had between their thighs, her knees, and his reawakened crotch in a stationary coach proved to be insufficient in a moving one.

Which meant that their thirty-minute ride home actually lasted an eternity and every fiber of his being yearned for her all the way.

Chapter
TWENTY

∝⊶⊷∝

When Lottie had taken an hour's respite in her room while Lady Frinton enjoyed her afternoon nap, the subsequent planned activity had been a ramble in the woods. That was why she had donned a summer walking dress and a pair of sturdy boots. By the looks of all the debutantes in their fashionable, floaty muslins and ridiculously large and overly decorated bonnets, they had believed the same. Even Lord Wennington, who still could not look at her without his eyes hardening, was braced for an arduous afternoon in the great outdoors helping his silly entourage over imaginary tree roots that those simpering girls would not be able to climb over without his manly assistance. However, it now appeared that there had been a change of plan and by the twin gleeful expressions on Lady Frinton's and Lady Wennington's faces as they called for the amassed to all gather round, the two older women were up to something.

Something they had neglected to tell Lottie.

"In honor of this windless afternoon, we are going to partake of one of my son's favorite sports—archery." Lady Wennington smiled at him and his eyes narrowed. "Please do not panic if you have never tried it before, as he will give you personal instruction before the tournament commences." Right on cue, all the silly girls began to twitter like the dawn chorus at the prospect.

"How exciting!" The entire shrubbery of silk flowers on the elder Miss Harper's hat wobbled as she bounced on the spot. "I am bound to be useless with the bow and will need plenty of instruction." A sentiment that was doubtlessly shared by the rest of this shameless gaggle.

As if she'd heard her, Lady Wennington continued with some bad news. "Fortunately, we have two proficient archers with us today who can help you learn the sport, including one who claims to shoot an arrow straighter than Robin Hood." She did not need to direct her gaze to Lady Lynette because all eyes swiveled her way anyway. "And thank you, Lady Lynette, for telling me that this morning over breakfast as you are personally responsible for giving me this wonderful idea."

Hoisted by her own petard and now in no position to dominate the viscount as she had so far all day, Lady Lynette's smile was tight as she acknowledged that with a regal nod of her head.

"Now if you will all follow me out onto the lawn." Lady Wennington waved a piece of paper. "I shall allocate the teams." The statement started a stampede as most of the debutantes did their utmost to get out of the French doors first.

Lottie hung back as a good lady's companion should and resigned herself to an afternoon of dull spectating while the young ladies all fell over themselves to make an impression on Guy. No doubt by being pathetically needy rather than shining at the sport. Once outside, she wandered to the bank of chairs that had been set up for the parents and felt a pang of pity for poor Guy, who stood amongst his wittering entourage only a few feet away, noting that he already looked like he wished he were dead. She couldn't blame him. It was doomed to be a long and, for him, a very trying afternoon.

"What the blazes are you doing sitting down, gal?" Lady Frinton unceremoniously nudged her from behind with the tip of her cane. "Go and compete."

"Absolutely not!" Completely forgetting her place, Lottie glared at her employer. "It wouldn't be proper. I am your servant, not a guest."

"Since when have you cared about propriety, Travers?" Unmoved,

Lady Frinton jabbed her again. "And remember your mission." Her conniving gaze wandered to the debutantes and back to Lottie as she whispered, "You are my eyes and ears, gal, and you can't do that from here." Before Lottie could argue, the old dragon flagged down her sister. "Constance! Which team is Travers on?"

Rather than issue Lottie with the reprieve she craved, Lady Wennington consulted her list. "Miss Travers is on Lady Lynette's team." Marvelous. Now Lottie wished she were dead too. "Have you ever shot an arrow before, Miss Travers?"

Lottie sighed as she shook her head. Because why on earth would she when archery wasn't a useful skill for either a farmer's daughter or a lady's companion? And the absolute last thing she wanted to do was take any begrudging instruction from that angry, hurt, and rude oaf, Lord Wennington. Or worse, Lady Lynette!

"Splendid! You are just in the nick of time for the lesson!" Lady Wennington gestured her over and arranged her at the end of the long line of debutantes awaiting their private moment with the viscount. Then she deferred to her frankly horrified son. "The floor is yours, Guy."

"Right," he said, eyeing them all with understandable trepidation. "Why don't I just demonstrate what to do and you all give it a go?" Ignoring the disappointment on the debutantes' faces, he grabbed a bow and set about showing them how to hold it and how to prepare the arrow.

Lottie could not help but admire the sublime visual sorcery that occurred in the muscles of his arms and shoulders as he aimed at the target and pulled back the taut string. Nor could she help noticing how many of the other young ladies ogled him too, experiencing a proprietorial but futile pang of jealousy as they did. However, she flatly refused to be party to the pathetic sigh they all emitted when his arrow flew through the air and hit the target straight in the bull's-eye.

"Who wants to give it a go?" His eyes widened as all of the debutantes took a rapid step forward, but it was the shameless Miss Maybury who dashed to his side and claimed him by grabbing his arm and clinging on like a barnacle to a boat. Even after a footman handed her a bow.

Guy extricated his sleeve from her grip and took several paces back, explaining the steps, which all seemed perfectly simple to Lottie.

Brace your feet. Clip the indented feathered end of the arrow—the nock—to the string in the center, align the pointy bit onto the arrow rest in the middle of the wooden bow. Raise your bow to a right angle with the ground until the arrow is perfectly horizontal, line up the target, pull back the string, release the nock from between your gripped fingers, and let physics do the rest.

Instructions which even an idiot could have followed the first time. But, of course, instructions that Miss Maybury struggled with at every juncture. She made such a hash of it that Lord Wennington had to step behind her and move her apparently useless limbs into the correct position. Something she made an absolute meal out of with a calculated expression of triumph that he could not see from his intimate position behind her.

The conniving witch!

But alas, it proved to be the standard for the next half an hour as desperate debutante after desperate debutante feigned complete and utter uselessness so that they could all flutter their eyelashes up at him pathetically while they basked in Guy's strong arms.

Then it came to Lottie's turn and he stiffened. "Let's see what you've got, Miss Travers." The way he said that made it plain that the six feet of ground that stood between them wasn't anywhere near enough space.

She sent him a defiant look back, marched to the spot, set her feet, aimed, and fired without waiting for his critique. By some inexplicable miracle, her arrow flew to the target and lodged itself in the outer rim, clearly surprising them both.

"That was an excellent first attempt, Miss Travers." From her position nearby, his mother clapped her hands. "You are a natural. With a few minor tweaks in your technique, you could hit the bull's-eye. Position her, Guy, so that she is perfect."

A nerve ticked in his cheek as he moved toward her, his expression a barely disguised mask of distaste.

"If I can shoot an apple off of your head with my father's bent and battered old pistol, I sincerely doubt it will take me long to master this without your help." Lottie threw him that barbed bone because she felt awkward enough and hurt enough already by his behavior. "All I need is some private time to practice."

"Oh, pish," said his mother. "Never be too proud to learn from an expert, Miss Travers."

"Just do as you are told, gal," shouted Lady Frinton from the spectators' chairs. "You are representing me, after all."

Trapped, Lottie had no choice but to raise her bow again and suffer his ministrations. The flesh on her back tingling with unwelcome awareness as he positioned himself behind.

"Line up your shot," he said in clipped tones much too close to her ear.

Lottie did as instructed and heard his sharp intake of breath before he used the tip of his index finger to briefly touch her elbow and raise it a millimeter. He then practically leapt back as if he feared he might catch some fatal disease from her.

"Now fire."

If they hadn't had an audience, Lottie would have rebelled. Turned around and given the stubborn wretch a piece of her mind for his continued childish petulance, but as all eyes were on them, she had no choice but to grit her teeth and do as she was told.

She was about to do just that when Lady Lynette piped up in a loud aside to Miss Harper that Lottie was clearly intended to hear. "Let us hope she hits it. I cannot believe that we are delaying the start of the tournament for Lady Frinton's servant when we *invited* guests are all chomping at the bit to begin. It isn't as if Miss Travers is one of us."

In her peripheral vision Lottie watched Guy stiffen at the insult and just knew that he was going to say something in her defense. While that gave her some hope that he might forgive her eventually if she persisted, she did not want him to cause any more of a scene, so instead shot him a warning look before she set her focus back on the target. Picturing Lady Lynette's face on it, she pulled back the string and let the arrow fly.

It missed the bull's-eye by a whisker.

Pleased with her own grace under fire, Lottie grinned at her achievement and could not resist a little gloat at Lady Lynette as she sauntered from the field. "I cannot wait to watch you beat that, Robin Hood."

———※———

*G*uy had no blasted idea why his mother had decided an archery tournament was the perfect way to while away an afternoon. He had shown no interest in the sport since he'd turned thirteen, when he had discovered horses and girls, and he wasn't entirely sure that giving a bunch of title-hungry debutantes weapons was wise.

The competition was certainly bringing out the worst in some of them but fortunately, his mother had decreed that he be a referee rather than a participant in this ridiculous battle. That suited Guy just fine as it allowed him to put fifty feet of distance between him and the debutantes as he needed to be stationed near the target.

Unfortunately, that also meant that the ladies used it as a blatant opportunity to parade their wares in front of him, which, as well as bloody awkward, was not without its danger. Several arrows had come too close to comfort thanks to the firer of them focusing too hard on him while they flirted with their eyes from afar rather than the target. But keeping extra vigilant was a small price to pay for not having to listen to them all, and watching them all fight for his favor was occasionally entertaining. It was also good for his poor, bruised ego and he sincerely hoped it made Lottie a little bit jealous.

"This is the last round!" hollered his mother for the benefit of anyone who had lost track of this tedious game. "And it is still neck and neck."

Being the last round, the two team captains stepped forward. Lady Lynette was one of them and, for reasons best known to his mother, Lottie was the other. A decision that had made the awful Lady Lynette dislike her opponent all the more and which he wouldn't have put past his dear mama to have made for her own amusement.

"Oh, for the love of God, can we get this over with?" Aunt Almeria practically screamed. "I'm bored stiff and want my tea."

Some words were had between his mama and the team captains and then his mother shouted to him again. "To speed things up, the ladies are going to shoot all their arrows at once rather than alternating."

Guy could not care less but nodded with what he hoped was enthusiasm while Lady Lynette positioned herself. As it wasn't her team's turn to go first, he could only imagine she had done it to put Lottie in her place. Lady Lynette clearly considered herself Lottie's superior, which was laughable really when the Valkyrie superseded her in every possible way. Looks aside, although it went without saying that Lottie was the most beautiful woman present, she was also cleverer, humbler, and much more interesting. It was too bad that she had proved herself so untrustworthy, however, as she'd be quite the catch otherwise.

Lady Lynette fired off her five remaining arrows in quick succession. All hit the target and all gave her a decent enough score that she gloated. Lottie would need to match her on four and score a bull's-eye with the fifth to beat her and, despite how disappointed he was in her, Guy found himself rooting for her regardless. In case she noticed, he pretended to tot up the score while she prepared herself. Watching her elegant, lithe rider's body take her stance through hooded eyes instead.

"That girl has severe delusions of grandeur." He had been so engrossed in staring at Lottie that he hadn't noticed Lady Lynette's approach. "I shall take great pleasure in knocking her down a peg or two in defeat."

Guy let his expression show how much he disapproved of that petty statement. "I happen to like Miss Travers." A lie because he was pretty certain he loved her. At least enough that just looking at her now hurt.

"Perhaps you are not as good a judge of character as I." Lady Lynette patted her ringlets. Tight, stiff, artificial curls that were no match for Lottie's natural, tousled locks. "But your generosity of spirit to your aunt's companion does you credit. One should always be kind to the servants."

Guy felt his teeth gnash but swallowed any sort of pithy response lest Lady Lynette work out that he was compelled to defend her honor because Lottie meant something to him. But he did take great pleasure in watching Lottie's first arrow hit the bull's-eye. "Now Miss Travers only has to match your last four shots to win."

"Hmm." The tight disdain pulling at Lady Lynette's features made her look ugly as Lottie's second arrow did indeed match. Proof, he supposed, that beauty was only skin deep as her rancid interior was poking through. "We'll see." Then she forced a smile. "If you don't mind, I would rather not waste this precious time that we finally have alone talking about her. Why don't we talk about you?"

"Me?" He did not mean to sound incredulous, but thus far, all he had ever heard this pompous deb talk about was herself. "I'd rather not. I am not the least bit interesting."

"Au contraire, my dear Lord Wennington, for I find you fascinating." To his horror, she brushed her hand down his arm, lingering as her index finger caressed the back of his hand. "Fascinating enough that I have quite forgotten all about the other two suitors who are vying for me back in town."

Guy's pulse ratcheted several notches in panic but before he found a polite way to sidestep Lady Lynette's obvious advances, an arrow whooshed past and thudded into the target with such force it shocked them both. It was all the excuse he needed to briskly put some distance between them as he glanced Lottie's way. She was so outrageously nonchalant as she met his eyes, it was plain to him that she had done it on purpose.

While he hoped, pathetically, that she had done so out of jealousy, he was grateful for the timely intervention even if she hadn't. "Well done, Miss Travers," he said while noting down her score. "Two more like that and she'll be victorious." Another arrow whooshed past and he enjoyed correcting himself. "Make that one. *This* is the decisive shot." Guy had hoped he had made it plain that he was on Team Lottie, and he was in more ways than one, but Lady Lynette had skin as thick as an elephant.

She closed the distance and touched his sleeve again. "I just want you to know, that if you were to throw your hat into the ring, I wouldn't be averse to your suit, my lord."

"I . . . er . . ." From fifty yards away, Miss Maybury's braying laugh startled him again and he jumped. "Bloody hell!" But as his head whipped around to the noise it became clear that she had also startled Lottie, who screamed. He had no idea why until he saw it. Whizzing directly toward him at speed.

Guy threw himself backward as the arrow whistled mere inches above his head, so close it was a wonder it didn't part his hair before he landed with a thud on his arse. Airborne and winded for the second time thanks to Lottie—but this time in front of an audience.

Chapter

TWENTY-ONE

~※~

*W*ith hindsight, especially after almost shooting him, asking Guy about Hercules's progress over dinner last night hadn't been her best idea. At the time, she had brought up the horse as a way to offer yet another olive branch to break his resolute stony silence toward her.

A silence that had only loomed louder and angrier since the unfortunate incident with the arrow. An incident which, of course, he had refused to allow her to apologize for.

She endured it through the soup course and all through the fish, which had been exceedingly awkward when she had been seated next to him for some reason, much to Miss Maybury's and Lady Lynette's chagrin. But when the main course arrived and he seemed intent to go without potatoes rather than ask her to pass them to him, she used the excuse of Hercules to break the deadlock.

That it had backfired spectacularly had kept her awake all night. But how was she to know that the mere mention of his horse would turn, so quickly, to his love of them (thanks to his aunt) and his large collection of them (thanks to his mother)? And then, before she could say anything to stop it, a planned invasion of the sanctuary of his stable by the seven fawning debutantes who insisted on going out riding with him today.

In a little over an hour, all thanks to Lottie, Guy would have to spend the rest of this glorious sunny morning keeping pace with the simpering Miss Maybury and the wittering Lady Lynette. Miss Yates, who Lottie rather liked, and the giggling Lady Alice, who was rapidly proving herself to be the oddest of the bunch thanks to her obsession with the ancient Egyptians and mummification in particular. The two Harper sisters were also coming, after significant pressure from their mother, so that they could show him their superior skills as horsewomen. As was Miss Horatia Babbage, who couldn't be more than seventeen and who so far hadn't said boo to a goose but whose father had bullied her into coming.

Of course, as it would be considered highly improper for a single gentleman to ride alone with so many single ladies, the dreadful mothers of Lady Lynette and Miss Maybury were tagging along as the chaperones. Because obviously they had been such exemplary chaperones so far to their shameless daughters.

In short, Lottie had inquired about Hercules and then sent him his worst nightmare all wrapped up in a bow.

"You're a brave woman to show your face here," said Bill with a frown as she stepped into the stable yard. "He's been cursing you all morning."

"I can't say I blame him—I'd prefer a plague of locusts over his admirers any day. In my defense, it wasn't intentional, and I have come here to apologize before I take Blodwyn out. Where is he?"

"Fetching Zeus. We've got Hercules calm and in with his mother already." He jerked his head toward the training paddock where both Arabians were basking in the sun. "Once his father is there, we're going to try to saddle the three of them all together."

"Do you think Hercules is ready for that?"

Bill shrugged. "We've been taking him out riding with his parents three times a day since you came up with the idea, and his nibs thinks it's as good a time as any and wants to give it a go while it's still quiet."

"Three times a day!" Lottie smiled even though that news hurt. She would have loved to be the one to accompany Guy on those rides, to finish what they had started together, but clearly she had ruined that thanks to her part in *the Surprise*. "And Hercules has been good with that?"

"Better than good. He's taken to it like a duck to water. Gallops like the wind beside his mother and doesn't fight the bit at all. All thanks to you. Training him alongside his parents was a good idea, Lottie."

"At least I did something good." She sensed Guy approaching and glanced up in time to watch his step falter when he noticed her. Then resolutely ignore her once again to put Zeus in the training paddock with the rest of his family. "I suppose it's time for me to get my head bitten off. Wish me luck."

Bill offered her a sympathetic smile. "For what it's worth, try to remember that despite his foul temper, his heart is always in the right place. I think he wants an excuse to forgive you. He likes you, Lottie." His expression grew more serious. "A lot. But he's a complicated soul and like his temperamental stallion, he spooks easily. Guy likes his world to be just so, and when something's out of his control, it unsettles him." He shrugged again in a way that let her know that he thought her apology this morning could go either way. "So bear that in mind when he bites and try to give him an excuse to forgive you if his hard head won't allow his ears to hear your apology."

"I will. Thank you."

Lottie wandered warily toward the paddock, where Guy had purposefully put his back to her as he sorted the tack. "I am really sorry about last night. Had I known that your besotted horde would go on the rampage, I never would have mentioned Hercules."

He did not answer, nor pause in what he was doing, so Lottie braced herself for the inevitable explosion.

"I am also sorry about the arrow."

"Trying to kill me, you mean."

"I wasn't trying to kill you! I was trying to save you!"

"By shooting me and thus putting me out of my misery?" He reached for another bundle of reins without turning around.

"By ending the tournament as quickly as I could to relieve you of Lady Lynette!" He snorted his disbelief. "I was aiming for the bull's-eye, Guy, and would have hit it too if Miss Maybury hadn't screeched directly in my ear and put me off."

He stalked to his horse, laden with tack, forcing her to jog behind him. "But most especially, Guy, I am so very sorry to my core that I never forewarned you about your birthday party." His spine stiffened with a jolt, confirming that she had hit the rawest nerve. "To begin with, when I thought you were just a storm cloud and I loathed you, I found all the subterfuge amusing. I will confess—and I am not proud of this—that even though I knew that you would hate the surprise, I was looking forward to seeing you suffer a bit. But then you made me like you, despite your curmudgeonly and standoffish disposition, and that complicated matters. I wanted to tell you, but I also work for your aunt, who had sworn me to secrecy."

Still without turning, he heaved a saddle onto Zeus. "How nice for you that, when push came to shove, you put money over principles, Miss Travers."

She wanted to shout at him for being so deliberately obtuse but held it back. Because she supposed he had hit the nail on the head—partly. She'd put her family first and ignored her conscience and decided to worry about tomorrow, tomorrow. But she'd had to. Guy was inconvenienced. They were in dire straits. Her wages put food on her father's table. "I am a lady's companion, Guy. A servant, just as Lady Lynette always reminds me! Can't you see that it wasn't my place to tell?"

"Bill! Tom! Come and help me saddle these blasted horses, you layabouts!" Guy lifted the second saddle onto Juno and, as Tom dashed across the yard to join them, finally gifted her with a look. It wasn't a forgiving one. "Are we done now, Miss Travers? Only I have a lot to do before the besotted hordes you galvanized arrive."

If he had been one of her brothers, she'd have jumped the fence and punched the stubborn wretch on the nose for his sulky petulance. But he wasn't, and he also wasn't in any sort of mood to listen, so she spun on her heel, hoping that he would be in a better frame of mind tomorrow.

She was only twenty yards away when she heard Hercules's bad reaction to the saddle and couldn't just leave them to it.

"Stop," she said in her most commanding tone as she marched back. "Let go of the reins, Tom, and give him a moment."

"We can manage this without you, Miss Travers." Guy held up his palm to cease her advance and she ignored it. Enough was enough. If the stubborn, rude oaf wanted a fight, she would jolly well give him one—but she would see to Hercules first.

Not caring that it wasn't ladylike, she climbed over the fence. "Hello, boy." She took the reins from Tom and slackened them before she stroked the Arabian's nose. "Are these nasty men trying to put something strange on your back?"

Hercules snorted as if to say yes. He'd stopped dancing and had leaned his big forehead against hers and, bizarrely, she could feel his uncertainty. "You love to gallop though, don't you? You want to learn too, I can tell." She could feel his frustration. Sense the fear of separating from his mother. His desire to please.

"Bill—climb up on Juno." She had an idea. Probably another stupid one, but it was worth a try. "And Guy, you need to mount Zeus."

She expected an argument but all she got was a huff and a glare so sharp it could kill. But he did as she asked and then Bill followed suit. "Let's take him for another run out with his parents. Try again another day." An instruction that proved Guy had grabbed hold of the wrong end of the stick.

"He's not ready for the saddle—but I think he is ready to ride." Her gut told her so. "Tom, come give me a leg up."

"You absolutely cannot ride an unbroken horse bareback, Miss Travers!" Guy's tone made Hercules jumpy. "I forbid it."

"You can forbid all you want, *my lord,* but I do not work for you so do not have to listen to your orders." If he wanted to match stubborn for stubborn, she would give him the battle! "Give me a leg up, Tom, or I'll just walk Hercules to the gate and use that to boost me instead."

"Or I'll have you physically removed for your own blasted safety!" Guy, typically, was spitting feathers, the stubborn wretch.

"You can try—but unless you chain me up in a dungeon and post a guard on me, I'll come back and do it while you are off riding with your eager hordes. That I can guarantee." She twisted to the boy. "Are you going to assist me or not?"

Poor Tom hovered, unsure of what to do, so she did as she had threatened and walked the horse to the gate. When Guy opened his mouth to protest again it was her turn to hold up her palm and glare, but she made sure that her tone was soothing for Hercules's sake.

"If I fall off and break my neck because you spooked this horse, then it will be your fault. Otherwise, it will be all mine and your conscience will be clear. But know that whether you forbid it or not, I am getting on Hercules at some point today regardless and I would rather do it while he is calm."

"Then on your own head be it." Guy wasn't happy and she didn't care. But she also knew that the chances of her being thrown were high. Higher still in this stupid riding habit that weighed a ton.

Still holding Hercules's reins, Lottie reached for the ties of her heavy skirt and undid them. The only man who didn't gasp at the sight of her breeches as the dratted thing pooled around her feet was Guy. That inconvenience dispensed with, she turned to Tom, who couldn't seem to take his stunned eyes from her bottom half. "I am ready now." She held back teasing him about his ferocious blush as the poor lad had likely never seen a woman's body without layers of petticoats before, so the sight of actual curves and thighs had probably overwhelmed him.

Tom scurried forward and cupped his hands while Lottie cooed reassurances to the horse as she gently raised herself up, all the while keeping her mouth close to his ear.

To everyone's continued surprise, including hers, Hercules barely protested as she carefully slid her leg over him. She gave him a moment to get used to her weight and then gestured to the men. "Start riding around the paddock. Let Hercules see what he needs to do next."

With a surly expression, Guy nodded to Bill and they both did as they were told while she sat astride Hercules and watched. She let a good minute tick by before she risked sitting upright and could feel his impatience. And it seemed to be impatience to join them rather than condemn Lottie to the dirt.

"Want to give it a go, boy?" She gently nudged his belly with her feet. "Come on."

The horse took a few uncertain steps forward, then tossed his head from side to side. But because she remained calm and encouraging, Hercules began to relax. When they set off again, there was one hairy moment when he suddenly ran to catch up with Juno, but she held on for grim death and the moment passed.

"Good boy," she said as they came up level with Guy and Zeus, who both looked like they wanted to jump the fence and gallop off as fast as they could, and she couldn't resist a dig. "You are so much better behaved than your father—but perhaps he's only contrary because of his rider."

He nudged Zeus into a trot, which encouraged his son to do the same, for an entire lap, doubtless just to test her mettle, and then they all fell into the same sedate rhythm. Lottie lost track of time and could have happily stayed where she was for the rest of the day, but Tom had been put in charge of keeping them on schedule.

"The ladies will be here in ten minutes, my lord."

She heard Guy groan as he pulled his Arabian up, then dismounted in one impressive athletic movement to come and assist her. As he took hold of the reins and secured them for her safety, he offered her the ghost of a smile that never failed to make her insides flutter. "You enjoyed that display of stubborn willfulness, didn't you, madam?"

"It is hardly my fault that I understand horses better than you."

He didn't deny it. "Even a stopped clock is right twice a day, Miss Travers." Because of course the stubborn wretch was going to punish her with formalities until he deigned to accept her latest apology. "Do you need my help to get down?"

"Did I need your help to get up?" Ignoring his begrudging offer, she swung her leg back but Hercules danced as she did, and lurched sideways so fast she lost her grip. She would have dropped to the ground by the horse's side in an ungainly backward lump if Guy hadn't caught her around the waist on the way down.

Self-preservation had her grabbing his shoulders and clinging on for dear life, but she had no ready excuse to explain why her gaze latched onto his and held. Why her breath hitched. Why the odd moment felt incredibly significant. Or why neither of them made any attempt to end the embrace until Bill appeared in their peripheral vision.

"I'm not sure such a public clinch is wise with all the ladies due at any moment—but there is nobody in the tack room if you two need some privacy." He winked as he sauntered away and left them both scrambling upright. "And you should probably put your skirt back on too, Lottie, unless you want to cause a scandal."

With perfect timing, Lady Lynette's voice drifted across the yard. "Yoo-hoo! Lord Wennington!"

Which meant that the only thing to do was to pick up her discarded skirt and run into the empty tack room before Miss Know-It-All saw her.

Chapter

TWENTY-TWO

L ottie waited a full ten minutes before she ventured back out into the yard. By then, it was a hive of noisy activity as Bill, Tom, and Guy tried to match horses to the overexcited hordes wanting one. There were more than the planned seven debutantes too, as not to be outdone, three others had decided to join the fray, and so the men were fetching and saddling additional ponies. Guy did little to disguise that he was losing his patience.

Lottie waded in to help, seeing as this ghastly group ride was all her fault, and decided that the best way to do that was by sending all the ladies already assigned mounts to the opposite side of the yard to wait rather than get under the obviously increasingly frustrated Guy's feet. Keen to show off her superior seat on a horse, Lady Lynette decided to mount Blodwyn to assist, snapping out loud orders for show while she tried to use Lottie like a sheepdog to herd them all together. The irony being that if Lottie had listened to her stupid instructions, then chaos would have ensued, but she allowed Lady Lynette to think that she was in charge because it was easier than challenging her. As her father always said, you couldn't argue with stupid, and that arrogant irritant was about as stupid as they came.

Miss Maybury, who had hung back on purpose to spend more time in the yard pestering Guy with inanities, was the last lady to join the rest. When he stalked off to fetch Zeus, Lottie helped Tom and Bill get everyone else mounted and hoped that went some way to giving him more of an excuse to forgive her. She was ready to wave them off when he returned with not one, but two Arabians. He was already seated astride Zeus but had a saddle draped over his shoulder.

"Put this on Juno." He tossed the saddle to Bill. "One of the chaperones needs her."

Lottie glanced back to where Lady Connaughlty and Mrs. Maybury sat perched on mares, ignoring their charges while trying to out-brag each other. "But the chaperones already have horses."

"Those are the *young ladies'* chaperones. *You,* Miss Travers, are going to be *mine.*"

Bill chuckled as he slapped the saddle on Juno's back. "They do say the punishment should fit the crime, but I think I'd rather prison." He shifted position to tie one of the straps and that was when Lottie noticed the lopsided leather and hooked pommel.

"But that's a sidesaddle!" She glared at Guy in outrage. "I loathe sidesaddles! Why can't I have a proper one?"

"Because you are a young lady in the company of other young ladies and it wouldn't be proper." He shrugged with a devilish smile, enjoying her protest more than was gentlemanly. "And if I have to suffer throughout this awful ride, it strikes me as only fair that you suffer too. Consider it penance."

"Penance! Penance is making amends. This isn't penance—it's torture." She flicked the hard pommel in disgust. "Worse than torture, in fact. Sidesaddles are incredibly uncomfortable. Unbelievably impractical. They throw your balance off and give you a crick in the neck. If you'd ever ridden on a sidesaddle you would know that they are an abomination that should be banned."

"But why would I know that when you are, technically at least, the one currently in the skirt?" He nudged Zeus forward to join the others and she swore she heard the scoundrel laughing.

They set off across the pasture at a sedate pace and remained that way for the next fifteen minutes because all the young ladies bunched their horses around his. That didn't please Zeus at all, and poor Guy had to work hard to control him while he made uncomfortable small talk with the debutantes. To her credit, Miss Yates was the only one who did not join the melee and instead chose to ride on ahead. Something she did with great aplomb too, the clever thing, as it meant that while all her rivals were scrambling to be noticed, she became the only one impossible to miss. The swan amongst the gaggle of hissing geese. It was a sensible ploy, even though it piqued Lottie's jealousy some. It was obvious Miss Yates was her main rival—not that Lottie was in any position to compete.

Unable to even dare attempt to compete, she hung back so that she could quickly intervene if things—or debutantes—got out of hand, but she needn't have worried. Guy veered off the pasture and took the group down a tree-lined path that naturally tapered until they all had to go in single file.

From the rear, she was rather left out of things and as a mere companion, nobody tried to include her, so with nothing else to do, she was forced to watch them all court his favor from afar. As, she supposed, a proper lady's companion should.

She would leave here with Lady Frinton in just four days. The morning after Guy's final unwanted birthday dinner. And then she might never see him again. Or only see him very occasionally if she remained in Lady Frinton's employ. Neither were conducive to fostering an unconventional romance—not that he had given her any cause to hope for one. In the heat of the moment, he had told her with his body that he wanted her, but that had been a purely carnal confession. She and he were never meant to be more than ships passing in the night, but she wanted to leave on the same good terms with him as they had enjoyed days ago. The thought of him still angry at her duplicity and still calling her Miss Travers upset her almost as much as accepting that he could never be hers.

As she stared longingly his way, she realized that at some point during her wool gathering, the path had widened again and the hordes were once more huddling around him. Worse, Zeus was playing up. She could tell by the way the muscles in Guy's arms bunched that the difficult stallion was fighting the reins.

Lottie kicked Juno into a trot and steered her up the verge to get as close as possible and was alarmed to see both Miss Maybury and Lady Lynette flanking him like sentries. So close to him that they would both be in danger if Zeus decided to flip. Then either they, or heaven forbid Guy, could be trampled.

"You absolutely must be my bridge partner tonight, my lord. I absolutely insist." Lady Lynette was too busy fluttering her eyelashes to see where she and Blodwyn were going. Lottie knew from experience that Blodwyn, as lovely and gentle a mare as she was, wasn't the brightest of horses and needed direction. "We will win, for sure, if we team up. If I say so myself, I am *quite* the card sharp. Bridge, whist, piquet—pick your poison, my dear Lord Wennington, for I am equally formidable at all three." Her practiced tinkling laugh was rapidly becoming as grating as Miss Maybury's braying one. "In fact, and I shouldn't brag . . ." She shouldn't, but she would. In perpetuity, if she went unchecked, so that nobody else could get a word in edgewise. "I have not lost a game in over a year. The trick with bridge is—" Good grief, did she ever pause for breath? Lottie couldn't intervene unless she did! "—to always check that—"

When Zeus snorted his displeasure, Lottie had no choice but to interrupt. "Have a care, Lady Lynette. His lordship's Arabian doesn't like to be too close to other horses."

Lady Lynette's head snapped around, her expression an ugly snarl. "How dare you give me instruction! Know your place, Miss Travers, and have more respect for your betters!"

"Now see here—" Guy, bless him, was about to take issue with the horrid snob, but had to turn his focus back to Zeus, who was now thrashing his head about as he sensed the fresh tension.

"I spent an hour admiring your lovely roses all alone again yesterday, my lord." With an astounding lack of awareness, Miss Maybury decided that now was the optimum moment to attempt to seduce him again. "I shall be doing the same again today." She reached across to caress Guy's arm and because he jumped at the contact, Zeus did too. It took him a few moments to bring the horse into line, but the Arabian was far too agitated to be properly placated. Hardly a surprise, when he had been bred to run unhindered and not to be caged in a prison of slower horses.

Which gave Lottie an idea . . .

---

*S*o shall we be partners at the bridge tournament tonight—"

Guy was about to scream his frustration at the hideous Lady Lynette when somebody else screamed instead.

A proper, full-bodied, bloodcurdling scream that brought everyone up short.

"Help me! I can't control her!" Lottie's eyes were wide with fear as Juno reared beneath her. Instinctively, he tried to turn Zeus to assist, but there were too many horses to do it quickly. "Oh! *Oh! OH!*"

Juno reared again and Lottie struggled to hold on. In a thunder of hooves, the usually placid Arabian then set off at speed straight past him.

Lottie pulled on the reins and did her best to calm her, but something had spooked the horse and she wasn't having it. She reared again, changed direction, and plunged into the trees, taking Lottie with her.

Guy kicked Zeus to follow, his heart in his mouth. This was all his fault! He'd put her on a sidesaddle for his own amusement and now she was in danger!

If she got hurt . . .

If he couldn't save her . . .

Bile stung his throat while tentacles of fear wrapped themselves around his ribs, the guilt so heavy it settled like lead in his gut. He had to save her. *Had to!* There really was no other option. A world without Lottie didn't bear thinking about.

As he broke through the other side of the trees, he was just in time to see her disappear over a small hill.

He gave chase, pushing Zeus as fast as he could, as Lottie flew across the pasture at a terrifying speed. Her trim body bent low over Juno to keep herself from being thrown. Runaway horse and rider disappeared again over the top of a bigger hill and by the time he reached it, there was no sign of them on the path.

He slowed Zeus slightly to look left and right, then, in desperation, checked the ground for any sign of hoofprints in the dirt to know which way to head.

He heard a whinny and as his head whipped toward the pond beyond, saw Juno. Riderless and munching on the long grass at the water's edge as if she suddenly didn't have a care in the world. He dismounted and ran toward her, scanning the area for any signs of Lottie's broken body on the ground.

But there was nothing.

TWENTY-THREE

❧❧

*G*uy felt sick.

Physically sick and impotent.

Had the horse thrown her into the water? Juno was too near the deep end not to make him panic that Lottie's heavy riding habit had sucked her to the bottom of the pond. Was he too late? Had she drowned in the minute it had taken him to catch up?

He was on the cusp of diving in to search for her on the bottom when he heard another sound.

"Psssst!"

Lottie's grinning face appeared out of the branches of the old weeping willow.

Relief warred with fury as she beckoned him over, giggling before she disappeared back into the canopy as if she was having a whale of a time, and he instantly realized that he'd been had. The menace had staged the whole thing and almost given him a heart attack in the process.

He stalked into the branches, wrestling an invasive one from his neck as he did. He warred between shaking her by the shoulders and hauling her into his arms, so settled for waving his arms like a maniac instead. "What the bloody hell do you think you are doing!"

"Saving you again, of course." She seemed to find his animated fury hilarious and pointed at him. "Oh my goodness, look at your face, Guy! It's a picture!"

"You could have killed yourself with that stupid stunt."

"Oh, stop being daft." She giggled some more when he loomed, incredulous. "I was in full control at all times, idiot, and thought that you, of all people, would have had the good sense to know it."

"You are questioning my good sense when you just displayed none!" He stalked closer and growled. "That was the stupidest, most reckless thing I have ever seen."

"Genius is what it was, and you know it. Juno is a darling. And who knew a horse could act?" That made her chuckle some more. "I couldn't have wished for a better accomplice. Juno should be on the stage, she is so good." While he struggled to find the right words to express his outrage, Lottie prodded him in the chest, her lovely cornflower eyes dancing with mischief. "This is the part where you thank me for my brilliance."

"I think it's more the part where I strangle you!" He raked a hand through his hair as he swallowed past the lump in his throat. "You scared me half to death, Valkyrie." And his poor heart had broken temporarily in two in the process when he had thought he had lost her forever. A truly hideous way to discover that he was more than a little bit in love with this duplicitous, disloyal, and infuriating hellion. Irrespective of what his sensible head told him, his stupid heart was all the way in. Somehow, he had to yank it back out. At least a little bit, for self-preservation until all his doubts were gone.

"A small price to pay for escaping the twin clutches of Lady Lynette and Miss Maybury—you are welcome." She gestured to the secret space encompassing them. "Thanks to my quick thinking, not only will it take them a little while to find us here, but when they do, you will be able to insist that you have to escort me home because I am in shock." She wafted the back of one hand to her forehead. "So shocked that I am having a touch of the vapors and could pass out at any moment." She swayed comically against the willow's thick trunk and Guy felt his lips twitching. "Somebody fetch the smelling salts."

"You, Miss Travers, are a blasted menace."

"But you like me." She circled him with a saucy smile on her face. "Admit it."

"No, I don't. You knocked me on my arse—twice—threatened to horsewhip me, covered me in hot soup, and almost murdered me with a blasted arrow, and I have known you less than a month! You, Miss Travers, have rapidly become the bane of my life and I loathe you." So much that in just three weeks he was already prepared to jump in front of a bullet for her!

"Is that because I've put you to shame with my superior riding skills—even perched on a sidesaddle, I am better on a horse than you will ever be."

He scoffed despite suspecting it was the truth after that impressive display. "I sincerely doubt that."

"Care to bet on it? Or are you too scared to go up against me in a challenge?" She stopped circling to put her hands on her hips, one golden brow cocked, blue eyes twinkling, goading him.

Tempting him.

Seducing him into ignoring all the warnings that his head was screaming about the need for caution and diligence before he flung himself fully into the dangerous ravine of love again.

"Set the challenge, time, and the place, Miss Travers, and I'll make you eat your words."

She pointed at the church spire way off in the distance. "What about a good old-fashioned steeplechase? Tomorrow. I'll meet you in the stable yard at dawn and commiserate in it once we're done because I shall be victorious."

"And the stakes?" His heart was racing again—but in a different way. With anticipation and excitement and, heaven help him, a healthy dollop of lust. Trust her to suggest a steeplechase. "What are we competing for, Miss Travers?"

She shrugged. "If you win, I will form a constant shield between you and the hordes. Turn myself into Miss Maybury's and Lady Lynette's annoying shadow, intercepting and thwarting every attempt they make to get near you, just like a good chaperone should. But . . ." She prodded his chest again. "If I win, you *have* to forgive me for not telling you about the surprise. And you have to start calling me Lottie again."

Whichever way he looked at it, Guy would win, because something powerful within, perhaps even a combination of his head and his heart, told him that he had to forgive her. "Do you expect a head start because you are a woman?"

"Absolutely not. Do you require one? I would be prepared to give you an entire minute—to give you a fighting chance. You are heavier, after all." She looked him up and down with mock disdain as she circled him again and somehow, he felt her eyes on his back. His shoulders. His arse. "And older."

"Don't be daft." He adored her cheek and her confidence. And the irreverent, playfully insulting way that she talked to him. He adored those characteristics so much more than he could all the fawning nonsense he had been subjected to by the blasted debutantes in the last few days. "Even if I start a minute later, I shall still leave you standing." All this sparring felt like flirting. Foreplay even, and God help him, but he liked it.

She shook her head, the light of battle in her eyes, and that made him wish it was dawn already. "We shall start together."

"Then you have a deal," he said, holding out his hand. She took it and shook it and then something peculiar happened and he could not bring himself to let go. *Kiss her,* said the screaming voice in his head. *Kiss her and to hell with it all.*

"Yoo-hoo!" He groaned aloud at the sound of Lady Lynette in the distance. "Lord Wennington, where are you? Is anyone injured?"

Hands still interlocked, and doubtless blissfully unaware of the effect that she was having on him, Lottie twisted into his arms as if they were dancing, gazed up at him, and grinned. "Let's see if you are a better actor than a horse, shall we?" Then she pretended to collapse into a standing faint against him.

"We are not going to pretend that you are overcome. It is a childish thing to do."

"Oh, for pity's sake, put away your storm cloud for a few minutes and have some fun, Guy. If I am not overcome, then we will have to continue the ride and—unless you beat me tomorrow—I have no obligation to save you from those two scheming sycophants. You will have to fend them off yourself because I am too shaken to continue." She feigned a faint again. "And you will be left all alone with them."

"Yoo-hoo! Lord Wennington!" Lady Lynette's feet, and several others, were now scurrying up the path toward their private sanctuary. "I am worried sick about you!"

"Not as worried as I am!" It was Miss Maybury's voice that sealed the deal.

"Very well—play the damsel in distress if you think that you can be convincing." It certainly wasn't a role that suited her. "I shall plead affronted ignorance if you fail."

Her response was a grin so infectious he chuckled and allowed her to tug him out of the shroud of the willow, where she swooned into her character. Then, bizarrely, enjoying himself immensely, Guy maneuvered her along the little path down the side of the pond while she did her best to be a deadweight in his arms.

"Miss Travers is in shock!" he shouted to nobody in particular as they came into view. "Does anyone have any smelling salts?"

"Not on me." Lady Connaughlty patted her riding habit to check. "But I have some back at the house."

"What about some water?" That came from the levelheaded Miss Yates. "A splash on her temples might revive her."

"What an excellent idea!" Guy couldn't resist one small act of petty revenge for the way Lottie had scared him half to death. Suppressing a smile, he solicitously deposited her limp and lifeless body on the soft bank, leaned over it to use both hands to scoop up as much of the chilly pond water as he could. Then chucked the whole lot in the vixen's face.

TWENTY-FOUR

❧

ut what made Juno rear?" His aunt Almeria, typically, wanted to know every detail and was interrogating Lottie like a Bow Street Runner. "She's normally such a calm horse, isn't she, Guy?"

It was only the four of them in the drawing room now since his mother had shooed all the rest of the guests out as soon as he had helped the still comically limp Lottie in. She had assumed that the menace had needed peace and quiet while she sipped a cup of tea laced with fortifying brandy in case she required the urgent attention of the physician.

"She is." Rather than embellish or assist the Valkyrie's lies, Guy decided it was more fun to watch her scrabble around herself now that the brandy had miraculously fortified her in record time. He helped himself to one of the jam tarts from the tea tray and took it to the fireplace at the back of the room so that he could watch her squirm from the best angle. She hadn't anticipated the Spanish Inquisition and that, in turn, made the situation all the more hilarious.

"Something specific must have spooked her." His aunt stared at Lottie expectantly, thwarting the menace's attempt to escape for "the little lie-down" she had claimed to need.

"I think it was the melee," she said, twiddling her fingers as she stood on the rug in the center of the room, her hair still wet from the pond water he had doused her in and the back of her dress stained with mud and grass. "The horses were all bunched together and one must have stepped too close." She shrugged, clearly uncomfortable with this aspect of her genius plan. "Then she ran."

"And you couldn't control her?" Aunt Almeria picked up her quizzing glasses to stare through, a sure sign she smelled something was off. "*You*—the Infamous Galloping Governess of Hyde Park?"

Infamous Galloping Governess of Hyde Park? How funny and fitting was that? And how typical that Aunt Almeria would know all Lottie's dark secrets too, then not care about them. She'd always had a penchant for the unconventional and this breeches-wearing bundle of energy of a galloping governess was certainly that.

"You found Juno more of a handful than Lord Chadwell's enormous Thoroughbred stallion?" His aunt was like a dog with a bone.

Lottie blinked. "Well . . . Er . . ." Then she did the oddest thing. She put her hand behind her back and crossed her fingers. "Normally, I would have managed it, my lady, but I was on a sidesaddle and I'm afraid the Infamous Galloping Governess has never ridden one of those." Suddenly, she was animated and not squirming at all. "For the first two hundred yards it really was touch-and-go that I might get thrown, but I managed to shift position slightly and cling on until Juno calmed down. And that was that, really." The fingers uncrossed and the hand dropped to her side.

"Then how did you end up on the ground in a faint if you weren't thrown, gal?" Sometimes, Guy adored his aunt Almeria. "That is how Guy found you, isn't it?"

He nodded as his aunt's quizzing glasses turned to him, taking more pleasure out of the Valkyrie's discomfort than was gentlemanly and not caring one jot. She had scared him witless with this lie and then had acted like a tragic Greek heroine all the way home after making him her accomplice, so she had this coming. It *was* fun to witness. The best fun he'd had in forever. "Indeed, aunt. She was as limp as week-old lettuce by the time I caught up with her and discovered her spread-eagled on the ground." *Get yourself out of that, Lottie Travers!* She wasn't the only one who could spin a yarn. "For a moment, I thought she was dead. But when I crouched down to check for a pulse, she moaned. Thank goodness, as I have no idea—"

"What did she moan?" asked his aunt, interrupting and inadvertently giving him one of the best early birthday gifts ever as Lottie shot him surreptitious daggers over her shoulder, warning him not to gild the gaudy lily further.

Guy paused while he wondered what the headstrong hellion would hate hearing the most. "It was a fretful and frightening moment, as I am sure you can appreciate, so I do not remember what she said verbatim— but it was something along the lines of '*Lord Wennington, you are my hero.*'" He shoved the jam tart into his mouth whole to stop the laughter from escaping.

"So you *were* thrown, Miss Travers?" His mother stared at her with concern. "Perhaps I should send for the physician because if you had a concussion rather than a faint, that could be dangerous."

"I wasn't thrown." Lottie's hand went behind her back again and her fingers crossed. "But it *was* a close-run thing and I genuinely feared for my life. Even with my superior skills on horseback, a panicked, bolting horse is a challenge." Her explanation and earnest expression were doubtless for his wily aunt's benefit. "However, after I managed to pull Juno up and climbed off her, it all rather caught up with me. I felt dizzy and sat down and then . . . I must have passed out. Probably because I didn't eat breakfast."

"Hmm." Aunt Almeria wasn't convinced. "You've never struck me as the feeble sort, either with or without a full belly."

"Usually I am not." Lottie's fingers were now crossed so tight, the tips of them were pink as she did her best to wriggle out of exposure. "But today really was quite the ordeal. Even for m-me." She managed to inject a distraught hitch to that last word and Guy almost spat out a mouthful of crumbs. "But I am fine now, thank goodness. Just feeling a little . . . well, fragile, I suppose."

"Oh, go and have a lie-down then!" Aunt Almeria shooed her away with a complete lack of sympathy and Lottie happily bolted.

That was when his mother and his aunt turned to him with twin do-you-think-we-were-born-yesterday expressions and Guy realized that he was about to be interrogated too. "I should also go." He wasn't stupid either. "I need to check on Juno. She's a valuable horse and might need some medical treatment herself."

"I smell shenanigans, Guy Harrowby," said his mother to his retreating back, "and, rest assured, we are not done with this yet!"

He could have gone back to the stables, but did not trust either Miss Maybury or Lady Lynette not to track him down and dominate his afternoon, so instead decided to take Zeus out to visit some of his tenants. Although he could hardly go dressed like this. He had donned a formal outfit for this morning's ride. Too formal for a casual catch-up with those who worked his land, and thanks to Lottie's mad dash, his cream breeches and once-shiny Hessians were covered in dust and mud. He needed to change first and was on the way to his bedchamber when Lottie's head poked out of her door.

"Thank you very much, Judas!" It was a toothless reprimand because it was accompanied by a begrudging smile. "You were more hindrance than help down there. Spread-eagled indeed! And do not get me started on the 'Lord Wennington, you are my hero' nonsense."

"You thought my improvised additions too much? My apologies for not being as natural a liar as you are." He shrugged, not bothering to hide his amusement. "Probably because I didn't realize that simply crossing one's fingers behind one's back canceled a lie out."

"Ah . . ." She colored slightly. "You saw that, did you?" Then she grinned. "I am aware that it is a wholly pathetic thing to still be doing at my age, but I am afraid I've been doing it for too many years to break the habit. It was something my older brothers always did to get themselves out of trouble with our parents and it's stuck. I am also a dreadful liar if I don't cross them."

"Yes—I noticed how all the um-ing and er-ing stopped the second you crossed them. It was fascinating." As was she. Every facet of her bold and unconventional character intrigued him.

She leaned her head against the doorframe, seemingly as keen to linger and chat as he was. "Do you think they believed me?"

"Absolutely not. Do you?"

"No." She sighed. "I am in for more questions once your aunt gets me alone again, aren't I?"

"Undoubtedly." Guy rested his back against the opposite wall. "Tell her the truth. My aunt Almeria has always had a warped sense of humor and will find that story hysterical. Just as she doubtless found hiring the Infamous Galloping Governess amusing. But I take it Lord Chadwell didn't."

She winced. "No."

"I went to Cambridge with his son."

Her expression instantly shuttered. "Are you and he friends?"

The mere thought of the wastrel had Guy pulling a face of disgust. "Absolutely not."

"Good." She edged back into her room, her sunny smile back, and gestured to her hair. "I'd best go fix the soggy bird's nest on my head before Lady Frinton comes to tear me off a strip. Can you believe that some ungentlemanly scoundrel thought it funny to almost drown me in half the pond? I certainly shan't be saving him from all his annoying admirers at tonight's bridge tournament. Instead, I shall amuse myself by taking a seat at the back and leaving him to their mercy while I eat jam tarts."

"I shall survive for one night unchaperoned." He shrugged, matching her playful tone. "After I beat you tomorrow, *Miss Travers*, my hordes will all be your problem because you will become my constant bodyguard who has to fend them all off." While his heart wanted him to linger longer and flirt with impunity, his sensible head told him that this seemed like the most prudent time to back away. "Enjoy your lie-down and your inevitable dressing-down, Miss Travers." He pushed himself away from the wall. "And thank you for saving me today."

"Good luck with tonight, Guy." She went to close the door then stopped, her expression suddenly serious. "Please keep your wits about you with Miss Maybury. You don't want to end up ruined."

Sometimes she said the darndest things. "Can a man be *ruined*?"

"He can be compromised into marrying a woman and I wouldn't put it past her to try." There was concern in her lovely eyes.

"I have managed to fend Miss Maybury off for at least two years all by myself."

"Maybe so, but I fear she has decided to up her game because of all the competition. Just know, that although you do not stand a cat's chance in hell of winning me as your chaperone tomorrow, I will come to your aid with her for the duration if she gets to be too much. The same goes for Lady Lynette. Send me a signal." She raised her right palm. "I solemnly pledge to do whatever it takes to protect your virtue."

"That is very decent of you." They shared a smile. For Guy at least, it felt profound. "I look forward to your sworn protection at dinner."

❦

The few gentlemen present, including Guy, went off to play billiards after the bridge tournament and, as it was close to midnight, the ladies then began to drift off to bed. Lady Frinton was one of the first to go, and Lottie had to attend to her before she could come back down and keep watch. As it wasn't the done thing for a mere companion to rejoin the esteemed guests without her mistress, she took herself off to the library. Picked a book and a chair nearest the cracked-open door so she could check that both Lady Lynette and Miss Maybury had retired to their rooms before she dared retire to hers.

The male laughter drifting down the hallway as she descended the stairs suggested that either the billiards, or more likely the port and cigars, weren't ending anytime soon. Nor was the excited ladies' chatter coming from the drawing room, so she settled in for the duration.

She was a whole chapter in when Lady Wennington poked her head around the door. "Do you mind if I join you?"

"Of course not—it is your house after all."

"Thank you. I am never in the mood to sleep after playing hostess but, I confess, I am all done with playing hostess tonight." With perfect timing, Miss Maybury's high-pitched, braying laugh pierced the air and

Guy's mother winced. "I am also all done with my favor being courted constantly. I never expected them all to try to woo Guy through me and, frankly, listening to them unsubtly brag about their suitability as my future daughter-in-law is all rather tiresome." Lady Wennington closed the library door with a conspiratorial smile. "I am honestly sick to death of some of them. As, I suspect, are you."

Lottie laughed. "As a companion, I obviously have no opinion, my lady."

"That is a great shame, Miss Travers, as I am intrigued to know it." She wandered to a table where a decanter sat and picked it up. "Can I bribe your opinion out of you with a little nightcap?" She pulled out the stopper and took a deep sniff, then sighed. "It's cognac, thank goodness, as I am all done with sherry too." Lady Wennington poured a generous snifter. "Can I tempt you to imbibe with me or are you one of those prim and pious, meek and mild young ladies who disapprove of vices?"

"I am not sure either prim or pious could ever be used to describe me, my lady." Lottie took a sip and was pleasantly surprised. She had tasted her father's brandy once and had hated it so much she had immediately spat it out but this was nothing like that. It was aromatic and smooth, warming her throat as it slipped down it. "It's nice, and, for the record, I am not meek or mild either." To prove that, she took another sip.

"Although, to your credit, you do try to be meek, even though it doesn't suit you." Lady Wennington poured another cognac for herself. "And you fail with such aplomb that I respect it. You have an irrepressible character, Miss Travers, and the rare gift of lighting up a room without even trying." Her smile said that she meant the compliment, so Lottie beamed back. Lady Wennington was an easy woman to like. She had all the mischief and boldness of Lady Frinton but without any of the sharp edges. "My sister tells me you grew up in a house full of men, which probably explains your lack of meekness. Are you a close family?"

"Very." Lottie took another sip. "Although as much as I love my four brothers, I could cheerfully strangle each and every one of them on a daily basis."

"I can imagine. My sister and I have a similar relationship." Lady

Wennington took a long swig and savored it, then sighed. "I always wanted a big family like yours, but it was not to be. Guy only turned up after my husband and I had given up all hope of a child, and although we tried and tried and tried . . ." Her brows wiggled naughtily. "We were never blessed with another. Do you want children?"

It was such an unexpected question Lottie's glass paused midway to her lips. "If I am lucky enough to get married one day—yes. But I am a companion so I am resigned to the fact that it might not happen."

"Oh, of course it will! Just look at you! You are quite the head turner, Miss Travers. You have character and brains alongside a feistiness that appeals." Lady Wennington toasted her with her glass. "What is not to like? Some lucky man is bound to snap you up soon."

"You sound like my father, my lady."

"Good parents want to see their children happy." She swirled the amber liquid in the brandy balloon and stared at Lottie over the rim. "On the subject of our children's happiness, and seeing as we are both already in agreement that Miss Maybury is awful, what do you think of Lady Lynette for Guy?"

Was this a trap? Did Guy's mother also dislike that horrid braggart like her sister did or was she inquiring because she thought Lady Lynette was enough to make Guy happy?

Lottie tried to put aside the sudden flash of jealousy to formulate a tactful answer. "Well . . . um . . ." There was no doubting that Lady Lynette had the best aristocratic credentials of the debutantes here. Her father was an earl and nobody had questioned her claims to be related to a duke, so Lottie assumed that had to be the truth. "What do *you* think of her, my lady?"

"Oh no," said Lady Wennington with a shake of her head. "I asked first and according to my sister, you are a keen and pithy judge of character, so I want you to be completely honest. My son's future happiness lies in the balance, after all, and I want to know which direction to misdirect him to and which cliff it is best to push him off of."

Oh dear. Guy wouldn't take kindly to more matchmaking. While she pondered how honest to be about that, Lottie took another sip of her cognac and decided to be brave. "I think Lady Lynette is absolutely dreadful and no match for your son at all."

The older woman threw her head back and laughed. "She is absolutely dreadful." She clinked her glass against Lottie's. "And I absolutely wouldn't give my approval if Guy wanted to marry her—not that he would, of course, because it's obvious that he loathes her. But if pigs suddenly flew and he declared her to be *the one,* I would have used my mother's veto and expressly forbid it."

"Guy would go stark-staring mad shackled to a stupid and silly woman like that." Lottie clamped her errant jaws shut. Thanks to the heady effects of the cognac, she had spoken without thinking and quite forgotten her place, but rather than be shocked at her impertinence or overfamiliarity, Lady Wennington leaned closer.

"You're right. I so want him to experience the same joy with a soulmate as I did with his father—but he needs someone who intrigues him, doesn't he? A challenge. Someone who gets under his skin and who sees right through all his bluster and gruffness. Someone who forces him to smile and who calls to his hardened heart so loudly the stubborn wretch cannot ignore her." Lady Wennington grinned at Lottie and then huffed. "I fear that none of the girls *I invited* here meet that quite specific criteria, despite all of my best efforts to find him the perfect match."

"You know what they say, my lady: *You can lead a horse to water but you cannot make him drink.* Your son has to make his own choice. He won't allow you to push him off a cliff, he'll have to decide to leap himself."

"You are right again, Miss Travers. Guy has to leap." Lady Wennington stared at her thoughtfully for a few seconds, then smiled. "While we await that miracle with bated breath, let us have another glass and you can entertain me with your pithy observations of all the other plainly unsuitable girls here. Then you can tell me the real story about how you sabotaged this morning's ride. Because we both know that you did."

Chapter
TWENTY-FIVE

*uy lost at billiards but didn't care. He had enjoyed the game, just as he had enjoyed the bridge tournament before it, despite having to put up with the all-knowing Lady Lynette for most of it. In fact, ever since his mad dash to rescue that menace who hadn't needed rescuing this morning, he'd had a spring in his step. And bizarrely, he also had . . . not butterflies as such . . . but an odd fizzing inside at the prospect of their reckless steeplechase tomorrow. In just a few hours . . . He pulled out his pocket watch as he reached the top of the stairs and realized that, technically, seeing as it was a quarter past one, it already was tomorrow.

Good grief, he needed to get his head down and sleep off some of this port or he'd be good for nothing when the sun came up!

But rather than hurry, his feet decided to slow as he approached Lottie's bedchamber, his vivid imagination punching through his tiredness to picture her in her bed. Or perhaps not, because dim light bled from beneath the door, tempting him to knock. To say . . . well, anything really as they hadn't had any opportunity to do more than exchange a greeting over dinner. His mother had rearranged the seating plans again, in her quest to give all the young ladies a turn to tempt him, so Lottie had been placed in the middle. Forcing him to lean slightly to even see her, which he'd found himself doing with alarming frequency.

What was she doing now? Propped up on the pillows reading, her golden hair loose. Or was she taking down her hair slowly, pin by pin as he had dreamt about doing more times than he cared to think about? Knowing Lottie, she would have no patience for the task and would do it in a hurry, but if he ever got the chance to do it, Guy would savor it. Use the task to thoroughly seduce them both and . . .

Hard just imagining it, he had to fist his hand to prevent it from knocking on her door, then give his feet a stern talking-to to make them move again and head where they were supposed to be going. And the sooner they got there, the better, because his rigid cock was suddenly in dire need of attention. Again.

Bloody hell, but he wanted her. He could listen to his head and be as cautious as he liked but that did nothing to lessen the yearning—no, craving—he had to touch the minx. Hold her close and keep her there.

Forever.

Forever was creeping into the fantasy more and more and he had no earthly clue how to halt it. How the blazes was he supposed to take his time getting to know her properly when his head warned him to slow down but his heart and, damn her, his body wanted him to speed things up?

Frustrated, Guy adjusted the uncomfortable bulge in his breeches, then quickened his pace. He was about to turn the corner into his hallway when, suddenly uneasy for some inexplicable reason, he stopped dead.

He had no clue why he was compelled to flatten himself against the wall and surreptitiously peep around the corner but he was bloody glad he did when he spotted Miss Maybury. Loitering outside his blasted bedchamber door, for goodness' sake!

Worse, she was in her nightgown as she idly paced, her neck craning constantly to check that nobody was coming. It was a frothy, lacy, brazen garment, much like the woman herself. The V-shaped neckline and sheer sleeves showed far more of her flesh than he ever wanted to see. And although she was carrying a book and glass of milk as props that she would undoubtedly use to claim that she hadn't been able to sleep and just happened to be passing, he recognized an outfit of seduction when he saw one. Except, conversely, it killed his painful erection stone dead. Guy felt his cock wither in his breeches and then continue to shrink itself inside, almost as if it was hiding from her in protest.

Dread settled in his bones as Lottie's warning rang in his ears. It appeared that she was right and Miss Maybury was going to attempt to compromise him if she managed to corner him. He knew that if just one person saw them together with her dressed like that, he would be in a very tricky situation indeed. Even if he dashed past and locked himself in his room, if she loitered for longer, then someone might think that she was just leaving it after a night of passion. Then he was done for.

Like his shriveled penis, the only sensible course of action now was to hide. He backed up on tiptoes, keeping his eyes on the hallway in case Miss Maybury heard him. As soon as he was well clear, he would seek out some help and then arrange for a footman posted outside his door every night for the rest of this awful house party because it seemed that he now needed around-the-clock protection. What the hell had his mother been thinking to invite fifteen desperate debutantes to stay?

A floorboard creaked beneath his boot and he froze.

"Hello?" Miss Maybury's hushed question made him panic. "Is somebody there?" The scheming would-be seductress was heading his way and he almost ran for his life, but that was when Lottie's bedchamber beckoned again for the second time in as many minutes—but for very different reasons.

Lottie would help him, she had said she would, so he grasped her doorknob and quickly slipped in. "Please don't scream!" He hissed that into the dim candlelight and thankfully, she didn't.

Because the bloody menace wasn't there! Despite solemnly promising to protect him!

"Hello?" Miss Maybury was on the hunt. "Lord Wennington. Is that you?"

Guy pressed his back against Lottie's door and held his breath as Miss Maybury wandered past, the shadows from her feet leaking beneath the wood and dancing over his toes. He twisted so that he could listen, for the first time in his life fully understanding how silence could be deafening. The petrified hammer of his heartbeat the only sound he could hear.

He was too scared to risk opening the door, so remained as still as a statue and barely breathing for at least a minute while he waited in limbo.

Had the noise spooked Miss Maybury enough that she had abandoned her quest?

Or was she out there still, prowling the halls like a tiger stalking its prey and waiting to pounce?

The shadows danced over his toes again, returning from whence they had come, and because he just knew she wasn't the sort to give up easily, he cracked the door in time to confirm that his worst nightmare had come true. The trail of her frothy robe disappeared back in the direction of his room, where clearly she intended to wait for the duration. But at least she hadn't seen him and had no clue that he was here.

He blew out a relieved breath and sucked in a calming one. As soon as Lottie returned from wherever it was that the menace was at silly o'clock in the morning, he would enlist her help to get rid of Miss Maybury.

Until then, he would make himself comfortable.

He sank to the mattress and took in his surroundings. It didn't take long because this was an annexed room intended for a servant to sleep in, albeit a servant of elevated status, so that they could be next door to their master or mistress if needed. It was also, to give his privileged family some credit, a nice room. The bed was comfortable, the plain linens and the upholsteries of good quality, and it had a small, matching wardrobe and dressing table. The big, open sash window overlooked the garden as well, which none of the guest rooms did, and the fragrance of the midnight dew whispered in on the cool night breeze. If he had been assigned this room at an inn, Guy would have been very pleased with it, but it irritated him now because this had been given to Lottie. His aunt's companion or not, she deserved better. And bigger. It was barely large enough to swing a cat in and there was no way you could fit two people in that bed—unless they were snuggled together, of course.

He would gladly suffer that if he could snuggle up next to Lottie.

At the thought of her, Guy's gaze began to focus on her things in the soft lamplight. Her brush tossed idly on the dressing table, surrounded by hairpins that seemed to have been scattered like confetti rather than placed in one of the jars or drawers made to hold such things. Her scent bottle remained open, the stopper right beside it. A shawl sat in a puddle on the end of the made, but not properly made, bed. A pair of breeches hung over the back of her chair, while the sleeves and skirts of several gowns poked out of the wardrobe door. It was, like the confounding woman herself, organized chaos. But oddly, when he was a stickler for everything in its place, he rather liked it.

That did not mean that he wasn't going to tidy some of it up though, because what sort of person left their scent unstoppered when it could spill? He stood and wandered to her dressing table to do just that, sniffing it before he did so and smiling at the overtly feminine fragrance. So juxtaposed to the men's breeches and riding boots that she wore so well but oddly fitting for a woman so unlike any he had ever encountered before.

He placed the closed bottle on the top corner of the dressing table, in the exact place where he put his own cologne on his, then set about gathering all the hairpins and putting them in the empty jar. A task that took him several minutes because over half of them had to be straightened because she had left them bent. He put her brush and the comb he had found under the dressing table side by side, then stood and pushed in the chair.

He had intended to leave his interference at that, but the neatened dressing table only made the discarded breeches still on the chair look untidy. So he folded them and went to put them away in her wardrobe, but the contents of the wardrobe exploded outward as soon as he opened the door. He would have stuffed it all back in as she had done but then everything would end up horribly creased, so he spent the next fifteen minutes folding everything properly. Then when even the sight of all her clothes finally neatly stacked still bothered him, he organized them according to purpose. It did not take that long because she hadn't brought that much with her. Her few evening gowns were all grouped together and hung up. Next came her traveling dresses and pelisses. Then day gowns and finally, so that she could reach them easily, her two riding habits, blouses, and breeches were put at the other end so that he could stand her riding boots in the space beneath.

As he did not need the torture that would come from intimately knowing her underthings, he closed the door on that heap of trouble and set to work on the bed. He was in the midst of plumping one of her pillows when the door opened, scaring them both.

"Why are you in my room!"

"Thank God you're back!" He gestured for her to close the door. "And where the blazes have you been till this time!"

She frowned, her face flushed. "Having Constance with cognac."

"I'm sorry?"

She frowned some more and rubbed her forehead. "I've been in the library." Her tongue seemed to have some difficulty with all the *R*s in the word "library." "Drinking *cognac* with *Constance*." She nodded, pleased that she had finally put those words in the right order.

"Till almost two in the morning! How much cognac did you drink?"

She reached for the mattress before she sat on it, looking delightfully befuddled as she blinked at him. "Enough to call your mother Constance but not quite enough for you to take advantage, so don't get any ideas." She pointed a swaying finger at him that dropped to his crotch. "The last idiot who tried to take advantage now sings like a soprano. And I broke my brother's nose once with just one punch."

"Duly noted." Although it was hard not to get ideas when she was seated on a bed less than a foot away from him. "I didn't come here to take advantage of you." He replaced her pillow on the bed and, as she had done earlier, raised his right palm. "You have my solemn pledge on that." But he wouldn't mind if she decided to take advantage of him.

She stared at the pillow and then at her dressing table. "Did you come here to tidy?"

"No." And now he felt silly for his obsession with order. "I came in here to hide from Miss Maybury and tidied up while I waited for you as something to do."

"But why are you hiding from Miss Maybury in *my* room?"

"Because Miss Maybury has laid siege to *my* room." He pulled a horrified face. "In her *nightgown*. And I don't want to be ruined."

Her lovely eyes widened. "Oh dear." And then she was incensed, shooting up from the mattress. "The brazen hussy! What an awful thing to do!"

"I was hoping you would get rid of her for me."

"Consider it done."

She was halfway to the door with murder in her eyes when he caught her hand—because something else wasn't right. "Why were you drinking cognac with my mother?"

"Because she asked me to."

"Why?" His mother was up to something, he could smell it. Although, being his mother, it would be unusual if she wasn't poking her nose into something.

"Because she knew that my story about Juno and the subsequent swooning was codswallop and she wanted to know what really happened." She sighed and swayed a little. "I had to tell her the truth."

"How did she react?" If his mother was going to put a flea in his ear tomorrow about cutting short that awful ride, forewarned was forearmed.

"She found it hysterical and poured us both another drink." Lottie patted both her flushed cheeks. "Cognac is heady stuff, isn't it? I've never had it before—but I liked it." Her anger at Miss Maybury forgotten, she smiled. "But it has made me a bit loose-lipped, I'm afraid." Doubtless exactly as his meddling mother had intended when she'd plied her with it. "And I accidentally told her about the incident with Lord Chadwell's son—and then how you and I first met in Hyde Park. She found both of those stories hilarious too." She patted his lapel, looking all contrite and tipsy and adorable. "I'm sorry, Guy, but she knows that I threatened to horsewhip you."

Suddenly, he didn't care about that. "What incident with Lord Chadwell's son?" Jealousy coursed through him. *Had she and he—*

"He's the one who now sings soprano," she said with a sage nod, and the jealousy was replaced with outrage for her. "And then got me dismissed."

"Then I shall be having words with him the next time I am in London!" Stern words before he wiped the floor with the libertine. "How dare he take advantage of you, the disgusting scoundrel." The red mist had descended. "I'll go tomorrow and—" She pressed a finger to his lips and giggled.

"I don't need you to protect my honor, Guy, because he picked the wrong woman to try to take advantage of. I have four brothers, remember, so know how to fight dirty if the need arises and believe me, I did. One of the advantages of being taller than the average woman is that your legs can kick higher and I sent a couple of things south that are meant to hang north." She sniggered through her fingers. "I blackened the fool's eye, too, and made his nose bleed and all with just this elbow." She waggled it. "He got his just deserts. I was honestly more upset at his father for dismissing me as I really liked being the governess to his daughters. But then, when all looked doom and gloom, your aunt hired me and here I am." She patted his lapel again with a slightly soppy grin. "So all's well that ends well. And speaking of libertines, I suppose I should go and deal with your prospective debaucher so you can get some sleep." She stood straighter and pasted back on her angry face. "Give me five minutes."

She marched out, ready to do battle, and he had to usher her back. "Rather than cause a scene and wake the whole house up, it might be better to use diplomacy and tact first. Quietly."

"Spoilsport," she hissed with an insulted flick of her head. "As if a grumpy, vexatious curmudgeon like you even knows the meaning of those words."

Guy left the door open a crack so he could hear the exchange, ready to leap out at any moment if he was needed. Especially if Lottie read her the riot act, which was a distinct possibility after too much cognac.

"Good evening, Miss Maybury." Thankfully Lottie started politely. Not too loud but loud enough that if the conversation continued, others would hear it. "What are you doing wandering this hallway? Are you lost? Only this is the family wing and your room is over on the other side of the house."

"I . . . um . . . must have taken a wrong turn after my visit to the kitchen." Miss Maybury's whisper was fainter. "After I fetched myself this hot milk." He had known that was a blasted prop!

"This house is a maze, isn't it?" Lottie again. "It took me days to learn my way around."

Miss Maybury said something else which he couldn't discern and then Lottie played a blinder. "Allow me to show you the way . . . No, it is no trouble at all . . . Hurry up, we don't want poor Lord Wennington, or one of the other fathers, seeing you in that nightgown, now, do we?"

Then it went quiet, so he assumed that she had saved the day and paced the small room for a few minutes while he awaited her return.

Lottie came back with a smug smile on her face. "She's back in her bedchamber and I might have accidentally awoken her mother next door by talking too loudly, so you are safe for now. At least from Miss Maybury."

"Thank you."

She tilted her golden head in the direction of his room. "But in case one of the others gets ideas, I shall be a good chaperone and escort you back."

They walked side by side in companionable silence, a journey that was far too short for Guy, who was rather enjoying tipsy Lottie. "Make sure you lock yourself in." Her soft whisper felt intimate as they reached his door at the end of the hallway. "And because I wouldn't trust Miss Maybury not to pick it, maybe slide a heavy piece of furniture in front of your door too and we'll think of a more reliable debutante deterrent tomorrow."

He nodded but wanted to touch her instead, so clasped his hands behind his back. "Thank you, Lottie, and . . ." Would it be wrong to suggest they go downstairs for another nightcap? *YES! Wrong and reckless and much too dangerous!* ". . . good night."

"I like being Lottie again." She beamed at him. "Does that mean that you conceded our race before I've had the opportunity to beat you?"

Lord, but she was beautiful in candlelight. Beautiful and oh-so-tempting he could barely stand it. "Of course not, *Miss Travers*, that was just a slip of the tongue."

"Of course it was." She gave him a playful push. "For heaven forbid you forgive and forget until you have squeezed every drop out of my penance. That you even insist on penance is churl-*lish*." She stumbled over that last syllable and chuckled some more. "Bloody cognac!" He liked loose-lipped Lottie a great deal too. "Good night, Guy." She turned, then turned back. Went to say something and, to his complete shock, took two steps forward and pressed her mouth against his instead.

He could taste the cognac on her lips, reminding him that she wasn't sober, and cursed the gentlemanly manners ingrained in him that forced him to stand passive rather than haul her into his arms like he wanted. Perhaps not completely passive as, while his arms remained nobly locked by his sides, his mouth responded. He was only human, after all, at least that is how he justified his restrained participation.

Lottie, on the other hand, was anything but restrained and bestowed upon him a hungry, thorough kiss, an intoxicating promise of more that was way too short. Then, no sooner as it had started but it stopped and she used his chest to push herself away. She blinked at him in shock, her breath as reassuringly ragged as his was, her fingertips going to her lips where he hoped he still lingered.

"What was that for?"

"I think I am a tiny bit drunk." She bit her lip, her eyes both stunned and shimmering with need. "Perhaps a lot drunk and getting drunker by the second."

"Cognac does that." God dammit. "Best you go sleep it off before you lose your head completely." Or he lost his.

"Yes . . . undoubtedly." She edged backward, her expression befuddled by the potency of the impromptu contact, just as he supposed his was. "Good night, Guy." She spun on her heel then and picked up her skirts, offering him one last indecipherable look before she scurried away. "Sleep tight."

Guy watched her go and then leaned back on the solid door for support as he choked out an ironic laugh. Exactly how the hell was he supposed to sleep now that all he could taste was Lottie and cognac?

And, as the return of the painful bulge in his breeches could attest, the former was definitely headier than the latter.

༭྄ྀ ྄ྀ༐

$\mathcal{S}$ ometimes, according to her big brother Stephen, the only way to deal with making a total arse of yourself (which he did often) was to simply take it on the chin. Therefore, as Lottie arrived at the stables a little bit after sunrise—and undeniably more than a little bit thick-headed and mortified by her behavior—she greeted Guy's wry, smug smile with a shrug. "Rest assured that lessons have been learned and I shall be avoiding all cognac going forward. It clearly brings out the worst in me."

Except it had actually brought out her. At least the part of her that wanted him in every which way possible. Guy consumed her—her thoughts, her dreams, her emotions, her desires, her body—in a way no man had before. After a fitful night of recrimination and soul-searching mixed with lust, she could not deny the feelings she had for him. Sometime in the last week she had been speared by Cupid's arrow and there was nothing she could do about it. That she was leaving in a few days and they were separated in station by an ocean only made it all so bittersweet. But she was here now, with him, and they were well on the way to parting as friends again, and that had to be enough. "I obviously apologize for the . . ." Her index finger circled her mouth because she really didn't want to have to talk about that kiss—because it had come from the heart. Her heart and a few other, mostly lower, body parts that had decided to join in. "As I just said, cognac is apparently my nemesis."

"Oh, I don't know," he said, chuckling now, as he finished saddling Juno, "it made you very entertaining. I thoroughly enjoyed all your swaying and slurring and swearing and impropriety." His gaze briefly dropped to her mouth but thankfully he made no mention of the kiss either. "However, if you are feeling too fragile this morning to compete, I do understand. You could save yourself the humiliation of a crushing defeat and simply concede now."

"On the contrary, I feel much better about racing you with the handicap of a headache. I would have felt bad about not giving you some sort of concession this morning." She sincerely hoped the crisp morning breeze would blow those alcohol-induced cobwebs out fast.

"Let's have a pointless rundown of the rules," said Bill, emerging from the tack room, regarding them both with an expression of bemusement. "To try and avoid any broken necks or exploding tempers." He waited for them to pay him their full attention. "Rule one—" He held up his meaty hand to count them off on his fingers. "If anyone starts before my signal, they are automatically disqualified and the win goes to the other. Rule two—no pushing, barging, or interfering with each other's horse in any way." He stopped counting to wag a finger. "There will be no cheating." He held up his hand again and raised his ring finger. "Rule three—the first rider to touch the churchyard gatepost is the winner. And rule four—and this is the most important one—whoever loses is not allowed to murder the winner and bury their body in the woods to save face. If one of you doesn't return, I shall personally call foul and then call the constable." He folded his arms. "Do you both agree to these rules?"

They nodded.

"Good. Then if you are both ready, make your way to the pasture so we can get this childish debacle over with." Bill had already set off.

"Shouldn't we warm up our mounts first?" With a little drummer boy drumming away with enthusiasm in her head, Lottie needed a couple more minutes of fresh air to feel ready. "We don't want to do either of them a mischief."

"Already done." Guy regarded her wryly, as if he could hear what her drummer was drumming to. "Some of us were here bang on sunrise, after all, as stipulated." Then he shot her a positively sinful smile before he leaned down with cupped hands to give her a boost. "Juno, Zeus, and I are all warmed up and raring to go."

"Splendid." Rather than let him see how inconvenient that was, Lottie grabbed the reins and hoisted herself up without his help. "Then may the best rider win."

"I will, *Miss Travers*."

She tried not to watch him mount Zeus, but because Guy's muscles did wonderful things as he climbed onto a horse, she couldn't help looking. Then looked some more as he led the way out of the stable yard because, honestly, his backside was a thing of beauty.

"It's a mile and a half across mostly flat country to St. Eanswythe's." Bill pointed to the church's steeple on the misty morning horizon. "And the ground is good, so hopefully, you'll return in one piece. In case one of you doesn't, know that I disapprove of this race, so expect no sympathy from me while the poor physician has to put you back together or if the undertaker has to lower your broken remains into your grave."

"Duly noted," said an impatient Guy. "Now can we get on with it?"

"Just one more thing." Bill folded his arms and gave them both a stern look, but with a naughty twinkle in his eye. "Do you need me or one of the maids to follow behind for the sake of propriety?"

Guy gestured to her breeches-clad thighs with a snort. "I think that ship sailed when Miss Travers forgot to put on her skirt this morning, don't you?"

"On your own heads be it then." Bill winked as he herded them to the starting line he had marked with handfuls of straw and, once satisfied they were both level, raised his handkerchief in the air. "On your marks, get set . . ." He paused for dramatic effect as both riders bent low, then paused some more. *"GO!"*

Being the most amiable of the two Arabians, Juno started quicker and was already flying by the time Lottie reached the boundary between the pasture and the next field. But no sooner had she passed through the gate than Guy and Zeus jumped the fence. By the look of determination on both of those faces, Lottie knew this wasn't going to be an easy race. But if they could jump fences, so could she, and she was a lighter load than Guy.

She nudged Juno faster and, spotting a huddle of grazing sheep in the distance, changed direction early to avoid them. A decision that put him temporarily in the lead, but which paid dividends when she hit a gloriously flat and unobstructed path that cut right through the next hedge.

Guy, on the other hand, decided to continue riding as the crow flew for longer than he should have, making the sheep shatter hither and thither when the ferocious Zeus jumped the hedge into their field and made them panic. A decision that gave him some unexpected obstacles to dodge, which slowed him down.

Lottie couldn't resist laughing at his mistake over her shoulder as she shot past, then almost rued her hubris as she turned back to find that the path curved and the next gate was shut.

It came up too fast and she only managed to jump it by the skin of her teeth, but already Guy was hot on her heels. With the St. Eanswythe's steeple looming ever closer and her pride at stake, she had to dig down deep to keep her lead. Her opponent was an exemplary horseman and Zeus was, despite his stubborn temperament, an exceptional horse. Probably one of the finest specimens that Lottie had ever seen. His powerful legs made short work of her lead and he gained on her with every step.

The path petered out and gave way to a couple hundred yards of the stubby, harvested stalks of wheat that were yet to be plowed in, forcing both riders to slow some. Then they both veered in different directions to avoid the dense clump of trees enmeshed in the next hedge before they could find a suitable section to jump. Thankfully, after that, it was pasture again, pretty much all the way down the gently sloping incline to the village.

"Come on, girl!" Lottie used her heels to encourage Juno to pull out all the stops for this last half mile and several yards to her left, Guy was doing the same. As their paths converged again, they were pretty much neck and neck.

She risked turning to check his progress and caught Guy grinning at her. She grinned back, then a bubble of joyous laughter burst out as the last remnants of summer sun finally burned through the dawn clouds and bathed them in warmth.

And he did the same. Tilting his handsome face to the sky to soak it all in. Both of them loving and living in this moment, and as well matched as riders as it was possible to be.

Lottie could have happily lived in the moment forever.

But like all good things, it had to end, and suddenly the church gates beckoned, and things got serious again. In the final seconds they pushed themselves and the Arabians to the absolute limit and, kicking up clouds of dust, they charged through the opening together. Simultaneously standing on their stirrups to slap the wooden archway as they thundered through it.

Guy slowed. "That was a bloody draw, wasn't it?" He was trying to look peeved but his eyes, alight with the excitement of the ride, made his angry expression unconvincing. He had thoroughly enjoyed himself and it showed. He was rumpled and windswept and so in his element it was a joy to behold. The jaded, guarded curmudgeon was nowhere to be seen this morning and so this was one of the memories of him that she would most treasure after she left. The man she was probably in love with doing what he loved and letting her see his true self in the process. "We hit that gate together."

"Sadly, I think we did." Lottie grinned as she gulped in some air, her lungs burning from all the exertion but elated, nevertheless. "But it was the best fun I've had in ages."

"Me too." Guy was panting too, his broad chest rising and falling as he slid off his horse and patted the stallion's neck. Zeus snorted in response and danced on the spot, clearly nowhere near as exhausted from the gallop as the riders were. "You are some horsewoman, I'll give you that. I cannot remember a time when anyone has given me such a run for my money. There were moments there when you almost had me."

"There were moments when you had me too." Now was one of them. As tired as she was, she still wanted to kiss him until they were more breathless than they already were.

He held out his arms to help her down and it took her last drop of effort not to either collapse in a heap into them or fling herself into them and attach herself to his mouth. After her scandalous behavior last night, she put some distance between them as soon as her feet hit the ground. If they were ever going to kiss again, it was his turn to instigate it. She wasn't Miss Maybury, after all, and she did have some pride. "Obviously, I'd have won if I hadn't overimbibed the cognac."

"For the love of God, be gracious in defeat, woman!" He rolled his eyes heavenward. "I haven't got the energy to argue with you now. It was a tie—and I hate it as much as you do, but I am big enough not to make any excuses about it."

Lottie poked out her tongue in response to that and Guy chuckled at her petulance as he gathered up both sets of reins to lead the two horses back out of the gates to the water trough. He was rummaging in his saddle-bag by the time she mustered the strength to follow. "But if I were to make an excuse, madam, I was the one carrying extra weight because I don't suppose you thought to bring any provisions after your overindulgence last night." He tossed her his water flask first and she caught it gratefully, not caring one wit that glugging from it wasn't ladylike. That ship had sailed around him too and she was too exhausted to feign any of the expected decorum that had never come naturally to her. Not that he ever seemed to expect it. Perhaps he liked her as she was? A thought that made her smile as she took a seat on the low wall that separated the churchyard from the lane.

"What provisions did you bring?"

He responded by chucking an apple at her, so she swapped him the water as he sat beside her while the horses—and they—cooled down.

Guy shined his apple on his thigh before he took a bite. "I haven't done that in years." His dark brows knitted. "Nine to be precise. I remember because it was just before my twenty-first birthday and poor Bill suffered the last of a series of drubbings." He smiled at that. "Although if you were to question him about it he'd say that he had to let me win because he feared for his job otherwise—but it isn't true. He just couldn't stand that I got better than him."

"When was the last time you were beaten?"

His nose wrinkled as he considered it. "Probably a decade ago. Bill again and he gloated all the way home with absolutely no fear for his job that day. You?"

"The same. A decade . . ." Where had all that time gone? Instantly her mind conjured images of home before she had left to study the Four D's at Miss P's school for ladies. She had been much wilder then. "Peter Clifton, the blacksmith's son, beat me by a head."

"Ouch," said Guy with genuine sympathy. "So close and yet so far."

"Although, in truth, I pulled up a tiny bit at the last minute." She held her forefinger and thumb apart a quarter of an inch. "And *did* let him win that day, so I am not sure that it counts."

"Why on earth did you do that?" As a fellow ridiculously competitive person, it was obvious that such a sacrifice was anathema to him.

"Ah . . ." She smiled at the vivid recollections of her and Peter climbing haystacks in her father's fields so they could stare at the sky together. "Because he was a handsome and mature young buck of fifteen and I was convinced that I was a woman at thirteen and I thought myself in love with him." And what a twit she had been then. Womanhood was blossoming but she'd still had the mind of a child. "It was all very serious, of course, as young love always is and we plighted our troths to one another behind a barn. My first kiss too . . ." She gave a dramatic sigh that made him smile. "I felt so grown-up and thought I had found my soulmate, only to have him reject me in the end, because life is cruel, and love is crueler." It was certainly being cruel to her now. What had Cupid been thinking to make her poor heart yearn for a forever with a man she likely could never have for longer than this week?

"Why did the idiot reject you?" Guy was genuinely perplexed and she took that as a compliment. "Aside from your infuriating character and problems with cognac, of course."

Lottie lifted her legs and pointed her toes. "Because thirteen was also the year of my growth spurt. And trust me, I grew like a beanstalk." Sadly upward but not outward as her bee-sting breasts had never poked out farther from her flat chest than they had when she was thirteen. "Peter was able to look me in the eye for our first kiss—but six months later I was at least six inches taller than him, and he took that personally." But like the twit she had been back then, she had done everything in her power to minimize her height. Including walking beside him with permanently crouched legs that ended up giving her a backache. "He left me for a shorter woman. Dilly James, the miller's daughter." She pretended to swipe a tear from her eye. "She was an acceptably petite five-foot-two. They are married now. She worships the ground he walks on and he happily towers over her while she does. And good luck to them. I am happy for them."

"I thought hell was supposed to have no fury like a woman scorned, so why are you not bitter?"

In silent tacit agreement, they'd retrieved their horses to amble beside them in the direction of home. "Because it turned out that that first kiss, which I had believed could not possibly be beaten, was quite a substandard kiss. More a wash than a kiss, so I got over him much too quickly to have been really in love. Thanks a great deal to Edgar Garrick, who knew how to do it properly."

"You fell in love with a man called Edgar?" Guy seemed appalled by the thought. Or jealous. The eternal optimist within her hoped he was jealous, because that offered them some potential. "Ed-*gar*." He then put on a comical falsetto which she presumed was supposed to be her. "'Kiss me, Ed-*gar!* Oh, how you make my young heart pound, Ed-*gar*. I love you more than life itself—Ed-*gar*.'" He made a disgusted sound and dropped the falsetto. "Now there is a name that thoroughly ruins the moment."

"Firstly, his parents gave him that dreadful name and he went by

Ed, which was much more tolerable. Secondly, his wandering eyes made him too unreliable a fellow to waste my time falling in love with. Probably because he practiced his craft at every available opportunity with whichever willing woman came along. He was too charming by half, the floozy, and buzzed from girl to girl like a bumblebee does flowers. But, in my defense, I kissed him before I realized that. And it was memorable enough to render the kisses of the next two gentlemen who came along as bland by comparison."

"Precisely how many men have you kissed?" Guy's eyes were looking resolutely ahead but his jaw was clenched, convincing her that he was just a little bit jealous. Although he had nothing to be jealous of as his kiss came at the very top of her rankings.

"Not as many who had wanted to but probably more than I should have." She shrugged, enjoying his irritation. Nothing riled a man up more than the competition of other men and, despite the depressing fact that a viscount was unlikely to compete for her in anything other than an affair, it was nice to know that he cared. "Remember that I am a farmer's daughter who grew up watching sheep or cows or horses indulge their passions openly without a care in the world, so I am not as easily shocked as most ladies are by the physical. A few stolen kisses here and there are tame in comparison to what was happening in our farmyard—and it is hardly my fault that I am such a fine specimen of womanhood that men want to kiss me, now, is it?" She flicked her hair and batted her lashes in the ridiculous way that Miss Maybury always did and his jaw relaxed a little.

"If all these men keep wanting to kiss you, why haven't you married one of them? Or have Ed-*gar*'s talented lips ruined you for all other men?"

"Much to my astonishment, nobody has asked." She flicked her hair again to make him smile. "Apart from the year that I secretly courted Stumpy Peter at thirteen—my brothers' cruel nickname for him, not mine—all my flirtations have been short and sweet. And because . . . well . . ." Seeing as they seemed to be friends again and friends should always be honest with each other, she admitted to the truth. "None of them felt right to want to explore the acquaintance further. I figured I would know when it was love"—Lottie touched her heart—"in here. Because everything would feel just right once I had found my soulmate." She knotted her hands together and sighed at her folly. Wondering why it was that her stupid heart had decided that in all her three and twenty years and close to three and ten kisses, only Guy felt just right when he was out of her reach. For eternity at least. That errant idea, as scandalous and improper as it was, was suddenly food for thought. "I am too selfish to settle down for less than those all-encompassing, all-consuming, overwhelming, passionate romantic emotions that supposedly only come with true love." The exact sort she was feeling for him. Which she supposed meant she was destined to end up with her heart broken very soon.

"Oh, good grief, you're a romantic!" He said that like it was an insult and she remembered that he'd had his heart broken too.

"I *am* a romantic. Unashamedly so. I fail to see what is wrong with that? I want what my parents had—what I hear your parents had—I want to be someone's everything and have them be my everything in return. Don't you?"

The storm raging in his eyes said that he did but his frown tried to convince her otherwise. He also, tellingly, deflected rather than answer her question. "Fairy tales are for fools."

"Then I am proud to be a fool." Lottie stuck out her chin and mirrored his expression of disdain. "But then I am a ray of sunshine who believes that dreams do, sometimes, come true and you are a crochety storm cloud with no joy in his soul." She nudged him with her elbow, seeing as they were walking together so close. "Why is that?"

"Because I am a realist and not an idiot."

Lottie sighed at that depressing response. "What was her name?"

His jaw clenched momentarily and then, to her surprise and relief, he huffed. "Florinda."

"Florinda!" She had to laugh at that awful moniker. "And you had the nerve to make fun of the name Edgar." She could not resist putting on her deepest voice and deepest scowl to parody him and lighten the honest moment enough that he might feel less uncomfortable about it. His whole body had stiffened as he mentioned her name and it still hadn't relaxed. "'You seem the sensible and unromantic sort, so be mine, *Florinda*.'" She rearranged her tongue and mouth after saying the name and then attempted an octave lower for levity's sake, raising her hand to the sky. *"But, soft! What light through yonder window breaks? It is the east, and Flo-*rin-*da is the sun."* Lottie pulled a face. "It has too many jarring and harsh syllables to trip off a breathless tongue."

"Once upon a time I found her name exotic." His lips twitched. "But I was young and foolish . . .'"

"Weren't we all at some point." She nudged him again. "Did you grow too tall for her? Or was she not a fan of storm clouds?"

He was silent again while he deliberated exactly how much to confide, and for a moment she thought he would clam up and deflect again, but he surprised her. "If you must know, she left me for a duke. An older and significantly richer duke."

"Ah . . ." She didn't want to let on that she had heard as much from his aunt and mother.

He slanted her an awkward glance. "Publicly. On my twenty-first birthday too."

"So you were *very* young and foolish."

"Very, and rushed in like a whirlwind, for goodness' sake, too blinded by my passions to notice that she was only using me as bait to hook a bigger fish." He growled at his old self. "Like an idiot, in front of most of Mayfair, I proposed in the middle of my birthday ball—and Florinda left it on the arm of the other man. It was all over the papers, so you probably read about it. Or saw the caricature." His shoulders slumped as if the weight of it all was still too heavy to bear.

"They mocked your heartbreak in print?"

"Indeed—*The Courting Jester* was too hilarious not to." Poor Guy. They hadn't told her any of that. "I'll give you three guesses who the weeping jester holding the ring was." He shrugged, attempting to make light of it and she was so moved she wanted to smother him in an embrace and weep for him. He had been used and humiliated in the worst possible way and that explained why a packed house party of society's finest was not his idea of fun. Or why he did not trust easily. Or why he thought love was for fools. "That's dreadful."

"It was a long time ago and I am over it," he said, not looking the least bit over it. "Although I am understandably jaded by the experience." Then he became all twitchy, and awkward, as if he regretted revealing all that and that split her heart right in two. As if he should somehow be ashamed of, or blame himself, for what that vile woman did to him. "Shall we ride the rest of the way? I don't know about you, but I've worked up quite the appetite thanks to our race. That apple was no substitute for a proper breakfast, and I would like to eat mine in peace before the hordes wake up." Quick as a flash, he had his foot in Zeus's stirrup before she caught the back of his coat.

"Stop." Lottie yanked him away from the horse and spun him around, and like a fox caught in a trap his eyes told her he wasn't happy to have his escape thwarted. "Don't you dare deflect or attempt to run away again because you are panicking about looking stupid. I do not think less of you because you got your heart broken. If anything, I am delighted to discover you possess one as you've kept it so well hidden! Now that I understand why, and you have allowed me to see some of the real you, I am not going to allow you to build another wall to shut me out again. Any more than I am going to allow you to carry all that hurt and shame and anger around inside of you where it has quite obviously been festering, as that isn't healthy."

His eyes narrowed, a sure sign that his temper was about to erupt and a storming-off was imminent, so Lottie reached out to take his hand and laced her fingers through his to prevent one. "Like it or not, I am your friend now and I am an even better friend than I am a horsewoman." He cocked a disbelieving brow, but it showed her that he was calming down. "Talk to me about it. Let it out. Lance that boil. Rant and rave all the way home if you need to. But you have to let it out to let it go, Guy."

"Easy for you to say when your reckless stupidity is not immortalized in print, Lottie." It was a half-hearted rebuff and, noticeably, he had dropped the formal "Miss Travers" that helped underpin his barricade.

"It hasn't been—yet—but I am the Infamous Galloping Governess of Hyde Park, remember, so I daresay it is only a matter of *when* and not *if* at this stage that my name makes the papers. Then we'll have even more in common than we do already."

He stared off into the distance, his hand squeezing hers. "You are not going to give up, are you?"

"On a friend? Never."

᠗

*G*uy had never wanted to talk about his *Courting Jester* debacle. It was all too humiliating, and, as they set off for home, he had been determined to find a way to change the subject as quickly as possible to avoid having to. But there was something about the way she listened— part sympathy, part irreverence, and part protective fury—that coaxed it all out of him anyway.

To his great surprise, over the course of just one short, leisurely half-hour ride, he told her more than he had ever told another living soul. How he and Florinda first met. That first waltz. All the public flirtations and private, heated trysts. Lottie had been honest with him about the men that she had kissed and didn't judge him for being so overwhelmed by his youthful passions that he had allowed the frisky appendage in his breeches to lead him astray.

That frank conversation had come about after he had politely tried to tell her that there had been more to his relationship with Florinda than flirting, and that had definitely clouded his judgment.

"There is nothing more determined to cover a cow than a randy bull during his first season," she had said sagely, and then instantly colored when she realized exactly what had slipped out of her mouth.

"It is quite all right," he had said, laughing during a conversation he had never dreamed he could ever have with a woman or find funny. "I am a farmer's son, remember, so I am not as easily shocked as most gentle-men would be by a farmer's daughter who always manages to say the right thing in her own inimitable way. I was that randy bull."

After that, he had been able to tell her everything. All the things about his doomed love affair that he had only ever kept to himself.

And for the first time, that everything also included the death of his father. A devastating chapter in his life which he had never thought formed part of the debacle but was actually so interwoven with it when he said it aloud, that Guy understood things better himself. The combination of grief and the new responsibilities inheriting his estate had left him in a vulnerable state before he met Florinda. That, in turn, had made him an easy target to exploit. He had needed something to fill the big, gaping hole left by his father, and she had allowed him to think that she was it.

In truth, by dissecting it with the help of Lottie's fresh eyes, he also realized that Florinda had not explicitly ever made any promises or dec-larations that might be construed as a promise. She had flirted with him, shamelessly, purely to make another man jealous. Did all she could to se-duce him, without actually seducing him, to keep Guy on the hook too. Those things were still true, calculated, and unforgiveable—but as she had used every wile at her disposal to lead him on she had never once suggested that she loved him. Nor had she ever hinted that they had a future together. Those things were all him. Because he had felt it—or more likely wanted to feel it to end the all-consuming pain of grief—he had manifested his own desires onto her. It was sobering to realize that he had had as much of a hand in his own downfall as Florinda had. Sobering but also enlightening.

By the time they reached the stable yard, he didn't so much feel cleansed of the hideous experience as a little lighter inside. A little less burdened by the past and, perhaps, a little less afraid of talking about it.

"I was about to send out a search party," said Bill as he came to greet them. "Who won?"

Lottie shrugged. "Neither of us—or both of us—depending on your point of view."

"By that, she means it was a tie." Guy was smiling, although why he was smiling when he had just dredged up the entire fetid riverbed of his past was beyond him. "We are both furious about it."

Bill gave him an odd look. "Yet neither of you look furious. I wonder why that is, eh?"

"Because it was stupendous," said Lottie, sliding off her saddle before Guy could get to her. "I'd throw the gauntlet down to race you to the church tomorrow, Bill, but I have it on the highest authority that you are no challenge."

"That's because I like my bones unbroken, thank you very much. I'm also not mad." Bill shook his head at the pair of them as if they were, as he led the two Arabians back to the pasture, leaving Lottie and Guy by themselves again.

"I suppose we'd best go change for breakfast." She said that with all the enthusiasm of someone who was as fed up with his mother's horrendous house party as he was. "Then it has been decreed that all the ladies are going to take a jaunt to the village to shop for last-minute frills in preparation for the big ball that will mark the end of your birthday ordeal. An entire morning of Lady Lynette's incessant sermonizing lies before me." She flicked him a withering glance. "I take it you have already made your excuses to get out of it."

"Urgent estate business, I'm afraid." He could not help grinning. "It's hard work being a viscount."

"I might beg your aunt for some urgent errands to run." Her lithe body deflated. "Before the reading salon later, although why anyone would want to hear anyone else read is beyond me. Will I at least see you there?"

"Sadly, an unexpected emergency will detain me just before it starts but I might make it back before it ends. Show face and all that, to please my mother." Then he winced. "But she has threatened to have me castrated if I do not attend tonight's dreadful *musicale,* so I shall definitely see you there. Lady Lynette is apparently a virtuosa on the violin *and* the pianoforte, so that should be something to look forward to."

"She's only an expert on two instruments? That surprises me when

I would have thought there would be none that she didn't excel at." Her irritation quickly melted into defeat. "Miss Maybury has threatened to sing, so that will doubtless be a treat too. The two Miss Harpers are singing after her. A selection of arias from Mozart. A *selection*. Because one being warbled isn't torture enough." Lottie's expression was so glum, it was comical.

"It could be worse." He used the tip of his finger to tilt up her chin. "They could be warbling them to you—it is in my honor, remember, and they do all want to marry me."

That brought her smile back. "And suddenly the world is a brighter place because I at least get to watch you suffer."

Guy realized that the finger that had tipped up her chin was still lingering on her jaw and reluctantly let it fall away. An action that, of course, she noticed.

"We keep having these odd moments, don't we?" Trust Lottie to face the issue of the increasingly magnetic attraction between them head-on. "Loaded looks here and lingering touches there." Her gaze searched his, waiting for him to either confirm or deny it and when he simply sighed she did too. "I suspect we've never finished what we've started. We keep getting interrupted or attempting to deny it or there is cognac involved, so it's all"—she clenched her fist to her tummy—"festering within and—"

"That is not healthy? I think when it comes to lust it bubbles more than it festers, but it is rather distracting." Which was putting it mildly. He wanted her so badly it was visceral, and yet his head still urged caution because this was all happening so fast. He hadn't known Lottie a month yet and already she had laid siege to his body and his soul.

She looked at him with such need in her lovely eyes. "Do you think if we just got it over with . . . bite the bullet, as it were, and just let all the lust out we might . . ."

"Are you suggesting that we . . ." Guy touched his mouth and she nodded. "Now?" He glanced around the open stable yard, incredulous. His head and his frisky appendage already engaged in all-out war. "Here?"

"Well, not here, obviously. But . . . perhaps if we get . . . um . . .

it . . . over and done with . . ." Had they really just descended into using the word "it" and hand gestures to communicate like prudes? When they had just discussed the ways that Florinda had figuratively and literally teased his cock and yet neither of them could mention the word "kiss" to one another! ". . . as quickly as possible, it might bring an end to our odd moments, don't you think?"

Guy thought it would be easier to throw snowballs in hell but nodded anyway. "It might."

And more likely it might not. He knew already a kiss wasn't going to be enough to satisfy his craving. Nor, he suspected, was burying himself to the hilt inside her. Guy didn't want a taste of Lottie, he wanted all of her. Forever—except how could he plan forever with a woman he hadn't yet known a whole month?

But, heaven help him, he wanted to kiss her. So much at this precise moment he was happy to grab any excuse to overrule the increasingly irritating fearful voice in his head that urged for less haste and more caution. "What do we do if it doesn't work?" Because he suspected he would be right back where he was days ago—years ago—ready to throw all caution to the wind once more for a woman he barely knew. "What if *it* just makes everything worse?"

She shrugged, blushing again, which he found delightful when she was usually such a supposedly unshockable farmer's daughter. "Cross that bridge when we come to it?"

Not the answer a man who preferred to be in control needed to hear.

"It's not much of a plan but I suppose it will have to do." Not quite believing how utterly reckless he was about to be, Guy grabbed her hand. "Follow me."

Because he was in a hurry, he practically sprinted her across the yard, through the deserted stables, right to the tack room beyond where they had both privacy and a back door to escape out of if they needed one. He let go of her to close the door and then they just stared at one another.

She at one end of the small room and he at the other.

The air between them so charged with pent-up lust and anticipation it was a wonder it didn't crackle. "Here we are then," he said.

"Here we are." Her cornflower eyes were darkened with desire. Her gaze dropped to his mouth and held.

Guy wasn't sure who moved first, or if, like they did at the church gates, they did it together, but they collided on a mutual groan and a tangle of arms, legs, and hungry mouths.

They did not waste any time on preamble. Things were too far gone for that, so instead they picked up exactly where they had left off when Longbottom had interrupted. Guy's hands filled with her bottom; hers in his hair.

When that proved to be nowhere near enough, their hands went wandering. Hers explored his chest and shoulders beneath his coat, then when the coat got in the way she wrestled him out of it. Guy smoothed his palms up her ribs, sliding them forward so that he could finally cup her breasts. She sighed into his mouth as his thumbs teased her nipples over her clothes, arching her hips against his erection and sending him out of his mind.

"Touch me properly." Lottie shrugged her arms out of her coat. "Touch my skin."

It was an invitation he could not turn down, so with no finesse whatsoever he yanked the hem of her blouse from the waistband of her breeches and slipped his hand beneath.

Her skin was as smooth as satin, the soft swell of her breast slotted perfectly in the center of his palm. He tested its weight before he allowed his fingers to tease her tight nipple tighter still. "Don't you ever wear stays, woman?" He tore his mouth away to watch the pleasure his touch was bringing her.

"I don't exactly have much to put in them, do I?"

He growled at that unnecessary apology, sliding in his other hand so that he could cup them both. "You are perfect, Lottie Travers. These are more than perfect." He pinched both nipples simultaneously and watched her eyes roll back in her head. "And so sensitive." If they hadn't been in the tack room, he would have peeled her blouse off there and then and worshipped them with his mouth.

"And you are so big," she said as her hands splayed over his chest muscles before one of them snaked its way down his abdomen and boldly explored the bulge straining against his breeches. "So—"

They froze at the sound of footsteps in the stables behind them. His hands still filled with her breasts and hers still flattened against his throbbing cock. Foreheads touching as their breath sawed in and out.

"All the stalls need fresh hay, Tom." Bill was clearly giving the lad his list of daily chores. "The water troughs need filling and then you need to take Blodwyn to the blacksmith. She's thrown a shoe and one of the ladies might need her this afternoon if they decide to ride rather than walk to the village. But Hercules needs a good session in the training yard first."

The footsteps retreated, meaning the coast was clear again, but the lull in proceedings seemed a good time to double-check that Lottie was still up for what they were doing.

"Do you want to stop?"

She gently massaged his crotch as her teeth nipped his bottom lip. "I want you to touch me some more."

"Here . . . ?" He squeezed her breasts, the unabashed pleasure she took from it killing him. "Or *there*?" He flicked his eyes downward.

"Definitely *there*. I ache for you, Guy."

Bloody hell, he was doomed. For how could any man resist such temptation?

"Oh, Lottie . . ." With clumsy fingers he undid the top few buttons on the falls of her breeches and then, because he wanted to remember every moment of this for the rest of his life, slowly edged his hand inside. His fingertips had just discovered the soft curls between her thighs when she caught his wrist.

"Wait . . . I want to touch you too. Can I?"

He choked out a sound: half relief, half need but definitely a resounding yes as he kissed her hard. "Yes! God, yes! For the record, Valkyrie, you never, ever have to ask." She smiled against his mouth, her fingers already unbuttoning his waistband. But as his dipped into the wet indent of her sex and she undid the final button of his falls, bloody Bill chose that moment to return and then thoroughly ruined everything.

"You're right, Tom. It is market day and the blacksmith is always busy. Get Blodwyn saddled up and take her now before the rush."

Guy glared up at the neat racks of saddles and tack and knew that their time was up. Lottie did too, because straightaway she severed all contact. "Oh, lord, we can't be found here!"

"Don't panic—there's a back door." But she was panicking and rightly so as two pairs of boots were headed their way.

As they had both shoved arms in sleeves, he grabbed her hand and dragged her out of the door to escape into the yard before they were caught in flagrante. As they sprinted across the yard, they were both in such a hurry to get out of the sight of Bill and Tom that neither of them noticed Miss Maybury staring at them agog from the stable doors.

Chapter
TWENTY-EIGHT

৵৶

"Travers!" Lady Frinton hammered on her bedchamber door while Lottie was trying to get ready for dinner. "A word in my room, if you please!"

As "a word" was usually code for chapter and verse as far as her employer was concerned, Lottie sighed at her half-done coiffure in the mirror as she accepted it was a lost cause. "I shall be right with you, my lady."

In the absence of anything different to wear in her wardrobe than the three evening gowns she had packed and worn at least once each, she had been trying her best to do something wonderful with her hair that involved a curling iron. The hope was that some fashionable ringlets would frame her face better than the few naturally wavy tendrils she usually left when she had to dress for a fancy dinner. It was a vain and pathetic attempt to compete with all the other young ladies who all had expensive and fashionable gowns aplenty to do most of that work for them. Not one of them had worn the same thing twice yet, not even Miss Yates, who was the only sensible one.

Lottie had never cared about such nonsense before, had always believed that she was confident enough in herself that she found all the hard graft that went into looking like "a woman," like curling irons and rouge and tightly laced stays, a pointless waste of her time. However, after this morning she wanted to be as attractive as she could be for him, just in case he was as keen as she was to finish their still unfinished business later.

She still couldn't quite believe how brazenly she had propositioned him earlier. It hadn't been her intention at all during their ride to do so. That had genuinely been more about rekindling their special friendship before she left. A friendship that she had convinced herself she was content to leave with—until her body decided otherwise again.

However, as soon as his finger had touched her chin and then lingered, Lottie had realized that while she was determined to leave here as his friend, she was now seriously contemplating grabbing anything else that might be on offer while she was here. And by anything else, after their kiss in the tack room, she suspected that she was prepared to offer him everything. After all, if she would have given herself to him this morning—and she was in no doubt that she would have if they hadn't been interrupted—it made no sense to do otherwise if opportunity knocked.

But was that wise when she was leaving?

If fate provided them with a chance to be alone, should she really throw all caution to the wind and give Guy her more than willing body on a platter for him to do what he pleased with?

She certainly had no doubt it would please her too. Her nipples instantly puckered at the thought of his hands on them and, over twelve hours after that sublimely passionate kiss, the sensitive bud of nerves between her legs was still absolutely distraught at being denied his touch.

And she had always subscribed to the old adage that it was better to have loved and lost than never to have loved at all. She wouldn't have kissed quite so many men if she hadn't been hoping that she would be hit by the thunderbolt and then live happily ever after.

Her feelings for Guy hadn't so much hit her like a thunderbolt—but they had snuck up on her quickly like fast-growing brambles and she was too entwined in them now to do anything about it. The die was cast. Her heart had been stolen and that was that. And while she would undoubtedly have to leave him, and then break all over again when she discovered that he had inevitably found some other lady of his class to spend his forever with, surely she would much rather live in the precious moments with him now than live with any regrets?

Even if it could go nowhere?

And wouldn't it be better to have something more scandalous to contemplate on her deathbed than all the things she hadn't done? Life was for living, after all, and right in this moment, she was sorely tempted to live it to the fullest and to hell with the consequences. Dive in headfirst and worry about tomorrow, tomorrow, exactly as she always did.

That philosophy hadn't steered her wrong yet.

Unless she counted the two times galloping across Hyde Park that had caused her to be dismissed.

Or all the other thousand times when her recklessness had backfired, as all the bruises, tellings off, and mortifying recriminations she had accrued over the years were testament to. Or how much she had hurt Guy by not telling him about *the Surprise.* How could she not consider the consequences for once when the consequences for her heart were bound to be dire?

Unconsciously, she rubbed her chest. She had never experienced heartbreak before. At least not the sort that came from losing the prospective love of her life, and if she did dive all the way in with Guy, it might end up being too much to bear.

Was she prepared for that?

Could one ever be prepared for that?

Or was it inevitable anyway—seeing as her heart was already his?

What to do? *What to do?*

"Travers! What the blazes is keeping you now, gal?" As that shout made the wall between her room and Lady Frinton's vibrate, Lottie would have to ponder the conundrum after she'd seen to her impatient employer's latest whim.

With a last sigh at her lackluster unfinished coiffure, Lottie grabbed all the loose tendrils, pinned them to her bun, and took herself next door.

"Yes, my lady?"

"There is no easy way to say this, and nor do I suppose should there be, so I shall just say it straight out." The older woman huffed. "Miss Maybury claims to have witnessed you having a tryst with my nephew this morning at the stables."

Oh, good grief, what had she seen? The heated kiss? Guy's hand on her breasts? Down the front of her breeches while she writhed against it? Hers brazenly exploring the length and girth of his impressive erection while her tongue was in his mouth?

Lady Frinton folded her arms. "I take it from your scarlet face and saucer-shaped eyes that her claim is true."

Lottie scrabbled around for any excuse that would keep her in her job. "It was a moment of madness, my lady, and it will not happen again."

"Oh, for goodness' sake, gal! I couldn't give a fig! What two consenting adults do *discreetly* in their own free time is nobody's business but theirs! Life is too short not to grab the moments of madness, as you so aptly call them, by the horns. So long as you are still running around at my beck and call when I expect you to, the pair of you can fornicate like rabbits for all I care."

"Then you are not going to dismiss me?"

"Of course not." Lady Frinton waved that away. "I merely wanted to warn you to be a bit more discreet, especially where the obnoxious Miss Maybury is concerned. She's a sly one, that one, and I wouldn't trust her as far as I can throw her. Despite the half an hour of her detestable company that I had to endure this afternoon and my assurances that she shouldn't read anything into two people running across a stable yard together as anything beyond them being in a hurry"—she paused to watch Lottie visibly relax at that clarification before she pointed a bony finger—"she is definitely on to the pair of you, and she is more than unhappy about it, so . . . be careful."

Lottie didn't know quite how to react or what to say to that, and fortunately she didn't have to.

"Why the blazes are you still gawping at me, gal? Go do something with your hair. You look as if you've been dragged through a hedge backward!"

No sooner had she stepped out of Lady Frinton's door than she collided with Longbottom. "Seeing as it has been sitting on the hall table for two days, I thought I'd best hand deliver this to you." He passed her a letter, looked her up and down. "Are you all right, Lottie?"

"Just a bit bemused, Longbottom."

He assumed, because she had just left their employer's bedchamber, that Lady Frinton was the cause. "I empathize. I feel like I've been permanently bemused for the last fifteen years. But ours is not to reason why, ours is but to do, eh?"

"Indeed." Except she had no earthly idea what to do next—with either Guy or Miss Maybury.

Her head spinning, Lottie took her letter into her room and stared at her youngest brother's scruffy handwriting on the front before she put it on her nightstand to read later when the spinning stopped. Then, overwhelmed with considering all the potential consequences of her increasingly complex situation, she picked it up and cracked the seal.

Dear Lottie,

I have no idea how you did it, Beanstalk, but sending Lord Wennington to the farm was a stroke of genius. Thanks to you, our father has a spring in his step, the cows are saved, Stephen's read every book on legumes that he can find and now considers himself the world's foremost expert on the subject, and we're all preparing the Field of Doom, ready to plant it in the spring.

I know Papa has already written to him to thank him, but can you thank Lord Wennington personally for me for the two cartloads of pea seeds that arrived so promptly the day after his visit?

It was obvious to me that they were brand-new despite all his claims that they were left-

overs moldering away in his barn, it was obvious
to the rest of the boys too, but we roughed up all
the sacks before our father saw them and he is,
thankfully, none the wiser. You know how proud and
stubborn he gets at any whiff of charity!

I dread to think how much Lord Wennington
paid for all those seeds though at such short
notice, but let him know from me that once they
grow, we'll repay him properly for his generosity.

Dan

P.S. I know there is no accounting for taste, but
from the soppy look he got in his eyes each time
your name was mentioned, I think it's fairly safe
to assume that Lord Wennington sent those seeds
because he likes you. Goodness only knows why.

She dropped the letter in her lap and shook her head. Just when she
had thought her feelings for Guy couldn't get any more complicated, the
wretch decided to rescue her family behind her back and not mention it at
all. Not even as a way to get his hands down her breeches!

How noble and utterly romantic was that?

---

*G*uy's mother had placed Lottie at the other end of the dining table
again, but each time their eyes had met, the unmistakable heat in
hers wreaked havoc on his body.

He liked that she wanted him. Almost as much as he liked that she
didn't play games. He knew, just from the way that her gaze devoured
him, that she wanted to finish what they had started this morning. That
she wanted to touch him and wanted him to touch her—and the sooner,
the better.

But imagining her as ripe and ready under the table as she had been this morning was not without its pain. Thankfully, his mother had placed Lady Lynette right beside him again and that alone kept stopping his pistol from firing and disgracing him beneath the tablecloth.

"Are you looking forward to our impending concert, my lord?" Guy offered the horrid woman a polite, noncommittal smile as he toyed with his trifle, wishing this interminable dinner over with so he could spend the rest of the evening with Lottie. "Are there any particular tunes you would like us to play?" She touched his arm and that instantaneously did wonders to deflate his painful cock. "What is your favorite?"

"I'll listen to whatever it pleases you to play." It wasn't as if he had a choice! He would be stuck there listening to it until the damned *musicale* came to an end to please his mother.

"Well . . . I thought we'd start with some Beethoven to wake us all up after this large dinner and then . . ." His ears immediately tuned Lady Lynette out again. She was wearing a gown cut too small to hold her copious breasts and, likely on purpose, a mountain of trussed-up cleavage spilled out of it which she *accidentally* touched often to attempt to draw his eyes there as she droned on. They weren't bad breasts. In fact, they were good enough that they might have impressed him two weeks ago, before he'd caught his first glimpse of Lottie's by the pond. But now that he had been fully converted to the small but oh-so-sensitive breasts camp, Lady Lynette's bountiful charms did nothing for him. Frankly, if Lady Lynette scooped them out of her bodice, laid them in his dessert plate, and smothered them in cream right this minute, he wouldn't care.

But when he got his hands on Lottie's later, he was keen to test his theory that she would climax just from having her breasts pleasured alone. Then he was keen to test how quickly she would come when he pleasured her down *there*. It seemed only polite after she had invited him to touch her *there* earlier. He would start with his fingers and then use his tongue—

A pair of hands clapped in front of his face, snapping him out of the erotic fantasy. "Come along, nephew!" His aunt was glaring at him and, to his mortification, while he had been wondering what Lottie would look like in the throes of Guy-induced ecstasy, half of the dinner guests had already left the table. Including Lottie. "You are going to sit with me."

That wasn't in his grand plan for the evening. "But . . ."

She hooked her arm through his elbow and dragged him up. "Your mother is saving us three seats at the front."

Like one of the condemned on their way to their execution, Guy shuffled into the next room where his mother sat beaming and beckoning. He searched the rows of seats for Lottie, hoping she had found one in the back so that when he came up with a believable enough reason to excuse himself mid-concert, she could easily slip out unnoticed behind him. Except Lottie had been commandeered by Miss Maybury's mother and father and was seated, sandwiched between them, right in the middle of the middle row. She shot him a frustrated glance as his aunt dragged him to the front, as unhappy about the situation as he was.

The universe was clearly plotting against them and at least another hour of sexual frustration loomed before him.

Except it wasn't an hour because the dire *musicale* droned on for two. By which time Guy was ready to murder someone. But somehow, he managed to thank all the ladies for their performances, beside his insistent mother, before he was able to make his excuses and leave.

He shot Lottie a heated look and she shot one back, and was almost out of the door when Mr. Maybury collared him. "I had a special bottle of port brought from home for all us gentlemen to enjoy over our billiards tonight, my lord." He tapped his nose. "Along with the finest cigars from Cuba."

"Sadly, you will all have to enjoy them without me tonight, Mr. Maybury—with my complete blessing, of course—as I have an early start tomorrow and—" His blasted mother jabbed him in the ribs before she trapped his arm like a vise.

"But you can spare our neighbor half an hour after he has been so generous, can't you, Guy?" It was more an order than a question because she was pinching the skin of his bicep hard. "You are the host, after all."

"Well . . . er . . ." Out of the corner of his eye he watched Lottie get spirited from the room by his aunt Almeria. She twisted briefly and caught his eye, and he could tell by her expression that she wasn't going to be allowed to escape anytime soon either. "Of course."

And because the universe wanted to punish him some more, it was another hour before he could escape the blasted billiard room. But at least the rest of the house was quiet.

Guy quickly checked every single downstairs room he could possibly think of where Lottie might be waiting for him, from the library to the linen closet, but all to no avail, then had to conclude that she had gone to bed like everyone else.

But did she want him in it?

He pondered that conundrum as he readjusted the insistent bulge in his breeches for the millionth time before he jogged up the stairs.

Wanting some mutual touching and satisfaction was a long way off from wanting him inside her and he didn't want to appear to be pressuring her into full-blown intimacies by knocking on her door. But on the other hand, what if she was waiting for him too so that they could finish the mutual touching they had started to their mutual satisfaction? Guy knew his way around a woman's body but he had never understood how their blasted minds worked. And he had no idea how to approach such things. If he were Bill, he'd likely know precisely how to handle this situation. Would know all the right things to say and would do it with such seductive, flirty charm he wouldn't look like an idiot. Guy, on the other hand, was in grave danger of looking like an idiot because, as he stood outside Lottie's bedchamber, he was halfway to tongue-tied already and he hadn't even knocked on her door.

Good grief, but he was pathetic!

Annoyed at the nerves that were getting the better of him, he lifted his hand to tap on her door and almost choked on his own tongue as it swung open and there she was. Her golden hair hanging all loose and enticing, bare toes poking out from beneath the hem of her robe, and the sultriest smile he had ever seen on her lips.

"What took you so long?"

"I'm sorry . . . I . . ." What the blazes did *what took you so long?* actually mean in this context? "Mr. Maybury wanted to talk about the black rust on his wheat and—"

She grabbed a fistful of his cravat. "Just shut up and kiss me." Lottie dragged his mouth to hers as she simultaneously yanked him inside.

꧁ ꧂

*L*ife really *was* too short not to live it to the fullest.

Lottie knew that her relationship with Guy might not last longer than the next two days, but she had decided that she would rather make the most of that time than ponder the inevitable consequences.

She poured everything into the kiss, pinning him against her bedchamber door as she turned the key in the lock, not caring one whit that she was being shameless. Guy didn't seem to mind either as he was all over her, moaning into her mouth as his hands explored her back and bottom.

"There is nothing under this robe, is there?" His voice rasped as he nipped at her ear, his breathing choppy and his body eager.

She arched her neck to give his mouth better access to it, her own voice thick with desire too. "There seemed little point in keeping my clothes on when I knew you were going to take them off."

"Oh, Lottie . . ." His sigh was hot and heavy against her skin. "You are killing me."

"That was my plan." She supposed propriety dictated that she shouldn't be quite so brazen and shameless, but she was enjoying it. Her nerves, as she had paced her bedchamber waiting for him and wondering if giving him everything was prudent, had dissolved the second his eyes had devoured her in her doorway as he stuttered inanities.

Watching him swallow.

Watching him flounder.

Watching him want.

There was something empowering about unmanning a man who usually kept all his feelings locked so securely inside. But unapproachable, stiff, and reserved Guy was nowhere to be seen now. Instead, what stood before her was a man who was putty in her hands. Hers to do what she wanted with.

And at this precise moment, she wanted it all.

"Consider it a birthday gift." She raked her fingers through his too-neat hair as she kissed him because she preferred him all windswept. "Would you like to unwrap it?"

Apparently, she really was going to bare herself to him—right now. Without snuffing out the candle as she had planned to do as she had paced, and wondering if this was the right way to tempt him.

"God, yes." His fingers instantly went to her belt and fumbled with the knot. Lottie loved that. Loved that she undid him so—but still left him to struggle with ties because she was enjoying the anticipation.

As the knot gave, the edges of the robe parted in the gentle dip between her breasts and he stepped back a little to take it all in. Tracing the pad of his index finger from her collarbone down to her navel, so slowly it made her shudder. She watched his eyes dip lower to the triangle of curls, and then he smoothed the flat of his hand down to cup them. "Are you trying to seduce me, Miss Travers?"

"I am." She leaned to brush her lips over his. "Is it working?"

"I was all yours at 'shut up.'" His fingers traced the same path back up her body. "That's a lie—you've tormented me since you knocked me off my horse. Every minute of every day." They slipped beneath the fabric to caress the tops of her arms. A part of her body which she had never realized could render her boneless if touched, and yet now it did. "You have no idea how many times I have imagined you naked." His lips whispered over hers, barely touching, and yet she still felt it everywhere. "Or how humbled I am to finally find out." He stepped back again as he slowly edged the robe from her shoulders until gravity caught it and it puddled around her feet.

His sharp intake of breath was its own reward and the subsequent sigh a benediction. "I knew you would be beautiful but—" Something different was swirling in his eyes alongside the desire. Wonder. Awe. Affection. "You are perfection."

As if she was something fragile and precious, he traced her flesh with just the pad of one finger. Her neck and shoulder. Her arm. The indent of her waist and the curve of her hip. Then finally the outer edge of one breast in gentle rounds until it was circling her nipple.

Lottie moaned, she couldn't help it, and tilted slightly to shift his touch to the straining tip, but he pulled it away. Then, with a wolfish smile she had never seen before, bent to take the whole thing in his mouth.

"Oh . . . *Guy* . . ." She gripped his head and arched against his tongue, every nerve ending she possessed dancing as it swirled around. Shuddering each time he gently nipped the sensitive bud at the end because each nip and flick caused ripples of need to pool between her legs.

He twisted to shift their positions so that her back was now against her bedchamber door, and plundered her mouth while his hands continued to torture her breasts in a kiss so carnal she quite forgot where or who she was.

As they came up for air, she became aware of the buttons of his waistcoat pressing into her flesh and realized that he was still fully dressed. She pushed his coat from his shoulders, started on the buttons of his waistcoat, but they eluded her touch because he was on his knees, kissing her belly.

Then lower.

And lower.

Lottie cried out as his tongue dipped between the folds of her sex and found that secret, shameless knot of nerve endings. Then, in one oddly lucid moment, realizing that anyone passing the door might hear her come undone, bit the back of her hand as he looped one of her legs over his shoulder. Her other hand groping for the doorframe for support as his tongue did its magical swirl again and she completely lost her wits.

She was so ready, her climax was almost instantaneous, slamming into her with such force, the walls of her body pulsed and contracted for an eternity before she emerged from the stupor. Only to find Guy, still fully clothed and on his knees, smiling up at her from between her thighs like the cat who got the cream.

"What took you so long?" He chuckled as he mirrored her words of just minutes ago.

"Sorry . . . I . . ." Should she be embarrassed for coming so fast?

Guy surged to his feet before she could finish that sentence and seared her mouth with a kiss that tasted of her. "I'm not. I intend for that to be the first of many."

As he kissed her, he lifted one of her legs and then the other so that she had to hook them both around his waist as he carried her to the bed. Then he gently lowered her onto the mattress, only to stare down at her. His gaze darkened with desire but his expression was a little uncertain.

"Would you like me to join you?"

That he felt compelled to ask, to await her invitation, touched her. "I can hardly seduce you otherwise, Guy, can I?" She twisted on her knees to reach for his hand and tugged him nearer. "Any more than I can seduce you with you all buttoned up." She sat back on her heels, her gaze raking the length of him. "So are you going to take your clothes off, or am I?"

"You are." His wolfish smile returned with a vengeance as he waited, passive, for her to take the lead again.

Their kiss was a leisurely exploration as she made short work of his waistcoat. He was beside her as she tugged his shirt out of his waistband, and he lifted his arms so she could pull it off. Their mouths parting for just a second while she tugged it over his head.

Then she took several moments to admire his chest. To explore its contours and its hollows. Enjoying the way his nipples puckered as she gently grazed the backs of her fingernails over them, and the crisp feel of the dark dusting of hair that narrowed in an intriguing line down his abdomen and through his navel.

Needing to feel his skin next to hers, she shuffled onto his lap, nestling her hips against the bulge in his breeches while she looped her arms around his neck. They both sighed as she flattened her breasts against his body, falling back on the mattress together and landing with her on top.

Instinctively she straddled him, her arms and hair forming an intimate cage around their faces as they kissed some more. The bulge in his breeches strained against her body as she gently rotated her hips to tease him. Except it teased her just as much and her body ached with need to have him inside her.

Guy, the wretch, was content to remain on his back simply kissing her even though his sawing, ragged breath told her that he wanted more too. But he was waiting for her, the noble wretch, and wasn't going to take their lovemaking to the next level unless she instigated it.

Instinct told her to unbutton his falls, which she did with clumsy, eager fingers. As she tugged the garment from his hips, the bulge sprang free in all its glory, and she had a brief moment of panic if everything would fit. Swiftly followed by the overwhelming urge to make it fit regardless. Because she ached so much. Yearned so much.

For him.

Suddenly in a hurry, she stripped his breeches from his legs as he toed off his boots, then straddled him again. Sitting on his thighs so that she could scrutinize his erection properly.

His eyes locked with hers as she touched him, closing slightly as she explored his length. His penis was warm and smooth, and yet seemed to have a core of steel as it twitched in her hand. She found a bead of moisture at the tip and rubbed it away with gentle circling movements that made his hips buck off the bed. Fascinating . . .

"Do you like that?"

"Yes," he said through gritted teeth.

"How about this?" She wrapped her fist around him and lightly squeezed, and he nodded.

"What about this?" She bent to kiss him as he had kissed her and he growled as he grabbed her and flipped her over on the mattress.

"If you do that then . . ." He groaned and kissed her. "It's been a while, Lottie, and I'm so close already I might explode . . . and I want to be inside you when I do."

And even though his body strained against hers, he still hesitated. Still waited for her permission to take what was already his. "I want you inside me too." She widened her legs and tilted her hips in blatant invitation, and he sighed her name. Then in one swift movement pushed himself inside.

---

*S*he made a little squeak and her eyes widened more in panic than pleasure and Guy froze. "Did I hurt you?"

"No . . . I just need a moment to get used to you. I've never . . ."

"What do you mean, you've never . . ." Guilt swamped him. Guilt because it hadn't even occurred to him. He'd never had a virgin before and assumed that it would be obvious. "Oh, Lottie, I'm so sorry. I didn't feel any sort of . . ." Bloody hell, what was the polite word for it? "Barrier."

"I ride horses a lot. Astride. Very fast. I'm not surprised it's not there."

They were both breathless. His damn body was still straining. So much it took every bit of his willpower not to move. "I assumed because you . . ." Guy closed his eyes, feeling awful. So what if she knew how to kiss or how her body worked? It was no excuse. "I shouldn't have made assumptions. Again. I'm sorry. Why didn't you tell me?"

"Because . . ." Her body softened beneath him as she hooked her calves around his. Her lovely eyes so trusting. "You might have decided to be all noble and wouldn't be here with me now."

Guy gently eased his body out, almost all the way, and then slowly slid it all the way back in. "Yes, I would . . ." He copied the action and pushed deeper, enjoyed the way her eyes widened with pleasure this time. "I'd have just used a little more finesse."

She smiled as she kissed him, her soft sighs music to his ears as she became more and more accustomed to his intrusion, his restraint agony. Sheer agony but in the best possible way. If it killed him, he was content to go like this. Her legs and arms wrapped around him, her perfect body awakening to a wholly new form of pleasure beneath his, and his cock hugged by the tight, slick walls of her body as he moved within her. Both humbled and overwhelmed that she had never granted this honor to anyone else.

He wanted to tell her that he loved her. That he was hopelessly, completely, head over heels gone. But those words wouldn't come because the usual blasted fear held them back and her eyes were heavy with desire again, her body quickening and arching and ready for more.

He used that as an excuse to not say what his heart begged him to.

Then her hands raked down his back and grabbed his buttocks, pulling him closer, and the weak walls of his restraint began to crumble bit by bit. But it was her lovely legs that finished him off. And how she tilted her hips so that she could hook them around him and there went his last rational thought. From then, like their steeplechase this morning, it was all about speed and haste and competitiveness. And, as usual, they were too well matched.

Almost.

Because the moment Guy felt the first tremors begin in her body, he was done for. The pressure in his groin reached a breaking point, white lights blinded him, and he called her name in gratitude over and over as he spilled inside her. Then hugged her close as she tumbled into ecstasy right behind him, thanking his lucky stars that he had finally found the one.

THIRTY

~❧~

*B*ill was helping Guy saddle the horses by the time she reached the stables. "Good morning, Miss Travers. Are you ready for your morning ride?" The devil asked that with a completely straight face and a sinful twinkle in his eyes. "I know how much you like a good dawn gallop."

"I do." Although they both knew that he was referring to a very different sort of ride. The one that happened an hour ago just as the first glimmers of sunrise shone through her bedchamber window, and it hadn't involved any horses.

"Fancy saddling up for an invigorating morning gallop, Valkyrie?" he'd asked in a sleepy, seductive voice as he had awoken and caught her propped on one arm watching him.

"I'm not ready to go riding just yet, Guy." She'd traced his lips with her finger, hoping that would be enough to let him know what she was actually contemplating.

"That's a shame," he'd said, whipping off the blankets, his manhood pointing rigid. "Because I am."

Then he'd taught her how to ride him until they had both collapsed into an exhausted heap on the bed. And now they were here. Trying to act like two people who hadn't spent the night nakedly entwined. Baring both their bodies and their souls while they found oblivion. "There is nothing more invigorating, is there, Lord Wennington?" She blew him a kiss as Bill bent to tighten the buckle beneath Juno's belly and Guy pretended to catch it and slip it into his waistcoat near his heart just before his head groom straightened and eyed them with suspicion.

"Please tell me the pair of you don't have plans for another race this morning?"

"No—I cannot speak for Miss Travers, but I'm still not over yesterday." Guy's lips twitched, so he spun on his heel to fetch Hercules, who was coming with them. "I am still worn out."

She stifled a giggle because they hadn't slept that much last night. They had been too busy getting to know one another properly, talking in between their several bouts of lovemaking, rather than waste such a perfect night on sleep. But while they had talked about their lives in intimate detail before they had met each other, everything from laughing over clumsy first kisses and youthful mistakes to the impact losing a parent had had on one another, in tacit unspoken agreement, they steered clear of any mention of their feelings for one another and their future. Leaving Lottie as uncertain about the chances of them having one as she was before she had given herself to him.

But he had loved her body with such reverence that it had felt like he cared. Felt like he cared a great deal, in fact. The ever-optimistic side of her character hoped that meant that a few nights of passion weren't all they would have.

But then again, the pragmatic, realistic side of her cautioned Lottie not to get her hopes up. She hadn't gone into last night expecting it to be the start of something beyond a night of passion. And he had certainly given no hint that he wanted more from her than what he already had, or that he expected their . . . affair, for want of a better word . . . to continue beyond the two days together that they had left. Even today's plan wasn't fully formed. Nothing at all in fact was planned for them beyond the casual "I presume I shall see you in the stable yard shortly?" that he had asked as he had kissed her goodbye at her door.

Should she bring it up equally as casually on their ride?

Or would that spoil things today when it was something better put off until tomorrow?

Right now, with the sun on her face, an Arabian, and a handsome man awaiting her, and her sated body aching in all sorts of new but not unpleasant ways, Lottie wasn't sure she was prepared to spoil this close-to-perfect morning at all. Content to live in the moment for as long as possible until she ran out of them.

Guy returned, a contented half smile on his face that was just for her. "Where would you like to go?"

"Wherever you want to take me." Because that was the truth. The ball was in his court, after all. He would have to make the grand gesture because he was the viscount and she wasn't the sort of woman to beg or trap him in a corner, no matter how much she loved him. He either came willingly of his own accord or it wasn't meant to be. She had entered into their intimate relationship with her eyes open and no expectations of forever, no matter how much the idea of a forever with him filled her with . . . excitement? Joy? Hope? With a serendipitous sense that he was precisely what her heart had been waiting for? Besides, as the old adage said, it was better to have loved and lost than never to have loved at all, so if she did leave here in two days and that was that, then she would still treasure the memory of their time together.

"Do you fancy meeting some of my tenants then?" Not at all what she thought he was going to suggest when she had been contemplating somewhere quiet and secluded where they could rip each other's clothes off again. "See the real estate through the critical eyes of a farmer's daughter rather than the visitor's version curated by my mother?" He kicked a stone gently with the toe of his boot, not meeting her eyes. "I would value your thoughts."

"I should like to see it." Which was true, she was curious—but still bemused by the offer when he must have known that she would let him have her again. As many times as he wanted before this thing between them had to end.

"Excellent." He seemed relieved. "Excellent." His eyes briefly flicked to hers, then back to his feet. "Then maybe we can work on Hercules together again? Seeing as you seem to have this magical touch with horses that nobody else possesses and the stubborn brute only listens to you."

"Of course."

"Good," he said with an odd look in his eyes. "That will give us plenty of time to talk."

"About what?" Did his suddenly serious intensity mean that he wanted to talk about them and the dreaded *F*-word that neither of them had yet acknowledged—their future? Butterflies flapped in her tummy at the prospect of one—or lack thereof.

"This," he said, awkwardly flapping his hand between them. Brow furrowed. Eyes troubled. Posture as stiff as the trunk of the old oak tree behind them and not the least bit encouraging that "this" meant the same to him as it did to her.

Bill returned, and Guy's uncomfortable expression shuttered.

"Do you two need a chaperone?" The head groom's eyes twinkled and Guy's cheeks colored.

"Haven't you got a stable to see to?" Guy tugged Lottie's elbow toward Juno and was about to help her up when a man she had never met before rode into the yard.

"I wasn't expecting you, Jack," Guy greeted the fellow with a surprised half smile and then immediately introduced them. "Lottie—this is Jack Foster, my estate manager. Jack, this is Miss Charlotte Travers. I was going to bring her to meet you in a bit but you've negated the need. Anything wrong?"

Jack tipped his hat politely, but his grave expression shouted that he had better things on his mind than making small talk with a stranger. "I'm sorry to bother you, my lord. But this is an emergency." Guy's spine instantly snapped to attention at that. "Granger has got wind of all your negotiations behind his back and has gone on the attack. He's summoned all the grain merchants for a secret meeting in Maidstone this morning. I only got word of it just now." He handed Guy a note. "He's going to try to convince them to form an alliance again to bring the prices we've already agreed upon down, hoping that the last-minute ultimatum now that the harvest is in will force our hand."

Guy scanned the missive and then crushed it in his fist, his postcoital awkwardness forgotten. "That bloody man!" He let out an angry grunt and then turned to her. "Forgive me, Lottie. But I need to go to Maidstone now!"

"Of course you do," she said, disappointed not to have any time with him but understanding completely. "You cannot let that money-grabbing merchant fleece all those farmers." It was on the tip of her tongue to ask if she could come with him. To stand by his side and support him while he went into battle to rescue the livelihoods of those farmers who, like her father, he probably barely knew. But it wasn't her place to, especially after the uncomfortable and not so cryptic "this" he was at apparent pains to quantify, so she waved him off instead.

With nothing better to do, she helped Bill exercise the three Arabians in the training yard and then went back to her room. She took her time getting changed and, at the usual allotted hour, went to Lady Frinton's room to help her get ready for the morning, only to find her not there. She was halfway down the stairs, ready to go to breakfast with all the other houseguests, when a footman approached.

"Miss Travers—Lady Wennington has asked to see you immediately in her private sitting room."

Lottie happily went. Over the time she had been here, she had grown to like Guy's friendly mother more and more. Especially after their session with the cognac. She had no reason to think that this summons was anything to worry about—until she entered the room, saw all the grim expressions, and felt the palpable chill in the air.

She expected Lady Frinton to be there with her sister, as they were practically inseparable, but she hadn't expected either Lady Lynette or Miss Maybury to be present.

"I shan't ask you to sit, Miss Travers, as this won't take long." Lady Wennington's tone was clipped. "But it has been brought to my attention that your behavior is not that which can be tolerated in this house."

Lottie swallowed, unsure of which behavior had offended. "I am afraid I am not sure what you are referring to, my lady." She looked to her employer for some clue, but it was Lady Lynette who spoke.

"When my dear friend Miss Maybury mentioned to me yesterday that she was convinced she had witnessed a tryst between you and Lord Wennington, I took it upon myself to keep an eye on you. I have long suspected that you have always had an ulterior motive here as you have never behaved in any way as a proper servant should, but I never thought that you would dare stoop so low as to attempt to seduce and compromise a viscount into marriage."

"I would never—"

Lady Lynette held up an imperious hand. "I saw him leaving your bedchamber this morning, Miss Travers. From my hiding place I witnessed you kiss him while you were scandalously wrapped in naught but a sheet. It was obvious that you had engaged in more than a kiss with one of your betters, you calculating harlot!"

There were a great many things Lottie wanted to take issue with in that, but her mind was whirring too fast to know which to tackle first.

"She's been on a mission to seduce him all week!" Miss Maybury had the nerve to appear shocked. "She turns up at the stables every single morning to bother Lord Wennington, shameless in scandalous breeches! She almost shot poor Lady Lynette here with an arrow to dispense with her as competition and we all saw the way she constantly stared at him last night." She pointed a quaking finger. "The invitation to sin was as bold as brass in her eyes and it was obvious she intended to lure him in. She's also done everything in her power to thwart the rest of us from gaining his affections at every juncture. Forcing herself into the prime spots in carriages and at dinner, and constantly using her wiles to divert him from our company—like Delilah tempting Samson."

"Except the temple is about to fall around your ears, Miss Travers." Lady Lynette looked at Lottie like she was something vile. "And you are about to properly learn your place. In my humble opinion, not before time too!"

"If I could say something . . ." Although Lottie had no earthly clue what to say to make this awful situation any better. There were too many truths wrapped up in Lady Lynette's and Miss Maybury's lies for it not to look bad. In desperation, she glanced at Lady Frinton, who had known that she and Guy were involved and had made it plain she thought it nobody else's business, but the old lady turned her head away.

As if she was so disgusted, all of a sudden, that she couldn't even look at her.

"The jig is up, Miss Travers, and your chickens have come home to roost." Miss Maybury made no secret of the fact that she was enjoying Lottie's discomfort. "You tried to snare yourself a viscount in the most underhanded manner and got found out."

"Indeed," added the awful Lady Lynette with some glee. "Although did you honestly think that *you* could snare yourself a viscount in such an egregious fashion? Surely you realized that a man of his station was never going to want more from a woman of your station than a quick night of passion?" She feigned a laugh and looked Lottie up and down. "A man of the stature of Lord Wennington was never going to marry a lowly, worthless servant like you."

Lady Wennington raised a finger, her expression so bland in its obvious disappointment, and silence descended like a shroud that the older woman let hang for several long and painful seconds.

"You have brought my house into disrepute, Miss Travers. And in doing so have insulted both me, my family, and my illustrious guests. Fortunately, Lady Lynette and Miss Maybury are in agreement that the best way to deal with this is discreetly, and so none of the other impressionable young ladies here are aware of your improper behavior. Your things are being packed as we speak, and my sister's carriage is being prepared to take you back to London."

"But—"

"There are no buts, Travers." Lady Frinton held up her palm. Lottie's fate apparently already decided. "If you go quietly and immediately, I shall pay you two months' wages as severance and write you a good reference."

"But—" Surely they did not expect her to go without saying goodbye to Guy? "Can't I—" Lottie found herself speaking to the old lady's palm again.

"If you do not, then you leave me no choice but to publicly condemn your actions as I throw you out, thus bringing shame on both your father's and Miss Prentice's houses too."

THIRTY-ONE

❧

hanks to all of bloody Granger's deviousness and postulating, it took almost all of the day and all of Guy's arsenal to get the rest of the grain merchants to agree not to renege on the deals he had already made with them. But in the process, he had made a powerful enemy and he knew already that next year's negotiations weren't going to be easy as a result. A looming prospect that would have ground him down usually, but which didn't seem quite as bad this evening now that he knew he had someone else in his corner who would understand.

Two heads were supposedly always better than one, after all, and in Lottie, he wouldn't just have a friend and lover—he'd have a clever and resourceful partner in crime. Someone who would love this land, and everything on it, as much as he did.

A thought that made him smile as he handed Zeus over to the waiting Tom in the darkened stable and trudged his way back to the house.

He had long missed dinner, but there was some sort of soiree going on in the drawing room as he snuck past it. As much as he would have preferred curling up in bed beside his good woman at this late hour, he supposed he owed it to his mother to show face after missing this afternoon's tedious planned picnic by the river. Besides, Lottie—his not so much as good but absolutely perfect woman—would be stuck in the drawing room right now too, so the cuddling would have to wait a little while anyway. But at least they would be in it together.

Who would have predicted that a month ago? For a man who loathed surprises, Lottie had been the biggest surprise of his life. The best surprise too. She was . . .

Well, everything actually.

Everything and more. Another thought that made him grin like the besotted fool he was suddenly delighted to be.

The idea of just seeing her tonight made him take the stairs two at a time and then clean himself up at record speed. He even put on cologne as he checked his reflection for the third time in quick succession, wondering if his green silk waistcoat would look better than this burgundy one, while feeling peculiar that he wanted to look his best for her. And more peculiar still that he had finally found someone he wanted to look his best for.

It was all alien.

The way he felt. The way he thought. The way he yearned. The hurry he was in to see her. Touch her. Taste her.

Talk to her.

Talking was at the top of his suddenly long list of things to do.

For all the confidences they had shared last night as they had lain in each other's arms, there were so many things still left unsaid. Important things. Life-changing things. Forever things. And as much as Guy feared saying them—and perhaps even feeling them—they very definitely had to be said. Then—hopefully—there were plans to make. People to tell, a life to create together, and he was impatient to just get on with it all.

Within ten minutes, he strode into the drawing room, his eyes scanning the room for the unconventional ray of sunshine who had made his jaded, shriveled heart beat again and was immediately accosted by the twin horrors of Miss Maybury and Lady Lynette.

"There you are!" Miss Maybury's arm wound around his like a serpent's. "Consider yourself press-ganged onto our team for charades as we are one short."

"What perfect timing as usual, my lord," gushed Lady Lynette, claiming his other arm. "For all the fun is about to start. Do you like charades?"

As his mother was watching and he was keen to prove to Lottie, wherever she was hiding in the overly crowded room, that he could banish away his storm cloud and have fun sometimes, he gritted his teeth in preparation of lying through them and smiled at his kidnappers. "Of course." Even though he would genuinely prefer to flay all the skin from his body and then bathe in acid than spend a moment in either of their company.

They dragged him, giggling, to the front of the room, sandwiching him between them as they all sat, still clinging to him. Then, to ensure he couldn't escape their clutches, both ladies leaned against him like proprietorial twin bookends. Simultaneously pushing their unappealing bosoms into his horrified biceps as they took it in turns to blow flattering smoke up his arse in a battle to outshine one another.

That position made it difficult to turn around to find Lottie, but he still found as many excuses as he could to do so during the game but spied no sight of her anywhere. At first, he assumed that she must have popped off to visit the retiring room but, not even when he had the floor a half hour later and was forced to mime something cringing to the crowd, could he spot her statuesque, tousled blond head anywhere.

Was she sick and had excused herself? Or had she feigned some malaise to get out of tonight and was already awaiting him in her bedchamber? Expecting him to somehow know that? Dressed in nothing but that robe again and so ready for him that she would fall on him like she had last night? New to the whole game of passion fueled by love, Guy honestly didn't know whether to feel concern for the menace or desire, so had to suffer feeling both in tandem for what felt like eternity. While simultaneously being repulsed by the overt flirtations of his charade partners.

Torture did not even begin to describe it!

When an interval was declared so everyone could recharge their glasses, he extricated himself from his awful teammates' clutches as fast as he could. Before he could leave the room, he had no choice but to slow to acknowledge his mother sipping punch by the door with Aunt Almeria.

"Have either of you seen . . ." He stopped himself from saying Lottie in case they asked a million questions about why he had suddenly dropped that formality. "Miss Travers." Although if he had anything to do with it, the menace wasn't going to be a *Miss* for much longer.

"She's gone," said his mother with a grimace.

"Gone where?" He hadn't expected that answer but immediately it made him worry. "Is she ill?" Because if she was, then he would need to get the physician here as soon as possible in case her malaise festered and she took a turn for the worse and died. A prospect that made his poor heart clamber up his throat to choke him.

"No," was all his mother unhelpfully said through flattened lips.

"Then has something happened to her father or one of her brothers?" Visions of all manner of farmyard accidents scurried through his mind and gave him further palpitations. "Should I saddle a horse?" Because family should always be there for family and those men were soon to be his. "What the blazes has happened!"

"If you must know . . ." Now his aunt was grimacing at his loud, panicked tone but whispering as if she were sharing a state secret and forcing him to lean closer to hear her above the hubbub. "I dismissed her."

"What!" Guy did not bother whispering that. "You . . . *dismissed her!*" Had the world—or his aunt—gone stark-staring mad? "Why the blazes did you do that?"

"Unbecoming and improper behavior." That curt but also hushed comment came from his mother.

"Scandalous behavior," added his aunt, pulling an outraged face. "So she had to go. Straightaway. She left this morning."

"And good riddance!" said his mother as Guy's head began to spin. Then she whacked his arm with the back of her hand. "And shame on you too, Guy Harrowby! For you are not without blame in this unseemly debacle!"

"Unseemly debacle?" A nerve ticked in his cheek as his temper began to rise. He would have allowed the top of his head to explode but he didn't want to cause a scene. Several guests were already staring and, instinctively, being a spectacle made him queasy. "What is that supposed to mean?"

"That you were seen, you stupid idiot!" His mother's hushed hiss was angry. Her eyes incensed as she grabbed his sleeve and yanked him into the privacy of the hallway. "Sneaking out of her bedchamber this morning!"

"I most certainly did not." Denial seemed like the most gentlemanly way to defend Lottie's honor despite all the ungentlemanly things he had done to her in that bedchamber. "Somebody malicious has told an outrageous lie and you have punished an innocent woman on the back of it. How dare you!" *Oh my god, oh my god, oh my god! Why hadn't he been more careful when it was his job to protect her?*

His aunt rolled her eyes as she closed the door on the drawing room and all the gawping faces therein. "We dared because another witness saw the pair of you kissing behind the stables, so I think it is fairly safe to say that that horse has well and truly bolted. Never mind that we'd all have to be blind not to see the covetous way you looked at her last night, so excuse us for not believing that self-righteous rot, nephew." Then she prodded him with a bony finger. "How dare *you* copulate with my companion when I finally found one that showed promise! Couldn't you dip your nib in another inkwell if you urgently needed to *write*?"

Nibs!

Copulating!

How dare they denigrate the beauty of what he and Lottie had shared as some sort of itch that had needed to be scratched! As if any blasted *inkwell* would have done!

He didn't care that his aunt was a frail old lady and rounded on her, his own finger jabbing the air between them. "Keep your filthy insinuations—"

His mother yanked him back to face her. "Whether you did or you didn't *write* with Miss Travers is a rather moot point at this stage. Especially when we both know that you did." His mother's finger made contact with his breastbone, and he grabbed it, more furious at her than he had ever been in his life. She snatched it away and wagged it. "A complaint was raised, and with you conspicuously absent from your own birthday party yet again, I had no choice but to deal with it in the manner I deemed most appropriate!"

"And the most appropriate way you deemed was to punish Lottie rather than me?" Guy had never come this close to strangling his meddling mother in his life. And poor Lottie . . .

Oh, good God! Poor Lottie!

And he hadn't been here to defend her.

"How could you be so callous?" Emotion choked his throat as he struggled to understand it all. His mother was a lot of exasperating things, but cruel wasn't usually one of them. "How could you be so unfair? And how bloody dare you!"

She bristled at that. "There are impressionable young ladies here!" She pointed a finger back at the drawing room. "From some of the best families in society and one of us had to think about this family's reputation!"

"And the best way you could think to do that was to publicly humiliate her?"

His aunt prodded him again. "Travers wasn't publicly humiliated! It was all done on the quiet, so kindly keep your voice down or everyone in there will know! Thankfully, only Miss Maybury and Lady Lynette are aware of your scandalous and inappropriate indiscretion, and they came straight to us with it, which was jolly decent of them. They even promised to take the secret to their graves so long as that temptress was removed from these premises with all haste."

Instantly, things slotted into place. Because of course only those two, of all the young ladies present, were despicable enough and desperate enough to sink so low.

"*They* insisted she be removed?"

His mother and aunt nodded in unison.

Jaws set. Noses in the air.

Unrepentant.

"You put the demands of two sycophantic, thwarted, scheming, abhorrent social climbers over Lottie's feelings?"

"Of course we did," said his aunt. "Lady Lynette's father is an earl, after all, and bloodlines matter."

"We did it for your own good, Guy." His mother had the gall to stroke his arm as if she loved him. "Once you've calmed down, you will realize that and thank us."

That was when the red mist descended.

The exact moment that nothing else mattered one damn over his perfect, beautiful, wronged soulmate.

Guy barged back into the drawing room and, oblivious to the wide eyes and gasps from his mother's awful houseguests, marched through the throng to the two worst who had wronged his woman. "How dare you!"

While Miss Maybury acted all innocent, the pompous Lady Lynette shrugged and stuck out her arrogant chin. "I dared because that brazen upstart needed to be put back in her place!"

"Lottie's place is next to me, damn it!" He pointed to the empty space beside him, sick to his stomach at how humiliated she must be feeling right now. "Whereas yours is as far away from me as is humanly possible!" He was aware that he was shouting. Aware that his arms were waving uncontrollably in the air, but he couldn't stop. "Pack your bags, the pair of you, and get out of my house!" Then as an addendum, he bellowed, "And if anyone is brazen here, it is you two, who, for the record, are not worthy enough to lick her boots!"

He spun on his heel and stalked back through the crowd and, with a visceral growl, straight past his mother in the hallway.

She grabbed his sleeve as he reached the front door. "Where are you going?"

He snatched it away. "To fetch back the woman that I love! And if you don't like that, Mother, then you can pack your bloody bags too!"

He then took great pleasure in slamming the door in her face.

ady Frinton's carriage had dropped her back at Miss Prentice's School for Young Ladies just before supper and Lottie had collapsed into the older woman's arms the second the front door had closed.

After the longest and most painful journey of her life, she had been too devastated and too humiliated to hold back the tears or to make up a more palatable story as to why she had been sent back in disgrace. Absolutely everything had spilled out in Miss P's little parlor. With Miss P on one side of her and Kitty and Portia on the other, none of them quite knowing what to say to make the awful situation better.

She had been exhausted by the time the tears finally stopped. Wrung out like an old dishcloth and in total despair, so they tucked her into bed with a hot toddy and a batch of fresh handkerchiefs and told her that things would all look better in the morning.

Except they hadn't and Lottie only felt worse.

For all her inherent sunny outlook, she had maintained realistic expectations of what she actually had with Guy. She had expected the imminent end of their romantic liaison. Had braced herself for the inevitable but natural conclusion to their relationship to come in just one more day after she left with her employer, because he was him and she was her and in the normal course of things, like oil and water, a viscount and a servant never mixed. He had said as much yesterday when he had awkwardly, almost apologetically, informed her that they urgently needed to talk. Never mind that not once during the many times they had made love had any actual words of love been uttered. But the abrupt, unexpected termination of everything without the closure of a goodbye had hit her like a speeding post coach. Leaving her battered, bruised, and grieving.

"I cannot bear to think what he has been told." That one thing had haunted her the most all night. That he had been lied to about her sudden exit as a way to turn him against her. "I cannot bear to think that he might have been convinced into believing that I actually always had a plan to seduce him into wedlock and now hates me for using him." Especially after a woman had used him with such cruel, selfish calculation before.

"Why don't you write him a letter and tell him, then? And tell him how you feel. He's bound to come here to fetch you if you confess that you love him." Kitty, bless her, had always worn rose-tinted spectacles when it came to the subject of love. She firmly believed that love conquered all, but while Lottie was an eternal, sunny optimist and hoped with all her heart that Guy would surprise her, she was also a realist. A noble one, apparently, with too much stubborn pride of her own.

"If he comes to get me, it has to be because *he* wants to. I will not do anything to try to force his hand."

"He's a viscount at the end of the day." Portia had always been more a pragmatist than a romantic. "An aristocrat. I hate to be the voice of doom but we all know that aristocrats only marry other aristocrats so that they can beget more. And thus keep their tight hold on the reins of oppression and power."

"But you *love* him," said Kitty with pleading eyes. "Love is always worth fighting for. No matter what the obstacles. You have to fight for him, Lottie. You *have* to."

"No, she doesn't," said Portia firmly. "She needs to protect herself and her reputation and both will be ruined if she tries to force a blue blood's hand."

"*If you love something, let it go.*" Miss P sighed as she recited the same bittersweet old adage that Lottie had recited to herself over and over again as she had stared at her old bedchamber ceiling last night. *"If it comes back, it is yours; if it doesn't, it never was.* I'm afraid I agree with Lottie and Portia, Kitty. Sending him any sort of letter would be a mistake. Aside from the fact that it would leave her with her dignity in shreds as well as her heart, this is, ultimately, a test of the strength of his feelings for her. If the viscount chooses the side of his peers or decides to believe them that Lottie was capable of that sort of duplicity, frankly, he doesn't love her enough at all."

"And I do have form when it comes to duping him." Guy had barely just forgiven her for helping to plan his surprise behind her back and he did have a tendency to batten down the hatches when his feelings were hurt. She could picture him now. Ruthlessly focusing on estate work like a lion with a thorn in his paw, seething on the outside and within at being made a fool of again. "He's been hurt by a scheming woman before too, so I don't hold out much hope of him coming around." She had to force herself to face that truth in order to accept it. No matter how much she wanted to put off thinking about it until tomorrow. Accepting it until tomorrow. "If he does . . ."

Stop hoping!

All the odds were stacked against them. Had always been stacked against them. Doubly so now that his mother was against them. Lottie sighed and blinked away the gathering tears. "Lady Wennington has already made it plain that she will not approve of any match, making it next to impossible that the pair of us can have any sort of future together. Not—to be fair to him—that he has ever given me any reason to believe that we did have a future together."

We need to talk about this, *Lottie.*

This.

Not us.

Not them.

Not the future. But the situation that had, by the morning after, made him so physically awkward he could barely look at her as he had flapped a stilted hand between them.

Unconsciously, she rubbed her poor, aching heart at both the memory and the conclusiveness of that moment. "He is also a viscount, as Portia has so rightly just pointed out, so therein lies another obstacle."

"Class shouldn't even be an obstacle!" Kitty was incensed at what she saw as Lottie giving up.

"But it is, dear." Miss P understood the utter hopelessness of the situation.

"This is why this country needs reform!" Portia wagged an enraged fist toward the heavens. "Why we'll probably have to resort to a revolution just like they did in France! Our archaic and unfair system of master versus servant has to be replaced!"

"Oh, do shut up, Portia," said Miss P with a roll of her eyes. "Do not use poor Lottie's heartbreak to fuel your desire to revolt!"

Portia winced and squeezed Lottie's hand. "I'm sorry . . . I just hate to see you hurt and wish I could do something to help it all go away."

"I know." Lottie squeezed her friend's hand back. "Your presence right now is more of a comfort to me than storming the houses of Parliament would be."

Miss P sighed. "That said, class is the single biggest reason why I have always cautioned my protégées not to dally with their masters." She brushed a hand over Lottie's hair. "Even if that is always easier said than done. It rarely ever ends well, as I know to my cost."

As this was the first anyone had ever heard about Miss P's romantic life, the three friends blinked at her, but it was Kitty who asked, "Did you fall in love with a viscount too?"

"Worse," said their mentor with a wistful smile. "The oldest son of a marquess. Saying goodbye to him was the hardest decision I had to make, no matter how inevitable I knew it always would be. He had to marry someone of his own ilk, and I had to let him. Neither of us would have ever been happy otherwise. His family thoroughly disapproved of me and made no secret that they would never accept me. Nor would the rest of the aristocracy either, as I was not from his world." A sad tale that so perfectly mirrored Lottie's, all of Miss P's repeated and vehement cautions now made sense.

"And he let you go?" Poor, romantic Kitty, who had always believed that life really could be a fairy tale if you willed it hard enough, shook her head in disbelief.

Miss P gazed off into nothing as the clearly painful memories assaulted her, making Lottie fearful that her current feelings of wretchedness might never ease, no matter how much time passed. "Edward said he was happy to leave that world behind for me, but I knew that once the first flush of passion faded, and the enormity of all that he had sacrificed to be with me sunk in, he would start to resent me for being the reason he had to make that choice." The older woman swallowed. Hard. As if her pain at losing the mysterious Edward was still visceral. Then she offered them a wistful smile that barely held. "The sad fact is, Kitty, love alone, sometimes, just isn't enough to beat all the obstacles in its way." She wrapped a comforting arm around Lottie's shoulders. "But the pain does ease eventually, dear. For at least most of the time. I found that keeping busy helps. That and ice cream." She rose to teach her next lesson. "The worst thing to do is to mope around waiting for someone to come who very likely isn't." And with that depressing but sobering thought, she left them.

"It is almost lunchtime and you didn't touch your breakfast. Do you want to go and get some ice cream?" Portia rubbed Lottie's slumped shoulders. "It might cheer you briefly."

"Or would you rather mope around here in case your viscount turns into a knight in shining armor?" That came from Kitty.

Lottie would rather mope. Curl herself into a ball and cry some more, but her friends were trying to help so she smiled. "Let's try the ice cream."

They took a convoluted walk around Hyde Park to get to Gunther's, one which forced Lottie to walk past the exact spot that she had first collided with Guy. It had been her choice to do that, as she had hoped that the quicker she faced all those things, the quicker her bludgeoned heart would start to heal. Kitty had laughed at the story and hugged Lottie tight when her eyes had filled with tears, and spouted more hopeful nonsense because she was convinced that Guy would not let her go. Because why on earth would any besotted man—and her friend was convinced that Guy had to be—let a prize like her go?

Rather than depress herself further by regurgitating all the same insurmountable reasons that she, Portia, and Miss P already had, Lottie instead fed the ducks at the Serpentine, because she knew that she needed every diversion possible to get through this awful day. It was close to three by the time they reached Mayfair's most famous confectioner's, and the shop was so crowded there was only one table left. The worst, most confined table in the restaurant that was squished right at the back. One that managed to be both geographically isolated and yet on full display at the same time. Most definitely not the sort of table to indulge in a quiet, unobtrusive bout of self-pitying weeping. The sort of weeping she suddenly very much needed to do.

"I hope they haven't run out of the raspberry ice." Portia eyed the severely depleted counter with a frown as the waiter hovered, unaware of Lottie's increasingly watery eyes because he was too busy staring at the ridiculously pretty Kitty instead. "That's my favorite."

"Sadly, we are out of the raspberry, miss." The waiter eyed Kitty with the same interest as Portia was giving the display. "But we have strawberry and that is equally as delicious. And we have lemon and plenty of the Parmesan ice if you fancy that."

Kitty pulled a face. "I have never understood why anyone would want a cheese-flavored ice cream. Parmesan ice is an abomination as far as I am concerned."

"Me too," whispered the waiter, now smoldering at Kitty with barely disguised attraction. "We are kindred spirits on that score. I suspect that is also why we always have plenty of it left." Kitty nodded, giggling, and encouraged, he edged closer. "I've not seen you in here before. Do you live locally?"

"Only temporarily. Again," said Kitty with her usual honesty. "I was dismissed by my last employer for daydreaming on the job. An accusation which would have been a travesty if it hadn't been true." She smiled at the waiter and the poor man practically melted into a puddle on the spot. "I do not suppose that there are any jobs open here? I might do better fetching the gentry their ice cream than I do watching their children."

"I could ask." The waiter gestured to the kitchen with a tilt of his head, clearly keen to impress. "And perhaps I could find a bit of raspberry ice for you and your friends here while I am about it?"

"Oh, that would be—" Always easily distracted, Kitty twisted at the loud tone of another waiter.

"As I have told you, sir—you must join the queue if you want a table!"

"And I have told you that I do not want a blasted table!" Lottie stiffened at the unmistakable sound of Guy's voice, her head swiveling like an owl's toward it. "I have urgent business with someone already at one!" She could see the hatless top of his dark head at the doorway over the crowds. "I insist that you let me pass!"

"Oh, for goodness' sake! Is nowhere safe from ruffians, nowadays?" Portia craned her head to see the commotion better. "This is Mayfair, after all. Home of all that is supposed to be superior. Does the word 'manners' mean nothing to some? Or the concept of queuing to wait your rightful turn? I'll bet that rude oaf is a duke or an earl or some such. Pompous and entitled and convinced the world revolves around him."

"As previously stipulated, there is a queue, sir . . ."

"Hang the blasted queue!" The ominous sounds of a scuffle filled the air as the restaurant full of diners suddenly fell silent.

"Oh, no, you don't, you blighter!"

Paralyzed with shock and her perennially warped sense of humor that was desperate to see how this unexpected turn of events played out, Lottie blinked at the sight of several waiters rushing to the front to assist their colleague. The over-pomaded head of the maître d' appeared in a small gap between the now craning heads of the sixty or so customers who were all mostly standing to get a better view of the altercation. "I must respectfully ask you to leave, sir, or I shall call the constable!"

"Call whoever you bloody well want!" She caught the tiniest glimpse of Guy laboring toward her, three waiters hanging from his arms and shoulders as he dragged them along with them before the crowd closed ranks and blocked her view. "Lottie! *LOTTIE!*"

Kitty squealed as her hands flew to her gaping mouth. "Oh my goodness! Is that *him*?"

"That's *him*?" Portia stood to get a better look too. "I knew he'd be a

blue-blue with all that imperious carrying-on." However, even her mili-
tant friend smiled at the kerfuffle. "I thought you said that he hated being
a public spectacle?"

"He does." Not that Lottie could quite believe he was making quite
such a public spectacle. "Being made a public spectacle, most especially
here in Mayfair, is his worst nightmare."

"But he is making himself one here for you, Lottie." Kitty clutched
at her heart. "Right in the middle of Gunther's. Just as I knew he would."
Her friend squealed again and their waiter, who mistook that shriek of
delight as one of fear, prepared himself to protect Kitty at all costs.

"Don't panic," he shouted, obviously panicked himself. "I will protect you from the scoundrel if he comes this way!"

"Do we look so pathetic that you think we need rescuing?" Of course
Portia would take issue with some misguided manly heroics. "Are you
aware that we women can look after ourselves?"

"LOTTIE!" As Guy pushed himself through the crowd, his three
restraining waiters still attached, their waiter launched himself at him
too with such force he knocked poor Guy to the ground. Being a big man,
Guy went down with a thud, dragging the tablecloth he had instinctively
groped for as something to stop his fall down with him. Several sundaes
and a large slice of chocolate cake followed. As the ice creams exploded
on his chest, the chocolate cake caught him on the chin and stuck. Melt-
ing ganache slipped down the side of his neck as he tried to simultaneously wrestle Kitty's waiter off him and sit up.

His stunned eyes narrowed as they locked with hers. "Where the
blazes have you been!" His handsome face like thunder, he batted one of
the ices from his chest, managing to only smear it further before he gave
up and pointed a dripping, sticky finger at her. "I've been everywhere
looking for you, you infuriating bloody menace!"

"Now see here, sir!" Kitty's waiter scrambled upright as the other
waiters dragged Guy back down before he could stand, his clenched fists
waving. "That is no way to speak to a lady!"

"He cannot help himself." Lottie could not resist teasing a little
despite the flock of nervous seagulls flapping in her stomach. "Guy has

always been a rude oaf." And he was here. *He was here!* "But his bark has always been worse than his bite so you should probably unhand him, gentlemen."

"He is also a viscount." Kitty's comment created a curious buzz in the already riveted crowd while she stood and smiled down at him. "You must be Lord Wennington." The buzz of the crowd got louder at that. Their eyes wide as furtive gossip ricocheted around the restaurant from behind futilely disguised hands as they all remembered who he was. Her hopelessly romantic friend, however, was beaming as she bobbed a curtsy before she offered her hand to haul Guy up. "I am Kitty Black-stone. One of Lottie's very best friends. I am so glad to see you because, obviously, I never doubted you would come for her. Our friend Portia here, on the other hand"—she gestured to Portia, who was eyeing Guy dubiously—"doubted you at every juncture because she is not a fan of aristocrats. It's nothing personal to you, you understand, merely a polit-ical point of principle."

"The days of inherited privilege are numbered, Lord Wennington," said Portia before her eyes narrowed. "As yours will be if your intentions toward my friend Lottie here aren't absolutely honorable."

Guy blinked at her friends, baffled momentarily by the both of them, then positively glared at Lottie as his irate finger jabbed the air. "I cannot believe you just left! With not so much as a by-your-leave!"

That was not the romantic speech she had been hoping for, although why she suddenly hoped for one when his just being here meant the world was a mystery. But she did. "It is not as if I had a choice! Your mother threw me out!"

"You should have known that I wouldn't have allowed that! Or that I would not accept that." He jabbed the air with his incensed finger some more. "You should have had more faith in me and stayed!"

"Should I? Why?"

"Because!" He threw up his sticky palms. "Because . . ." He glanced around the shop and winced at all the gawping faces staring back, drop-ping his voice a little as if that would somehow give them more privacy after he had already created the most almighty public scene. And he had made an equally public fool of himself.

For her.

Despite that being his worst nightmare.

How romantic!

"Because you knew how I felt about you, woman!"

"I have no earthly idea how you feel about me, actually. Absolutely nothing was said."

He went to argue, paused, and then shouted some more. "You knew I wanted to talk to you before I left!"

"About 'this,' as I recall it. 'This.'" Lottie stood and folded her arms in case she was tempted to fling them around his neck and thank him for coming, which would not do at all until all her hopes were properly confirmed. "Whatever 'this' was supposed to mean."

"Well, by 'this' . . ." He flapped an awkward hand between them again, his voice rising. "I obviously meant that I wanted to talk about us!" The hand rotated ahead. "Going forward. And I wanted to show you around the estate properly. And you bloody well knew that I wanted you to help me train Hercules!"

"And he bought your family all those peas," said a grinning Kitty, butting in.

"Yes, I did." His angry, ice cream–covered finger jabbed again. "I bought your family blasted—" He stopped shouting for a moment and winced again, remembering that that was yet another thing he had neglected to mention to her in the last few days. He raked a hand through his hair, oblivious that he was coating it in icing and melted ice cream, and sucked in a calming breath. "Lottie . . . I—"

It was at the precise moment that the constable charged in.

"Is this the rude gentleman that you would like me to remove?" The constable looked first to the waiters and then to her.

How steam didn't shoot out of Guy's ears was a miracle. "I am not a rude gentleman, I am her fiancé! And I'd like to see you try and remove me!"

"Is he?" The constable frowned at Lottie.

"Not that I am aware," she replied as a giggle threatened to escape. Before it did, Guy's temper snapped.

"If you think that you can just ruin me for all other women and not marry me, Lottie Travers, you have another bloody think coming! We are getting married, Valkyrie, and that is that!" Noticing that his arms were flailing, he folded them and glared.

"Give me one good reason why."

His brows knitted into one dark, solid line and he threw up his palms again. "Because I bloody love you, don't I." Most of her insides melted on the spot as both Kitty and Portia sighed beside her. "And you love me too, don't you?"

She wanted to say yes but Miss P's words of caution still echoed in her ears. She could not make him do something that he would ultimately regret. She would not be able to bear that. "Your mother does not approve of me."

He walked toward her and took her hand. His stormy eyes intense. Vulnerable. His thumb caressing the sensitive flesh of her palm and instantly setting her nerves dancing. "Do you love me, Lottie?"

"I am a companion and you are a viscount and—"

"For the love of God, woman, just answer the question."

Should she be honest or should she, like Miss P had with her marquess, set him free of all the obligation he felt so that she wouldn't have to be that obstacle between him and his family? "I don't know."

He grabbed her arms from where she had hidden them behind her back. "Say that again where I can see that your fingers are uncrossed, because I know you cannot lie if they aren't."

"She loves you." Kitty interrupted again. "Stop trying to be noble and just tell him the truth, Lottie." Then as an aside to Guy, her incorrigible friend said, "She's been in bits since yesterday. Absolutely heartbroken. In all the years I have known her, I have never seen Lottie so besotted by a man."

"Me neither," added Portia begrudgingly. "But I'll make sure you're the first to the guillotine if you break my friend's heart!"

"Oh, do shut up, Portia," said Kitty, dragging her away. "You are ruining the most perfect romantic moment."

"Well?" Guy smiled as he traced a finger down Lottie's cheek, coaxing a smile from her too. "Do you?"

"I might." His smile quickly stretched into a grin while Lottie's faded. "But your mother—"

"Let me deal with my mother."

There was a cough and suddenly Longbottom appeared from the crowd. "On the subject of Lady Wennington . . ." He held up a letter, which Guy went to snatch, but the butler pulled it away. "I was told that I had to hand this personally to Miss Travers at the opportune moment, my lord. Her and no one else."

He handed it to her with a wink. "You'll want to open that now, Lottie, and know that I would have told you if I could have, but Lady Frinton pays my wages and I have mouths to feed too."

Lottie cracked the seal, then read the missive's contents with an increasingly dropping jaw.

My dearest future daughter-in-law,

Please forgive me for all the horrid things that I said to you yesterday. I never meant a word of it. However, we both know how stubborn my exasperating son is. It was obvious to me that there was a frisson between you that first day you threw all that soup over him. But when Longbottom informed my sister that he had caught the pair of you kissing and then Guy ran away sulking, we knew that we had to intervene. I will confess, Almeria and I did everything we could to thrust the pair of you together, but neither myself nor my sister had any hand in Miss Maybury's and Lady Lynette's malicious complaint.

However, once they made it, it seemed a waste not to use the great gift that those two awful idiots had given us . . . after all, if I want my son to turn left, he will always stubbornly turn right!

But you were right too, dearest Lottie.

Guy always had to leap off the cliff himself. But he turns thirty today and I am impatient for him to start his life with you, so please do not hate me for pushing him to that cliff's edge. Or for tossing you so shamelessly over it to encourage him to follow.

You will understand all my necessary machinations better when you become a mother too. Tell my irritating son that I sincerely hope that he makes that day come as soon as possible as he owes me a house full of grandchildren!

With love,

Your Meddling Future Mother-in-Law

P.S. Kindly tell my stubborn son that it was all for his own good and he is welcome!

As Guy had read the same words as she had over her shoulder, Lottie turned to him and waited for him to explode. Except he didn't. He simply shook his head as if all his mother's machinations were par for the course and grabbed her hand.

"Now that that problem is dealt with, can we go back to Kent where we belong? I loathe blasted Mayfair and all the blasted people in it." He glared at all the gawping diners for a moment before he started to drag her toward the door. Expecting her to meekly follow when she had never been meek a day in her life and wasn't about to start now.

"Wait!" She planted her feet before they left the shop. "I am not sure I can marry you. Not with the gaping chasm between us." She held out her hands a foot apart.

He frowned even harder than he had been, if that was possible. "You know that I have never been one for airs and graces and I have certainly never given a damn that you are a confounding companion, Lottie Bloody Travers. You *know* that!"

"Just as I've never given two figs that you were a vexing viscount." She was going to enjoy teasing this quick-tempered man for eternity. "I was more thinking about the unbridgeable chasm between our outlooks. I'm a delightful ray of sunshine and you wander around with a perennial angry storm cloud hanging over your head—and I worry that we are going to drive each other to distraction as a result."

"Of course we are!" He more growled that than said it. "You've driven me to distraction since the day you knocked me off my blasted horse, woman, and I am resigned to the fact that you likely will until the day I die. But—"

He hauled her into his arms, not caring that he was smearing her in ice cream and chocolate cake too, or that absolutely everyone, inside Gunther's and out, was staring at the scandalous public spectacle he was willingly creating.

"You do know what happens when sunshine collides with a storm cloud, don't you, my infuriating, headstrong, reckless, and equally vexing Valkyrie?" His scowl morphed into that rare smile she adored so much. The twinkle in his dark eyes a sinful promise as they dropped to her lips. "Bloody rainbows, that's what."

Acknowledgments

Some books are difficult to write and some simply fly out of your fingers as you type. This was the latter. I adored Lottie, Guy, Lady Frinton, Lady Wennington, and all those awful, desperate debutantes from the very first to the very last page. However, as easy as it was to write, I would be remiss to not mention the wonderful people around me who helped make *Look Before You Leap* happen.

As always, my long-suffering husband, Greg, has to come first in the thank-yous, as he's the one who has to talk me off the ledge each time I reach that tricky part in every single book where I am convinced it is the worst thing that has ever been written. A thank-you also goes to my editor, Sallie Lotz, who never fails to make suggestions that make each story better, and my agent, Kevan Lyon, who believes in my stories enough to want to sell them.

I also couldn't do this without my wonderful, talented writing friends who are always ready to celebrate and commiserate the roller-coaster journey of every single book that I squeeze out. Because only a fellow writer truly understands that the struggle is sometimes real—especially if it is fictional! Jean Fullerton, who will always drop everything for a phone call to help me put the world to rights (and vice versa when this writing malarkey gets us down). Lucy Flatman, Liam Livings, and Alison

Rutland—thank you for all the laughter, no matter how manic, loud, and inappropriate it all often is.

Finally, a massive thank-you to all my readers, both new to me and old, because your appreciation of the stories that come out of my odd brain genuinely means the world. And just in case you've ever felt inclined to message or email an author and tell them how much you enjoyed their work, please—just do it! Those precious words make all the days we authors spend bashing our heads against our desks waiting for our own words to come worth all the pain of writing them.

About the Author

Kat Moran Photography

When **Virginia Heath** was a little girl, it took her ages to fall asleep, so she made up stories in her head to help pass the time while she was staring at the ceiling. As she got older, the stories became more complicated, sometimes taking weeks to get to the happy ending. Then one day, she decided to embrace the insomnia and start writing them down. Now her Regency rom-coms (including the Wild Warriners and Merriwell Sisters series) are published in many languages across the globe. Thirty-two books and four Romantic Novel of the Year Award nominations later, it still takes her forever to fall asleep.